JEHOVAH'S WIND

A JACK SANGSTER MYSTERY

JEHOVAH'S WIND

A JACK SANGSTER MYSTERY

LEWIS HINTON

The Book Guild Ltd

First published in Great Britain in 2023 by
The Book Guild Ltd
Unit E2 Airfield Business Park,
Harrison Road, Market Harborough,
Leicestershire. LE16 7UL
Tel: 0116 2792299
www.bookguild.co.uk
Email: info@bookguild.co.uk
Twitter: @bookguild

Copyright © 2023 Lewis Hinton

The right of Lewis Hinton to be identified as the author of this
work has been asserted by them in accordance with the
Copyright, Design and Patents Act 1988.

All rights reserved. No part of this publication may be
reproduced, transmitted, or stored in a retrieval system, in any form or by any means,
without permission in writing from the publisher, nor be otherwise circulated in
any form of binding or cover other than that in which it is published and without
a similar condition being imposed on the subsequent purchaser.

This work is entirely fictitious and bears no resemblance to any persons living or dead.

Typeset in 11pt Adobe Jenson Pro

Printed and bound by CPI Group (UK) Ltd, Croydon, CR0 4YY

ISBN 978 1915853 042

British Library Cataloguing in Publication Data.
A catalogue record for this book is available from the British Library.

For my children, remembering how much you all loved Dartmoor when you were little

"God blew and they were scattered"
Queen Elizabeth the First on the defeat of the Spanish Armada

INTRODUCTION

The year is 1970, the month June, and Jack Sangster, special investigator with the Granville Institute, a philanthropic organisation dedicated to helping troubled youngsters, is in Devon, having been asked to assist in the case of a lost child.

A former naval commander and oil executive, Sangster was originally taken on by the Granville Institute for his empathy with youngsters, along with exceptional people and organisational skills. But… his true talent lies in resolving difficult, sometimes apparently insoluble cases, especially when there are missing children involved. Sangster often works closely with both the Department of Education and the police on such cases.

Sangster's hometown is Chester, but he can be sent anywhere on assignment. As the story opens, we flash back to an incident in Ireland during the Second World War, when Sangster was a serving naval officer, and then fast forward a quarter of a century, to find an older Sangster starting his search at a remote moorland hotel…

BALLYSHANNON COUNTY DONEGAL 1944

SATURDAY, APRIL THE 29TH 12 NOON

"Those poor airmen never stood a chance. Seven souls lost."

"I guess you're right, Phil," I said, looking across Donegal Bay towards the River Erne's windswept estuary as the Mammoth, the world's largest floating crane, groaned under the weight of its as-yet-unseen undersea charge. "But they'll be bringing the plane up now, so we'll soon know for sure nobody managed to bail out."

"Wonder what went wrong, those big seaplanes are so reliable, aren't they?"

I thought for a moment as he spoke.

"Everything goes wrong sometimes," I eventually answered. "And if you're in a plane in the air when it does go wrong, well…"

"Suppose so, Jack, but… ah, look, up she comes."

We watched from the bridge of our ship as the enormous carcass of the Sunderland flying boat broke the sea's surface, sending spray all around. And as the still-intact fuselage and broken wings were raised higher, the dead machine began to weep water in what looked to me like giant tears. A signal lamp from the Mammoth then began to flash, and a few moments later a crew member appeared behind us waving a piece of paper.

"Message from the Mammoth, sir," he said, and after saluting, offered it to me.

"You'd better take that note, Phil. The Old Man being ashore makes you senior officer on board."

"Guess so, Jack." Phil took the note and held it at length from his nose (even then, when we were both yet to turn twenty-nine, he was long-sighted). "Says the crew are all dead and the crash is likely due to a bird strike." He shook his head. "Like I said, poor airmen, I…" Phil then held the note even further from his eyes and let out a gasp. "My goodness…"

"You alright there, Phil?"

"Seems like… yes, says here the divers found a shipwreck. A warship underneath the flying boat."

"Never heard of a navy ship going down here."

"I know you've got an encyclopaedic knowledge of naval history, but nevertheless—"

"As far as the Admiralty Digest says," I interjected, "there's nothing registered as sunk in these waters, I'm sure."

"No, Jack, not a modern ship."

"Sorry?"

"It's… well, you're not going to believe me."

"Phil, you're the steadiest bloke I know. Of course I'll—"

"Jack," he interrupted, "it's a wooden ship, and if the divers are right, a… well… I still can't believe it."

"Believe what, Phil?"

"Well, by its size and shape, more than likely from the Spanish Armada."

4:30 PM

"Those chaps seem to have awfully weak bladders," whispered Phil as we sat in the bar of Flannagan's Porter House in Ballyshannon and watched one of the locals jump down from his stool and virtually run to a door on the other side of the room. The man was part of a group who sat next to an ancient-looking radio at the end of the bar, all avidly listening to a crackling broadcast that every now and again degenerated into a high-pitched whine as the signal wavered and knobs were frantically adjusted to reset the machine. Within the hour Phil Anson and I had been watching them, several of the group had done this same thing, suddenly running to the side door then reappearing again after a few minutes. Each time this happened the group would then stop sipping their beer and huddle closer around the radio for a short time, before sitting back on their stools again to resume drinking.

"Amount of stout they're getting through I'm not surprised," I answered, watching six more glasses of creamy-headed black liquid being passed along the counter by the landlord's daughter. As she handed the last pint over, the shrill bell of a phone rang.

"Flannagan's… er… yes… yes, they're here… I'll let them know… right away… yes… bye bye." She turned to us. "Lieutenant Commander Anson and Lieutenant Commander Sangster?" We both nodded. "You're wanted back at the hotel. Urgent, so they said."

"Thanks, Maureen," said Phil, downing the last of his pint. "By the way, could you help me with something?"

"Sure that depends," she answered in a sing-song local brogue, that to my ear wasn't quite Northern or Southern Irish, whilst giving Phil the merest hint of a wink. "On what it is you want me to help you with."

"Come closer, Maureen," whispered Phil, beckoning with his finger as she leaned over the bar. "See that lot at the end there?"

"Yes."

"Have they got some sort of, well, you know, bladder problems?"

"Sure I wouldn't like to say," Maureen replied, stepping back a little.

"But they keep running to the loo, through that door." He pointed across the room and Maureen let out the loudest of guffaws, a deep and echoing noise quite out of keeping with her pretty face and slight frame. Then she began to snort, before managing to collect her composure well enough to talk again.

"Bladder problems," she sobbed. "Bladder problems. That's a side entrance to the bookie's next door. They take turns to place the bets then come back and listen to the race on the radio there. Saves them going outside and getting wet, it…" She sobbed with laughter again. "Rains a lot in Ballyshannon." Snorting once more, she then called over to the group by the radio.

"Hey, these two want to know if any of you lads got problems with your waterworks?"

The group all turned and one, much bigger than the rest, shouted back, "Waterworks, what d'you mean waterworks? You two fine British officers wouldn't be taking the michael now, would you?" He and his friends stood up and glared. He was even bigger than I'd thought.

"No, no, no," Phil called back. "Misunderstanding, must be leaving." He tugged my jacket sleeve. "Enjoy your afternoon's racing, gentlemen, and thank you, Maureen." With that he put on his cap, saluted and fairly ran for the front door.

"Bye," I added, doing the same.

"Better get back to the hotel sharpish, Jack," said Phil as we walked down the hill past the bookmaker's shop front. I looked over my shoulder, but the street was empty.

"I think they've stayed inside the pub for the next race."

"Good thing too, Jack, our uniforms aren't too welcome around here. And I'd almost forgotten about horse-racing since the war broke out. I guess they still do it here in Ireland."

"But asking the barmaid about bladder problems? I mean, come on, Phil, you—"

"Perhaps I should have thought twice." He laughed. "But anyway, sounds like the Old Man wants us. Must be something up for him to call the pub like this."

*

I had also wondered what that 'something' might be, as it had seemed that our work here in Ballyshannon was done. The flying boat had been successfully raised intact and safely stored in the hold of our salvage ship, the bodies of the crew were all retrieved and laid up with appropriate dignity pending return to their loved ones, plus the necessary paperwork was completed with the local authorities. This last task was particularly complex and arduous, but it was an inconvenient fact that the plane had crashed into Donegal Bay, waters belonging to a neutral country. Procedures had to be followed to the letter if the Royal Navy was to be permitted access.

We entered the lobby of the Imperial Hotel, to be greeted by Mrs Slattery, a fearsome manageress of a certain age who made no bones about resenting her establishment being requisitioned for use by the British.

"No mud on your shoes, is there?" she snarled. We both looked down and shook our heads. "Well, you're wanted in the back parlour." Mrs Slattery jerked her own head towards the back of the hotel, Phil and I murmuring our thanks before proceeding down the hall, whereupon the sound of heated voices grew ever louder. I recognised the distinct tones of the 'Old Man', Commodore (First Class, as he often reminded his subordinates) Baines, a bear of a man famous for his quick temper. Baines commanded the flotilla that had been dispatched from Belfast to retrieve the flying boat. Our company comprised a destroyer, salvage auxiliary, an ocean-going tug, and the Mammoth, requisitioned from Liverpool docks for the duration, more than enough vessels to disquiet the neutral Irish.

"Hats off and best foot forward," said Phil, his knocking on the door barely audible over the shouting inside. We entered to see Baines and two other officers (young sub-lieutenants, both looking distinctly frightened), along with several civilians, crowded round a table, which was strewn with charts and what looked like chunks of blackened wood.

"Come in, you two," shouted Baines. "Now, you were both present when the flying boat was salvaged?"

We nodded in unison.

"And you found fifty-cal—"

"Er, yes, but sir, we—" Phil began, only to be drowned out by Baines' booming tones.

"See, now as I was saying, Mayor Gallagher, there is no escaping the fact that fifty-calibre ammunition has been found in the wreckage of the flying boat. This plane didn't crash due to engine failure; it was shot down."

"I don't care what you say, none of our lads fired a shot and there's been no Germans here in Ballyshannon."

"But the ordnance, Gallagher," Baines yelled, holding up a barnacle-encrusted point-ended shell just under six inches long that I immediately recognised as a fifty-cal round. "Luckily, this one didn't go off."

"I don't fecking care, there's been no shots here and no harbouring Germans in Ballyshannon." Gallagher banged his fist on the table. "And for you to accuse us, after Ireland, a non-belligerent, let you bring your warships into our waters, let you billet your men in our town. It's a fecking disgrace." He then spat on the floor, as the indignant Baines turned an ever-darker shade of purple. "In fact, I'll be reporting this to the Dail, in Dublin, directly. You'll have a diplomatic incident on your hands before you can sing 'God Save the King', Baines, make no mistake."

"Why, you insolent—"

"Excuse me, sir," I interrupted as politely as I could.

"What is it, Sangster?"

"May I, er… examine that shell?"

"If you must," snapped Baines, passing the oversized bullet to me. I looked closely at it, sensing immediately there was something wrong. This was indeed a standard fifty-cal round, but odd-looking for two reasons. Firstly, it was barnacle-encrusted to an extent that would usually only happen over a long period in the sea. Must be something about these waters, I told myself. Second, it had a blue tip, which I'd never seen that before, the paint very much faded but still visible.

"And this shell was found in the flying boat?" I asked.

"No, dammit," said Gallagher. "If I hear right, this shell and many others like it were found in the planking of the old wooden shipwreck beneath. Some had gone off judging by the damage around the bullet holes, and some were unexploded like this one." He grasped a chunk of wood, which almost crumbled to powder in his hand. Inside was a similar shell. "Look, here on the table. This is what the divers brought up."

"So the flying boat was strafed, and some of the shells hit the shipwreck," said Baines.

"No bullets were fired here," shouted Gallagher.

"If I may explain, Commodore, Mister Mayor," I said, holding up the shell. "I think I have the answer."

"Go on, Sangster."

"Some of these Sunderlands are modified to hold a waist-mounted machine gun, and that gun would be fully loaded and primed during any reconnaissance runs, do you agree?" Both men nodded. "So, I suspect in this case, the aircraft came down after hitting a flock of birds, the M2's firing mechanism was set off during the crash and the gun, completely unmanned, then peppered the galleon wreck with shells as the plane settled on the seabed. Total coincidence that the sunken flying boat settled on an old wreck, but there it is, see." I held up another chunk of wood and squeezed until it too crumbled to reveal another barnacle-covered cartridge case. "Embedded inside the planking. Must have come from our plane."

"Hmph," grunted Baines. "You satisfied with that, Gallagher?"

"Sounds like common sense to me," the mayor replied. "I'll forget your accusations if you, your men and your ships leave Donegal without delay."

"Consider it done." Baines held out his hand, and the mayor shook it but without looking the commodore in the eye, then turned and beckoned to his companions to leave.

"That means tonight," called Gallagher over his shoulder as the door slammed. Baines was about to speak when the door opened once more. "And you lot don't touch any of that wood, Baines. It's part of an archaeological find belonging to the Republic of Ireland. I don't want Britannia's Huns carting away Irish heritage, alright?"

"Of course, we'll leave everything here for you." The door slammed again, and Baines sighed, falling back into his chair. "That seems to have been resolved. Didn't know they had M2's mounted on Sunderlands, mind you." He sniffed. "Should've, though, so good thinking, Sangster."

"Thank you, sir."

The commodore's pleasure was short-lived, however.

"Well, don't just stand there like a pair of lemons. You heard that Mayor Gallagher, so get the men back to the ships, we sail on the evening tide."

"Yes, sir," we saluted together, then turned to leave.

"Oh, and sir?"

"Yes, Sangster?"

"May I keep this?" I held up the blue-tipped shell.

"Can't see why not."

I slipped it into my pocket. I wasn't quite sure why.

*

"How did you know there was a waist-mounted fifty-cal on the flying boat?" asked Phil as we walked down the hall.

"I didn't."

"Didn't?"

"The boat that crashed is an old Mark Two Sunderland. If it had a waist-mounted gun on it at all it would usually be a three-o-three, not a fifty-cal."

"You sure?"

"Positive. The Yanks' Catalina seaplanes might have a fifty-cal but never a Mark Two."

"Catalina, huh." Phil frowned, before brightening up with a smile (he was always one to discard potential problems if a plausible excuse came up). "Sorted that row with the mayor out, though. He wasn't going to back down and we all know what Baines is like when someone tries to square up to him."

"Yes," I said, feeling the shape and rough texture of the shell in my trouser pocket.

"But," said Phil, tugging my sleeve to stop me walking, "if those shells didn't come from the flying boat, where did they come from?" He scratched his chin. "I mean, that wreck's lying in well over a hundred feet of water. The only way bullets would embed that far into wood planks is from close-up shooting. Firing from the surface would never reach that deep."

"That's what's bothering me, but better not worry the Old Man with it."

"It'll all come out in the inquiry, Jack."

"I'm not so sure." I remembered previous inquiries, and the need for crystal-clear evidence to confirm any findings.

"Why?"

"Well…" I said slowly. "The mayor said he didn't want the stuff on the table touched, so apart from the single shell I have in my pocket, the navy's got no evidence. The Irish, on the other hand, have the shell-embedded planks from the wreck but don't have the plane wreck to check its guns."

"The way you put clues and evidence together, Jack, there's a career waiting for you as a detective, maybe in Naval Intelligence." I laughed, but he went on. "People have said it before and when I hear you, I think they might just be right."

"Oh, come on, Phil. I'm just saying this is an odd one and there's no immediate answer, but also no evidence the English and Irish are likely to share."

"Set to remain a bit of an unsolved riddle then."

"Yes, and the navy doesn't like riddles, Phil, so best we keep our heads down and hopefully it all gets forgotten and the crash put down to a bird strike."

"Mum's the word, Jack, but like I said, you're a sleuth in the making."

DARTMOOR DEVONSHIRE 1970

MONDAY, JUNE THE 22ND 5:30 PM

The gloom grew as the road gained height, winding up from Plymouth towards the high moorland. Houses became fewer with each bend I drove around, until only fields and woodlands lay either side, and what had been a sunny afternoon in the coastal town was now overcast, the air thick with mist. Finally, even the woodlands gave way, the landscape becoming one of open heather-covered hills interspersed with rocky outcrops, and although there were still several hours of daylight left, low-hanging cloud rendered the far horizon grey and indistinct.

As the road topped a hill, squat terraces and block-like buildings within high stone walls came into view, which I guessed belonged to the infamous Dartmoor prison, their form seemingly embraced by the darkening sky. And coincidently, just as I passed a sign welcoming me to Dartmoor, thunder rumbled in the distance and almost immediately afterwards, rain fell on my head. I pulled up by the side of the road and jumped out, raising the hood of my car just as the heavens opened. By the time I was safe and dry and back in the driving seat, the downpour was hammering against the roof, a thick curtain of water on the windscreen making visibility beyond a few yards all but impossible. I switched on the headlights and drove very slowly forward, tyres making a spray, the tarmac now having become a torrent. Crawling ahead, I encountered only a few oncoming cars, their lights shimmering in the rain as they approached, snail-like along the flooded road. After some minutes of this, I saw what looked like two bonfires, alight on the moor despite the storm.

A moment later, the sign I was looking for came into view...

Wyvern Arms Hotel

...and crossing the river, I turned through a pair of stone gateposts to find a rambling collection of joined white-walled buildings. Pulling up on gravel by a porticoed entrance that appeared to be the main door, I now saw a second bridge, a much older double-arched stone crossing hardly wide enough to carry a small car and presumably now disused by all but walkers, cyclists, or horse riders. A wide lawn stretched away to the right, leading, as far as I could see through the rain and occasional lightning flashes, down to a river that ran parallel to the hotel building.

Either side of the hotel doorway stood a thick stone pillar, and by each of these an ornate iron fire pit that to my mind, wouldn't have been out of place next to the Roman Colosseum. These sheltered fire pits burned brightly, explaining the illusion from the road of bonfires on the moor and giving the hotel an atmosphere both welcoming and ethereal.

Above the entrance, swinging with rhythmic thuds as it was thrashed by the rain, hung a sign, proudly stating the hotel's name over a painting of a red dragon. I watched as the front door opened to reveal the figure of a woman, silhouetted by yellow light shining from within.

Grabbing my coat from the passenger seat, I stepped into the deluge and went to the car boot, pulling out my bag before running towards her, jacket held overhead in a vain attempt to stay dry.

"Mr Sangster, is it?" she yelled, as thunder clapped above us.

"That's right."

"Come on, let's get you out of this awful weather."

I followed her through another set of double doors and into the common room, as I found out later it was called, a wide space supported by more stone pillars, with a bar at one end, and a large open fireplace at the other. The place was cluttered, almost to distraction at first sight, with numerous wall hangings, everything from old portraits to farm implements, silver trophies, stuffed fish, birds, and animals. And the furniture said 'cosy' in my mind, with well-used oak chairs and benches, numerous and non-matching tables of much the same type as the chairs, and several very well-used by the sagging cushions and cracked look of the upholstery, brown leather Chesterfield settees. The room was full of people (there was no enjoying the outdoors on a day like this), some in groups, such as a set of middle-aged men, a fishing party, judging by a waistcoat one wore that was covered in fishing flies, some solitary guests, and several couples. But the most striking thing to me was that the whole place rang with conversation and activity. Perhaps, I thought, this was due to its being a refuge from the storm, but my underlying sense of the room was of somewhere that would always stimulate busy company, as I watched uniformed waitresses coming and going and an immaculate-looking barman with a white jacket and slicked-back hair busily serving an unending queue of guests.

One couple particularly caught my eye, a middle-aged man and woman, both with long and rather unkempt brown and grey flecked hair, wearing sandals and floor-length gowns held tight at the waist by a rope. His gown was bright green and hers a light magenta colour. The berobed pair seemed to be arguing intermittently, turning away from each other now and then to sip their drinks. Both held pints of beer, and not the first of the afternoon, judging by their demeanour and a number of empties on the table next to them.

My hostess, who beckoned me towards a reception desk, was tall and slim. I remembered being measured at six foot one in the navy and she seemed close to my height. She was rosy in complexion, blue-eyed and with long blonde hair drawn back from her forehead with a white 'Alice Band'. She wore an off-white Aran sweater with blue jeans tucked into brown riding boots, and, although I always found it hard to judge a woman's age, looked to be in her late thirties, very early forties at most.

"So Mr Sangster," she said, sitting down behind the desk as a venerable and ancient-looking grandfather clock next to us struck the hour, "welcome to the Wyvern." The word 'Wyvern' was shouted over the deafening chime.

"Thank you, Mrs Merrivale," I said back, after a pause to let the chiming stop. "And please call me Jack." I held out my hand.

"'Scuse me, Missus," said a voice from behind, its shrillness making me quickly turn to see a waitress, a slight girl of about twenty, with hair tied up in a bun underneath a white cap. "Can we still serve cream teas, it being gone six and all?"

"Who's asking, Tilly?"

"Those three old ladies in the corner, Missus." She gestured to a panelled alcove by the window where three very elderly women sat in a row, waving as they saw us look round. "Mrs Curtice says—"

"Never mind what Mrs Curtice says, give them the teas but don't overdo it on the cream, we're running low."

"Missus," said the waitress with a nod before scurrying off along the corridor.

"Sorry, Jack, busy afternoon. Bad weather brings everyone indoors, now where was I?"

"Going to need another barrel of bitter, Ma'am," came another voice from behind, this time from the Brylcreemed barman. "Can you ask Whiddon to keep bar till I come back?"

"He's not turned up yet, Joe. Should have been here by six, but I haven't seen him."

"How about Tilly?"

"She's just gone to the kitchens for more cream teas, Jenny as well. Leave the bar unattended until you've changed the barrels. Guests'll just have to wait."

"Missus." Joe nodded.

"Oh, and Joe."

"Missus?"

"No more drinks for our two druid friends, they've had quite enough for one afternoon. Let them go upstairs and sleep it off."

"Missus," Joe repeated solemnly.

"Really busy, as you can see," Mrs Merrivale then said to me as he walked away to the sound of complaints from the unoccupied bar. "Now, where was I again?"

"We were making introductions and you were signing me in."

"Of course, and I'm Mercedes," she responded, before finally shaking my hand (which, I realised, must have been outstretched for about a minute). "Owner here for my sins." She gestured around the room with open hands, then pointed to herself. "And please call me Mercy, everyone else does."

I remembered that conversation in the coming days, especially the way Mercedes Merrivale spoke to me almost from the outset as if we'd known each other all our lives, and which at the time I simply took for that easy confidence pub and hotel owners so often seem to possess.

"Well, er… Mercy." I laughed. "Don't think I don't appreciate it, but do you always come out personally to meet your guests?"

"Ah, well, no, Jack, but the weather was so bad and some people here are expecting you, so I kept an eye out for a green open-top E-type. I had the fire pits lit as well, so you could see us from the road."

"People expecting me?"

"Yes, two police officers, plain-clothes. They're in the lounge right now."

"Alright, but look, could you hold them off for a bit longer so I can change?" I shook water from my jacket. "I'm soaked, even from that quick sprint from the car to the door."

"Of course." She winked. "I'll give them another coffee and say you'll be down in twenty minutes." She offered me a pen and paper. "Now just sign here, and no deposit needed because everything's paid for by, er… now who was it?"

"The Granville Institute."

"And what do they do?"

"Assist troubled children. I, er… specialise in problem cases."

"Do you now?" She looked hard at me. "Anyway, this was left for you." She held up an envelope (thick and brown with an HM Government crest on the back), which on opening proved to contain, as expected, a mandate for the institute to investigate the disappearance of local boy Christopher De Coverley, signed by the Chief Constable of Devon and Cornwall and the Head of Plymouth Social Services.

But… the envelope also contained something I hadn't expected, an Official Secrets Act form, already filled out with my name, address, and job title, as well as employer details for the Granville Institute. Along with this was a white, pre-franked envelope with a Whitehall address printed on it. I scribbled my signature, wondering what on earth could merit me needing to sign such a document, then folded the paper into the envelope, which I licked and sealed as fast as I could to avoid the contents being seen.

"Could someone post this for me?"

"Of course," Mercy said, placing the envelope in a pigeonhole behind the desk. "Now come on Jack, room seven, it's an en suite, I'll show you the way."

We walked back through the common room and past the couple in the coloured gowns, who had resumed arguing, then up a staircase. As soon as we were out of sight of the bar, Mercy turned to me and laughed.

"You saw those two in the robes?"

"The ones you don't want to have any more drinks?"

She nodded.

"They're druids, or so they claim."

"Hmmm… I suppose that explains a lot."

"And they're on their honeymoon," she whispered behind her hand. "But insisted on a twin room, separate beds, you know?"

"How romantic." I laughed.

"They were married just yesterday, or as they described it, 'handfasted.'"

"Where?"

"In a field at the back of the hotel. It has some old standing stones in it which they say have mystical powers to bless their union."

"As I said, how romantic."

Mercy laughed out loud at that, showing immaculately white and even teeth as she did so.

"Yes, our back field's a horse paddock, so besides standing stones, it's full of, well, you can imagine what…" She let out a 'phwoar' noise. "But that field is the best place to watch a sunset, and yesterday was the summer solstice as well."

"Ah, yes, important to druids. What are their names, by the way?"

"Well, she is called Fidelma, and he's Ballar. They said these aliases were… now what was it?" She scratched her head. "Yes, that's it, their 'Craft Names.'"

"And their surname, Mercy?"

"Dike, another Craft Name, I suppose."

"The Dikes, eh?" It was my turn to laugh. "Are they going Dutch with the hotel bill?"

"Sorry?"

"You know, dike like the ditches in Holland?"

"Oh, er… yes."

I suddenly felt awkward. There were two alternative emotions I felt when a woman failed to understand one of my jokes. The first was disappointment, the second embarrassment from knowing I had tried and failed to be witty.

"Very droll." Mercy then grimaced, giving me a twinge of the latter emotion. "Their real name's Atkinson, Janet and Colin, it's on the reservation letter they sent with their deposit."

"I like Dike better."

"Me too," she said, opening the door to room seven. "Here we are. Come down as soon as you're ready. The TV lounge is on the left of the common room, along a corridor just past the bar."

I walked into the bedroom, closed the door behind me, and was about to open my suitcase when I heard a knock.

"Yes."

"Only me again, Jack," said Mercy, craning her head around the door. "It's just that—"

"Come in, please." She entered, closing the door behind her.

"I wanted to say that I know why you are here."

"Er… it's rather confidential, I can't—"

"It was me," she interrupted.

"Sorry?"

"Who called the police."

"I was told it was an anonymous tip-off."

"I didn't give my name but had to call, couldn't wait any longer." She dabbed her eye with a handkerchief. "I mean, a boy, missing on the moor for who knows how long, and a father who simply won't cooperate."

"You did the right thing by calling, so let me talk to these police officers downstairs and get the full picture. Then perhaps we can meet later, and you can tell me more about it?"

"Yes, let's, but it'll have to be after dinner's done and most of the guests have turned in. Can you wait up that late?"

"Sure."

"Good, and now I'd better go back down. Full sitting for dinner tonight, lots to do. You'll dine with us?"

"Starving and looking forward to it."

"About eight then, and," she said with another wink, "proper clothes, Mrs Curtice can't abide sloppiness at dinner."

"Sloppiness?"

"Yes, so it's jackets in the dining room, please. No jeans or shorts and tie optional."

"Who's this Mrs Curtice?"

"Oh, you'll find out when you meet her tonight." She laughed from the hall. "And just remember, no sloppiness."

Yes Missus, I said to myself as she left me alone in the room.

7 PM

"A special investigator no less," observed the detective inspector, examining my card, her mouth curling down at the corners as she spoke, forming what I could only take as a sneer.

"That's right," I replied. "Granville Institute."

"And which kinds of investigation do you specialise in?"

"I look into cases involving troubled children, often missing."

"Well, it seems you have gained a reputation for, how did my superiors put it… yes, that's it, they said you 'have a knack for seeing things the police miss.'"

"Did they?" I said flatly, feeling more and more uncomfortable at her unspoken resentment.

"Said it was you found that girl down near Truro last month, the one all over the news. Buried alive by all accounts."

"Look, Inspector Hawke, I had this assignment foisted on me just yesterday evening, out of the blue, and it's been a long drive from Chester." She looked at me with one eyebrow raised. "Yes, and longer than it should have been. After the motorway stopped, back in Bridgewater, there were roadworks on the A30 and I had to take a detour via Plymouth." I sighed as she continued to stare. "So can we please discuss the case in hand?"

She lowered the raised eyebrow. "You, er… have a written mandate, I believe?"

"Yes," I said, offering the paper to her.

"Never actually seen one of these before." She looked the document up and down then passed it back to me. "Someone on high must really want you working the case. Any idea who?"

"Certainly came at very short notice," I replied, keen to avoid saying too much. "But please, let's discuss the case itself now."

"Very well," she said with a shrug. "Eccles, move those coffee cups and get out the papers on the De Coverley boy so we can let Mr Sangster have a read."

The detective constable meekly emptied a cardboard folder of loose documents onto the table. As I was about to pick the first one up, the door opened and Tilly the waitress appeared.

"Mrs Merrivale wants to know if you'd like any more coffee?"

"No, girl, we wouldn't," snapped the DI. "And please remind Mrs Merrivale that we were promised this lounge would remain private. No more interruptions."

"Yes'm," said Tilly, looking at the ground and reversing out of the door as she did so.

"Are these documents for me to keep, Inspector Hawke?" I asked once Tilly had gone.

"They're all copies, so yes."

"Then I'd rather read them later, and while we're here, listen to your account of the situation. That OK?"

"I suppose so, providing we agree specific actions and demarcation lines for the ongoing inquiry."

"Oh, demarcations lines, yes, of course. Actions too."

"Very well, and you'd better sit back then, because this will take me some minutes. Eccles?" She held up her cup and the constable immediately refilled it from the coffee pot. He then went to pick up the milk jug, but she waved him away. "No, no, I'll pour, you always put far too much in. Just sit down over there and take notes."

I topped up my own coffee, sat back as instructed, and regarded the DI, whose singular looks, I felt, matched her demeanour. Dressed in a dark grey trouser suit and black brogue lace-up shoes, she was a spare-framed woman in her early forties with sharp facial features and page-boy hair, which she had styled using almost as much grease as the white-coated barman Joe wore. I also noticed a polished ebony cane topped with an ivory goat's head leaning against her chair (for help with walking or just for effect?). DI Hawke's most striking accessory, however, was a black eye patch, shaped like a cat's eye, and worn without a strap or any other visible means of support. Then there was her make-up, thick blue eyeshadow on the exposed eye, and bright red lipstick contrasting with heavily powdered porcelain-white skin, all of which only exacerbated an already almost emotionless demeanour. I found myself wondering whether the inspector's doll-like face might crack if she laughed (I guessed I would never find out).

"So, Mr Sangster," she began, "if you've quite finished appraising me?" I nodded, feeling my cheeks colour slightly. "Here's what we know thus far."

*

"Christopher De Coverley is the son of Doctor John De Coverley, who lives at Foxtor House, where I think his family has resided since, er... when was it, Eccles?"

"Elizabethan times, Ma'am."

"Exactly, and it's just a few miles from here, close by the Highmoor Research Centre."

"The Ministry of Defence facility?" I'd heard of this Highmoor Centre, scene of anti-nuclear protests and featured in TV documentaries. A remote place of government secrets, or so it was portrayed by the press.

"That's right. A lot of research started there after the war, and the current superintendent is Sir Peregrine Frere."

"And De Coverley's connection?"

"De Coverley began working at Highmoor when it first opened, at the end of the war. Being who he is, it was natural the doctor would end up there, I guess."

"Being who he is, Inspector?"

She looked at me with open disdain, as if my ignorance was hard to believe.

"To spell it out, Sangster, the foremost nuclear physicist in the land who just happens to reside within walking distance of the Highmoor Centre."

"And," I said, trying not to react to her acid glare, "how old would Doctor De Coverley be?"

"Er... Eccles?"

"Born early 1917, Ma'am, so fifty-three."

"And the missing boy?" I asked her.

"Fifteen."

"And how long since he was reported missing?"

"Two days, Sangster, but that's not quite the point." She picked up one of the sheets from the file. "Apparently, Christopher hasn't been properly seen for some weeks. You see, even though our enquiries at his last school showed the boy was a model pupil, since January, the father insisted on home-schooling his son. Christopher was also being tutored in specialised subjects by Professor Septimus Frere, Sir Peregrine's brother. Septimus lives over by Yelverton."

"Ma'am?"

"What, Eccles?"

"Shouldn't we mention to Mr Sangster that the Freres are uncles to Mercedes Merrivale?"

"Yes, yes, Eccles." She waved her hand at the DC. "On her mother's side, Sangster. Anyway, if I may continue, Eccles..."

She went on to say that Septimus Frere was a recognised authority on Sir Francis Drake and the Spanish Armada, a former Cambridge history professor, and now curator of a museum dedicated to Drake.

"So this Septimus is well qualified to tutor the boy, who you say hasn't been, how did you say, 'properly'..." I looked at the DI for confirmation and she nodded, "seen for a long time?"

"Not close up, to talk to. Some people claim to have seen Christopher from a distance, but that's all."

"So, Inspector," I said, thinking perhaps some fundamental questions needed asking, "what about his home life, siblings, relatives, his mother?"

"Ah, yes. No siblings or close relatives bar the father. Mother dead, car accident late last year. Very close by here, it happened. Swerved off the road, she did. No other vehicle involved."

"Drinking, or some history of medical problems. Epilepsy, perhaps?"

"No, from what I remember the autopsy didn't show anything untoward and she had no medical problems if I remember right."

"There's been a few crashes on that road, Ma'am," said the detective constable from his corner. "And no good explanation for them."

"Don't be silly, Eccles." The DI waved a dismissive hand. "Just keep writing your notes and Mr Sangster or I will let you know when we want help."

"One moment, Constable, how do you mean, 'no explanation'?"

"Just more than normal, sir." Eccles looked at me oddly as he said this, so that I wondered if he was holding something back, perhaps just from me, perhaps from the DCI as well. "Cars swerving for no reason, that is, I reckon—"

"It's dark and narrow along there," interrupted DI Hawke. "And with an inverse camber at one point. People just need to be more careful."

"If you say so, Ma'am, but that's a treacherous stretch all the same."

"Anyway, Mr Sangster, to stay on the subject, social services have been unable to see the boy, and the tutor—"

"This Professor Septimus Frere?"

"Yes, and he says he hasn't seen Christopher for, er… how long, Eccles?"

"More than two and a half months, Ma'am."

"Was this boy a troublemaker, you know, the kind to run away?"

"As I told you, model pupil according to his school reports," said the DI, shaking her head. "And there's no record of him ever having run away before."

"And girls," I asked. "What about girls?"

"Girls?"

"Well, er… some lads that age, they tend to like older girls, and older girls may sometimes feel the same. Was there anyone who—"

"The boy was close to Melissa Merrivale."

"Mercedes' sister?"

"Sixteen-year-old daughter."

"I see, and the girl's father?"

"Not around. I've been working this patch a few years now, and Mercedes has always been on her own." The inspector sniffed with what I thought indicated disdain. "Always seemed none of the local blokes were good enough in her eyes."

"OK… but what puzzles me is why Doctor De Coverley wasn't the one to report his son missing."

"Me too," agreed the DI. "When we spoke to him, De Coverley said the boy had run off and would likely be back. Claimed he had no idea where Christopher would go."

"You searched the house?"

"Yes, outbuildings and all," said Eccles. "Nothing, and Doctor De Coverley was pretty angry when we did it. Didn't seem worried about the lad at all, though, did he, Ma'am?"

"Not for you to say what a member of the public might be thinking, Eccles," she snapped back.

"So if I may summarise, Inspector…"

I went on to say that as far as I could tell, the case revolved around a previously very steady and dependable boy who had apparently disappeared, and a father, well known and nationally respected, from an ancient local family, who refused to cooperate with the authorities to prove his boy was safe.

"Very succinct, Sangster, that does more or less put the whole thing in a nutshell," said the DI when I'd finished. "Now let us agree who will do what next."

"Do all these documents give me the contact details of the people we discussed?"

"Addresses and phone numbers are all there, including photos and background notes," said Eccles. "We've interviewed them all."

"Well, I'm formerly assigned to the case now, so I'll go and talk to the people you mentioned. John De Coverley, Septimus Frere, his brother Peregrine, and er… the daughter, what was her name?"

"Melissa, and don't miss Mrs Merrivale either. She may know something."

"I won't, Inspector, but what are your next steps going to be?"

"We'll do door-to-door, take any calls from the public, post pictures around of the boy, and generally keep our ears to the ground. You'll report in every day?"

"Of course. Phone call at noon unless we need to talk at other times?"

"Sounds reasonable, Mr Sangster, but I'm still intrigued."

"By what?"

"Why did they bring you in?"

"Don't I seem competent?"

"Oh no, you seem very good, even if you are a dilettante." I could sense it was hard for her to accept me, and it seemed she'd felt compelled to qualify the compliment by calling me a dilettante. "And believe me, my chief super's well pleased to have you here. CID's always short-staffed and you cost him nothing."

"Glad to hear your chief super likes to keep an eye on the pennies."

"Yes," she sighed. "But why send someone like you, the best the Granville has if I read the reports right, to find a missing kid in Devon?"

"Well, I—"

"Now don't be modest," she said, standing up and leaning on her goat-headed cane. "And truth be told, I do feel outsiders like you can pose a threat to proper policing, but you're too good for this case."

"I'm not sure," I said, considering how I could best answer this, whilst feeling gratified her question came from the heart, "that I'm too good for any case where a missing child is concerned, but I know what you mean, and honestly…"

"Yes?" asked the DI, now entirely focused.

"I've no idea myself why they put me on this case."

7:45 PM

"Mr Sangster?"

I looked around to see Tilly standing in the door frame. "Call for you, sir," she said, prompting me to look around the room for a phone. "Downstairs, sir."

"Very well." I tidied the papers given to me by DI Hawke, which were spread across the bed, slipped on my blazer, and followed the waitress down the stairs. She pointed to an alcove opposite reception where a table and studded green leather telephone seat stood, a chair of the hemi-spherical type that surround the occupant. "You can take it there."

"Thanks," I said, walking over to the seat as the phone on the table began to ring. "Hello?"

Sitting down, I heard payphone pips and then the familiar and slightly breathless voice of my wife.

"It's me, Jack, and this'll need to be a quick call, I only have two shillings in coins." Her voice had an edge to it, and I could guess why. We were all set to travel together when I'd received an instruction from my boss to go to Devon immediately. He had even, and very uncharacteristically for the richest miser I had ever met, offered to refund my plane ticket to Tel Aviv and cover the cost of my wife's flight as compensation.

"Did you make it to the airport OK?"

"Yes," she replied flatly. "I'm through customs now and in the lounge. Just got to wait for the flight, I—"

"Look, I really am sorry about having to leave so early this morning." I waited for her to reply but there was silence. "I got a three-line whip from Sir John last night. Never been spoken to like that before, so God knows what's so important about this case." More silence. "What else could I do?"

"Told your boss where to get off, that's what. Told old Granville it's not every day your wife flies off to bury her grandmother."

"Please understand, Sarah," I sighed.

"I do, darling," she said, her voice softening. "It's just such a shame you're not with me."

"You've Rachel with you."

"Not quite the same."

"Well, look, you'll be back home before you know it, so try and relax on the plane, have a good old chat with your sister, and I'll see you soon." As I spoke, the sound of an airport announcer could be heard echoing in the background.

"Eight forty BOAC flight to Tel Aviv now boarding at Gate Seven."

"Oh, my flight's being called. Have to go now."

"Alright, and I'll likely be out and about tomorrow, but please, leave a message at the hotel to say you arrived safely. Yes?"

"OK, and you take care as well. I can't help feeling anxious about this assignment, the way they gave you so little notice, and the way Sir John described it. What did he say again?"

"Er… something like, 'Can't tell you more now, but this is vital to the national interest, Sangster, vital, I say.' He sounded quite flustered."

"Something's not right, I can feel it, I—"

The pips went again, drowning out what she said next, after which the phone went dead.

*

"Er... Mr Sangster, room seven."

"Yes, yes, one moment." The woman standing by the dining-room door waved me to one side. She was dressed in a formidable green taffeta evening gown and wore a glittering tiara in her grey/blue permed hair. In her hand was a clipboard, which she scrutinised through a pair of horn-rimmed glasses.

"Now then," she said, removing the glasses and addressing Mr and Mrs Dike, who stood defiantly before her in their Druidic robes, "I can see your names here, but I'm afraid you simply don't meet our dress-code requirements. Look." She gestured to a sign stating:

Ladies' and Gentlemen's Dinner Dress Code
Dresses, skirts, or smart trousers
Jackets, collared shirts, creased trousers, tie optional

"Well, these count as dresses," shouted Mrs Dike, pointing to her robe.

"The dresses, Madam," said the woman (Mrs Curtice the 'stickler', I presumed, as mentioned by Mercy), pointing at Ballar, "refer to the ladies' apparel, not the gentlemen's, and in any event, a garment made of, what is it..." she waved one hand dismissively at Mrs Dike's robe, "sackcloth tied up with string, hardly constitutes a dress. No." She shooed them away, now using both hands. "I'm afraid you'll have to eat in the common room or your bedroom. The bar menu is very comprehensive and available for room service."

"Why you old—" shouted Mrs Dike, before being interrupted by a soothing voice.

"Now what's all this?" I looked round to see Mercy, quite transformed from the jeans-clad outdoor girl that met me at the door less than a couple of hours before. Now, she wore a low-cut ankle-length black velvet dress with matching choker; her straw-coloured hair was up, her make-up perfect, and in high heels she definitely stood taller than me. "Mother, it's five past eight. Shouldn't you be starting your recital?"

"But these two—"

"No buts, now you go over to the piano and I'll handle this."

"Very well, my dear, you know best, I'm sure." Mrs Curtice sniffed, handing her daughter the clipboard and pencil, then picking up a glass on the table next to her and downing the contents before looking at the empty vessel with apparent confusion. "Oh, and Mercedes, tell Gurney to bring me another gin and tonic, would you?"

Mercy nodded.

"And you, young man," Mrs Curtice said, pointing at me.

"Me?"

"Yes, you. A few years ago we'd have expected gentlemen to wear a dinner jacket, not a blazer. It's sloppy, everything's sloppy these days."

"I'm sorry."

"It's easy for you younger generation to let things go."

"Mum," Mercy laughed, "I'm not exactly a spring chicken, and nor is Mr Sangster."

"Chicken, you don't know the half of it. Why, I had my menopause—"

"Alright, Mum," said Mercy, tapping her mother's arm.

"No, no, it needs to be said." Mercy took a step back and looked at the ceiling. "I had my menopause at twenty-seven."

"Was that alright, gynaecologically, you know?" asked Mrs Dike, her eyebrows raised some way towards her hair line.

"Course it was." Mrs Curtice raised her empty glass. "I drank my way through it."

I tried to contain my laughter, but a snort came out.

"And you can be quiet, young man," shouted Mrs Curtice, slapping my cheek. "Sloppy," she then added again.

With that, as Mercy mouthed 'sloppy' to me, grinning as I rubbed my face, Mrs Curtice folded and placed her glasses in her cleavage, then slowly turned and walked away through the dining room, stopping to talk to some of the guests before sitting down at a grand piano in the corner.

"So we're not good enough for you?"

"Of course you are, Mrs Dike. Mrs Curtice is a bit of a stickler for rules, but she means no harm. Now please, take that nice quiet table in the corner. Tilly, show Mr and Mrs Dike to table twelve, please."

"Yes'm," said the waitress, then solemnly led the robed couple away.

"You look a bit smarter than the drowned rat I met at the door," said Mercy when they had gone. "Navy tie?"

"You recognise it?"

"Yes, Al… my husband, was in the service."

"Ah," was all I said in response. Usually I would have asked more about someone in the navy, but at that moment thought better of it, remembering DI Hawke saying Mercy's husband hadn't been around for some years. "And you, well, you do look…" I paused, involuntarily looking her up and down, not quite knowing what to say next.

"Yes, I do look what?" she said after a few moments, gesturing encouragingly with her arms.

"Quite stunning."

I immediately thought of Sarah as I spoke, but also felt justified. If this woman trusted me then she would open up, and despite only having been at the Wyvern for a short time, I already felt Mercedes Merrivale had much more to tell me about the case.

"Oh, Jack." She blushed. "Now then, there are a few people dining alone tonight, so I've put you all on the same table. Hope you don't mind."

"Not at all, lead on." We crossed the room, accompanied by the sound of *Moonlight Sonata*. Mrs Curtice, fortified, I noticed, by another G&T supplied by the ever-reliable Tilly, had begun to play. "Your mother, er… she is your mother?"

"Oh yes." Mercy laughed. "She rises around four most days, spends a couple of hours dressing then holds court in the kitchens and the dining room. Luckily, she is a lovely pianist, although I have to keep an eye out for, well…"

"When perhaps it's time for her to, um…?"

"Yes, I know, stop playing." She gestured to a round table where all but one of the six seats were occupied. "Excuse me." The guests looked up. "This is Jack Sangster, and he's come down today from Cheshire. Isn't that right, Jack?"

"That's it."

"Now, Jack, let me order you a drink."

"When in Rome." I shrugged, thinking of Mrs Curtice. "I'll have a G&T."

"Everybody else alright for drinks?" The group nodded in unison.

"Then," said Mercy, "if I may, I'll leave you to make your introductions."

I sat down and looked at my dining companions, three men and a woman.

"Jack Sangster, a pleasure to meet you all."

"Peregrine Frere," said the man to my left, holding out his hand. He was in his sixties, ruddy-faced with a full head of white hair, and wearing a three-piece tweed suit. Somehow his name was familiar, but I couldn't place it.

"Miles Edgerton," said the man on my right, now extending his hand. I shook it, feeling the strength of his grip. Miles looked in his early forties, with thinning dark hair, a broad frame, and I guessed tall, his figure that of a wrestler or rugby forward.

"Jane Ustrix," announced the woman opposite, perhaps in her early thirties, dressed in a bottle-green trouser suit, with minimal make-up and her hair in a tight bun.

"Septimus," said the last of the diners, a man of sixty or so wearing a blazer with a crest on the breast pocket. He leant over the table to shake my hand. "Septimus Frere."

That's it, I thought. The two brothers mentioned by DI Hawke.

"Peregrine there is my elder brother," Septimus added, confirming my thoughts. "Sir Peregrine, I should say," he added with a twinkle. "Now what brings you all the way from, um… somewhere in Cheshire, you said, now where was it?"

"I didn't say, but Chester."

"Ah, yes, Mr Sangster, now don't tell me…"

"He fancies himself as a bit of Sherlock Holmes." The brother laughed, Miles Edgerton agreeing with a grin.

"Now let me see." Septimus looked me up and down. "Yes, I perceive you are visiting our locality to, er… may I be frank?"

"Oh, you may," I said.

"To look for a love child, from a liaison some years ago. Perhaps here incognito. Am I on the right track?"

The other guests began to laugh and so did I.

"I'm afraid you're not quite 'on the right track', Septimus." I chuckled. "Not really."

"Well, you would say that."

"I would." I laughed again, as Tilly handed me my drink. "But cheers, pleasure to meet you all." Everyone then raised their glasses, except Septimus, who sat erect and glared. I felt guilty for laughing.

"Please, Septimus," I said to him as he continued to stare, "tell me how you arrived at that conclusion."

"Seems pointless now," Septimus muttered, lowing his eyes.

"Proceed, Septimus," his brother said, gesturing with outstretched hands. "Enlighten us all."

"Very well," Septimus sighed. "You aren't wearing a wedding ring, Sangster, but you seem personable, ahem." He cleared his throat. "Even handsome, some would say, so odds are you're married and have removed it, hence likely pretending to be single and checked in under an assumed name." I held up my left hand and regarded the empty ring finger (none of the men in my family wore wedding rings). "Plus, you're travelling alone, and I saw you enter the hotel earlier carrying a small case, so no luggage that would indicate you're here for fishing, rambling, or even the hunt."

"Go on." I nodded.

"You wear a Royal Navy tie, and those are navy buttons on your blazer, but unless you're top brass, you're too old to be anything but retired, and last but not least."

"Yes," came a chorus from the other diners.

"I didn't mean to eavesdrop earlier, Sangster, but I couldn't help overhearing you speaking to the detective inspector as you were walking out from the hotel lounge." He held his finger in the air and raised his voice. "Saying, and I quote, 'anything else you can do to help me find this child.'"

I wondered for a moment how he knew DI Hawke was a detective, then remembered the police had interviewed Septimus two days before.

"And in summary?" asked his brother.

"Sangster is retired RN, sometime based in Plymouth, now returned, and seeking his love child."

"Tell my brother if he's even close," said Peregrine, looking at me and winking. "Please?" Septimus glared again.

"Well," I said, worrying that any answer might be construed as laughing at Septimus, "he is on the mark in certain ways. I am retired RN, commander for my sins, and don't hunt, fish, or even ramble very much. Plus, I am here to find a missing child, but not mine, I—"

"Prawn cocktail, sir?" asked the waitress. "Or a summer salad?"

"I haven't ordered yet, but yes, prawn cocktail would be nice."

"Set menu tonight, sir," she said, placing the dish in front of me. "And wine, white or red?"

"Oh, white, please."

"Whose child then?" asked Miles, as the other starters were served and wine was poured.

"It's a little delicate, but—"

"*Bon appétit,*" said Jane Ustrix, and the rest of the table raised their glasses.

"Mmmm?" Miles continued to ask, despite his mouth now being full.

"The De Coverley boy, Christopher. Up at, um…"

"Foxtor House." Sir Peregrine completed the sentence then pointed his fork at me. "And why did they send you all the way from Chester to find him?"

"I work for the Granville Institute, and…" I went on to explain my job, as a special investigator into cases of troubled youngsters and how I'd some experience of finding missing children. The most recent of these wasn't too far away, a girl in Truro (all except Jane Ustrix said they had read of the case in the papers), and I'd been assigned to work with the Devon police to help find Christopher. I didn't stress the oddness of the De Coverley case, with its apparent urgency and inexplicable concern from the highest authorities. And luckily, they didn't ask.

"Well, Sangster, you've sat at the right table," said Sir Peregrine. "Hasn't he, Septimus?"

"I suppose so."

"I oversee the Highmoor Research Centre, where Christopher's father works, and Septimus has been the boy's tutor since the turn of the year, although…" He pointed to Septimus. "My brother hasn't seen the lad for some time."

"That's right, but I imagine you knew all that, Sangster, and that's why you are sitting here tonight," Septimus added, whilst chewing a mouthful of prawns.

"No, this is just a coincidence," I said. "But a lucky one. I'd planned to come and see you both as soon as I could, given you know the De Coverleys so well."

"Main courses?" The waitress's voice reverberated in my left ear. "We've jugged hare, fresh river trout, or, er… a potatoey gratin thing."

"I'll try anything once, so jugged hare, please."

The others followed my lead, except Jane Ustrix, who ordered the 'potatoey gratin thing'.

"My brother and I are, as they say, suspects then?" said Septimus, voice elevated excitedly when he pronounced 'suspect'. "Potential child abductors even?"

"We were already interviewed by the police," added Sir Peregrine. "Very rude detective inspector. Woman with one eye."

"Of course you're not suspects. I, and the police, just need to try and get a picture of the whole thing, see the lie of the land, talk to people who know the lad. I mean…" I lowered my voice, trying to calm the atmosphere. "Don't want to underplay it, but Christopher De Coverley's likely just run off. Happens nine times out of ten with kids of his age."

"Dartmoor," said Sir Peregrine, looking hard at me, "isn't a nine-times-out-of-ten sort of a place."

"Er…" I was saved from having to think of an apt reply by the return of our waitress, pushing a heavily laden serving trolley.

"Bonne continuation," said Jane, raising her glass, and after toasting back, my dining companions and I set to with the main course. Jugged hare, despite my reservations, turned out to be delicious, served on the bone in a rich red wine gravy, along with roast potatoes and cauliflower cheese in plentiful supply on a centre of table platter.

"Let's not talk shop for a while, let's talk about us," she then said, and the party complied, making more detailed introductions. Miles, it seemed, was the master of the local hunt.

"Fox hunting?" I asked.

"No, otters."

"You hunt otters?"

"Oh yes, we've a fine pack of otter hounds hereabouts, and we've a hunt tomorrow." He waved his hand towards the other tables. "Most of these people are here for the hunt, or should I say, hunts."

"How do you mean?"

"What he means," said Peregrine, "is both the Princetown Fox Hunt, that's them over there, we call them 'Foxes.'" He pointed to the other side of the room. "And the Highmoor Otter Hunt, that's us." He spread his arms, gesturing to the diners close by. "All except Septimus, who's an honorary Otter tonight as he dines at my side."

"No love lost between Foxes and Otters," added Septimus. "I'll be riding with the Princetown tomorrow. My brother and I have different ways when it comes to hunting."

"And you, Jane?"

"Oh yes, I will join the hunt."

She surprised me with this, as I'd guessed she was a vegetarian (summer salad and potatoey gratin thing).

"I see."

"It's a matter of research," she then added.

"Into what?"

"I'm a folklorist by profession, and in this case, the Wild Hunt."

"Ah," Miles laughed, "you'll be hoping to visit Wistman's Wood then."

"I, er… couldn't say," Jane stuttered, then stared down at her plate, as Septimus looked hard at her.

"That wood's famous for being haunted by Sir Francis Drake, isn't it?" he asked, glass simultaneously raised to the waitress for a top-up.

"That elegantly introduces you, eh, brother?" Sir Peregrine pointed at Septimus.

"I'm a history professor, not a dabbler in hocus pocus, but I suppose it does, yes."

"Yes what?" queried Jane.

"My speciality is Drake. I'm curator of a museum dedicated to Sir Francis."

"Given over our family home to the thing," said Sir Peregrine.

"Sir Francis Drake really used to live in your family home?" I asked.

"No, Sangster, Drake lived at Buckland Abbey, a few miles away, but Septimus wishes he'd lived in our home, do you not, brother?"

"Nothing wrong with Reynard's Hall honouring Drake," answered Septimus, tapping his breast pocket. "This crest's taken from his drum."

"And if you give Septimus a couple of scotches," said Sir Peregrine with a twinkle in his eye, the whole table looking on in eager anticipation, "he'll recite Drake's Drum for you as well, word-perfect."

"Drake's Drum?" Miles Edgerton looked confused.

"It's a poem," snapped Septimus, as the waitress appeared again.

"Cheeses or cake?"

"What's the cake?" asked Miles.

"Black Forest gateau."

The rest of the table took the cake, whilst I asked the waitress about the cheese.

"Dartmoor farmhouse, sir, bit like cheddar."

"Just that, no other cheeses?"

"No, sir."

"Then I'll have it, I like cheddar."

"It's wrapped in nettles, sir."

"Does it sting?" Septimus laughed.

She solemnly shook her head.

"Accompanied by a glass of port, sir?"

"Sounds like a good thing all round," said Sir Peregrine before I could say no. "Port wine, gentlemen?"

"And gentlewomen," said Jane, as the others nodded their approval. "Although I'll have a cream port if you have one, I—"

She was drowned out by Mrs Curtice calling loudly across the dining room. "Well, ladies and gentlemen, I'd just…" she stopped to drink from a large wine glass, "like to thank you for listening tonight, and especially thank those who didn't dress in a sloppy way." She swigged again from her glass, looking particularly hard at the Dikes' corner table. "Sloppy, as I say, but anyway…" she emptied her glass, "I'll finish with some boogie-woogie."

"Oh God," whispered Sir Peregrine, covering his eyes. "She's either going to be amazing or embarrassing."

"Or both," added Septimus under his breath.

"This is called…" said Mrs Curtice, whilst building up to an almost classical crescendo with a high-noted climax, "the 'Swanee River Boogie.'" She then, and unexpectedly which made it all the better, hit the low notes, thumping out a boogie bass. This way of musically sneaking up on the listener, judging by the cheer that went up, delighted the diners, even more so when she accompanied this with the 'Swanee River' melody. The audience clapped for some minutes when Mrs Curtice finished playing, at which point there were several cries for more, but it was not to be.

I saw Mercy take Mrs Curtice by the arm, letting the woman bow before escorting her, staggering more than a little, from the room.

"And gentlemen, you may smoke," she called out as Mercy led her through the door. The time had come, as Mercy had said earlier, for her mother to stop.

*

"So, Sangster," said Sir Peregrine as we sipped our coffee, "I suppose you'd like to meet up at some point."

"I would appreciate it, and I'd like to meet with Doctor De Coverley."

"He'll be at the centre tomorrow, so perhaps late afternoon."

"Not earlier?"

"No, I—"

He was interrupted by Miles Edgerton, who stood up and clinked his glass with a spoon.

"Ladies and gentlemen. I'll be brief because we have an early start in the morning, and just take this opportunity to thank you again for supporting the otter hunt."

"And the fox hunt," came a shout from across the room, and I looked up to see a ruddy-faced man, hand cupped around his mouth. "You forget us on purpose, Edgerton?"

Edgerton's cheeks turned a deep shade of red, and he pursed his lips as if to say something back, before presumably thinking better of it.

"And if I may continue," he went on through gritted teeth, "we'll be assembling at seven thirty as usual, the weather forecast is good, so I raise my glass…" I saw that the 'Foxes' all kept their glasses firmly on the table, whilst the Otter side of the dining room enthusiastically raised theirs in reply. "To our friends of the Princetown Hunt." Here Edgerton managed a watery smile as he looked towards the ruddy-faced heckler. "And," Edgerton went on with a beaming smile, "to the Highmoor Hunt and a splendid day's hunting for all."

There was a deafening round of applause, with knives and glasses hitting the tables, the noise only dying down after several minutes. The general effect of the toast, however, was to signal the end of the dinner and encourage the diners, both Foxes and Otters, to begin leaving, so that before long the room was largely empty. After a time, the group at my table stood up to leave as well.

"Sangster," said Septimus, "I could see you tomorrow afternoon at Reynard's. Say, two o'clock?"

"That would work well, thanks." I took out my notebook and jotted down the time, then looked at his brother. "And you, Sir Peregrine?"

"Come to the Highmoor Centre a little after that, around four?"

"Very well."

"I'll make sure they have a pass ready for you."

"Thanks to you both, and goodnight."

10 PM

"Well, goodnight, Mr Sangster," said Jane Ustrix as she stood up from the table.

"Miss Ustrix," I answered, before mentally kicking myself for assuming her a spinster.

"Jane, please," she answered back, and without contradicting me.

"Then please call me Jack, and if I'm not being too nosey," I asked, as we walked towards the dining-room door, "why would you ride with a hunt when you are clearly against animal cruelty?"

"Very perceptive of you."

"Not really." I laughed. "Judging by your choice, of courses."

She grinned and nodded as we negotiated the dining tables, where guests in various states of inebriation were standing up.

"And you know, Jane, before today, I had no idea there was such a thing as an otter hunt. Foxes, yes, and they even hunt hares on foot and with beagles near where I live, but otters, well, I—"

"Human nature, I guess, Jack. The cleverer and bigger the animal, the more complex and satisfying the hunt." She frowned for a moment. "Satisfying for some people at least. You, for example."

"Me?"

"You hunt perhaps the most satisfying quarry of all."

"Do I?"

"You hunt lost children."

"Never thought of what I do that way," I said, pausing to think. "But yes, I suppose it is satisfying when it works out alright." I paused again, remembering that it didn't always work out alright. "Anyway, this Wistman's Wood. Why are you so keen to go there tomorrow?"

"Now you are being nosey."

"Sorry, it's a side effect of my job."

"Ah well," she whispered. "If you want to know, I'm looking into a very different kind of hunt."

"Different, how?"

"Buy me a nightcap and I'll explain."

"OK," I said, looking around for Mercy. "Just a quick one, if you don't mind, what'll it be?"

"Whisky, please, neat. You decide which one."

I left the choice to Joe Gurney, who presented me with a twelve-year-old Macallan single malt. Shuddering to think what this would look like on my expense claim, I took a tonic water for myself, thinking tomorrow might be a long day.

"There we are," I said, sitting down beside Jane on a wide oak settle wedged into a bay window. "Barman says it's a very fine one, twelve years old. What were you doing in 1958?"

"Graduating, so cheers, Jack."

I raised my tonic glass in response, as guests marched past us through the common room, footfall and conversation filling the room with a blanket of noise as they filed up staircases, down halls, and along corridors on the way to bed.

"Now just briefly, because I need to be getting to bed as well, but you asked why I would ride with the hunt."

I nodded.

"Well..."

Jane, it seemed, was a research fellow and lecturer at Oxford ('Somerville College, Jack, exclusively petticoats'). Preferring to let her continue to talk, I didn't mention that my wife was an alumnus and very likely up at the same time At that moment it seemed best to hold my cards close to my chest and see what I could learn. Jane's subject, she said, was English folklore, especially from this south-west region, and in particular the Wild Hunt.

"I don't suppose you know about the Wild Hunt Jack, let me—"

"Ah ha," I interrupted. "Now I do actually. Only a few weeks ago I saw a ghostly-looking black dog on Bodmin Moor."

"You really saw a… what do the Cornish call it… a Dandy Hound?"

"Sorry." I shrugged. "A local man thought it must have been a Dandy Hound running with the Wild Hunt, but it turned out to be someone's Great Dane, slipped its leash. Not remotely ghostly, I'm afraid."

"Oh dear," she said, face visibly drooping. "But people take that sort of thing seriously around here. Know these spectral dogs as Wish Hounds in Devon, say they turn anyone who sees—"

"Yes, I know, turn anyone mad that looks them in the eye. My wife says it worked on me."

Jane laughed, before going on to explain that there had been numerous sightings of the Wild Hunt in the locality, not just in antiquity but right up to the present day, including quite a number this very year. The hunt was said to glow and spit fire, the baying of the hounds accompanied by a terrifying din from the huntsmen's horns, and its leader none other than Sir Francis Drake.

"So," she said at last, "what better way for me to get a feel for the Wild Hunt than join an actual hunt?"

"And this Wistman's Wood?"

"An oakwood, last remnant of the ancient forest that once covered all of Dartmoor." She sipped her whisky, then whispered, "Where the Wild Hunt is still said to ride. The name Wistman may derive from '*wisht*', same word they use for the ghostly hounds."

"And *wisht* is local dialect for what?"

"Haunted."

Perhaps it was the late hour, or the atmosphere of this remote hotel, but despite her relating what were no more than country superstitions, I felt a little shiver. Then Jane downed the last of her drink, raised her voice again, and broke the spell.

"Of course, the hunt's been seen in plenty of other places, including the area around Fox Tor. In fact, they say—"

But I never found out who 'they' were or what 'they' said, because all at once the sound of shouting came from the entrance to the dining room, followed by Mr and Mrs Dike, holding up their robes and almost running. They were followed by a diminutive moustachioed man in an enormous chef's hat, white shirt, checked trousers, and apron, the latter liberally stained with all colours of food. He brandished a meat cleaver and screamed out at the terrified couple.

"*Insulter ma cuisson, veux-tu? Tu es un cochon et ta femme laide dans son sac pour robe n'est qu'une truie. Te donner ma cuisine c'est comme servir de la confiture à des cochons.*"

Jane, clearly understanding him, laughed out loud whilst we watched the Dikes find themselves cornered by the bar. And as the apparently berserk little chef ran up to the clearly terrified druids, meat cleaver still raised, Ballar/Colin jumped behind his wife and cowered. Immediately afterwards, as Anton's mouth opened again, doubtless to scream some other insult, Joe Gurney grabbed the chef's arm from behind and relieved him of his weapon, then stood in front of the Dikes. A moment later Mercy appeared from the dining room.

"That'll do, Anton," she said, and very calmly given the circumstances, I thought. "Now what's all this about?"

"I'll tell you," shouted Fidelma/Janet. "All we did was politely explain to this, this…" she looked the chef up and down, "this maniac, that a hare is an animal to be revered in our religion, not eaten, and that he had committed a mortal sin by jugging it for supper." She spat. "Whatever jugging is."

"Pah," spat Anton in return. "You insult my cooking you insult me, I…" He went to punch Ballar, who had reappeared from behind his wife's robes, but was restrained again by Joe.

"Now, Anton," soothed Mercy, "these people are druids, and it may not be the same for you and me, but I daresay the hare is sacred to their religion, which is… what's it called?"

"Wicca," snapped Fidelma.

"Quite," Mercy continued. "And I'm sure the Atkinsons." Fidelma coughed loudly. "I mean, Dikes, meant no harm at all."

"He meant harm to us." Fidelma sniffed.

"Joe, please take Anton back to the kitchens." Joe nodded, turned the chef, who was still muttering curses under his breath, around, then frogmarched him away. "And only give him his meat cleaver back in the morning."

"Right you are, Missus," Joe called back over his shoulder.

"And Mr and Mrs Dike, how about a drink on the house?"

"Have them sent up to our room," Fidelma replied. "Two pints of bitter, and a couple of whisky chasers."

"I'm going outside for a smoke," came Ballar's muffled voice (he was still standing behind his wife).

"Best place for you," Fidelma shouted, then, nose in the air, ascended the stairs. Ballar, meanwhile, made a rapid exit towards the front door.

"Alright," said Mercy to the remaining guests who, bedroom-bound, had stopped in their tracks at the sight and sound of the fracas. "Show's over, goodnight, everyone." The audience plodded silently out of the room, leaving only myself and Jane.

"I saw you laughing, Jane. What did the chef say?"

"Well, a hare is sacred to the Wicca religion, so I daresay those two in the robes were genuinely upset if they thought the Wiccan Rede had been transgressed." I decided not to ask her what that meant. "But," she went on, "what they said to incense that little man so, well, if I'd been a fly on the wall—"

"Yes, but what did he say back to them?"

"Er…" She smirked. "Something like, 'Insult my cooking, would you? You are a pig and your ugly wife in her sack for a dress is no more than a sow.' And let me see… yes, 'Giving you my cooking is like serving jam to a pig.'"

"Lucky these druids don't speak French."

"Isn't it, but anyway, goodnight, Jack."

"Goodnight, Jane, and good hunting."

10:30 PM

"So, Jack, high drama at the Wyvern."

"Mercy, there you are." I looked up to see my hostess standing smiling, a brandy balloon in either hand, and felt a little pang of guilt, as I often did when socialising to get information for a case, but… the brandy also looked welcoming.

"Yes, here I am." Mercy passed me one of the glasses before sitting. "Ah, silence at last," she sighed at the now empty room. "They're all in bed, and God, I do love this time of the evening." Mercy sighed again, leaning back in the settle and crossing her legs, split skirt falling open to reveal black stocking tops and perhaps an inch of white skin above. I couldn't help but look, and she saw me. "Oops, and I thought it was blue stockings you preferred."

"Jane Ustrix, you mean?" I answered, privately telling myself off for so obviously reacting, whilst also wondering if the leg-show was done on purpose.

"Sorry, that was a silly remark. It's been a long day." She covered herself and sipped her brandy. "Let's walk out. The night's fine now, and I love the river on a fine night at this time of year. Let me show you why."

With that we left the now almost deserted common room, Mercy calling back inside as we stepped out into the night air ('make sure the fire pits are properly out and cut the downstairs lights now, would you, Joe, we'll find our way back alright'). Walking across the driveway and onto the humpbacked old bridge, we stopped at its crest, high above the river, which seemed to me still illuminated by the hotel's lights.

"Thought you told Joe Gurney to cut all the lights?"

"I did, you're seeing fireflies over the water. Always give a show at midsummer, look."

And she was right, here was a show, with numerous little points of yellow light, which suddenly came into focus now I was looking for them. 'Myriad', a poet might have said. The fireflies swarmed, moved, and shimmered so that the river course, perhaps five yards across and fifty yards long between the two bridges, reflected bright in the night. The fireflies shone all the more given this remote spot's only other sources of light were a gibbous and partly cloud-obscured moon, along with a few dim glimmers behind hotel bedroom curtains.

"Are those fishes under the bridge?" I pointed to three dark shapes in the water beneath us, hanging in the shadow of the arches.

"Why yes, they're trout." Mercy tugged my arm. "Look, you often see them hide under the bridges when there's sunshine, quite still and facing upstream." She peered down towards the water. "I guess when the fireflies are out at night, they do the same." She leant further over the bridge parapet. "Hide from predators, that is, and, oh…"

Suddenly, there was a splash and one of the fish was pulled away, a dark form breaking the surface for a few seconds then disappearing again.

"What was that?" I said, jumping backwards.

"Just an otter, Jack." She giggled as I wiped droplets of spilled brandy from my tie. "More than likely Old Soldier by its size."

"Old Soldier?"

"Wiley old dog otter, enormous thing."

"And he bests the local hunt?"

She nodded. "Yes, and he'd best get a good night's sleep if he knows what's good for him. They go out at first light."

"Do you hunt?"

Mercy shook her head. "I do ride, but not to hounds. Don't approve, although it's such a part of the Wyvern tradition that I'm obliged to host the hunts, both otters and foxes." She laughed. "They're grown men and women, but sometimes, on days like this when we have both of them here, keeping the peace between the two hunts is like trying to stop two gangs of football hooligans from tearing each other's throats out."

"I'd noticed." I laughed back. "But what in particular don't you like about hunting?"

"Hmmm... fox hunting just seems barbaric, so if you want to keep fox numbers down why not just shoot them? And the otters, well... the fishing lot say otters deplete stocks, but there are so few otters around nowadays that hunting them doesn't seem necessary, just cruel."

I looked along the almost silent river for a moment, imagining how the noise of dogs and hunting horns must seem to an otter on the run, remembering Jane Ustrix's words: "The cleverer and bigger the animal, the more complex and satisfying the hunt. You hunt a most satisfying quarry. Lost children."

This made me suddenly wonder why Mercy had felt compelled to report the boy missing, so I asked her outright.

"Well... I feel a bit responsible for him. I've known the De Coverleys all my life, you see, Chris, his dad John, and his wife Irene. She was—"

"Yes, I know, killed in a car crash."

"That's right, last year, on the road up to Postbridge, that way." She pointed past the second bridge. "Don't like that road. Anyway..." Mercy then told me how, after the crash, John De Coverley had thrown himself into his work at the research centre, so much so that he was rarely seen, and at the same time withdrawn his son from school in Plymouth to be home-tutored. The boy was taught English and classics by Septimus Frere, she said, confirming what the DI had told me, with his father teaching maths and sciences.

"The thing is, Jack, I found out from Septimus quite by accident that Chris hadn't been coming for lessons."

"How long?"

"Oh, since about Easter. We also used to see Chris here quite a lot, but he stopped coming to the Wyvern around that time as well." She smiled. "Even though I think he's quite sweet on Mel."

"Mel?"

"Sorry, my daughter Melissa, she's about his age. It's just that…" Mercy narrowed her eyes. "It doesn't add up. I even drove to Foxtor House—"

"Where they live?"

"Yes. I asked how Chris was and John gave me very short shrift. Said the boy had flu and I shouldn't come inside for fear of catching it."

"When was that?"

"A week ago. Then last Friday I called round again, and John told me Chris had gone. That's when I decided to contact the police."

Her being the one to call the police rather than the father, plus the man's apparent unconcern at his son's disappearance, were really bothering me now.

"And would you say John De Coverley is a good father?"

"Oh yes, he dotes on that boy." She then stood close to me, eyes wide and level with mine. "Jack, we only met today, but I can trust you, can't I?"

"Of course. Anything you say is in confidence providing…"

"Providing what?"

"That nothing illegal's happened."

"Well…" she said, taking a long draught of her brandy, "I think somehow Mel's involved."

"Really?"

"Yes. You see, she's been going to see Chris at Foxtor house, or so she says."

"Nothing odd in that."

Mercy drained her glass, then stared across the moor towards Princetown. "Jack, over there."

I looked and, for a moment, saw a red glow illuminate the horizon. It lasted just a few seconds but was unmistakable.

"Wonder what that was," I said, peering over the bridge in the direction of the glow. "Gone now, though, you were saying…"

"Mel told me she'd been there on Saturday morning and seen Chris. She obviously didn't know that he'd already been reported missing Friday evening. She lied to me, Jack."

"That is odd. I'll need to talk to Melissa, but let's not jump to conclusions. Where is she, by the way?"

"Oh, staying over at a school friend's house in Plymouth. She'll be back tomorrow evening."

"I'll see her then."

"Alright," said Mercy. "But there's another thing. Uncle Perry told me he saw Chris in the garden of Foxtor House on Saturday morning as well."

"So perhaps the boy isn't missing, and it's the father whose lying?"

"John didn't seem to be lying to me."

"Then we have a conundrum, but I'm sure the cold light of day will help. Shall we?" I held out my arm.

"Yes," she yawned, "it's late." Mercy turned, then lost her footing, a stiletto heel catching on the loose gravel of the bridge.

"Oh," she cried, instinctively grabbing me so that her face was almost close enough to touch mine, her breath warm against my lips, her perfume all-pervading. We both stared for a moment (or perhaps an age), then Mercy pulled away, coughed, and muttered something about high heels being the death of her. And along with those sensations of scent and female closeness, it seemed to me once again that perhaps manipulation was Mercy's main motive. This suspicion was quickly followed by the conflicting thought of Sarah, travelling alone to a strange land for the burial of her most closely related ancestor, whilst I was standing by a Devon river sipping brandy with a beautiful woman in the moonlight. I shuddered, then inhaled a deep draught of the night air and held out my arm, which, after a moment's hesitation, Mercy took with her hand.

"Come on," I said. "We should go back inside."

*

The silence felt awkward as Mercy went to open the front door, and I was about to speak when suddenly, headlights dazzled us as a car pulled into the driveway, crunching to a halt on the gravel. I saw a familiar robed silhouette as Ballar Dike then stepped out, slammed the door, and waved the driver away.

"Wait for me," he called to us. "Don't lock up yet."

"After you," Mercy whispered to him, as several upstairs lights came on. "And please, be as quiet as you can. Guests are sleeping." He held his fingers to his lips, tiptoed across the common room, then disappeared up the stairs.

"Lucky the man wasn't locked out," I said, as Mercy replaced the brandy glasses behind the bar. "Might not have been anyone to hear him knocking."

"There's Whiddon, the night porter, but he's as deaf as a post."

"Where is he?"

"Er…" Mercy looked around the deserted common room, then held up her finger. "Oh yes, Joe said he hadn't turned up at all this evening. Our druid friend might have spent a chilly night in one of the back stables if we hadn't been outside the door."

"And what will his good lady have to say in the morning? After all, Ballar Dike was just going out for a smoke, wasn't he?"

"That's what he said, Jack, and I'll say goodnight." She walked back along the corridor towards the lounge. "My rooms are this way," she then murmured. "Throw the light switch when you go up the stairs, please."

TUESDAY, JUNE THE 23RD
7:30 AM

Sir Peregrine Frere looked down from his saddle as I stood panting, hands on knees.

"You're an early riser, Sangster."

"Been running, I—"

"Now don't tell me," came a voice from behind. I turned to see Septimus Frere, resplendent in blue coat tails and a bowler hat, a long pole in his hand reaching almost above his head. I noticed it was tipped with a cruel-looking metal barb. "Doctor's got you on a regime of callisthenics, for a liver condition, I perceive."

"Liver condition?"

"I noticed you didn't accept any refills of wine with your meal last night and took only one small glass of port. Mercedes always serves fine wine, so a sure-fire sign that you were trying to abstain."

"Ha," I said with a mix of laugh and wheeze. "I just like to go easy on the booze, and as I said just now, I've been running."

"You're certainly huffing and puffing fit to bust."

"These moorland roads are hillier than they look in a car," I gasped.

"Stirrup cup, sir?" Tilly raised a platter laid with silver goblets up to Sir Peregrine, who took one with a smile and a nod. "And you, sir?"

"Oh, don't mind if I do," said Septimus, appearing to forget about his deductions. "Mmmm… Mercedes keeps a decent sherry in her cellar, just like her dad before her. You having one, Sangster?"

"God almighty no," I shouted, then saw Tilly wince. "I mean, no thank you. A little early for me."

Tilly walked away, offering her platter to others in the crowd, and I looked around. There were perhaps twenty horses milling in the driveway of the hotel to my right, their riders mostly dressed in black jackets, and a few in hunting pink. There were also plenty of people on foot, some dressed in the blue bowlers and tails like Septimus, one of whom I recognised as Miles Edgerton. Others wore no uniform but were clearly dressed for walking, with stout boots and gaiters. Each walker carried either a stick or hunting pole (like Septimus), with quite a few also holding long-handled whips. Between all these riders and walkers went the hotel staff, carrying platters like Tilly's or helping the riders by tightening saddles or handing up riding crops, including one young man whose only job seemed to be collecting up horse manure and dog dirt into a wheelbarrow. And amongst them all, barking, sniffing, occasionally fighting, were the fox hounds. Then, through the hounds' baying, I heard a different bark, deeper, more resonant, and looked to my left to see two open-backed and rather ancient-looking lorries, painted in the same shade of blue as Septimus' tail-coat. These lorries were both loaded with what I could only assume to be otter hounds, large, powerful-looking animals with long fur and wide jaws.

Suddenly, the morning mist was cut by a shrill trumpeting, emanating from a hunting pink clad rider astride a magnificent white stallion, turning circles on the gravel whilst blowing his horn. I recognised him as the ruddy-faced diner who had called out during Miles' speech.

"Ladies and gentlemen."

The Master of the Hunt, as I saw he clearly was by the way the other riders went silent as he spoke, brandished the horn and addressed his fellow hunters in a schoolmaster-like manner. "We ride towards Postbridge, so follow in line. Now, hoo-gaze!"

As he shouted 'hoo-gaze' there was an outbreak of horn trumpets, whereupon the master made for the old bridge at the trot, hounds baying around his horse's legs, the rest of the riders and walkers following him in a line. The sound of hooves, dogs, people, and horns, at first deafening, gradually faded as the clattering entourage crossed over the bridge before turning right towards Postbridge. A few minutes after that the Princetown Hunt could be heard no more, and I watched Miles Edgerton, who had been staring at the line of horses as they filed across the bridge, raise his own horn to his lips.

"Ladies and gentlemen." He blew his horn again, which to me sounded tinnier and generally inferior to the Princetown master's horn. "We've had a sighting phoned in this morning, over near Fox Tor, a big chap, so they said, and I think we all know what that means." At this, talking broke out amongst the otter hunters, and I heard the name 'Old Soldier' mentioned more than once.

"I know," said Miles, holding up his hand. "We've lost him up there by the tor countless times, but perhaps today will be our lucky day and we'll finally catch the bugger." Whoops and roars of laughter went up. "So," he continued, "we'll take the Princetown road, then cut across towards Whiteworks, park up there, and hopefully pick up a scent in the Swincombe River. Now remember…" he blew his horn once again, "we've a fine morning once this mist clears, but we're headed for Fox Tor country with its hidden mires that'll suck you under as soon as look at you." He blew his horn yet again. "And as the saying goes, 'Where rushes grow, ponies fear to go,' so please, stick with the pack and follow my lead. Now, to the trucks and hoo-gaze!"

With that the hunters downed any unfinished drinks and rushed towards the two lorries, climbing into the vehicles, and jostling for places on benches around the sides. The dogs were tethered in the middle. Once all were aboard, engines coughed into life and the backs of the lorries were raised by hunters, who immediately afterwards ran and jumped into the cabs. I then watched the Highmoor Hunt bump up the drive, gravel groaning under the pressure of the truck tyres, otter hounds barking, blue bowler hats of the sitting hunters just visible over the lorries' sides, and the hunters' poles protruding up from each lorry like the spines of a porcupine.

"Been for a run, Jack?"

"Oh, morning, Mercy, yes." I looked towards the Princetown road as the Highmoor Hunt lorries disappeared through the gates and calm returned to the Wyvern Arms car park. "Aren't they on a wild goose chase?"

"Sorry?"

"Well, we saw that otter you called, er…"

"Old Soldier?"

"Yes, last night by the bridge here, and Fox Tor is several miles away, isn't it?"

"Oh, a big old chap like Old Soldier can easily make a few miles in a night. And anyway, he's been seen up by Fox Tor many times, so they think it's where he has his holt."

"That's his nest, right?"

"Yes, but…" she smiled, "I still didn't tell them we saw Old Soldier last night. Thought it would, you know…"

"Tip the odds too much?"

"Exactly, Jack, those hounds can track a three-day old scent in water, and they can keep going all day, so Old Soldier needs every bit of the help he can get." Mercy pointed to the dining room. "Now then, breakfast?"

"Give me half an hour," I said, looking down at my sweat-stained T-shirt. "I need a bath first."

"Yes," she said, wafting her hand across her nose in an exaggerated manner, "I believe you do."

8:30 AM

"Egg white omelette, just as you ordered sir," said Tilly, looking at my plate with an expression I thought more appropriate to someone ordering roast baby, which was no real surprise to me, as my egg white omelette habit was generally considered odd. "And brown toast." She set the plates down at my table in a bay window of the dining room. "Anything else, sir?"

"Would you have a newspaper I could read?"

"Yessir."

I sat and ate in silence, taking in the view from the window, looking across the lawn to the river and the bridges. The day was now clear of the morning mist, blue sky and white clouds giving no hint that the moor could turn ugly at any time to deliver downpours like yesterday's.

"Finished, sir?" asked Tilly after a time. I nodded. "*Western Morning News* alright?"

"Thank you, Tilly."

She cleared my plates, while I spread out the newspaper and began to read. The journalists covering national news seemed incensed that the Prime Minister of only a few days, Edward Heath, was pledging Britain to join the European Economic Community ('A generation ago they bombed our cities and now our PM wants to cuddle up to them'). The paper also frowned on Heath's intention to push through the previous government's plans to replace pounds, shillings, and pence with a decimal system ('It'll never work'). However, the editorial column was more upbeat, because today, it said, Prince Charles would receive a bachelor's degree from Cambridge ('The first royal to receive that particular honour and a credit to our modern and relevant monarchy').

I smiled at the journalist's words, thinking of all the inner-city kids I'd dealt with, some bright as a new penny, some not so, but all of them with some trait that stood out, something where you could say, "That kid could be different." What chance for a degree from Cambridge for them?

"Get off your high horse, Sangster," I muttered to myself, then paged through the rest of the paper, which was mainly filled with ads and local articles.

'*Repeat break-in and theft from Devonport Naval Arms Depot*', read the first headline.

The next, '*Princetown residents to sue South Western Electricity Board over power surges*', was an account of household appliances burning out due to sudden electrical spikes, a substation failure plunging the town into darkness and even claims of moorland fires ignited from electrical sparks close to power lines. There then followed an article I found particularly interesting.

'*Historical site attributed to Drake debunked*' went the headline. The article went on to explain that an excavation by Professor Septimus Frere, the museum curator, and claimed by him to be a secret arsenal belonging to Sir Francis Drake, had been found to contain modern ordnance. A quote from a Doctor Stewer, of Plymouth Polytechnic, noted:

> *These twentieth-century fifty-calibre shells, crucially, lay underneath artifacts such as cannon balls previously dated as Elizabethan, thus proving the cache to be contemporary. It is a matter of record that I always cast doubt on Professor Frere's claims as to the antiquity of his find, and…*

The account didn't give any explanation as to why someone might bury modern shells under old cannon balls, and, having read enough, I folded up the paper and walked towards reception, where Mercy was addressing a circle of staff.

"Now then, everyone knows what they have to do. Hunt will be back here about noon, and I'd like two of you, Tilly and Jenny, outside waiting with stirrup cups, James and Richard to help dismount the riders, and the rest inside to take the guests to the dining room."

"But Missus," came the imploring voice of Anton the chef, now resplendent in a newly laundered apron, "I need the fresh meat and game now, and it is already thirty of nine. I must prepare a luncheon for fifty guests by noon."

"Delivery will be here soon, I'm sure, now come on, everyone." She clapped. "Lots to do." The group dispersed about their various tasks, and Mercy turned to me, about to speak, when Joe Gurney tapped her on the shoulder.

"Phone, Missus."

"Hang on, Jack," she called, and went to the reception desk, where I saw by her frown that the caller bore bad news. "Yes, yes, I'll come... anything I can bring? Yes, one moment, I'll get a pen..." She took some brief notes. "I'll be with you as soon as I can. Bye."

"Everything OK?"

"It's Whiddon, Jack," she said, grabbing a green waxed jacket from a peg behind her. "That was the district nurse, he's fallen from his bike. Been in hospital overnight and now they've got him home but she's short on a few things, wants me to do a shop." Mercy pulled on her jacket. "I'll need to get over there, and I don't know what to do, what with this big lunch on and everything..."

She picked up her handbag, then began talking quickly to Joe, before walking towards the door.

"I'll see you later, Jack, maybe this evening?"

"Hang on," I said, running after her, thinking a car journey with just the two of us would surely be a great opportunity to find out more from my hostess. "I've nothing on until two today, let me drive you."

"You sure?"

"Sure."

"Well, thanks. We'll go to Princetown first for the shops and then back across to Postbridge, near where he lives. But there's no time to lose, come on."

"Can I just get my jacket first?"

10 AM

As we walked out of the front door, a honking filled the air. 'Davy's Family Butchers, Yelverton' I read on the side of a large white van that drew up next to us. The driver pressed the horn twice more, then leaned out of his cab.

"I got twenty-five pheasant, a whole suckling pig, and thirty fresh trout here, plus three cases of mixed fresh veg. Where you want 'em?"

"Joe," Mercy called behind her. "Van's here with the delivery. Get Anton and a couple of others to help unload, would you?"

"Right you are, Missus," came the reply from within.

"Hood down, Mercy?" I asked, as we came to the car. "It's a nice morning."

"Why not? I think… yes, I've a headscarf in my pocket." She pulled out a white silk square and tied it over her hair while I took down the car hood. After a minute or so we were out on the road, and a few minutes later were pulling up outside the general store in Princetown.

"Just wait here, would you?" said Mercy, fumbling in her handbag for her shopping list and purse. "See you in a sec."

*

"Looks like you've bought up half the shop." I squinted sideways at the bulging carrier bag between Mercy's knees as we set off again.

"Oh." She looked at her list. "It's just, er… bread, butter, cheese, veg, some cans of soup, biscuits, plus extra lint dressing. Nurse said old Whiddon had almost no food in his house and he's going to be laid up for a few days yet."

"And he fell off his bike, you say?"

"Yes, on his way to us last night. Came quite a cropper, it seems."

"Hit and run?"

"No idea."

We drove on, back past the hotel before taking a left fork at the sign to Postbridge. The road was open, bare moorland either side, sloping down to a shallow valley bottom with a narrow stream crossed by a small, flat bridge. I sped up, feeling, as I always did when the sun was shining, the roof down, and my foot on accelerator, exhilaration as the speedometer needle edged clockwise, forty, fifty, sixty, seventy. Then, suddenly, as we came to the bridge, I felt the wheel turn. I pulled hard left to compensate, whilst slamming on the brakes, but the steering somehow pulled against me, the force of it all shaking the entire chassis and making me see double as I looked down, almost as if there was a second pair of hands holding the wheel. Brakes screeched and tyres squealed, the car sliding diagonally before eventually coming to a halt, half on the road, half on the verge.

"You OK, Mercy?" I was breathing heavily as I looked at her ashen face.

"I'm, er… OK, yes, but what happened?"

"I don't know, I just lost control. It was the wheel, it—"

"Pulled for no reason at all?" She looked at me, eyes narrowed, almost angry, it seemed.

"No need to be sarcastic. Perhaps I was driving a little fast, but I never—"

"I wasn't, Jack," She put her hand on my shoulder. "Being sarcastic, I mean. This is a bit of an accident black spot, people have, er… lost loved ones near here." She paused, looked down at her feet for a moment, then raised her head again. "Lost loved ones," she repeated.

"There was no warning sign that I saw."

Reversing back onto the road, I looked at the dark score marks from my tyres along the tarmac and shuddered at what might have been. "Anyway," I said as brightly as I could, "let's get going, but nice and slowly, and I'll put the radio on?"

"Nice and slowly," Mercy echoed, as the radio blared into life.

"*This is the Jimmy Young show*," came the familiar chirpy Gaelic tones of the DJ, whilst an accompanying jingle sang '*BBC Radio Two…*'. "And this is for our lads as they make their way back home," he went on, followed by the slightly suspect baritones of the England World Cup squad telling us how much they would be thinking about the folks 'back home'.

"Oh dear," I sighed. "Thought they'd stop playing that once Brazil had won."

"Me too." Mercy laughed.

"Now," said the DJ, as the music finally faded out, "*here's the latest one from Elvis, so off we jolly well go, with 'I've Lost You'. Take it away, Mr Presley…*"

"Do we keep going straight?" I asked, as a slow ballad began to play a combination of melancholy lyrics and melody that somehow brought Sarah to the front of my mind ('she's just gone to Israel for a few days, Jack, of course you haven't lost her').

"Yes," answered Mercy, bringing me back to the moment. "Keep going about a mile, then you see a signpost saying Wistman's Wood and after that a track on the left. Whiddon lives at the top of that. Turning is hard to see."

"OK," I answered, remembering this was the place Jane Ustrix had been so keen to visit.

"*That was Elvis, and now for Jim's pick of the month*," announced the DJ, as the gentle ballad faded and an electric rhythm blared out. "*Yes, it's last week's number one from Norman Greenbaum, 'Spirit in the Sky'…*"

"Here we are, Jack." I turned down the radio as Mercy put her fingers to her ears and exaggeratedly screwed up her eyes, before pointing to a sign standing by a concealed entrance to a narrow track. "About half a mile up here towards the wood."

We bumped along, snaking to avoid potholes before arriving at a bushy thicket, then rounding a bend to see a dishevelled-looking caravan. The van was painted in faded and flaking lime green, with grimy windows, a crooked TV aerial that looked as if it might fall off the roof at any time, and next to that an enormous chimney, from which thick black smoke billowed. This movable residence, I thought, may well have been the height of luxury in about 1930 but now stood neglected and clearly immobile, with one wheel replaced by bricks and various makeshift patches on the sides and roof. To compound the sense of permanent dwelling, several small wooden sheds stood next to the van, one an outside privy, I guessed, by its size and shape, and all equally in need of repair. By these was a 'lean-to' shelter with a tarpaulin for a roof, chicken wire all around, straw and earth on the ground, and a wooden hen coop tucked in the corner. The coop's occupants, heard but not seen, clucked to greet us.

I stepped out of the car to see two bicycles propped up against the side of the caravan, the nearest a gleaming scarlet-painted machine with a large basket on the front, a woman's bike, judging by the lack of a crossbar. The other cycle was old and black, with, as we would have called them when I was a child, 'sit up and beg' handlebars. Canvass panniers slung either side of the rear mudguard, which, I noticed, had no reflector light on it, and there was no sign of a lamp on the front either. What struck me most, though, were the wheels and frame, all badly buckled, perhaps beyond repair.

Helping Mercy climb out of the passenger seat by holding the groceries as she stood up, I was suddenly shocked by a ferocious barking. At this, the carrier bag fell from my hands, its contents spilling out over the ground.

"Oh, Christ," I shouted, looking round to see the source of the noise, an enormous dog with long and matted grey-brown fur. The otter hound, similar to the dogs in the hunt lorry, albeit somewhat bigger, older, and more unkempt, stared at me, continuing its deep-throated bark, until Mercy climbed out of the car, whereupon it silently wagged its tail.

"Bayliss, you old rascal," Mercy said, leaning down to stroke the animal, which licked her hand in return. "How's your master?" She began to walk towards the caravan, the dog lolloping after her. "Oh, Jack," she then called over her shoulder, "you've dropped the shopping."

*

Whiddon lay forlorn in his bed, a wooden fourposter which stood behind curtains draped across one end of the caravan, which I found out later he'd constructed the thing from a regular bed himself, nailing a plastic sheet on the top to protect from leaks coming through the caravan roof. Whiddon was old, perhaps well over eighty, with, I guessed, given it was mostly covered with a bandage, a head of sparse white hair that grew in long wisps, likely uncut for some time. His eyes were a glassy blue, alert but wandering slightly, and his face was ruddied to an almost purple hue. Nevertheless, several nasty bruises could be seen on his cheeks and chin.

"Oh, Whiddon." Mercy bent over the bed and felt his forehead. "You have been in the wars."

"Aye, Missus."

"He fell off his bike yesterday, down on the main road," said Miss Pickles, a smartly uniformed district nurse and, as she proudly announced to us, owner of the red bicycle. "Picked up by a passing motorist, and very lucky you were too, weren't you, Whiddon?" She shouted this last sentence in the manner I'd seen some people use with the very old.

"Alright, Nurse, I've got my Deaf-Aid in," Whiddon snapped back, touching his ear. "And depends on what you mean by lucky. I was driven off my bike, driven, I tell you."

"Was it a hit-and-run driver?" I asked.

"No, young man. It was the hunt."

"But the hunt didn't start out until this morning."

"Not them, the Wild Hunt. Came galloping across from Wistman's Wood, red glow followed by flashing lights. Knocked me clean off, they did."

"And you, er… saw these ghostly horsemen and hounds?"

"Aye… well, not exactly, but I heard them, felt them. That were enough."

"I, er… see," I said, disquieted by the memory of the red glow Mercy and I had seen the night before from the old bridge.

"Well, ghosts or no ghosts, Mr Whiddon," said Nurse Pickles, placing a cloth against the old man's forehead, "you just rest up here for a few days and you'll be right as ninepence."

"It was the Wild Hunt, I tell you."

"Course it was," she soothed, continuing to mop his brow.

"Why would I lie?" said Whiddon quietly, and it seemed to me he was speaking to no one in particular. "Why?"

"You've just had a shock," said the nurse, as Whiddon slumped back against his pillow. "Whiddon's thoughts do wander a little, but pay no mind, he's been like that a good while, it's not due to this fall." She pressed her finger to her lips. "He just needs to sleep for now."

We both nodded, tiptoed out of the caravan, which was difficult to do without making a noise, as it creaked and moved with every step, then settled back into the car. We were about to leave when Nurse Pickles came to Mercy's side window, bicycle in hand.

"I'll be away now. He's in reasonable shape, but will you have someone look in on him, Mercy?"

"Course. We'll keep an eye on Whiddon, don't you worry."

*

"Who will you get?" I asked as we drove away.

"Pardon?"

"To check up on Whiddon."

"Oh, there'll be plenty of volunteers. Tend to look after our own here in Devon."

"I'm sure." We drove on, coming before long to the low bridge and the tyre mark imprint from our earlier escapade.

"It would have been somewhere around here where he fell," said Mercy as we passed the spot where the car had veered off the road, so that I instinctively held tight on the wheel as we did so. "Maybe Whiddon's too old to be biking around."

"Could have been some sort of seizure, although didn't the nurse say a doctor had given him the all-clear as regards brain damage?"

"Bit worrying, though." Mercy nodded. "Not many cars come along this road, especially on weekdays and outside the school holidays, so he could have been lying there all night."

"Would it have been dark when he fell?"

"Maybe."

"Must have been a car or a lorry then." I shrugged. "Headlamps blazing, horn blowing, unlit road, coming up at speed on an unsuspecting cyclist without lights. Might well have seemed like the hounds of hell to Whiddon."

"Hmmm..." Mercy shook her head. "You know, it doesn't quite make sense. Longest days of the year right now, sunset's about half nine and Whiddon usually comes to us before seven." Mercy screwed her eyes, nose, and mouth up in a way I had already come to think of as her 'puzzled face'. "And Whiddon's as down-to-earth a man as I've ever met. Bit superstitious, perhaps, but plenty of people up here are."

"So you are saying?"

"Oh." She shook her head again. "I don't know, but he's alright, Jack, that's the main thing, now what's on the radio?" I pressed the button, to hear strains of cowboy music with haunting vocals fading out…

The BBC Radio Two jingle then cut in, followed by the ever-happy tones of the DJ. "*That was '(Ghost) Riders in the Sky'.*" This elicited a slight shiver down my spine as I thought of Whiddon and his Wild Hunt. "*Jim's signing off until tomorrow, so it's bye for now, but before the twelve o'clock news, here's the new number one, 'In the Summertime', from Mungo Jerry.*" A lively tune extolling the delights of fine summer weather struck up, a tune that I'd heard many times in recent weeks. "*And Jim's sure,*" the DJ's voice blared out over the song, "*that wherever you are, listeners, the weather is going to be fine for you too.*"

Mercy gazed up at the sky, where dark clouds were beginning to build up across the horizon, then looked across at me and half smiled.

"Not on Dartmoor, it isn't."

12 NOON

Pulling into the driveway of the hotel, the scene looked similar to the one I had encountered on returning from my morning run, with horses milling about, trays of drinks being offered round by Tilly and Jenny, and riders dismounting. Some, like the hunt master, swung effortlessly off their horses, some were helped down from their saddles, and some reached the ground using a set of wooden steps, the hotel staff wheeling this complex-looking apparatus to each rider that needed it.

With her customary 'oops', Mercy jumped out of the car, telling me she hadn't realised the hunt would be back so soon, before running over to the crowd. I put up the car hood, then went to follow her.

"Mr Sangster," said Joe Gurney, appearing from a side door, "message for you."

"Yes?"

"Lady rang, just said to tell you that…" He took a slip of paper from his pocket. "Let me see, yes… tell you that she was safely in Tel Aviv and everything's fine. No need for you to call."

"Great, thanks, Joe." I felt a sigh of relief Sarah had arrived without incident. Flying to Israel these days wasn't always safe. "Oh, and I need to use the phone, so can I go in this way to slip past all these people?"

"Course." He grinned. "Door leads through to the back hallway behind reception. And if it's too noisy to use the payphone in the front of the common room, just dial from the hotel line by the big leather chair and make a note of your call. We can put it on your room bill."

*

"Devon and Cornwall Police, Crownhill Station, how can I help you?"

"Oh, hello, can I speak to Detective Inspector Hawke, please?"

"And your name, caller?"

"Sangster."

"And the detective inspector will know what the call is about?"

"She's expecting me."

"Very well, Mr Sangster, I'll put you through to her."

Several clicks later I heard the familiar clipped tones of DI Hawke. "You're fifteen minutes late."

"Sorry for that, I didn't know we were on a strict timetable."

"Noon means noon, but never mind. What have you to report?" I resisted the temptation to tell the DI I didn't actually 'report' to her or any other police officer, making a mental note at the same time to set out the ground rules of our working partnership before too long.

"I've two appointments this afternoon, one at Reynard's Hall—"

She cut me off. "Why there? It's just a museum."

"Professor Frere, the boy's private tutor, remember, the notes in the envelope you gave me?"

"Oh yes, of course." She made no apology for overlooking what in my view was the most basic of case facts. "And the other appointment?"

"Highmoor Research Centre. I'll be meeting both the boy's father and Professor Frere's brother, Peregrine."

"Ah yes, he's overall in charge there."

"I hadn't realised they were brothers until I met them last night at the hotel."

"Wasn't it in the notes?"

"No, but anyway, that's my day, so not much to report yet. You?"

"Well, we resumed house-to-house interviews again this morning." She then yelled, presumably across her office, deafening me so that I held the receiver away from my ear, "Eccles, anything come up from the house to house yet?"

"Nothing in yet, Ma'am," came the faint reply. "We've posted up mug shots in shops, bus stops, stations, and so on as well."

"He says nothing's in yet, Mr Sangster, but I do have something else for you."

She then told me of an eyewitness at the Devonport Naval Arms Depot who described two figures very like Doctor De Coverley and his son driving a van, away from the scene of a recent robbery.

"We were wondering if you could go there, check the witness out, ask some questions."

"Isn't that police work?"

"We're stretched," DI Hawke answered quickly. "And anyway, they don't welcome civil police there. You being independent, ex-RN and all that, I just wondered…"

"Yes, I suppose I could perhaps—"

"Good, that's settled then," she interrupted. "I'll pass you to Eccles so he can give you the details. And tomorrow's call, twelve o'clock sharp, yes?"

"I'll do my best." The phone was then passed to DC Eccles, who gave me the number of the person to call at Devonport, a Lieutenant Jolly.

*

"Hello, is that Devonport… Commander Sangster… that's right, Sangster… no, I'm not, I'm retired… yes, that's right, Plymouth CID suggested I call… yes, I need to speak with your Lieutenant Jolly… yes I'll hold." After a time the switchboard operator came back on the line.

"Transferring you now."

"Hello, Commander Sangster?"

"That's right."

"Lieutenant Paul Jolly. How can I help you, sir?"

I explained who I was, a little of my assignment to look for the missing boy, and the suggestion by the police that I come and see him.

"Certainly, sir, I could see you this afternoon if you like."

"Tomorrow morning's better, if that's convenient."

"Nine thirty, sir?"

"Fine."

"Good. I'll have a badge waiting for you at the gate, and please bring some form of photo ID. Now is that all, sir?"

"Yes, thanks."

"Then I'll see you tomorrow. Good day, sir."

If only they were all that straightforward, I sighed to myself as I replaced the receiver, wondering whether I should call in to head office. "Hmmm," I muttered. "Might catch Sir John before he goes to his club for lunch."

"Mayfair 625 7701."

"Hello, is that Polly?"

"Mr Sangster." I always liked to hear the soft and familiar tones of Sir John's marvellously reliable personal assistant. "Lovely to hear from you. I guess you're after Sir John?"

"Yes, is he there?"

"I'll just check… yes, but he's about to leave for lunch. Oh, Sir John," I heard her call.

"What is it, woman?" boomed my boss, eccentric millionaire, founder of the Granville Institute, and, amongst many other things, bon viveur extraordinaire whose sacred lunches waited for no man.

"Sangster, is it a quickie? On me way to the club. Meeting the new Home Secretary, chap called, er… Polly, who is he again?"

"Reginald Maudling, Sir John."

"Write the name down on a slip of paper for me pocket, would you, Polly?" I smiled at yet another example of Sir John's complete indifference to the status of the people he met. "Anyway, Sangster, what is it?"

"Well, you asked me to call in about the De Coverley case."

"Oh God, so I did." Sir John's tone of voice changed at the sound of De Coverley's name. "Any luck yet?"

"No, but I've a few people to see, including the father. Police aren't much help, though. Want to leave everything to me, which is a first."

"Well, they've had this one dropped on them out of the blue, may not know how worried the people on high are by the lad's disappearance. And by 'on high' I mean the very highest in the land."

"I know, Sir John, you told me when you called on Saturday. Instructions from the Prime Minister himself."

"Yes, and he seemed mighty concerned. Inherited this De Coverley business from the other chap, what was his name?"

"Harold Wilson, Sir John," I heard Polly shout.

"Yes, Sangster, Heath inherited it from Harold Wilson apparently. Top of his to-do list when he entered Number Ten."

"But Sir John, that can't be."

"Why ever not, Sangster?"

"Because Wilson left office just last Wednesday, and Edward Heath came in Thursday. The boy was only formally reported missing Friday. How could Heath have inherited the case?"

"Well, he did, made no bones about it apparently, so what does that tell you?"

"Er... that the government has been interested in De Coverley Senior and/or Junior for some time, and there may be more to this case than meets the eye?"

"You've hit the nail on the head as ever, Sangster. I'll test the water with this Maudling chappie, so call me later, should be back from lunch about five. I wonder..." I heard him humming to himself, something close to the tune of Jerusalem, "if he'll give any hints as to what's so important about one missing lad. Couple of bottles of club claret should loosen him up – now I must fly. Good hunting."

"Just one more thing, Sir John, I—"

"Sorry, Mr Sangster," came Polly's voice, several decibels quieter than Sir John's. "He's gone."

"Oh well, I suppose my May expenses claim will have to wait. Bye, Polly."

*

I walked towards the common room, then suddenly remembered I'd forgotten to note down my calls, so returned to the telephone chair and scribbled the details on a piece of notepaper. Nobody was on reception, so I left it in the Room Seven pigeonhole.

"Jack." I turned around to see Jane Ustrix standing behind me.

"Jane, how was your hunting?"

"An experience, but a fruitless one."

"Fruitless… ah, you mean the hunt didn't catch an otter."

"Bloody right they didn't," shouted Miles Edgerton, walking past us towards the dining room. "Old Soldier gave us the slip again, up by Foxtor Mires. Thought we had him this time. Oh well." He rubbed his hands. "At least there's Anton's roast pheasants to help us get over it."

"And the Foxes?"

"You'd have to ask them, supercilious bastards," growled Edgerton, making me guess that the fox hunt had had more luck that morning, but said nothing. Looking into the dining room, I spied a long table, laid not only with the pheasants in question but also plates of trout and a whole roast suckling pig, its distended belly stuffed with peas and carrots. Anton was busily carving and serving, members of the hunt filing past and piling their plates high with the feast. I couldn't help feeling a pang of pleasure at the thought of Old Soldier once again besting this gluttonous gathering, tinged with a pang of sorrow for his foxy cousin, who presumably hadn't.

"You joining them?" I asked Jane.

"No, I have to change, and anyway, they've nothing there bar a few parsnips, carrots, and garden peas that I'd want to eat, which anyway came out of the pig's innards." She grimaced. "Even the potatoes are cooked in goose fat. You?"

"No, I, er… have things on this afternoon. Will grab a sandwich, full stomach would slow me down."

"Well, perhaps I'll see you this evening. I'm going for a lie-down then will perhaps take a ramble if the weather holds." She turned towards the staircase.

"Oh, Jane?"

"Yes."

"I met someone today who claims to have seen your Wild Hunt."

"Really? Do tell."

I related the story of Whiddon blaming the fall from his bicycle on supernatural dogs and riders. "And wait for it, this happened close to your favourite Wistman's Wood."

"The otter hunt didn't go anywhere near the wood today, Jack." She grabbed my arm. "But I must go there, even more so if there's been a recent sighting."

"You, um…" I gently removed her hand from my sleeve, "wouldn't have gone up there with that hunt on any day. It's high ground, not a place for otters."

"Yes, I realise that now, I was expecting a horse ride, foxes, and so on." She looked at the floor for a moment, then pointed to her feet and legs, which were wet and caked with mud. "It's embarrassing, I joined the wrong hunt."

"They went through marshes?"

"Rivers, marshes, ponds, mires, ditches, you name it." She laughed. "It was the fox hunt that went to Wistman's Wood." I laughed in return. "But if you're ever going up there…"

"I'll bear that in mind, Jane, but right now I do need to go. Have to be in Yelverton for two."

2 PM

"So, Sangster," said Septimus, standing outside the main door of Reynard's Hall, "no need to show me pity."

"Pity?"

"I perceive by your slightly hunched shoulders and downward stare that you are trying to disguise your sympathy."

"Sympathy for what?"

"Oh." He looked at his feet. "You've not heard that we drew a blank today?"

"I see, yes, Miles Edgerton did say the hunt was unsuccessful."

"That damned animal," he said between clenched teeth. "We sighted him, you know." He dabbed a tear from the corner of his eye, making me realise the hunt was even more important to some people than I'd thought.

"So I believe."

"Old Soldier disappeared, up near the mires. We got caught up with a couple of ramblers and when the hounds got back on the scent he'd vanished into thin air. Hounds were confused, we were confused."

"Just sounds like the animal has a strong sense of self-preservation."

"Ah." Teeth still clenched, his words spat out in an angry whisper quite out of keeping with Septimus's usually benign countenance.

"This one's different to any I've chased down in my life. When we lost him, tempers were high."

"I'm sure."

"I tell you, when he saw those ramblers, Miles Edgerton swore he'd happily kill anyone who got between him and Old Soldier. By the look on Miles' face, I think he meant it as well." I raised my eyebrows and Septimus coughed a little, then softened his voice. "Ahem, anyway, you didn't come here to talk otters."

"Christopher De Coverley. I'm trying to get a mental picture of the lad. Find out what makes him tick."

"Well, I can tell you what I know." He turned towards the door. "Not sure how much it will help, but can we talk as I'm walking if you don't mind? I have to check an exhibit inside."

"Of course."

I followed Septimus, into an enormous hall with an oak-beamed ceiling perhaps thirty feet high at its ridge and standing on a plinth in the room's centre, a huge and intricate model sailing ship ('Drake's *Revenge*, Sangster'). Septimus walked on, until we arrived at a large, panelled room, where a portrait of the great sea captain hung.

"Sir Francis was a contradictory character so I don't truly know what to think of him." Septimus stared up at Drake. "Did things like hang his own brother-in-law from the yard arm of his ship, participate in the barbaric slave trade, commit acts of what can only be called piracy, orchestrate mass murder of Spanish civilians, but achieved some of the greatest feats of navigation in history and saved England in perhaps her darkest hour."

Almost breathless from reeling off this list of Drake's good and bad deeds, he pointed to a glass case underneath the portrait. "Now here's the new display case, what do you think?"

I looked at a large, decorated snare drum sitting inside.

'Drake's Drum', stated a simple sign underneath.

"That's the same crest I saw on your blazer last night, Professor."

"Correct, this is a copy of the original, accurate to the last detail." He stared at the case, pulling out a pair of glasses to examine the contents more closely. "I'm sure there's a message in the drum's decoration somewhere, if only we could read it. Sir Francis had the drum sent back from the Caribbean when he was dying, you see. Said if it was brought home, he would come back from the dead and save England in her hour of need."

"Didn't see any sign of Drake during the Blitz, or the Battle of Britain, never mind that quarter final England just lost against West Germany in Mexico."

"Alright, Sangster, it's just folklore."

"Sorry."

"Come on, I need to check something at the dig outside. You may find this interesting." We walked back to the main door and out into the grounds. "This way, Sangster." Septimus pointed towards a walled area, where I could see a tent-like structure. "Mind you," he said as we trudged across the grass, "Drake did seem to believe in reincarnation, coming back from the dead." We walked on. "Now here we are, this is the dig. We discovered a cache of weapons when surveyors were checking the grounds for a possible site to build a tourist guest house."

"I see." I looked into a pit about eight feet deep, with a wooden ladder propped up against the side. "Down there?"

Septimus nodded, and we climbed to the muddy pit bottom, where I suddenly sensed irrational claustrophobia. Someone could take the ladder away and leave us here. I shook myself and saw there was a tarpaulin in front of us, which Septimus removed in the manner of a magician pulling away a tablecloth whilst leaving crockery and cutlery unmoved.

"Voila."

I saw row on row of neatly stacked cannon balls, a little rusty but generally intact.

"How did these stay in such good condition?" I asked. "Assuming they're from over four hundred years ago."

"Wrapped in sackcloth then buried, and no records of this place exist as far as we know, so Drake must have wanted it left alone by looters."

"And how do you know it's Drake's?"

"There were documents, in a lead box. Stated the cache was left here by the owner of the house on the instructions of Drake, and I quote." He pulled out a notepad and read from it. "'So that when, in some future time, I be needed, then such weaponry as suffices to defend England shall I have at my disposal.'

"Look." He showed me the notebook.

"Copied directly?"

"Yes, from the documents found here. We're having them dated by the British Museum, but I'm sure they're the right age."

"So why do people doubt this site was Drake's?"

"Because," sighed Septimus, "there was, how shall I put it… an anomaly." I looked at him, and he pointed to the ground. "Under the cannon balls."

"Under?"

"See?" He bent down, then, with a heave, lifted one of the cannon balls to expose a cartridge belt of modern-looking shells, fifty-calibre, if I guessed right. "It's like this everywhere we've looked, thousands of them, underneath the round shot."

"May I see one?"

"Certainly," he said, dropping the cannonball again and passing me one of the bullets. "Keep it, we have enough and to spare, as they say."

"This looks very old, but it can't be."

"Yes, soil and damp must have aged it, Sangster. Anyway, we found no sign this cache had been disturbed, but logic tells me it must have been, given Elizabethan cannon balls are laid on top of modern ammunition." He pointed to the rows of shells. "Someone hid thousands of rounds here." He rubbed his chin. "Hmmm… I thought maybe the IRA, or some criminal organisation, and we reported the find to the police, but they drew a blank."

"Right, well, in any case, criminals don't generally have access to a fifty-cal machine gun, terrorists, maybe, but…" I recalled a windswept Saturday in County Donegal more than twenty-five years previous. "I've, er… seen something like this before."

I fingered the bullet, which was rusty and apparently aged, but still showed faint traces of blue paint on the tip.

"Where, er… where did you see it?" Septimus's voice raised an anxious octave as he spoke.

"Oh, all I meant was I've seen shells like this that were weathered by the elements, especially the sea." I tried to sound as calm as possible, the Donegal shells disquieting me to the point where I needed time to think rather than discuss with the professor.

"Understood," Septimus muttered, seeming to relax again. "You do see some odd things when certain soils and so on get to work on buried artifacts. Anyway, all done here, Sangster?"

"I think so."

We climbed out of the pit, much to my relief, and walked back towards the main building.

"Anyway, have a good drive back," said Septimus as we arrived at my car. "And I'll be seeing you soon at the hotel, I'm sure."

"I haven't asked you much about Christopher yet. What sort of a lad was he?"

"Oh, no, you haven't."

"And?" I raised an eyebrow at the professor.

"Oh, typical fifteen-year-old. Tall, sporty, popular with the girls, I would imagine."

"And academically, his ability, his interests?"

"Christopher is a fair academic all-rounder, but very interested in history. Lad showed great flair, Sangster."

"History?"

"In Sir Francis actually. Fascinated by Drake's obsession with reincarnation."

"How's that?"

"Well, you know the poem 'Drake's Drum'?"

"No, but your brother said you'd recite it given half a chance." I laughed. "And a few whiskies."

"I'm sure Peregrine has all sorts of things to say about me." He laughed back. "But seriously, it's almost as if Drake thought he might be able to travel forward in time and save England from some future peril."

"How does it go?"

"'Drake's Drum', you mean?" I nodded. "Well, like this…" I cursed myself for mentioning the poem and was about to try and change the subject, but too late.

"Drake's in his hammock, slung 'atween the round shot, Cap'n art thou sleeping there below?"

On the word 'below' Septimus raised his arm and shouted, so that I almost jumped. He went on to complete the poem, finishing with a flourish.

"And if the Dons sight Devon, I'll quit the port of Heaven, and we'll drum 'em up the Channel as we drummed 'em long ago."

"Er… very rousing," was all I could think to say.

"Oh yes," Septimus said, now quite out of breath from his poetic exertions. "And the drum's said to beat by itself whenever there are momentous events that threaten England, and his remarkable confidence with the Armada, playing bowls on Plymouth Hoe."

"I was always taught," I said, wondering too late if I was sounding a little pompous, "that Drake knew the tide was unfavourable, so when given news the Spanish fleet had been sighted in the channel, Sir Francis nonchalantly declared he would finish his game of bowls first, then set sail to defeat the Armada. Done for morale's sake, my teacher said."

"Perhaps, because we know Drake was a canny politician. And that incident fascinated Christopher, especially when I explained to him that England should have lost against the Armada."

"Really? I thought with the weather against it, and with our superior ships, we—"

"You, Sangster, as a naval man, should know better," Septimus interrupted, with something close to a sneer. "And I promise, read between the lines of official history books and you'll see the odds were totally against the English." He wagged his finger to emphasise what he said next. "The Spanish couldn't possibly lose."

"But they did, otherwise we'd all be speaking Spanish."

"Yes, and that was of great concern to young Christopher." Septimus looked at his feet as he said this, seeming to consider for a moment. "Would you wait, Mr Sangster, while I get something?"

I looked at my watch. "Yes, I have a few minutes before I need to start out for your brother's research centre."

"Thanks, I won't be long." Septimus went back into the house and returned a few minutes later with an ancient-looking leather-bound tome.

"This is a record kept by Drake's equerry, one Peter Pearce, a manservant Sir Francis had with him in later life."

"And it's genuine?"

"So far as we know, a sort of diary."

"Interesting."

"Yes, and it's been in the library here since Drake's time." He opened the book. "Now there are two passages that interest me, and these same passages, I may say, fascinated young Christopher." He licked his finger and carefully leafed through the pages. "Here's the first, all spelt wrongly, of course, with some words clearly missing and the grammar all astray, you know how they wrote in those days?" I nodded. "So, I'll relate the passage to you as it was doubtless intended to sound." Septimus put on a pair of steel-rimmed glasses and began to read out loud.

> *"My master, when in his cups, would oft regale his guests with fantastic tales of those days of the Armada, and in particular, Sir Francis being a man blessed with the utmost piety, of God's wrath against those who might wrong England and her queen. And it did fascinate me to hear him tell of 'Jehovah's Wind', that in the hand of the righteous, would destroy any enemy of the realm. It was Jehovah's Wind, my Lord did tell me, that gave him such confidence as to complete his game of bowls on the Hoe when told of the Armada's approach. 'Pearce my old lubber' he did say. 'With Jehovah's Wind in my hand, I knew the battle won before ever we set sail.'"*

"So, Drake had the confidence in battle of those that truly believe God is on their side. Nothing new there, Septimus."

"And this second passage caught Christopher's attention even more. Now let me see…" He leafed carefully through the delicate parchment pages. "Here we are.

> "I now quote directly of my master's own words to me, and though what he meant by them I cannot tell, my lord spake thus: Pearce, he did say, I am assured by my friend and confidant Reynard, that I may come again in some future time, should England need my help. I read Job Fourteen with comfort, and having been shown such wonders by Reynard, can only think this to be true, and a great joy to take to my grave."

"A bit cryptic. Who was this Reynard?"

"That would be Reynard Hill, a close friend, even to the extent he was gifted this house by Drake. Buried here in the graveyard too."

"A contemporary then."

"Hill was some years younger than Drake, and apparently, first appeared in Devon at the time of the Armada. Where he came from, records don't say, but his line lives on still, and you will know where, I daresay."

"Will I?"

"Yes, Hill's only child, a daughter, married one Ahab De Coverley, owner of Foxtor House. De Coverleys have continued to live there ever since."

"And Job Fourteen, what's that?"

"I suspect you're not a believer."

"If by that you mean do I go to church, I'm afraid the answer is no."

"If you did," said Septimus, "you'd know Job to be a book in the Bible, and if I recall verse fourteen correctly, it says something like… 'If a man die, he will live again, All the days of my service I would wait until my relief should come.' That's it."

"And you think Drake, with his religious mania, hung on to this idea and thought he could come back to life, go forward in time even?"

"Pious, yes, but a religious maniac, no, and practical to the last was Drake." He closed the old book. "But my point to you was that these passages held some significance for Christopher, may even have some bearing on why he disappeared. You asked about the lad and I'm telling you what I know."

"Of course, thanks."

We walked slowly back towards the car park.

"Could we go via the graveyard, Professor?"

"Of course, Sangster," answered Septimus. "I imagine you now want to see Hill's last resting place."

"Very perceptive of you." I laughed, as we turned into a walled area covered in grass and gravestones.

"This is it," said Septimus, stopping by a headstone, now bent sideways with the ground's shifting over time and bearing faded writing:

Reynard Hill – died 1653
Beloved husband and father
In sure and certain faith of the resurrection

"Funny thing," said Septimus as we viewed various other inscriptions in that solemn and personal way one so often does with graves. "All the other stones here show a birth date as well as the date of passing."

There seemed nothing else left to say, so we walked slowly and silently on.

"Thank you," I said as we arrived at the car park. "Much appreciated." We shook hands, and I turned to open my car door. "Oh, and Professor, when did Christopher stop coming to you?"

"He was due to come again after Easter, but I didn't see him, so what would it be… twelve weeks or so. Shame, such a passionate lad as well. Didn't always agree with him, mind you."

"On what for instance?"

"Otter hunting, for one thing."

"At his age?"

"He was dead set against it. Even joined in with a group of hunt saboteurs, along with that lass from the Wyvern Arms. Hmmm…" He paused for a moment. "Yes, as I recall it was Christopher and friends who stopped us getting Old Soldier on at least two occasions."

"Thanks again."

And as I climbed into to my car, for all the talk of Christopher, I began to feel Melissa to be just as close to the heart of things. She hadn't disappeared, after all, so if I could just talk to her…

4 PM

"Jack Sangster, Granville Institute," I said, handing my card to an armed security guard at the gate of the Highmoor Research Centre. "Sir Peregrine Frere is expecting me, I believe."

"One moment." The guard went into a small sentry box and began, as far as I could see through the box's tiny window, to rifle through papers.

I looked around.

The place certainly was secure, with electrified perimeter fences, as stated by signs showing a stylised bolt of red lightning, topped by razor wire. Parallel with these fences and running as far as I could see in both directions from the gates, was a white metallic tube, set on stilts about a yard above the ground. This tube dipped either side of the gates, presumably buried underground to allow vehicles to pass, and try as I might, I couldn't for the life of me guess the structure's purpose. Beyond the gates sat several square concrete buildings, a tall mast, high-tension power cables that led over the fence and across the moor, and most noticeably, an enormous white radar dome perched on a small knoll above the main complex and looking like nothing so much as an outsized golf ball.

"Any identification, perhaps with a photo?" asked the guard, having come back out of the sentry box with a paper in his hand. I showed my passport. "Sign here," he said, handing me back my passport, along with the paper and a ballpoint pen. I duly signed.

"Thank you, we'll open the gates, and you just go on up there." He pointed to a broad driveway that led through the middle of the complex. "Sir Peregrine's office is in D Block, the guard on the door will show you in." Moments later the gates swung open, and another guard waved me through.

The concrete buildings seemed larger than they looked from the gates as I drove along the central drive, passing several blue Land Rovers with the Centre's logo painted on the sides, along with some green camouflage-painted military vehicles. There were numerous guards dotted around the place, as well as soldiers. Security here really is tight, I thought as I pulled up by D Block, which I recognised from the massive letter D painted on the building's side wall, so what are they so worried about?

I stepped out of the car to be met by another uniformed guard.

"Good afternoon, Mr Sangster, I'm Jones, assistant to Sir Peregrine."

I nodded, then followed him into D Block.

*

"Mr Sangster, come in, and welcome to Highmoor."

"Good afternoon."

"Take a seat, please," Sir Peregrine Frere said, gesturing to a swivel chair in front of his desk. "Now if you'll just excuse me a moment." He pored over a ledger, using a pair of reading spectacles as a handheld magnifying glass above one of the entries, before shouting into an intercom on the desk. "Jones, we've got an entry here for, er… fifteen thousand rounds of fifty-calibre ammunition, Royal Ordnance Factory in Cheshire."

"From when, sir?" crackled the reply.

"March, Jones, and they've sent a chaser letter for the costs. Any idea why we bought it all?"

"Would have been for the ballistics department, I'll need to check."

"Very well." Sir Peregrine looked up. "Tea, coffee, Sangster?"

"Coffee would be nice."

"Coffee and biscuits for three, please, Jones," he shouted back into an intercom. "Sorry," he smiled, "volume on this thing doesn't work too well. Now then, did you manage to find Reynard's Hall alright?"

"Yes, thank you. A magnificent place."

"I'm pleased you like it. Our family home, you know, Septimus and I grew up there, along with our five sisters." I now understood Septimus's name and reasoned he must be the youngest of the seven Frere siblings. "We sold to the National Trust not so long ago. Septimus only agreed on the proviso he could maintain the museum and live at the hall in perpetuity."

"And you?"

"Oh no, I live over in Tavistock."

"With your wife, who doesn't approve of otter hunting?"

"You are a bit of a sleuth, Sangster, how did you guess?"

"Visible wedding ring but invisible wife, at last night's hunt dinner and this morning at the hunt itself." I immediately thought this sounded smug and decided to change the subject. "Your brother seems very attached to the hall."

"Yes, the Drake connection excited him even as a boy, became an obsession…" He shook his head with a wistful expression and whispered, "As you will have observed, and it goes some way to explaining Septimus's lifelong bachelorhood." He then brightened his tone. "Now, Sangster, is there anything you would like to discuss before we call in Doctor De Coverley?"

"I would like to understand more about what you do here."

"Cigarette?" I shook my head as Sir Peregrine took one from a box on the desk, then picked up a heavy-looking silver table lighter. "Well," he said, drawing in smoke and sitting back in his seat, a high-backed black leather armchair that gave him the air of an interrogator. "I'm afraid details are classified, but in broad terms, we do research into nuclear weapons. Don't make the weapons, you understand, just research them." He blew a smoke ring. "Oh, and we also justify our existence by testing conventional naval weapons systems, everything from small-arms ballistics to the big stuff."

"And you have radio-active material stored here, weapons-grade plutonium and the like?"

"Ah." He shook his head. "Classified as well."

I took this answer as a yes.

"And how long has the centre been open?"

"Since the war, although…" He paused to stub out his cigarette. "That's not strictly true. The original centre was sited across the moor there." He stood up and pointed out of the window, to a hill perhaps two miles away, where a squat grey building could be seen. "The current centre opened when I came, in 1956."

"And who ran the original centre?"

"My predecessor was a Henry Weaver. He died just before I came in, so I never knew him, but John was with Weaver throughout."

"John?"

"Doctor De Coverley."

"Sorry, of course. Now, if I may ask, how was John's relationship with his son?"

"Oh, very good as far as I could tell. Saw them together regularly, and you know that John had the lad home-schooled after his mother… well, I suppose you heard what happened."

"Yes."

"Car crash, out towards Postbridge. Tragic."

"And can you think of any reason the lad might run off?"

"None. John and the boy were as thick as thieves, and Christopher's disappearance is only recent. Plenty of us have seen him in recent weeks, out by John's house."

I suddenly felt a rush of adrenaline.

"You've spoken with the boy in the last few days?"

"Not spoken with per se," said Sir Peregrine, lighting another cigarette. "But I've seen him, out in the garden when I visited John. Several times."

"When was the last time?"

"Oh, now let me see…" He scratched his head, cigarette ash landing on his nose in the process. "Whoa," he shouted, furiously brushing his face. "Hot stuff. But when? Hmmm… it would have been last Saturday morning. I dropped by to check some results of a test we ran on Friday night."

"I see." I tried to look inscrutable whilst remembering that this was the second supposed sighting of Christopher after he had been reported missing by Mercedes. "Did you actually go inside Foxtor House?" I then asked (for no particular reason except that it instinctively felt relevant).

"No, we talked outside. Yes…" Sir Peregrine lit yet another cigarette. "John actually appeared from round the back of the house. Often does that, now I come to think of it, haven't been inside his place for many a month."

"And can you say what Doctor De Coverley does here at the centre, if that's not classified as well?"

"You'd better ask him yourself, but Sangster."

"Sir Peregrine?"

"You should know John De Coverley is not a well man." He leaned towards me and whispered, "Cancer, so go gently, please." I nodded, as he leaned back again and shouted into the intercom, "Jones, can you ask Doctor De Coverley to come up, please?"

"Yes, sir," came the faint reply.

"And Jones," Sir Peregrine shouted again, even louder this time, "where's my bloody coffee and biscuits?"

"On it's, er… on the way, sir," crackled a traumatised-sounding Jones. "Be there, er… in, er… one minute."

*

"Sangster, this is Doctor John De Coverley," said Sir Peregrine, as a tall man with thinning grey hair, slim and gaunt in the face, entered the office. He wore black-framed glasses and a white lab coat over a brown suit.

I stood up, partly from countless years of expected etiquette, but more, I think, because De Coverley's general facial look and demeanour demanded it. Here, I thought, was a man who understood more than I, and more than he was prepared to say. A man for whom at least a hem of the curtain that shrouds the mysteries of existence had been raised. A man who knew things, and those things did not necessarily make him happy. Then there were the eyes, hollow, with an air of despair that only the terminally ill can impart. But there was also a defiance in De Coverley's eyes, a sense that perhaps he could somehow cheat death. This was a lot to assimilate in a split second, but it was how I felt at the time, and I spent some hours trying to analyse my feelings after that first sight of De Coverley without coming to any better conclusions. I took a breath.

"Jack Sangster, pleased to meet you, Doctor De Coverley." I held out my hand.

"Sangster."

"John's our, well… let's all sit down, have a cup of Jones's delicious coffee and… oh, custard creams, we are honoured today."

Sir Peregrine picked up a biscuit and dunked, whilst I noticed De Coverley remove a small jar from his pocket and take out a pill.

"Now then, Doctor, could you explain what you do here?"

"I can't say too much," De Coverley answered, swallowing the tablet with a sip of tea.

"Classified?" I sighed.

"I'm afraid so, but in summary, I work with particle accelerators."

"John's the best in the land, perhaps the world."

"That's, er… particles… er…" I stumbled for words. "I'm not sure what that means actually."

"Don't worry." De Coverley laughed. "It's an arcane subject. Basically, we accelerate subatomic particles to great velocity, close to the speed of light, and at times allow them to collide. You may have noticed an oval track running just inside the perimeter fence."

I remembered the tube-like structure I'd seen by the gate. "Yes, I think I saw it."

"Well, it's a vacuum tube. Two miles around."

"And for the purpose of, er... accelerating these particles."

"Oh, a variety of applications. One objective is to send a particle faster than light."

"So," I said, trying to think quickly, "if they collide, in your..."

"Accelerator," helped Sir Peregrine.

"Thanks, yes, then if particles travelling at light speed collide head on in your accelerator, they hit each other at twice the speed of light?"

"No." De Coverley shook his head. "Quantum physics doesn't quite work like that, but I can say we've sent particles faster than—"

"I don't think we need more of the details," said Sir Peregrine, giving De Coverley a look that said the doctor had spoken too much. "Anyway, Sangster, explain to John why you are here."

"I'm here to help," I said, wanting to be as tactful as possible. After all, this man, very ill and recently bereaved from his wife's death, now had a missing son.

"With what?"

"Your son's disappearance." I handed him my card. "I'm with the Granville Institute, we look into—"

"Yes, I've heard of it, and you. You're the chap who found that girl down in Cornwall."

"That's right, and now I've been assigned to help find Christopher."

"By whom?"

"Well, er..." I didn't want to mention that the instruction appeared to have come direct from senior government. "The police are quite short-staffed, it seems, so we were brought in."

"I see, Sangster." De Coverley nodded as he said this, but I could tell he was nevertheless sceptical by a look in his eyes, a look that was hard to describe but familiar to me all the same.

"Now just a few questions, if I may." De Coverley nodded again. "Firstly, was your son in any trouble?"

"No."

"Do you have any enemies who might want to harm you through the boy?"

"No."

"And if I may ask, do you have private means enough that Christopher could be a ransom target?"

"We have a valuable house—"

"I was thinking more about cash in the bank."

"No."

"And was there, perhaps, a girl on the scene?" I leaned forward, to encourage more than a one-word answer.

"Girl, er…" He shook his head, this time perhaps a little too much, I felt. "No."

"Or… I have to ask, a boy?"

"Heavens no."

"And you decided to home-school him?" De Coverley nodded yet again. "Why was that?"

"Oh," he answered, looking sideways in a manner I'd come to know over the years as a sign of possible disingenuity. "I, er… wanted the company after Irene passed, and felt I could teach Chris everything he needed."

"Everything?"

"Well, science-wise, yes, but for classics and so on, we had Professor Frere over in Yelverton."

"So I understand." I paused for a moment, wondering what it would take to get more emotion from this man. "And were you worried when your son didn't turn up to lessons with Professor Frere?"

"I didn't know."

I found this hard to believe given how close father and son were, and decided to press De Coverley a little harder.

"And I have to ask, was all well between you and your son?"

"Absolutely." He looked out of the window, almost detached from the conversation, and hardly the anxious parent I'd expected. "Chris and I were always close, and more so since his mother passed." De Coverley continued gazing out of the window, towards the derelict building on the hill Sir Peregrine had shown me earlier. My instinct, when watching De Coverley's eyes, was that this place held some importance for him.

"You've been with the Highmoor Centre for a long time, I believe?"

"Since its inception, Sangster, in the last years of the war."

"Starting in that building across the moor?"

"Well, I—"

"John's quite attached to the Old Centre, aren't you, John?" interjected Sir Peregrine. "We were going to have it pulled down, but John insisted we keep it. What did you say about the place?"

"Oh," said De Coverley, still gazing away from us, "just that we should preserve it as a reminder of the scientific progress made in those post-war years, and as a monument to Henry Weaver."

"Cost us more to make it safe than pull it down." Sir Peregrine laughed. "Had to fence it off, brick up the entrances, and so on."

"Why's that?" I asked.

"Place sits over a mineshaft. Very deep, very dangerous. And of course, we cleared it of equipment, but the structure hasn't been maintained. Unprotected, the Old Centre might be fatal for some rambler who chanced on it by accident."

"I'd been thinking you'd turned it into some sort of museum."

"No, Sangster, no. Place is all bricked up, as I told you."

As he said this, I found myself wondering why such a remote and inhospitable spot was chosen for the centre in the first place, so asked the question.

"This remote location is certainly good for security," answered De Coverley. "Just as it is for the prison, but there are remoter places, like the Scottish Highlands and Islands."

"Then why?"

"It's the geology. Do you know what a pluton is?" I shook my head. "Well, many millions of years ago, granite was laid down from volcanic lava all along the south-west peninsula of Britain and even out into the sea. Perry, haven't we got a Geological Survey map in here?"

"Er... yes, I believe so." Sir Peregrine opened a large cupboard. "Here we are." He pulled out a map, held in a roll by an elastic band. "Now look," he said, spreading the map out on his desk, "you can see what John's talking about."

This map, I realised as he spoke, was a geological representation of Devon, Cornwall, and the sea to the Isles of Scilly and beyond. And although clearly intended as a map, what I was looking at showed no roads, rivers, towns, place names, contour lines, or other familiar features. Rather, the land was covered in patches of colour, reds, greens, blues, browns, and yellows. The seas were mostly purple, with areas of lighter and darker shading, and although there was plenty of text, it was meaningless to me.

"Now look," said De Coverley, pointing to patches of red, "these are places where the granite appears at the surface, but they're all joined together below ground." He traced his finger across the surface of the map. "A bit like an iris rhizome, with a single root underground but different stems poking up through the soil."

"I see," I muttered, feeling I did not 'see' at all. "And why do these, er… plutons, was it?" De Coverley nodded. "Stick up?"

"Granite's hard, and the softer rock surrounding it eventually erodes, leaving the outcrops. We've got them all down the peninsula." De Coverley pointed to the red patches whilst naming them, one after the other. "Dartmoor, Bodmin Moor, St Austell, Lizard, the toe of Cornwall, the Scillies, and another undersea granite outcrop called Haig Fras."

"And these areas of high land are all connected, you say?"

"Together they form the Cornubian batholith," said Sir Peregrine.

I bet they do, I thought, refusing the temptation to ask what that meant, imaging these men thought me ignorant enough.

"And," said De Coverley, rolling up the map again, "plutons exhibit many interesting qualities."

"Such as?" I asked.

"They carry great mineral wealth for a start, like tin and copper. For us, though, the interest lies in the geological structure itself, and the rock's suitability for our kind of research. I'm not sure there is any better location in the world for what we do here."

"Makes sense to build the centre on Dartmoor then," I said, as De Coverley replaced the map on its shelf.

"Indeed." He locked the cupboard, then went back to gazing out of the window at the Old Centre.

"Anyway, Sangster, is there anything else we can do for you today?"

"No, I don't think so, Sir Peregrine…" I then looked back towards De Coverley. "Oh, and Doctor?"

De Coverley broke his gaze and turned to me.

"Yes, Sangster?"

"Just one more thing. Your son, where do you think he is?"

"Well, I'd say he's just gone off for a few days. Be back here any time, I should think."

"Had he ever run away before?"

"No."

"Anything else you can think of?"

De Coverley then gave me what seemed a very odd answer. "I'd say he hasn't gone very far, not very far at all, if you think in distances. In fact, I'm sure he's quite close by, nearer than some of us might imagine."

*

I couldn't think of anything further to say so made my farewells before being escorted to the car by Jones, a pleasant young man, clearly local by his accent, and with a healthy cynicism for his bosses.

"Bit of a tartar, Sir Peregrine," he said, when I mentioned the shouting down the intercom. "But he's dedicated, means well, just gets a bit mixed up at times."

"Like that order he couldn't remember?"

"Sir Peregrine will sign anything you put in front of him. Problem is that he forgets what he signed."

"And Doctor De Coverley?"

"Now he's an odd one. Works all the hours God sends, keeps himself to himself, and pretty well lives over the shop."

"How do you mean?"

"That house, couple of miles away, over by Fox Tor. They say his family's been there for about four hundred years. Doctor De Coverley's what you might call a gentleman scientist."

"And have you met his son?"

"Couple of times. The lad spends a lot of time with his dad, that's for sure, and with that tall girl. See the three of them together quite a lot."

"You, er… remember her name?"

"Um… she lives over at the Wyvern Arms hotel, now what was it…"

"Melissa Merrivale?"

"That's it, and I tell you, it's funny but…" He began to laugh to himself. "She's so tall."

"Like her mum?"

"Yes, she's tall as well, but Melissa, with that short haircut, you couldn't hardly tell the difference between her and Christopher. 'Cept close up, of course."

"Thanks, Jones," I said as we arrived at the car. "And I can make my own way from here," I added, feeling details like the girl's height to be wandering a long way off the point.

"Safe journey," Jones replied as I stepped into the car.

Pulling away down the driveway, I looked in the rear-view mirror to see Jones giving me a wave, then began to ask myself questions, three whys and a how, out loud.

Why was De Coverley so apparently indifferent about a missing child, his own son?

How could De Coverley not have known his son was cutting lessons with Professor Frere for twelve weeks?

Why did De Coverley seem so fixated on the derelict building up by the tor?

And why did De Coverley lie to me about his son not having a girlfriend?

5:15 PM

"Mayfair 625 7701, Granville Institute."

"Polly, it's me, Jack Sangster."

"You want," she said slowly, "to speak to Sir John?"

"Well, yes," I said, confused by her tone. "He did ask me to call back after five."

"He did, didn't he, but… well."

"Is everything alright?"

"Yes, Mr Sangster, but I think it might have been rather more than a couple of bottles of club claret."

"I see. Is he in a fit state to take a call…?"

"Suppose so, but be warned." I heard tell-tale clicks as she transferred me to Sir John's office.

"Sangster, how zugh devil are you?" roared Sir John.

"Oh, I'm fine, thank you, I was just ringing—"

"Jusht ringing about what? It's gone five."

"As you asked, to see how lunch went."

"Oh, splendidly, that Maudling's not such a bad cove after all. Sense of humour, not like the last bore of a Home Secretary, Callaghan. Maudling likes his claret too." I'm sure he does, I thought, listening to Sir John making slurping noises, doubtless from drinking the fine cognac he always kept in his office. "Anyway, Sangster, it's gone five, you know, what can I do for you?"

"Did you, er… discuss the case?"

"Which case?"

"Mine."

"What's wrong with you? Why have you got a case?"

"No, not about me, about the De Coverley boy."

"Ah, the De Coverley boy." There was a long pause.

"Sir John?"

"Yesh, now I remember. De Coverley… case and so on."

I thought I heard him snoring down the phone. "And…"

"Oh, yes, bad business, Sangster. Seems the defence of the realm, no, defence of the free world's tied up with the lad's disappearance."

"Why?"

"Not sure, but that Reginald more… more… more."

"Maudling?" I asked.

"That's him. Got quite agitated about it all, had to calm him down with a brandy in the smoking room."

"What did he say?"

"That whatever…" Sir John slurped again down the phone. "That's the father he was speaking about."

"Yes, Sir John?"

"Er… whatever the De Coverley father was up to, it could change everything, and that the boy's disappearance might be proof of that." I heard Sir John making his trademark 'hmmph' down the phone, a noise that usually preceded some demand. "Said someone's got to get to the bottom of it at all costs."

"Then why us? Why not the cream of Scotland Yard, MI5, the army, for heaven's sake?"

"Seems you got quite a rep with that last case with that girl down in Cornwall. MI5 know who you are now, and they like the idea of your softly softly approach. That's what Maudling said, anyway." Sir John 'hmmphed' again. "I'm sorry to get you into all this, Sangster, but it's going to be about as high profile as they come, so I shouldn't cock it up if I were you."

Thanks a lot, I thought, but merely asked, "Anything else?"

"Well, I pressed him on whether it was just the local police and the Granville Institute on the case."

"And?"

"No proper answer, but Maudling did say, now what was it, yes… that they were 'hedging their bets.'"

"Did he?" I wondered what the government might be doing behind our backs, even behind the backs of the Devon police.

"Anyway, Sangster, we'll talk again in the morning, now jusht a moment while I top myshelf up." I heard a bottle cork pop and the gurgling sound of liquid poured into a glass, then nothing.

"Sir John, you still there?" I asked after about half a minute, but the only sound to be heard was snoring.

"Polly, it's me again."

"Mr Sangster?"

"I had to ring back, Sir John seems to have fallen asleep."

"Well, you won't be able to speak to him now. I'll wake him at six thirty, before I leave. He can sleep at his club."

"It's you I wanted."

"You wanted me?"

"Yes, I need a favour, a bullet sending by courier."

"Sounds exciting."

"Not particularly." I laughed. "There's a plastic bag in the top left-hand drawer of my desk at home. It contains an old bullet. Is there anyone you might be able to call in Chester who could collect it?"

"Your wife's at home, is she?"

"No, she's out of the country."

"There's a key, perhaps?"

"Yes, under a flowerpot in the back garden, it's…" I explained exactly where the key and the bullet could be found.

"OK, now who could I, er… yes, I do know someone. Did you ever meet Mavis Stephens?"

"Of course, Polly. Spoke to her not so long ago, Director Johnson's secretary at the Chester education department. Very competent lady."

"We're both members of PA England, a sort of network of

secretaries, and I met her at a do last Christmas, in Birmingham. I could ask Mavis if she'd get the key and put it on the night train parcel service. Now let me see… one moment, I have the schedule somewhere." I heard the rustle of papers. "Says here you'd get it in Plymouth by nine o'clock tomorrow morning, if you can collect from the station." She waited for me to answer, but I was distracted by what I would do once the bullet arrived. "Will that be OK, Mr Sangster?"

"Perfect, Polly," I said, feeling the shell in my pocket, the rusty bullet from Drake's arsenal that shouldn't have been there, whilst experiencing that brief spasm of warmth that so often comes when some annoying practical problem is solved by someone else. "Just perfect, and send my warmest to Mavis, would you?"

6 PM

"Jack." Mercy held a small box up in front of me. "I, er... have a little favour to ask, I'm so busy, and I wondered, could you—"

"Take those pills up to Whiddon?"

"How did you guess?" She looked genuinely surprised.

"Must be clairvoyant, or..." I shook my head. "Overheard you just now in the common room actually."

I'd seen Mercy talking to Nurse Pickles when I returned from the Highmoor Centre, the nurse asking if someone could take the tablets up to Whiddon because she had another patient to see in Princetown. Mercy had said how busy she was, but that 'something would be done'.

"I know it's a big ask of a guest, but you've met him, and you know the way. I've nobody here I can spare, so would you, Jack?"

"Of course, Postbridge Road, turning to Wistman's Wood."

"Oh, thank you. Now, he's to take these twice a day, once in the morning once at night. Alright?"

"Uh huh." I nodded, trying not to grimace, whilst musing that the price of keeping Mercedes sweet was rising by the day.

"Thanks so much, Jack. I owe you another after-dinner brandy."

*

"Excuse me." I felt a tap on my shoulder, turning round to see Jane Ustrix. "I'm sorry, but did you just say you were going to Wistman's Wood?"

"I did, well, near there, anyway. Delivering some tablets to an old man, he's laid up in bed."

"It, er... wouldn't be the one who saw the Wild Hunt?"

"Well..."

"It is, isn't it?" she said, almost jumping up and down on the spot. "Would you take me with you?"

"I'll only be popping in to the see the old man."

"I'd really like to see the place where he sighted the Hunt, and well, I thought..." She put her hands behind her back and moved from side to side, looking to me like a schoolgirl asking to be excused homework. "It's a nice evening, so perhaps a quick look at the wood afterwards?"

"Er... yes," I said, thinking this detour might slow me down but in the moment unable to rustle up an excuse to say no, whilst a thought also tickled the back of my mind that I might learn more about this rather enigmatic woman. "Ready to go now?"

"Just let me go upstairs and grab my walking boots, Jack."

*

"This is a lovely car," said Jane, as we drove along the Postbridge Road (once again, I held tight on the wheel as we passed over the bridge).

"Thanks, I like it, and here's where Whiddon says he saw the Hunt, by the way."

"Hmmm..." She looked either side of the car as I slowed to cross the bridge. "Doesn't look that special, but anyway, this car, it's a car of dreams, we've nothing like this back home, I..." She suddenly checked herself, and I noticed her cheek redden. "Of course, I mean I haven't anything like this at home. Can't drive, anyway, and... oh." She pointed to the left. "There's the sign to Wistman's Wood."

I swung into the lane and a minute later was parked outside Whiddon's caravan.

"Wood's a little further on, I think, now wait in your seat, I won't be a minute." I climbed out of the car, then walked towards the caravan as the passenger door slammed shut.

"I must talk to him, Jack."

"Must you?" I sighed. "He's quite frail."

"I'll be brief. And gentle."

"Come on then." I knocked on the caravan door, heard a grunted 'come in', then entered to find Whiddon, still with his head bandage on but now sitting up and watching Wimbledon on a tiny television set that might well have been bought new to watch the Queen's coronation.

"Ah, it's you again, young man, and Mercy…" Jane stepped in behind me. "Oh, you're not Mercy, who are you?"

"This is Jane, she's another guest at the Wyvern Arms. Come to keep me company."

"Be quick, whatever you're here for, I'm watching this Virginia Wade, fine young English lass." He winked at me. "Fine pair o' legs too."

I looked at the veritable snowstorm on his screen, the only clues to the set showing Wimbledon being the clicking of balls and the roaring of the crowd. I wondered how he could tell whether this Virginia Wade had any legs at all, let alone whether they were 'fine'.

"Well, I won't keep you, Mercy just asked me to drop these tablets off." I placed the box on a shelf. "Now you take one at night, and one in the morning, for five days. Can you remember that?"

"I'm not senile, young man."

"Of course you're not, Mister Whiddon," interjected Jane. "And I hear you saw the Wild Hunt last night."

"See that? Double fault. Match point to Virginia."

"Let him watch it, then ask," I mouthed to Jane.

"Oh yes," shouted Whiddon, as a roar from the crowd indicated Miss Wade had won, although I still couldn't make out a thing on the screen. "She's in the third round now."

"Mr Whiddon," said Jane. "The Wild Hunt?"

"Seen it as well, have you, young woman?"

"Not me, you, last night. What was it like?"

"Came down from the wood, flashing lights all around me, made my skin tingle, terrible din."

"Did you see anything else?"

"No, but it was the Wild Hunt, I tell you, just like I told the copper who interviewed me at the hospital. He reckoned I was hit by a car, but I know what I saw." Whiddon slumped back in his chair. "Now, I really can't talk anymore."

"I'm sorry, I didn't mean to tire you out," said Jane.

"Tire me out, ha." Whiddon let out a wheezing guffaw. "Can't talk 'cos it's mixed doubles on now. Even more skirts and legs. Bye bye."

*

We drove slowly on along the track for several minutes, until the rough road petered out into scrubland.

"This is as far as I can drive."

"That looks like a boundary fence, Jack, and there's a gap just to the left, see? Must be Wistman's Wood on the other side."

We climbed out of the car, walked through the fence gap and into the trees, a thick tangle of oaks, heavily in leaf as would be expected in June, but stunted, as if the very ground beneath was poisoned. For all that, it would have been hard to tell what was happening on the woodland floor, strewn as it was with dead leaves, lichen-covered rocks, and bracken, so that nowhere was the actual ground visible.

"Mind your step, Jane," I said, almost missing my footing on some hidden and loose boulders.

"I'm fine, I… ugh, watch out, Jack." She grabbed my arm and pulled me back, then pointed to a patch of moss in front of us, where a writhing mass of patterned serpents lay hissing. "Adders, aren't they revolting?"

"Guess they live here and we're the intruders," I said, looking down at the snakes, perhaps ten of them in all. "Reckon they're out courting."

"Courting?"

"Yes, Jane, there'll be one female and a load of suitors vying for her favours."

"How does she decide?" Jane asked, staring at the adders and grimacing.

"You tell me, how does any woman decide?"

"Ssss." She drew breath, sounding very like a snake herself. "I couldn't say."

As she spoke there was a rumble of thunder in the distance.

"Come on, Jane, let's keep going."

We circled the adders, and after another fifteen minutes or so of walking, the trees cleared and we found ourselves on a rocky summit, the wood canopy spread out around us, and further away the moor, undulating on all sides. Looking towards where we'd come from, a faint column of smoke, doubtless from Whiddon's chimney, could be seen rising up through the trees, and beyond, a ribbon that was the Postbridge Road cutting its way back towards the Wyvern Arms.

"What's that?" said Jane, pointing down towards a glinting light in the trees on the other side of the valley.

"Not sure." I peered in the direction of her finger to see the light vanish, then appear again. "Reflection of some sort, in fact I'd say it could be the sun on binoculars." I looked again. Were there figures by the trees next to the glint? "Must be a peeping tom, spying on us from afar." I laughed.

"It's so peaceful here, Jack, I can't imagine anyone wanting to… ouch, my hair, I…" She touched her neck, shouted again, and held her hands against her ears. "Ah, that noise."

I felt it too, first a tingling sensation in my hair, then searing pain and a noise like thunder, not coming from the sky, or even the ground, but (and I would still struggle to describe the source of that noise) from within my own head. Then I felt stabbing pains in my arms and legs, and heard more noise, this time a shrill trumpet that accompanied each stab.

"Jaaaack," I heard Jane scream, as the wood around us seemed to come alive, the trees lit with a blue light the like of which I'd never seen before, a snake-like spark winding itself around trunk and limb, jumping from branch to branch. She kept screaming, but in the chaos the words sounded like a foreign tongue to me, thick consonants with long guttural vowels. I felt my head begin to spin and, falling myself, watched Jane collapse to the ground, as an orb of blue light hovered above her, before gliding away into the wood.

"My God, Jack, are you alright?" I opened my eyes to see Jane standing above me.

"Yes." I blinked. "You OK?"

"I think so." She rubbed the back of her head. "What the hell was that?"

"I've no idea, but let's get back to the car, now."

We said nothing more to each other, then fairly ran down through the wood, past the mossy patch of adders, which still hissed but seemed of no consequence now, and finally through the fence to the car.

"White lightning storm, I suppose," said Jane breathlessly as we bumped back down the track. "I've never met anyone who's seen one, but they do exist." Despite still being winded from our run to the car, she seemed remarkably calm given what had just happened.

I did not feel calm.

"But… I saw a sphere of blue light float over your head, I swear it."

"Ball lightning, Jack, well-known phenomenon. Rare, though, so you can count yourself lucky to have seen it."

"Lucky, eh?" I thought myself anything but lucky, feeling drained to the point of losing the desire to speak.

"Look, is that the Dikes?" She pointed to two figures trudging along the road in the distance. As we drew close, I could see it was indeed Ballar and Fidelma, both in their robes, which were billowing out from behind as they walked. Fidelma was bent low by a large rucksack, whilst Ballar, carrying nothing, as far as I could see, stepped ahead, tapping his way along the side of the road with a long wooden staff.

I slowed down and waved, and the Dikes waved back, Ballar smiling and raising his staff in salute, Fidelma grimacing.

"I know it sounds awful, but for God's sake don't offer them a lift."

"You're forgetting," I said to Jane with a wink, "this car's a two-seater."

"Jack." She smiled. "How much do you know of druids?"

"A little," I said, remembering a case the previous year where I had reluctantly learned more about paganism than I should have liked.

"Well, I know a little about modern druids myself, their Wiccan faith and the lore that surrounds it, and, well…" She leaned over and whispered to me, "The Dikes talk absolute rubbish. It's as if they've read a couple of books on witchcraft and picked out some words to bandy about."

"Well, it takes all sorts."

"But do you, er… not think they might be fakes?"

"Oh." I shrugged, wondering if she had some other reason to doubt the pair. "Perhaps that's just the way they want to dress, trying to go back to a simpler way of life, commune with Mother Earth and so on."

"Or they're not what they seem, maybe something more devious?"

"I doubt it," I said, unsure of my words as I remembered Ballar getting out of the car at midnight. "And why not be a druid?" I continued, instinctively feeling I shouldn't let Jane know I had doubts. "I mean, it's harmless, and there isn't any serious witchcraft around these days."

"Isn't there?" she whispered again, this time leaning forward even closer and staring at me. "Not even in Wistman's Wood?"

We drove the rest of the way back to the hotel in silence.

"See you at dinner, Jane," was all I said as we entered the common room.

"Yes, see you at eight."

9 PM

I arrived in the dining room an hour later than I'd planned, prompting Mrs Curtice to stop her piano-playing when I entered, so for an excruciating moment the whole room stared at me. Then she continued with the strains of 'Do You Know the Way to San Jose' and the diners gradually resumed their conversation. Just as I was cursing myself for oversleeping whilst having laid down on my bed to close my eyes for what was supposed to have been just a few minutes, Tilly appeared.

"Mr Sangster, we saved a place for you with Miss Ustrix, on that table by the window." She pointed across the room to where Jane sat alone, staring at a bowl of soup. "I hope that's alright."

"Lovely, Tilly," I said, still aware of some residual stares but relieved the table was about as far away from Mrs Curtice and her piano as the dining room allowed. "Did I see trout on the menu?"

"Yes, sir, wild caught. Anton cold-marinates the whole fish in fresh rosemary, melted butter and garlic, seasoned with sea salt and cracked black pepper, then he bakes the fish with almonds."

"I wouldn't have it any other way."

"Sir?"

"I mean, yes, I'll take the trout, please, and no wine tonight, just a jug of water."

*

"'Scuse fingers," I said to Jane as I extracted a last trout bone from my teeth. "Delicious but bony."

"Fish bones are one occupational hazard I don't have to cope with." Her face creased with laughter for a moment, then dropped into a frown. "That was a thing in the wood, wasn't it?"

"Thing's about right, I don't have the words."

"Just a natural phenomenon," she said quickly and with a tone of absolute certainty. "We're lucky to have seen it."

"And luckier to come out unscathed." I still felt a real sense of danger at what had happened and wondered where this confidence of Jane's came from. "So, you know about these things?"

"A little."

"Bit outside your area of expertise, isn't it?"

"Oh." She shuffled her cutlery, giving off an air of discomfort. "Picked up some knowledge on the way, you know how it is." I nodded, whilst thinking that I didn't really 'know how it is'. "But you could imagine how someone might think that was the Wild Hunt, especially if it happened in the dark."

"Yes," I said, nodding again. "Very much so."

"Dessert, cheese, coffee?" offered Tilly, clearing our plates.

"Just coffee for me, please, but Jane, do go ahead with a pudding if you'd like."

"I'm going to be very naughty, Jack," she said, then turned to Tilly. "And have some more of that Black Forest gateau we had last night."

"Yes'm, so that's one coffee, one gateau."

*

Jane was just finishing a last mouthful of cake when Mrs Curtice gave her customary bow, then left the room. This time her thank-you speech was more muted, there was no boogie encore, and she left under her own steam. It was then I realised I hadn't seen Mercy all evening.

"Is it a Scottish name?" I asked, as Tilly removed Jane's cake dish and cutlery.

"Sorry?"

"Ustrix, never heard that name before."

"Er... perhaps a long way back." She shuffled her napkin, and again, it was almost as if my most innocent of questions caused her discomfort. "Although," she then laughed, "Ustrix also means 'she who curls hair using heat' in Latin."

"And were you up at Somerville before you took your research fellowship?"

"Is this twenty questions, Jack?" Jane looked at me quite sharply as she said this.

"Sorry." I held my hands up. "I'm naturally nosey. Didn't mean to pry."

"It's alright, and yes, I'm a Somerville alumnus. You?"

"Dartmouth as a teenager then straight into active naval service. Not a formal academic qualification in sight, I'm afraid."

"They matter less and less the older we get."

"Maybe, although your knowledge on everything from folklore to atmospheric physics puts me to shame."

"Just got that kind of mind, Jack, retentive memory." She stood up. "Now then, if you don't mind, it's been a long day, so I think I'll turn in."

"Alright, then sleep well."

"Perhaps I'll see you at breakfast?"

"Sorry, early start, have to be in Devonport tomorrow."

"What's on in Devonport?"

"Visiting the naval armoury there," I blurted out. "Looking into an arms theft a few nights ago."

"I thought you were here investigating the disappearance of a child?"

"Unrelated," I said, feeling my change of tack must seem unconvincing. "Someone asked me to check into it, being former RN and all."

"How is the search for that, er... no, I forget his name... that missing boy?"

"It's Christopher, and I'll be dropping into his school to chat with the headmaster in the morning as well, maybe shed more light on the lad that way."

"But how are you finding the investigation?"

"To be honest, about as confusing as I've ever encountered," I answered, still somehow reticent to tell her more. "A real puzzler."

*

I sat in the bay window settle, looking across the common room, alone except for Joe Gurney at the bar and the Dikes sitting in the corner. They'd nodded to me as I passed, but now sat silently in front of their pint pots, having had another argument, I imagined. The silence was broken as the front door opened and I heard Mercy shouting.

"Why didn't you call if you were going to take the late bus?"

"Didn't think I needed to, Mum," came the answer, as a girl came into the room. She was easily as tall as Mercy, dressed in jeans and with a boyish haircut.

"Well, you'd better get straight up to bed, oh." Mercy looked at me. "Didn't see you there, sorry about this, Jack. Mel, this is Mr Sangster, he's an investigator, here to help the police find Christopher."

I stood up and held out my hand. "Jack, and you must be Melissa."

"Worked that out all by yourself, Mister Investigator?" she said, walking past without looking at me or taking my hand.

"Sorry, Jack, we've had a bit of a ding-dong."

"Sounds like the brandy should be on me." I signalled to Joe Gurney, who held his hand up. "Two cognacs, please, Joe, on my tab." I sat down next to Mercy. "Want to talk about it?"

"Not really, except that she was due home straight after school but didn't show up until now, last bus, and I've a sneaking suspicion..." she dabbed her eye with a handkerchief, "that Mel's been doing something she shouldn't."

"How do you mean?"

"She wasn't at her friend's in Plymouth last night, I phoned the mother." She dabbed her eyes again. "And Mel hasn't been there on most of the other occasions she's claimed to be sleeping over."

"Any idea where then?"

"No, but there's a boy involved, I'm sure." Joe placed two brandy balloons in front of us and Mercy cupped one in her hands, swirled the brown liquid, then sipped. "And a couple of months ago I'd have said it was Chris De Coverley, but he's disappeared, so now I'm not sure." She sipped again. "Not sure who she's seeing, that is."

"I know my job's looking for kids," I said, placing my hand on her shoulder. "But I've no children myself, so I'm afraid I can't help much with a parent's intuition."

"Don't want to burden you, Jack, it's just, well… with the way a mother is, and being on my own, plus the business and all, sometimes it's…"

"I know, hard to cope." I raised my glass to her. "Although for what it's worth, you do cope, and quite brilliantly."

She raised her glass in return and we clinked.

"I try, ahem." She blushed and cleared her throat. "So how was Whiddon?"

"Oh, just fine. Sitting up watching the tennis."

"And I saw you drive off with that woman from room twelve, Jane Ustrix." Mercy coughed again, then sat back from me.

"She was keen for me to show her Wistman's Wood."

"I'm sure she was."

*

I sat up in bed, wide awake and once again cursing the early evening nap.

"Alright, Jack, if you can't sleep, might as well use the time for something. Let's go through what we know." I began to count the salient facts on my fingers:

Christopher De Coverley was missing, and the authorities were unnaturally concerned with his disappearance.

The boy's father appeared relatively unconcerned, and it was Mercy who had actually contacted the police.

Christopher seemed to have disappeared about twelve weeks ago, but people nevertheless reported seeing him from a distance since that time, even after he had been officially declared missing.

Melissa and the boy were clearly close, and Mercy couldn't properly account for Melissa's movements in recent months.

Christopher was interested in history, Drake and the Armada especially, as well as animal cruelty, given he was a hunt saboteur.

I then tried to list things that just might be more than coincidental:

Many places in this locality seemed connected, with Christopher the common denominator: the Highmoor Centre, the Wyvern Arms, Reynard's Hall, even Devonport Docks.

There seemed to be odd natural, or even unnatural, forces at work on the moor: unaccountable power fluctuations in the Princetown area, a bizarre 'white lightning' storm in Wistman's Wood, Whiddon's encounter with the Wild Hunt, surely something akin to the white lightning, as well as the red glow near Fox Tor I'd fleetingly seen the previous evening.

Doctor De Coverley had said the geology of this part of the moor, and the whole of the south-west peninsula of England in general, was unique and special.

Drake's secret weapons cache, that Septimus Frere seemed convinced had remained untouched since Elizabethan times, contained thousands of modern shells, but with no reported theft or other leads to criminals, who could possibly have put them there, and why?

All these latter points didn't seem directly connected with the case, but nevertheless niggled the back of my mind. One point did seem clear, albeit inexplicable.

"Defence of the free world's tied up with the lad's disappearance," I remembered Sir John saying, albeit drunk at the time but by no means incoherent.

"How could this be?" I said to myself with a stretch and a yawn, eyelids involuntarily drooping as the bewildering array of characters I'd met in the last two days jostled with each other for attention in my mind.

Perhaps I'm more tired than I feel, was my last waking thought that evening.

WEDNESDAY, JUNE THE 24TH
8:30 AM

"Sign here, please, sir."

I scribbled my name and took the envelope from the clerk at the luggage office. Fingering the insides through the brown paper, the shape and texture indicated the package did indeed contain the barnacle-encrusted fifty-calibre shell I'd kept from all those years ago.

"Good for Mavis and Polly," I said to myself as I left Plymouth Station. "Done me proud as ever."

A few minutes later I arrived at the gates of the Devonport Naval Arms Depot, which guarded a red-brick building that could have been any anonymous office block (I'd been warned there were no signs, and that the facility, with its deadly contents, was deliberately made to look as innocuous as possible).

I gave my name through an intercom, and as the gates silently slid open, I smiled to think that this bland camouflage hadn't been too successful stopping robberies recently.

"Commander Sangster," said a uniformed officer, stepping out of the front doors to greet me, then saluting. "Welcome to Devonport."

"You must be Lieutenant Jolly," I said, returning his salute after a few seconds (the action no longer came naturally to me).

"Come this way, sir," he said, and I followed him into the building, through several corridors, until we arrived at a small office, where a fearsome-looking moustachioed NCO sat at a table smoking. "This is Provost Marshal Spinks, sir. Spinks, meet Commander Sangster, here to investigate the break-in at the armoury."

"Sah," said Spinks, springing to attention and saluting.

"As you were, Spinks."

"And no need to stand on ceremony on my account," I added, saluting back before sitting down. "I'm retired, so please, just take a seat yourself and tell me what you saw the night of the robbery."

"Go on, Provost Marshal," said Jolly.

"Well, sir," Spinks barked, sitting in a more relaxed pose but still speaking in a formal manner. "My lads were doing the rounds the other evening, when—"

"The rounds?"

"Checking the perimeter, doors, windows, last thing at night, sir."

"Of course," I said. "Please, proceed."

"Well, an alarm was tripped near the armoury. As I was on my way to the scene, I saw two figures climbing into a van, then drive out through the main gates, which were open, by the way."

"Colour of the van?"

"Dark grey, blue, hard to say, sir."

"Why would the gates be open?"

"I can't say that either, sir. Only way you could get through would be with some kind of force, explosive or whatever."

"But there was no noise and no damage to the gates?"

"No, sir."

"Then how?"

"A code, I suppose, sir, if someone knew the combination." Spinks seemed to think very hard as he said this. "It's a push-button lock, you see."

"And you say the two people you saw fitted the descriptions of Doctor De Coverley and his son?"

"They did, sir, so I thought nothing of it, especially as the gates were open."

"How d'you know what they look like?"

"Doctor De Coverley visits regularly, and sometimes he brings his son. I've seen that boy grow up from a nipper to the tall lad he is now."

"And you saw their faces, did you?"

"No, sir, not in that light, just their silhouettes."

"You're sure it was them, though?"

"Never forget a silhouette in my business. Picked up many a drunken rating of an early morning who made a run for it down Union Street the night before."

"The commander doesn't know Union Street, Spinks," said the lieutenant. "Don't talk in riddles."

"Sorry, sir, I—"

"No need to apologise." I laughed. "Been down Union Street a few times myself when I started out, dodged the MPs when I could as well."

Spinks then made a noise I guessed was the nearest he could get to a laugh.

"Will that be all, sir?"

"Just one thing, why did you not send anyone out after the van or alert the civil police?"

"Once we knew there'd been a robbery we did, sir, but by that time the thieves were well away."

"And De Coverley?"

"We contacted him, of course, sir, but he was elsewhere at the time of the robbery."

"But you said you recognised him and his son by their silhouettes."

"Thought I did, sir, but I must have been mistaken."

"But you say you're good with silhouettes, Spinks. Ratings running down Union Street and so on?"

"First time for everything, I suppose, sir. Doctor De Coverley had a cast-iron alibi. Provided by the daughter of a pub landlady up on the moor."

"Melissa Merrivale, perhaps?"

"Why, er… yes, sir."

"And did you inform the police?"

"Not at the time, Commander Sangster," said Jolly. "You know we manage our own dirty laundry in the service. No reason to call in the civvies, at least not immediately. We did eventually file a routine report which the local coppers would see, though." He turned to the provost marshal. "Oh, and thank you, Spinks, that will be all."

"Sir." Spinks stood, saluted, then marched out of the room.

"Not much changes over the years," I said to Jolly. "Those provost marshals used to put the fear of God into us junior officers."

"Still do." Jolly laughed. "But was that helpful, sir?"

"Oh, very helpful. And if I can ask, what exactly was stolen?"

Jolly opened a cardboard folder and ran his finger down a list. "On this occasion, just a maintenance kit. Took us a while to realise anything had gone missing."

"Maintenance kit?"

"Yes, box of tricks with everything needed to keep a fifty-cal working in the field. You know, grease, oil, new firing pins, cleaning rods for the barrel, that sort of thing."

"And the other theft?"

"Let me see…" He turned the page over. "Twenty-third of March."

"What was taken?"

"Hmmm… yes, very odd. Says here…"

"Go on, Lieutenant."

"They stole an antique machine gun we had on display. Sort of museum piece."

"What type?"

"Browning M2, inter-war vintage, Belgian Fabrique Nationale model."

"Very early one then?"

"Yes, and rather unique, with twin guns and a belt feeder either side. Must have been a fearsome thing in its day."

"And was it decommissioned?"

"I'm afraid not, sir. Fully operational and regularly maintained."

"OK, but why would someone steal that when you have so much new weaponry around?"

"We asked ourselves that same question, sir."

"And?"

"Well, the antique gun wasn't heavily guarded, so easier than some to steal."

"A machine gun left unguarded?"

"Not unguarded, but like I say, museum piece on display, so not held in the main armoury."

"Anything else?"

"We could only think that the thief had no way of maintaining a modern gun or acquiring new parts."

"Why?"

"Well those old Brownings jammed a bit, but they were primitive."

"How do you mean, primitive?"

"Simple, really easy to maintain with a basic kit like the one that was taken, so good for an outfit with no modern equipment or expertise. Steal a modern weapon and you'd need an expert team with the newest equipment to keep it in good working order."

"Terrorists?"

"Don't know, sir, but we informed the security services just in case."

"And you think the two robberies are linked?"

"Looks like it, sir, although the thieves didn't take any ammunition, so I'm not sure what they could do with—"

"Lieutenant?"

I felt in my pocket and pulled out the shell Professor Frere had given me, then opened the envelope from the train station. The barnacle-encrusted bullet from my desk at home fell out on the table.

"I'd like these two analysed, is that possible here at the base?"

"Certainly. We've a small ballistics lab on site, but it will take a while, the team's very busy. You'd be much better going up to the Highmoor Centre in Princetown. They've a much bigger ballistics facility."

"Can we keep this within the service, please, Jolly?"

"Very well, sir, if that's what you want."

"Thank you," I said with relief, as despite all the facilities at Highmoor, I somehow didn't trust De Coverley or Sir Peregrine to do the analysis. "And I need the results tomorrow latest."

"Impossible, I'm afraid, sir, you see—"

"Lieutenant," I said softly. "Will it make any difference if I say this is at the express request of Admiral Philip Anson?"

"Well, sir, I—"

"Shall we call him at the Admiralty?" I held up the receiver from the desk phone. "You can dial."

He leaned over and replaced the receiver. "No, sir, that won't be necessary. We'll, er... prioritise your request. You'll be wanting to know if we have a match for the weapon or weapons that fired these rounds, I take it?"

"Correct, plus anything else your technicians may think worthy of note."

"Report will be ready tomorrow, sir. Where shall I have it delivered?"

"I'm at the Wyvern Arms hotel, near Princetown, but I'd like to telephone you and save time."

"Two o'clock tomorrow, sir?"

"Excellent, we'll talk then." I shook hands then went to leave. "Oh, and Lieutenant, why would Doctor De Coverley visit this depot so regularly?"

"Er... can't say too much, but we do deal with nukes here, sir."

"I see."

10 AM

"The headmaster will see you now."

A trim, red-haired young woman with thick glasses and an unforgiving lime green twin set (were school secretaries made on a production line somewhere, I wondered for a moment?) gestured to the door in front of me before knocking and turning the handle.

"Thank you, Miss Urquhart."

I stood up and entered the room, annoyed with myself for feeling the slight sense of trepidation that always accompanied first meetings with headteachers, meetings common enough with my job, but nevertheless somehow always daunting throwbacks to my own school days.

"Welcome to Devonport High." A small and somewhat corpulent man with a bald head and a smile that was entirely undaunting, offered his hand to me. "Royston Spears, headmaster."

"Jack Sangster," I said, shaking the hand then passing him my card. "And thank you for seeing me."

"My pleasure, and I've heard of the great work the Granville Institute does for youngsters, so I'm only too happy to help." He pointed to a chair by his desk. "Now please, take a seat and let me know what I can do for you."

"I've been assigned to help find a former pupil of yours, Christopher De Coverley."

"Ah yes, Miss Urquhart did mention it. One moment." He flicked an intercom switch. "Miss Urquhart, could you bring in the file on the De Coverley boy, please?"

"He left at Christmas, I believe?"

"That's right, great shame, but his father insisted. I know the under-sixteen's rugby team miss him, now I'll need to wait until—"

"Here we are, Headmaster." Miss Urquhart placed a cardboard folder on the desk. "The De Coverley file."

"Thank you. Now then, let me see..." He turned over several sheets, mainly school reports, then looked up at me. "Yes, a bit of a loss to the school academically as well. The lad was a good scholar, especially on the humanities side."

"Humanities?"

"Yes, the arts, like English, classics, and so on. A bit surprising given his father is such an eminent scientist, but this, for example..." Spears held up several handwritten sheets. "A prize-winning history essay, written just before the boy left us. Showed he had a real feel for the Elizabethans."

"The Armada and Francis Drake, perhaps?"

"Er... yes, Sangster, exactly." He raised his eyebrows when I guessed correctly. "Showed a passion for that period, according to the teacher's comments."

"And his conduct, was he a troublemaker, problems with other pupils, teachers, anything like that?"

"Not at all. Very popular with peers and staff alike."

"And no record of truanting, I suppose."

"None at all."

"Well, Mr Spears, I think that's all, unless there's something else you think might help?"

"I don't think so, although..." He held the history essay up and ran his finger along the last few lines. "This is a very odd comment from the teacher, look."

I took the sheet and read the last paragraph:

De Coverley's essay on comparative firepower of the English and Spanish fleets is meticulously researched, with insightful comments. However, I cannot concur with his conclusion that a single superior weapon brought the English a decisive advantage. I explained to him that no contemporary weapon could ever have outweighed the numerical superiority of the Spanish, hence the English victory remains a mystery, at best put down to unfavourable weather or bad naval strategy. Despite my arguments, Christopher De Coverley continues to insist that the English fleet possessed such a weapon, enabling their surprise defeat of Spain, at that time the world's undisputed superpower. When I said I thought him naïve but admired his self-belief, and felt he would go far, De Coverley replied, and I quote, "Oh, much further in and further back than you could possibly imagine." He was not forthcoming as to his meaning. For all that a very promising pupil.

"Odd indeed," I said, not quite knowing what to make of this enigmatic comment myself. "But thank you anyway, you've been very helpful."

"As I say, Sangster, my pleasure, and do let us know if… I mean, when you find Christopher. We all liked the lad, and there's more than a few here at Plymouth High would want to see him turn up safe."

11 AM

"*So off we jolly well go,*" chimed the perpetually chirpy Jimmy Young as I drove past Princetown, the open hood letting elusive moorland sunshine stream into the car to soothe my face with its warmth. "*Here's an oldie for Maxine Crosby from Chester.*" I wondered for a moment if it was the Maxine who served in my local pub, the Jolly Miller of Dee Tavern. "*Happy birthday, Maxine, and this is for you. Herman's Hermits and 'I'm Into Something Good'.*"

I heard the record crackle as the DJ placed his needle down (definitely an oldie), followed by a deep and happy upbeat rhythm, the singer's melodic Manchester tones ringing out to remind me that Maxine, in a very confidential moment late one evening, telling me that her real name was Susan Shufflebotham (she pronounced it 'Shuffle Bottom').

"I wanna be a club singer, Jack, and Susan Shuffle Bottom hasn't got the same ring to it, has it?" I'd felt forced to agree and was sworn to secrecy for the price of a free scotch and, a little more embarrassingly given we were in the public bar, a kiss on the cheek. I then remembered Herman wasn't the Hermits' lead singer's name either. Peter Noone, I thought he might actually be called.

Shouldn't I use a racy alias as well, I wondered. "Hmmm…" I said out loud. "Sherlock Sangster, Jack Holmes, Jack Poirot, Hercule

Sangster, Miss Marple." I shook my head and laughed, before looking ahead to see a figure standing by the roadside. I took a double-take, then realised it was Jane Ustrix.

Her strawberry-blonde hair, previously always tied up in as tight a bun a possible, now hung loose around her shoulders, and in place of her formal trouser suits she wore a floral mini skirt, calf-length black leather boots and a denim jacket. The lenses of a large pair of binoculars protruded from a yellow suede handbag she held by a shoulder strap.

"Jack," Jane shouted as I pulled up beside her. "How lucky, I need a lift. The buses around here come every two hours, and then only if they feel like it." She walked over to the car. "Sorry, that's only if you're proceeding back to the hotel," she added.

"Course I'm 'proceeding' there, jump in."

"Lovely, as soon as I saw you I hoped you would pass by the Wyvern Arms."

Herman and his Hermits continued at full belt as I opened the passenger door.

"So Jane, what have you been up to?" I switched off the radio as she sat down and pulled the door shut.

"What do you mean, up to?" She fumbled with her seatbelt.

"Observing something to do with folklore?"

"Why observing?"

"Those binoculars."

"Oh, ha, I see," she said with a slightly nervous-sounding giggle, looking down at the floor and the open backpack. "I like to carry them in wild places like this, just in case I see something interesting."

Must be heavy to lug around, I thought, but said nothing.

"So what was on in Princetown?"

"I, er… came for a morning walk, around Fox Tor."

"You must have seen the Highmoor Research Centre then."

"That blocky place behind the barb-wire fence?"

"Yes." I laughed. "Ministry of Defence building. They're all the same."

"And that round building on the little hill down there." She pointed to the Old Centre, which lay to our left in the distance. "That's got barb wire round it as well. Do you know it?"

"Abandoned military facility of some kind, I guess." Feeling disinclined to say any more about the Old Centre, I looked quickly at her out of the corner of my eye. Yes, I thought, quite a beauty when she let her hair down, and there was no denying the woman's intellect, but something about Jane Ustrix's manner, and perhaps her voice, seemed subtly wrong.

"And you?" she asked after a time.

"As I told you last night," I said, remembering I'd let slip where I was going, "Devonport armoury."

"Oh yes, your case."

"Not the case, but a separate investigation."

"Of course, and you went to the boy's school as well."

I nodded and we drove on, coming after a time to the hotel gates.

"Jack, any idea what they did at that place, you know, the old building on the little hill?"

"Not sure, Jane," I said, stepping out and opening the car door for her. "Now sorry, I have to run."

11:30 AM

Whatever it is, I said to myself as we entered the hotel, something about Jane Ustrix doesn't ring true. Perhaps the odd vocabulary; 'proceeding' instead of simply 'going', 'barb' instead of 'barbed' wire, 'passing by' when she clearly meant stopping at and going into the hotel. And even if this odd way of talking was nothing in itself, there was Jane's undue interest in the Highmoor Centre and my activities, as well as a detailed knowledge of subjects like physics, well outside of her professed sphere of expertise. She also showed apparent discomfort when questioned on what seemed to me quite minor matters.

Then I watched Jane making her way across the common room, quite transformed from the 'blue stocking' Mercy had called her, almost a different person, as if the tight hairstyles and the stiff trouser suits were just a disguise. And Jane's mini skirt and boots that showed no sign of mud looked hardly right for a walk on the moor.

All of these things, and more that I couldn't quite put my finger on, caused disquiet.

I walked past reception to the padded leather telephone chair and instinctively looked around to see that I wouldn't be overheard, although the chair was designed to muffle most of what was said, and the corridor was anyway empty. As I sat down, I remembered giving

Jane her malt whisky nightcap in the bar and asking what she was doing in 1958. "Graduating", she'd replied. And she'd said her Oxford college was Somerville ('All petticoats'). Jane should therefore definitely be a contemporary of Sarah's. I paused for a moment, then dialled the operator.

"Israel, a Tel Aviv number, please… yes, charges to go to Yelverton er…" I looked at the circular label in the middle of the phone dial. "232959… yes, the Wyvern Arms hotel."

"It's day-time, so premium long-distance rates, that OK, caller?"

"Yes."

"Then please hold." I waited, clutching the silent receiver for about a minute. "I'm sorry, caller, but all lines are busy to Tel Aviv. Can you try later, perhaps off-peak?"

"OK, will do, thanks." I sat back in the phone chair, frustrated. I needed to find out more about Jane Ustrix, but how?

"Velinda," I exclaimed, standing up and making the Dikes, who just at that moment walked around the corner, cry out.

"Ugh," shouted Ballar. "Didn't see you there, Sangster, but anyway, who's this Velinda?" He made some sort of circular passing motion with his hand as he spoke the name. "Water goddess, perhaps, or the dominant deity in some sort of fertility incantation?"

"No," I laughed, "just an old friend."

"Oh," he said with a crestfallen frown. "Well, must be getting on, come along, Fidelma." With that the two druids continued on their way, whilst I dialled again.

"Hello… yes, Velinda, it's me Jack… well, thanks… yes, on Dartmoor… that's right, I'd like you to check with Somerville whether they have a Jane Ustrix at the college, research fellow in English Folklore… call back in twenty minutes… great, bye for now."

Velinda Flimwell was the principal (Sir John was too progressive to allow the title headmistress) of the institute's residential academy for gifted children, a converted manor house near Truro. I had been heavily involved in the academy's establishment and, in the process, come to know Velinda had strong links with Somerville College.

During my last case, which, like this one, had attracted government attention, I had also come to suspect Velinda of having some sort of link to the security services. She was still by far the best person I knew of to ask about Jane Ustrix, but I resolved only to tell her what I wanted her to know and expected anything I did say to be passed on.

"Passed on to someone I've already met?" I then asked myself. 'And if so, what might happen as a result?'

After a coffee in the common room, where the Dikes, now looking fully composed after the shock I'd apparently given them by my outburst whilst in the phone seat, sat at their usual table next to the fireplace ('we're off out this afternoon to choose our autumn wands from the woods, it's traditional in the time after the solstice). I solemnly nodded, trying to show my appreciation of this doubtlessly grave activity, then walked back to the telephone chair.

"Velinda, it's me again."

"Jack, well… I'm afraid I've drawn a blank. You did say Jane Ustrix?"

"That's right. Research fellow."

"Sorry, they've never heard of her. I spoke to the vice principal at Summerville, Alice Royall, old friend. She's quite sure there's no Jane Ustrix amongst the research fellows. Quite sure."

"And is she an alumnus?"

"Who, Alice or this Jane person?"

"Jane."

"You didn't ask so I didn't ask. Would you like me to—"

"It's alright, Velinda, you've already been incredibly helpful. Cleared up something important for me."

"I saw in the paper today there is a boy missing up on Dartmoor, is that you?"

"Investigating, you mean?"

"Bit of a coincidence if you're not. Never took you as one for hunting, shooting, and fishing."

"I might be here for the rambling or bird-watching."

"Whatever you say, Jack." She laughed. "Anyway, you keeping well?"

"It's good country for running around here, and I'm managing to go for a run when I can, so all in all, not too bad at all, thanks." I looked at my watch. Twelve o'clock. "Look, Velinda, sorry, I have to dash. Thanks again, and talk soon, I hope."

"Bye, Jack, and I'm sure you'll find him, you always do."

I hope she's right, I thought as I put the phone down. And did Jane Ustrix being an impostor simplify or complicate things?

Right now, I wasn't sure.

12 NOON

"Yes, Inspector, two o'clock." I explained I would be calling the Devonport ballistics lab then to find out more about some fifty-calibre shells they were analysing, and hopefully shed more light on the robbery. I chose not to mention the link to Reynard's Hall and the shell found in the timbers of the Spanish Galleon wreck from Donegal as being from the robbery as I guessed DI Hawke would not have given credence to this and, as a consequence, believed nothing else I said either.

"Alright, Sangster, what more have you got for me?"

"Spoke to the De Coverley boy's old headmaster. Lad seemed a model pupil."

"Nothing untoward that might explain him going missing?"

"No."

"What else, Sangster?"

"That Doctor De Coverley doesn't seem too worried about his son. I mean—"

"Yes, we found that when we interviewed him as well. Very strange, eh, Eccles?" I heard what sounded like Eccles faintly agreeing across the room. "And?"

"Well, I'd like you to find out what you can on a Jane Ustrix... yes, U-S-T-R-I-X... yes, with an X."

"Who is she?"

"Says she's a folklore researcher, but…" I told the DI about my conversation with Velinda, as well as my odd instincts about Jane.

"Alright, can't be too many with that surname, we'll run a background check. Eccles…" She barked instructions at the DC. "Results should come back by this evening, maybe even this afternoon. Eccles," she then shouted again. I heard a muted mutter.

"Yes, Ma'am."

"Get out of the room, the grown-ups need to talk."

"Ma'am?"

"Leave, Eccles, you imbecile, I need to speak privately to Mr Sangster."

"Yes, Ma'am."

I heard the office door slam as the DI began to speak again, this time almost in a whisper. "Sangster, have you had wind of, er… anyone else sniffing around our case?"

"Why do you ask?"

"Just the importance the powers that be are attaching to it. I had a memo from on high today, asking me to report progress." She rustled some papers, presumably including the memo in question. "And when I say on high, I mean Everest-type high. Never had that before."

So, I thought, now you're scared, Inspector, you want to be my ally.

"And Sangster, my point is that they only allocated me and you."

"And Eccles."

"Eccles doesn't count." She sniffed. "And even you and I are too much. I mean, I wouldn't come in on a case like this unless social services and uniform had drawn a blank, and you… well, like I said before, you're too good for a lad missing all of a few days."

"So what are you saying, Inspector?"

"I'm saying that when I piece everything together, I think the government consider this important enough to put us, plus perhaps others on the case as well. They wouldn't put all their eggs in our little basket, Sangster, would they?"

I quickly counted all the people I'd met in the last few days, and though there were quite a few, most were local, or one night only guests, so unlikely to be police or from some government agency. The Dikes, I'd heard, were 'from up country', but they hardly fitted the bill, and anyway, they had a legitimate reason to be on Dartmoor, with the solstice and the mystic, as they saw it, landscape blessing their marriage. That left only one person.

"Jane Ustrix?"

"Top of my list as well, but we can't do much until the background check results come in."

"Could be others, not staying at the hotel."

"Of course," the DI almost shouted. "But we haven't seen anyone suspicious, and it's not as if the area is seething with people." She shook her head. "No, let's start with Miss Ustrix. We'll talk again when we know more."

12:30 PM

"Message for you from…" Joe Gurney unfolded a slip of paper, "Professor Frere at Reynard's Hall. Asked if you could come over to him at three."

"Did he say what about?"

"No, sir, now would you like a drink?"

"Just a glass of water, Joe," I said, sitting on a stool by the bar. "And is there a snack menu, sandwiches, that sort of thing?"

"No lunch-time bar menu as such, sir, but you're a guest, so if you'd let me know what you'd like, I'll go and ask in the kitchen."

"Not sure. Can you find out what's on offer, please?"

As he left the room, I felt a heavy hand on my shoulder, turning around to see Miles Edgerton looming.

"Only drinking Adam's ale, Sangster?"

"Afternoon, Edgerton, and yes, just water, busy day today."

"Come on, have a drink with me." He looked at the beer pumps. "Is Joe Gurney about?"

"Gone to the kitchen."

"Never mind, I'll serve us." He opened the counter hatch and walked behind the bar.

"Thanks, but not for me right now." I watched Tilly looking apprehensively across the room as Edgerton began to pull a pint of beer.

"On Dartmoor, a real man never refuses a drink when it's offered," he said, lifting his glass and appraising the foaming brew within. "And you don't know what you're missing, because I pull a better pint than Joe," he added. "Just needs to settle, oh… hello, Joe."

"Staff only behind the bar." Joe Gurney stared at Edgerton, then held up the counter hatch and pointedly beckoned. "I'll bring your drink to your table, Mr Edgerton."

"Very well." Edgerton walked across to a corner table, opened a briefcase, and laid out a map, a ruler, a pencil, and notepad. "Come and join me anyway, Sangster," he called out.

"Anton says they can do beef, cheese, or ham, sir," came a voice from behind the bar.

"You know, Joe," I said, looking at Edgerton and thinking this a chance to interview the man without his knowing it, "I think I'll leave the sandwich for now."

"Very well, sir."

"And let me save you a trip."

"Kind of you, sir." Joe winked, as I picked up my water and Miles' glass.

"Ordnance Survey maps of the area?" I asked Edgerton, placing his pint on the table.

"Planning the rest of the season's hunts. We'll do three more."

"Only three?"

"Bloody Devon County Council."

"Sorry?"

"Reduced the number of hunts. Claim otters are endangered. I could kill that committee, every man jack of them."

"Are they?"

"Are they what?"

"Endangered, otters, I mean."

"I'll tell you this," said Edgerton, taking a long draught of ale. "Old Soldier will be endangered when I've finished with him, look." He pointed at the map, on which were drawn pencil lines, criss-crossing the moors, and all converging on the area around Fox Tor. "This is everywhere we've seen him in the last three seasons."

"Interesting," I said, an excuse to talk about the boy unexpectedly presenting itself. "These lines cross near where the De Coverley boy lives."

"Aye, and I'm glad he's out of the way." Edgerton said this without a trace of concern. "Troublemaker, that lad."

"Because he tried to sabotage the hunt?"

"Put us off the scent of Old Soldier a few times, so yes."

"But you'll still be going back to that same area?" I asked, pointing to where the lines converged.

"Old Soldier's been seen there many times before, so he'll be seen there many times again, I shouldn't wonder."

"How can you be sure it's the same otter you see every time?"

"Oh, I'm sure, Sangster. Big bugger, Old Soldier, no other like him."

"Don't the members of the hunt expect you to vary locations, go to other places as well as this locality?"

"They can expect," said Edgerton, draining the last of his ale, "all they like, but I'm master of the hunt." He banged his glass down on the table. "Now, I'll just get myself another of these. Sure you don't want one?"

"No, really. I'll get one for you, though." I lifted the empty glass and waved it at Joe Gurney.

"There we are, sir," said Joe a few moments later as he very deliberately exchanged a full glass for Edgerton's empty one. "A fresh pint, poured by hand, courtesy of the barman."

"Don't know his place, that Gurney," muttered Edgerton, sipping his beer as Joe walked away. "And pretty soon I'll be going behind that bar whenever I please."

"Really?"

"Sangster." Edgerton looked over his glass at me. "Mrs Merrivale and I have had, well…" he regarded the beer, momentarily lost for words, "what you might call, an understanding, ever since Aloysius passed on."

"Really?" I repeated.

"Yes, really," he snapped. "And the whole county knows she's spoken for, and that I'll be running the Wyvern Arms once she's ready to tie the knot."

"Really?"

"Yes, really." He banged his glass once again, this time sloshing some of the contents over his map. "Damnit, now look what you made me do." He began scraping droplets of ale off the sheet with a beer mat. "And I've seen you talking to her, Sangster."

"To Mercy?"

"It's Mercy now, is it?"

"I'd better leave you to your planning," I said, standing up.

Edgerton stood up too, nose an inch away from mine. "And Sangster," he snarled through beer-laden breath, "like I told you, the whole county knows she's spoken for, and so should you if you know what's good for you."

This prompted Joe Gurney to lift his counter hatch and walk towards us. "Everything alright, sir?"

"Yes, Joe. Mr Edgerton here was just explaining what's good for me."

2 PM

"Thank you," I said, taking a bag containing a sandwich, crisps, and a bottle of ginger beer from the young woman behind the counter of the Princetown general store.

"That'll be two shillings exactly," she said, ringing open an ancient-looking cash register.

"Could you change a fiver?"

"Think so." She fumbled inside the till and held up four pound-notes, a ten-shilling note, and four florins. "That's four pounds eighteen shillings change."

"Sorry," I said, taking the money then handing her back one of the notes. "You couldn't change this ten-bob note for some more florins, could you?"

"Er…" She opened the register again and rattled the cash drawer. "Yes, that should be alright. Here you are." She handed me five more two-shilling pieces, then shut the till with a clang. "Need the phone, do we?"

"Long distance," I answered. "And thanks again."

*

I put my lunch bag into the car, then squeezed into the call box outside the shop door, pulled out the slip of paper with the Devonport number from my pocket, and dialled.

"Lieutenant Jolly, please." After the usual questions I was transferred.

"Commander Sangster, how are you today, sir?"

"Oh, fine, thanks, Jolly. Got the results from the lab?"

"Sorry, sir, we've had a bit of a problem."

I felt as if my heart had dropped a beat when he said this. The two shells were, I felt, somehow essential to understanding Christopher De Coverley's disappearance.

"What sort of problem?"

"Two lads from the lab are off sick. I hadn't realised. We're backed up right now, and your tests will have to wait until tomorrow."

"Didn't I already say, Jolly," I snapped in my frustration, "that these tests were at the request of Admiral Anson?"

"They could be at the request of the Queen, and it still wouldn't make any difference, sir." I heard Lieutenant Jolly mutter something that sounded very like 'impatient bastard, pulling rank' under his breath.

"I'm sorry, it's just that... well, I don't want to sound over-melodramatic, but getting these results quickly may even be the difference between life and death."

"Understood, sir. Providing at least one of the technicians comes in tomorrow, I can have the results for you by five."

"Thanks," I said in what I hoped came across as a conciliatory voice. "I appreciate it."

"Until five tomorrow then, Commander. I'll look forward to your call."

*

"Hello, Operator, yes, I'd like to call Tel Aviv... yes, Israel. It's..." I opened my notebook and read out the number. After being questioned once again about premium rates, then waiting through numerous clicks and pauses, I heard ring tones, the welcome sound of the phone at the other end being picked up, and then pips.

"Go ahead, caller. You're connected." I thrust a florin into the slot and held another ready.

"Hello, this is Jack, Sarah's husband... yes, Sarah... oh, Rachel, hello, how is everything?" Sarah's sister gave me a quick account of their flight and accommodation, then called out, "Sarah, quick, it's Jack." I heard the pips go again and slotted in another florin.

"Jack, it's so lovely to hear from you. Everything OK at your end?" I said yes, deciding not to go into details given we were on a long-distance call, then asked her about the funeral.

"Well, we had the interment this morning. It was all a bit sad even though Bubby had lived to a ripe old age." She then went on to describe the service, and how she and Rachel had to take the place of daughters as they were orphans, tearing holes in their dresses over the heart to signify mourning. Several sets of pips and florins later, I realised we were running out of time and change.

"Sarah, sorry, but can I ask you something?"

"Sounds ominous." Her voice changed, and I detected that lower register my wife used when she was uncomfortable. "What is it?"

"You graduated when?"

"You mean from Oxford?"

"Yes."

"Class of '59."

"Would you have known the girls in the year above you?"

"Some. Have you met one of them down there in deepest Devon?"

"Well, yes and no."

"Sorry?"

"Jane Ustrix. She might have graduated from Somerville the year before you."

More pips and another florin, then a long pause from Sarah.

"No, I didn't know a Jane Ustrix... wait a minute, that name does sort of ring a bell." She paused again, long enough for the phone box to devour another coin. I looked at my hand and saw there were only three florins left. "There wasn't a Jane in that year as far as I know," Sarah said finally. "But there was a name that sounded like Ustrix, now what was it, er… Ustrzycki, that's it."

"Really?" I never ceased to wonder at Sarah's memory. "And she was in the year above you?"

"Yes, a Polish exchange student, from Krakow, I think."

"Remember anything about her?"

"Not much except… yes, she was studying a weird combination of subjects. Now what were they… um… English folklore and quantum theory." The pips went again. "That's how I remember, because the pairing was so odd."

"Can you think back to what she looked like?"

"Er… mousy, I think, kept herself to herself, but might have been quite a stunner if she had smartened up, worn nicer clothes and make-up, you know."

"And her first name?"

"One of those Polish-Christian names with lots of consonants." I inserted another coin, my last but one. "Hmmm… now what was it?"

"Look, Sarah, thanks, but I think we're almost out of time. Are you alright?"

"Dying to get home, darling, but yes, I'm alright. You?"

"Yes, I'm fine, although this case is a baffler."

"That call you got from Sir John on Saturday. Seemed terribly important. What did he say again?"

"He said something like 'this is vital to the national interest, Sangster, vital.'"

"And even you are baffled?"

"Yes, but I'll get to the bottom if it, I…" The pips signalled I needed to insert my final florin.

"Oh, Jack, how is the player?"

"Sorry, Sarah?"

"The cassette player, did you use it much yet?"

Sarah was referring to the in-car cassette tape player we had installed in the Jag. Originally intending to just buy a radio as the car hadn't come with one when new, we had visited the car dealer to see this very latest of gadgets proudly on show. 'Perfect for madam's E-Type' the oily salesman had crooned to Sarah, and I had thus been persuaded to have the thing fitted, a small mercy being that I didn't have to look at it, as the unit went inside the glove compartment, there being only space for a small radio on the dash. Unfortunately, the salesman forgot to tell us that there were almost no '*Musicassettes*', as the pre-recorded tapes were apparently known, yet available, so you had to either record something at home or buy from a very limited range. We had no cassette recording machine at home so had been given a demonstration tape by the dealer, *Mantovani and his Orchestra's Greatest Hits*. As a result, I had used the new radio far more than the cassette player.

"Oh, um... great."

"Alright, darling." Sarah giggled, before changing to a more serious tone. "But like I say, I've a feeling about this one, so do be careful. Now, I'd better let you go, I love you, and... oh..."

"What is it?"

"Janezcka, that was the girl's name. The one at Somerville."

"Sure?"

"Quite sure. Sounds a bit like Jane, doesn't it?"

"It does, Sarah, I..." The pips went again, followed by a continuous ring tone as the line cut off.

"It certainly does sound like Jane," I said to myself as I climbed into the car. "Time for a word with Miss Ustrix, but first, Professor Septimus Frere."

3 PM

I pulled up outside Reynard's Hall to see a sign by the gates telling visitors the house and museum were closed on Thursdays. The gates were open, though, so I carried on, parking by the front doors. Clearing the crisp packet and sandwich paper from the passenger seat, and draining the last of the ginger beer, I climbed out of the car and walked up the steps. What could it be the professor wanted to tell me so urgently, I wondered as I rang the bell?

My excitement was dampened when there was no answer, and after ringing several times, I turned to leave, idly pushing the hall's massive doors as I did so. To my surprise they swung open, responding to my fingers with little more than a mild creak. Perhaps Professor Frere was in after all?

I walked through the deserted great hall, with its galleries and portraits, and dominated in the centre by the massive sailing ship model. I then turned along the oak-panelled corridor leading to the drum room. If Septimus was anywhere I guessed, he would be there.

And I was right. Even outside the drum-room door I could hear conversation. The discussion seemed one-sided, though, as no other voice could be heard. I opened the door as quietly as I could, then looked across the room to see the professor standing alone, staring up at the portrait of Drake.

"No, Sir Francis, you may sleep longer," he was saying. "No peril to threaten England's shores today. Now, did I mention that my brother Peregrine has been—"

"Ahem," I coughed, "Professor Frere?"

"Ah, Sangster, you came." He turned around and, cheeks reddening visibly, walked quickly towards me. "Goodness, is that the time?" He looked at his watch. "I was, er… just, er… just practising for our Christmas extravaganza. We put on a show for the visitors every year in the festive season, bring the past back to life, so to speak."

"A little early to practise for Christmas, isn't it?"

"Never too early to start." He placed his hand on my shoulder and began to guide me back through the door. "Got to get it right, you know." He closed the door behind us. "Now, I was just about to take afternoon tea. Would you join me?"

"Love to, thanks."

We walked through a maze of corridors and stairs, coming finally to the entrance to a large office on the first floor, where an elderly woman in a black and white uniform stood, head facing towards the floor.

"May we have another cup, Maisy?" said Frere. "Mr Sangster here will be joining me."

She gave a faint nod and walked off down the corridor, head still thrust downwards.

We entered the professor's study, a long room, the walls, where there weren't shelves, panelled in the manner of most other parts of the hall.

"Take a seat, Sangster." He gestured to a small table by the stone fireplace, where a tray was set for tea. "Please."

I looked at the proffered chair, one of two that had seen better days, arranged either side of the table. The stuffing in the upholstery was uneven, the light red-patterned cloth faded, the wooden armrests pockmarked with age and use. I sat down, feeling the seat cushion give way so that I landed quite a way lower than expected. I silently gave thanks that I wasn't holding a cup and saucer.

"These chairs, Sangster, are from the early days of the hall. Been redone a few times, of course, but there is a good chance that your backside is, er… following in the footsteps of Sir Francis himself." He sipped his tea. "As it were." He sipped again. "And as you can see, this room reflects my two great passions in life."

And the room certainly did reflect at least one passion, as almost everywhere I looked I saw some reminder of Drake. Numerous books, old and new, with some connection to the man and his times lined the shelves. In the corner stood a life-sized stone bust, along with several ship models, whilst the walls were adorned with more portraits, framed charts, and several seascape paintings of ships and naval battles. All these spoke of the Freres' near-obsession for the famous, or infamous, Elizabethan sea captain.

"And Sangster, sorry for Maisy Whiddon's slightly, ah, odd demeanour, but she's a wonderful woman, been at the hall such a long time."

"Whiddon, you say?"

"That's right. You might have met her brother at the hotel, but no…" He paused to drain his teacup. "Don't like tea, Sangster?" he then asked, peering over the rim at my empty hands.

"No cup."

"Ah, of course."

Just then, Maisy returned with my cup, poured for me then left the room, and all without looking up from the floor.

"A little shy, Sangster, as I was saying, and you won't have met her brother because he had a cycling accident a few days ago. Nothing serious, thank God, although it was on that devilish Postbridge Road."

"Why devilish?" I asked, remembering my skid onto the verge two nights previously.

"Place just seems to see more accidents than it really should. De Coverley's wife, you know, very tragic." I nodded. "Anyway, how are your investigations going?"

"Coming along," I said. "But Professor, why did you want to see me?"

"Ah, that's to do with my second passion, look." I wondered what this 'second passion' could possibly be, as he spread his arms wide and turned to the far corner of the room. Then I realised. Amongst all the spectacular Drake paraphernalia, I'd overlooked this corner, which I could now see was entirely given over to Sherlock Holmes and his creator, Sir Arthur Conan Doyle.

"I'm afraid I don't really read Conan Doyle."

"No, no," he said, rubbing his hands, eager eyes open wide. "That's of no consequence, my point is that you're an investigator, a special investigator at that, and veteran of many cases."

"Yes, but—"

"And just like Holmes, you're not police. Would you say, Sangster," he went on, looking at me straight in the eye, "you are, just like the great man himself, a consulting detective?" He emphasised the word 'consulting'.

"I'm not very clever at all, Professor. Really, I'm not."

"But you do solve cases?"

"Well, yes."

"And by all accounts, some that have stumped the police, so tell me, how do you do it?"

"Well…" I decided to humour him, not least because I intended to pump him for information as well. "I do, and I suppose because, well… I care about kids. That's why I took the job in the first place."

"There must be more to it than that." He leaned forward. "Your methods, for example?"

"Well, I gather the facts first, then double-check them. Very important to do that."

"Yes?" Frere leaned further forward in his chair.

"And I try to put myself in other people's shoes. Perhaps the missing child, the people around the child, the people I suspect, maybe even folk who at first seem uninvolved."

"And then?"

"I piece things together as the facts unfold, try different theories until eventually the right one fits."

"And?"

"And the case is solved."

"You'll have seen that I try to make deductions in my own small way…" The corners of his mouth drooped, and he looked at his feet. "But they rarely work. What's your secret, Sangster?"

"Um… if there's anything then it may be that I'm good at following my instincts, and I have an eye for observing detail, but the most important thing could be…" I thought for a moment. Yes, it was an interesting question, one I hadn't considered before. "I talk to people," I eventually said. "And they talk to me."

"Just that?"

"Yes. People will always give themselves away in the end, and other types of research are all very well, but you learn most of what you need to know in a case from others."

"Fascinating. Have you any instincts about this case?"

"Perhaps, and perhaps you can help me with them."

"Fire away." Frere rubbed his hands again.

"Drake, you say, was completely confident of winning against the Armada, even though he should have known victory was impossible?" He nodded. "How could that be?"

"Have you heard the phrase 'God blew and they were scattered'?"

"Queen Elizabeth talking about the Armada right, the storm that drove them into the North Sea?"

"Correct, but that's somewhat apocryphal, let me explain. You're familiar with the Armada?" He pointed to a large chart on the wall beside us, showing the British Isles and a dotted line in the sea around them, presumably the course of the Armada.

"A little, but I tend to focus more on more recent naval history."

"Ah, you're a naval historian too?"

"Strictly an amateur," I said with a smile. "Do a little writing."

He smiled back.

"Then let me refresh your memory. If you look at the chart you will see where…" He told of the Armada first being sighted off Cornwall, of beacons being lit in a chain along the coast to raise the alarm, and the English fleet sailing from Plymouth, preceded by Drake's famous game of bowls. The object of the Spanish, Frere said, was not to land in England directly but to pick up a large army in Flanders, then sail up the Thames estuary and invade. The would-be invaders were harassed by the English all the way up the channel, eventually anchoring off Calais, only to be attacked with fire ships, vessels laden with gunpowder that were sent unmanned and aflame into the enemy fleet. The Spanish scattered, with a decisive action against the English coming just off the French coastal town of Gravelines the next day.

"Yes, Professor, I was aware of that—"

"And," he almost shouted, now thoroughly engrossed and ignoring my protests, "after the English engaged that final time, the Armada was too far downwind to turn back down the channel." He stood up and pointed, triumphantly, I though, to the chart. "So, with the weather worsening by the hour, the Spanish were forced to sail up the North Sea, around the coasts of Scotland and Ireland, then limp back to Spain as best they could. Did you know that many a ship from the Armada foundered off the Irish coast?"

"Actually," I said, deciding the best way to get him to stop telling me things I already knew was to change tack (as it were), "I was present when a wrecked galleon was discovered off the coast of Donegal."

"Nineteen forty-four, Ballyshannon, the *Santa Extrana*?"

"Yes, my ship was part of a salvage flotilla, except we didn't know at the time that was the name of the galleon."

"Oh, Mr Sangster, how lucky you were. Before you found her, the *Santa Extrana* was one of only three lost Armada ships. Now there are just two left unaccounted for."

"I suppose I was honoured."

"You were, Sangster, now let me talk of Jehovah's Wind."

The Dutch Republic, Frere then explained, supported the English, and caused celebratory medals to be struck in honour of the Armada's defeat. One medal bore an inscription, '*Flavit Jehovah et dissipati sunt*', which translated as '*Jehovah blew his winds and they were scattered*'. The phrase became so popular it was soon attributed to Good Queen Bess herself, and the storm that wreaked havoc upon the Spanish fleet became known as the 'Protestant Wind'.

"And Drake, Professor? According to those diaries you read to me yesterday, Drake thought he commanded the elements, controlled Jehovah's Wind, as he put it."

"Not the elements, Drake respected those too much, but he did have an unerring belief in his invulnerability and somehow, his immortality. Let me show you the last-but-one passage from that manservant's diary, it's always intrigued me."

Septimus opened a drawer in his desk and lifted out the leather volume he'd read from the day before. Then he put on a pair of reading glasses and leafed through the pages. "There are a few 'thee's and 'thou's, so I'll read it in the plainest English I can, now here goes…

"*My master's drum arrived today, shipped along with his baggage from the Caribbean…*" Frere then told of the servant causing the drum to be kept safe on his master's orders until the day Drake was needed to defend England from mortal peril, at which time he would return. The manservant also described an instruction from Drake to 'cut away the likeness of Jehovah's Wind from the *Revenge*' ('the Elizabethan Race Galley he sailed against the Armada, in case you didn't know, Sangster') and destroy this likeness so that '*no man may see the secret of my victories*'. The passage also noted that Drake explicitly asked that the ship itself be kept intact, and that his friend Reynard Hill should come to inspect it and ensure Jehovah's Wind had been removed and destroyed as ordered.

"But the *Revenge* was wrecked, wasn't she, in the Caribbean?"

"You do know your Elizabethan naval history, Sangster." He tugged at his greying forelock in mock reverence. "Yes, and Drake was no longer in command of the *Revenge* when it was broken up completely after being captured by the Spanish. But," he laughed, "that passage refers to a ship model, not the real thing."

"The one in the great hall downstairs?"

"The very same."

"Any more to tell?"

"Only a short piece where the servant relates how news of Drake's death came to Reynard's."

"Died of dysentery, didn't he, very quickly?" Frere nodded. "Buried at sea, in a lead-lined coffin by all accounts."

"One minute he was very much alive, next minute dead, and you know, Sangster," he looked over at the bust in the corner, "to this day nobody's ever found Drake's coffin, and it was indeed lead-lined, as you say." The professor held his finger up. "So ask this, why, when you are in perfect health, would you carry such a heavy thing on a sixteenth-century sailing ship thousands of miles from home?" He continued to stare at the bust. "I have to wonder whether Sir Francis faked his own death."

"Professor," I said, looking at my watch whilst thinking the man was now drifting into flights of fancy, "this has been fascinating, but I really have to go, so if you could just—"

"Of course, Sangster, and thank you for sharing your insights on sleuthing. You are the real thing, I'm just a dilettante."

"Funny, dilettante's just the word the police sometimes call me, but you haven't said why you wanted to see me in the first place."

"Ah." He slapped his forehead. "Bless me, so I haven't."

"And?"

"I need ground-penetrating radar."

"I'm sorry." I laughed. "You need what?"

"The last entry in the diary of Peter Pearce, look." He carefully opened the book at the last page and pointed to the final paragraph:

> *The interment to take place in the grounds, under the auspices of Reynard Hill, the spot to be recorded, so that Jehovah's Wind may be exhumed at such time as England is in mortal peril.*

"What could that mean, Professor?"

"The words 'interment' and 'exhumed' usually relate to a body, so perhaps Drake himself is buried here at the hall."

"But the entry you just read out clearly refers to Jehovah's Wind rather than a corpse."

"Either way, I know the navy has this ground-penetrating radar, so I wondered if you, with your connections, could, er…"

"I'm a civilian, Professor, retired from the navy long ago."

"But Commander Sangster, if I may call you that, imagine what such a discovery could mean?"

If a cache of fifty-calibre shells was buried by thieves in the grounds of Reynard's, I suddenly thought to myself, then perhaps those same people had hidden other things here as well. And given the navy was still trying to recover a dangerous stolen weapon, might they perhaps provide the wherewithal to help recover it?

"Alright, I'll check, but no promises, and it may take time. That kind of equipment's not to be bought in the average hardware shop."

"Thank you, Mr Sangster." He stood up, beaming, and offered his hand. "Now, can you find your way out? I have some papers to finish off."

"It is a bit of a rabbit warren, I'm not sure—"

"Maisy," shouted Septimus, opening the door and calling down the landing. "She'll be here in a minute to show you out."

The inscrutable Maisy duly arrived and, on instruction from Septimus, led me through the house, head down as usual, until we finally arrived at the great hall.

"One moment, Maisy," I said, walking over to the centre of the room and looking closely at the magnificent model. Yes, sure enough, a portion of the stern poop rail had been carefully cut away. It looked as if there had been some sort of bracket below the cutaway section (I could see two small holes and a tiny wooden framework), but whatever had been attached, Jehovah's Wind or otherwise, was long gone.

"Thanks, Maisy," I said.

"You're welcome, sir."

I jolted. Not only could the diminutive maid speak, but she did so with the Dartmoor brogue of Whiddon, voice perhaps a little higher but otherwise identical, as if Whiddon himself were in the room.

"I, er… saw your brother. He's doing well."

"Oh, I know, sir, he told me. You're the chap with the green sports car and a different woman every time you visit him." Maisy evidently had a sense of humour. "And sir, don't worry about Septimus, he's talked to Sir Francis like that as long as I can remember. Don't mean he's batty in the head or anything."

"I never thought he was, Maisy, and thank you for the tea."

As I drove away, the thought of discovering whatever was buried at Reynard's Hall began to excite me, my instincts once again telling me the fifty-cal shells, and perhaps even the hall and the ancient artifacts within it, had some bearing on Christopher's disappearance.

I determined to do what I could to get hold of the necessary radar equipment that might help find out and, grinning to myself, realised a single phone call to the right place might well do the trick.

4:30 PM

"Jay's will have to start charging you commission," said the girl behind the counter at the Princetown general store as I asked to change yet another note. "Who d'you keep phoning anyway?"

"Oh, lots of people, it's part of my job."

"You a copper?"

"No, I look for missing children."

I glanced at a notice board beside the counter to see a picture of Christopher De Coverley and a message to contact Plymouth police with any information. One of Eccles' 'mug shots' no doubt. The girl saw me looking.

"You're the one they sent to look for Chris De Coverley, staying up at the Wyvern Arms, aren't you?"

"Yes." Gossip clearly moved fast hereabouts, and I saw no reason to cover it up.

"Any luck?"

"Not yet, and it's difficult. He didn't go to school, you see."

"Why's that matter?"

"Well, after talking to the parents, that's where I normally start. Teachers, friends, and so on."

"He was a special one, him," she said, passing me ten florins across the counter.

"Special, how?"

"Dad," she called. "I'm popping out."

"Alright, Verity," a faint voice replied through a door in the corner. "Be back soon, though, there'll be nobody to wait in the café if I'm serving at the counter." I looked across the shop to see a small annex laid out with tables.

"There's no customers in for now and I'll just be a few minutes," she called back, then pointed to the door. "Come on, walk with me down the road."

We left the shop and began walking slowly along the street, Verity stopping me with her arm as we passed a police station.

"What's your name?"

"Jack Sangster, yours?"

"Verity Jay."

"Well, Miss Jay, is there something you'd like to tell me?"

"I'm nearly twenty-one, Mr Sangster, so you won't think the worse of me, will you?"

I looked at her, black hair blowing in the breeze, light make-up, short skirt, boots, and blouse seeming very much (as far as my old eye could tell) in line with a twenty-year-old 'Miss 1970'.

"Why would I?"

"I'm a bit lush on Chris, you see, or at least I was."

"I see, but, if I may ask, why did you stop being… what was it, 'lush' on him?"

She looked at her boots and blushed. "He's fifteen, Mr Sangster, and I…"

"And you told him you couldn't see him again?"

"No, Chris just disappeared." Verity began to cry, and I offered her my handkerchief. "Left me, he did, without a word."

"And did you try to—"

"Course." She sniffed. "I phoned, went to his house, even wrote to him, spoke to his dad, but got nothing."

"Nothing?"

"No, and it's been all of twelve weeks now."

Those twelve weeks again, I thought.

"Perhaps he's left the district?"

"No." She blew her nose. "Chris has been seen in the last few days, over at Foxtor House."

"And Melissa Merrivale?" I immediately wondered if this was the wrong thing to say.

"Her." Verity laughed. "Stupid kid thought Chris liked her."

"And did he?"

"His dad certainly did. Don't know exactly why, but maybe because her family owns the Wyvern Arms?"

I thought back to the angry young girl I'd seen arguing with Mercy the night before, then looked at Verity, softly spoken and, as I could, imagine a TV advert for farm produce might boast, the very flower of young Devon womanhood. The choice for Christopher seemed simple.

"Look," I eventually said, placing my hand on Verity's shoulder as we turned back towards the shop, "I'm no expert, but I do work with a lot of young people and, well… teenage lads aren't always reliable." She kept on crying as I spoke. "Perhaps you need to move on?"

"That's just it, Mr Sangster," Verity whispered, pressing her hands across her abdomen. "It's been twelve weeks, and I can't move on now."

"I, er… I'm not sure what to say, perhaps you should—"

"Please, don't say anything more." She held her hand up as we arrived back outside the shop. "I just felt that if anyone might be able to find him it would be you."

"I'm going to do my best," I said, handing her my card. "My very best."

5 PM

"Admiralty… yes… Commander J.G. Sangster here, can you transfer me to Lieutenant Joyce Yorke?"

"Putting you through to the lieutenant now," said the operator, after bombarding me with yet another barrage of questions.

"Hello, Joyce."

"Jack, is that really you?"

"It is. How are you?"

"As fine as can be expected, working for the Queen's Navy." She laughed. "Suppose you want the admiral?"

"'Fraid so."

"I'll connect you now, and please, come up to town soon, with that lovely wife of yours."

"Do my best, Joyce."

I waited as the receiver clicked.

"Phil, yes… it's me, look, I need to be quick. Is there any way I could get my hands on…" I explained, feeling something of a fool, that ground-penetrating radar was what I wanted.

"You what?" Phil guffawed down the phone.

"Once again," I said, holding the hand set away from my ear, "GPR is what's needed."

"You have to be joking, Jack, and how on earth would you know the Royal Navy's even got that kind of kit?"

"Someone told me it does, Phil, but that's not the point."

"Don't shout down the phone, Jack, but do enlighten me. What is the point of this call?"

"Got ten minutes?"

"I suppose so, fire away..."

Philip Anson was a friend, someone I had known since my teenage years at Dartmouth college, and someone I had relied upon during the war (on at least one occasion with my life). I left the navy in 1946, whereas he carried on, eventually rising to the lofty rank of fleet admiral, but whatever our current circumstances, I knew I could tell Phil anything.

"I've got a missing boy, and..." I explained the situation as far as I could, Phil becoming very loud when I mentioned Drake and the hidden cache containing modern shells. I then reminded him of our salvage mission to retrieve a sunken flying boat.

"Yes, of course I remember that day in Ballyshannon. Don't have your complete recall for detail, though, Jack, so how's it bear on your current case?"

I told him of the stolen M2, and the similarity to the bullet we found embedded in the Spanish Galleon.

"You kept that shell all these years?"

"I did, and the old professor at the museum is convinced there are more to be found if he can get his hands on ground-penetrating radar."

"Alright, old mate," said Phil with a sigh. "I know where you're going with this one, and you're in luck, as it happens..."

And it seemed I was in luck. Phil was due to visit Devonport at the end of the week to inspect an Antarctic survey ship which was equipped with the latest portable ground-penetrating radar unit.

"GPR's great for penetrating ice, apparently, and HMS *Endurance* doesn't sail for a few days, so if your old professor wants the kit in the meantime, then it's his. Give Lieutenant Yorke the name and address where we should deliver, would you?"

"Will do, and I've been liaising with a Lieutenant Jolly in Devonport if you want to assign him."

"May as well send him up to show this professor of yours how it works. Oh, and Jack, I'll need your lot, what are they called?"

"The Granville Institute."

"I'll need them to sign for it, just in case. It's worth over ten thousand pounds, I believe."

"That much?"

"I suppose you still want to go ahead?"

"Yes," I said, envisaging Sir John, pen in hand and steam coming out of his ears as he saw just how much money he was underwriting. "And I'll make sure someone signs who is good for the cash."

"That's that then, Jack, now where are you staying in Devon?"

"Place up on Dartmoor. You?"

"With you, of course. Give Lieutenant Yorke the details of your hotel as well, and we'll sink a few whiskies Friday night."

*

"Hello, Professor Frere... yes, Sangster here... yes, your GPR... that's right, ground-penetrating radar... it'll be with you tomorrow... yes, tomorrow, and you'll have it for a few days... don't worry, the navy will send someone to train you in its use... ha, suppose I did work a small miracle... no need to thank me... I'll call again to see it's arrived... and a very good evening to you too."

Replacing the receiver with a satisfying clunk, I couldn't remember ever feeling quite so smug.

5:30 PM

"Oh, Christ," I shouted to nobody in particular at the sight of the white Rolls-Royce parked outside the main door of the Wyvern Arms.

"JG 1," I then read out loud from the number plate. Sir John had come here, unannounced, to check up on my progress. I knew he was worried at the high-level attention the case seemed to attract, but this was ridiculous, wasn't it?

Then I looked up to see more vehicles, several of which were police cars. As I opened my car door, a siren wailed from behind as a police van pulled up. Adding to the confusion, I saw Mercy flailing her arms by the hotel door.

"Coming, Mercy," I shouted, sprinting across the car park. "What the hell's happening?"

"They descended on us, Jack. That one-eyed detective, and she's brought half the Plymouth police force with her by the looks of things. Arrested Jane Ustrix and took her to the billiard room."

"Arrested?"

"Yes, and your boss, at least I think he's your boss—"

"Six foot four all round and looks like something from a Dickens book?"

"That's him." She nodded. "Anyway, he arrived as well. Sitting in the bar now."

"Let's go in then," I said, taking a deep breath.

*

The common room was quiet as we entered, with only a few guests, but including the Dikes, who sat silently at their customary table. A tall, uniformed chauffeur I recognised him as Vassen, Sir John's driver and, where necessary, bodyguard, stood at the bar talking to Joe Gurney. Next to him was a slim young woman with long brown hair.

"Polly," I shouted. "What on earth—"

"Here as Sir John's… what did he call it… I'm his 'aide de camp', that's it."

"I bet you are, but it's great to see you anyway." I threw my arms around her, the intensity of the last few days making a familiar figure all the more welcome.

"Lovely." She laughed. "But that's not like our reserved Jack Sangster, is there something in the water here on Dartmoor?"

"We, er… haven't been introduced." A voice like ice spoke over my shoulder. "Mercedes Merrivale, and this is my hotel."

"Polly Darlow, Granville Institute."

"Old friends with Jack, I suppose?"

"I work with him," said Polly slowly. "Now, Jack, your presence is requested in the billiard room, and Sir John's already in there."

"I'll show you the way," Mercy said, before being quickly stopped by Polly.

"Sorry, Mrs Merrivale, the police were quite clear. Just Mr Sangster."

"Huh," said Mercy, staring hard at Polly. "Well, anyway, Jack, billiard room's down the hall near the TV lounge. Can't miss it."

*

"Sangster, there you are," boomed Sir John, standing, hands on hips, by the doorway. "You know this young lady, I take it?"

He pointed to Jane Ustrix, who sat, head in her hands, at the end of the billiard table, which was strewn with papers, some with printed text, others looking like graphical blueprints of some kind. DI Hawke sat on a chair next to her, and behind them stood Eccles and several uniformed officers.

"Yes." I nodded. "And I wasn't expecting you, Sir John. What's happening?"

"I decided to drop in on my way down to Truro, and glad I did. Seems there's all sorts of shenanigans going on here."

"Ahem." DI Hawke coughed. "If I may talk to Mr Sangster?"

"Oh, er… of course." Sir John stepped aside and gestured to me. "Do proceed, Inspector."

"Thank you. Now Sangster,, what do you know of this person?"

"Hmmm… I know she's not a research fellow, although she did graduate from Somerville college in 1958."

"Anything else?"

"That she is Polish, and her real name is Janezcka Ustrzycki."

DI Hawke looked up at Sir John. "Your man Sangster's on the ball, he really is." Sir John began to mutter something about the institute only hiring the best, but she spoke over him. "Nevertheless, we have more."

"Do tell," I said.

"I think," the inspector replied, "that Miss Ustrix should tell us in her own words." She looked at Jane, who said nothing, eyes firmly fixed to the floor. "We can stay here all evening, Miss Ustrix," she shouted. "And then all night at the station, and the next day, and the next night, and so on. Do you get me?"

Jane looked up at me with an imploring expression, and I noticed bruising on her cheek and forehead.

"What have you done to her?"

"There was a scuffle during the arrest. Now Miss Ustrix, are you going to—"

"Alright," Jane said. "Just take these off me, will you?" As she spoke, I noticed for the first time that she wore handcuffs.

"Do it, please," I said. "She can't cause any harm."

"Ma'am?" queried Eccles.

"Oh," DI Hawke waved, "very well, take them off her, Eccles."

Cuffs removed, Jane placed her hands on the table.

"My name, as Mr Sangster rightly says, is Janezcka Ustrzycki, and I am SB, there is no point in denying it."

"Polish secret service?" I asked, jolting at the surprise.

"Yes, Mr Sangster, Służba Bezpieczeństwa. Now, I've been asked to tell my story, so if you wouldn't mind?"

"Sorry."

"Very well, it began..." Jane told us how she and her mother had fled Poland shortly before the war. In their haste, they were forced to leave Doctor Jan Ustrzycki, her father and one of that country's most renowned physicists, behind. She was only two when she arrived in London, growing up under the anglicised name of 'Jane Ustrix'. Twelve years later, Jane's mother died, leaving her alone and without support. It was then that Jane's father sent for her, and she returned to Poland, where, little by little, she learned of her father's remarkable story.

Doctor Ustrzycki had been identified as a key scientist by the Germans at the start of the war, and allocated to a secret weapons project, developing one of Hitler's *wunderwaffe* ('that's miracle weapons, if you were wondering, Mr Sangster'). Doctor Ustrzycki had been teamed up with another brilliant physicist, an Austrian named Heinrich Weber, and their speciality was gravity, or more precisely, anti-gravity. By the end of the war, Jane said, they had come close to perfecting a device that could deflect gravity.

That device was called *Die Glocke*, or The Bell in English.

The facility where they worked was deep in Poland, sited to be far from Allied bombing. In the chaos of the Third Reich's last days, with Hitler already dead and the sound of Russian gunfire getting closer by the hour, Ustrzycki and Weber realised the situation was hopeless and struck a deal with the British. They would deliver the Bell to the allies in exchange for asylum for themselves and their families.

Loading the Bell onto a truck at the dead of night, Weber drove to a rendezvous point where a British transport plane would take the device and the fugitive families to safety behind Allied lines. Meanwhile, Ustrzycki was to fetch Weber's family and meet Weber at the plane.

Jane didn't know details, but it seemed the Russians were further advanced than expected and ambushed Ustrzycki before he could reach the rendezvous. The British plane took off with Weber, Jane, and her mother, and the Bell, whilst Weber's family and Ustrzycki became prisoners of the Russians.

The Russians disposed of Weber's wife and three children, but they valued Ustrzycki and set him up with the best facilities to continue his work. Without Weber he never managed to recreate anything like the Bell, though, and by the time Jane was reunited with him, Ustrzycki had all but given up trying. She also said her father's experiences had left him a broken man, dying not long after she returned to Poland.

"But," she said with a sigh, "I did inherit some of my father's talents in physics, and this, along with my fluent English, brought me to the attention of the SB. I was recruited and sent to Oxford on an exchange programme."

"So all this is very well, but what, young lady," said Sir John, as I guessed Jane's story had already taken longer than his usual attention span, "brought you here to Dartmoor?"

"The SB learned that the Highmoor Centre might be using technology developed by Weber and my father. With my knowledge and English background, they naturally assigned me to investigate, and so," she held her hands up, "here I am."

"And you know nothing of the disappearance of Christopher De Coverley?"

"Nothing at all. My interest is entirely in the Bell, although my handler did say the boy's disappearance might be related to its whereabouts."

"And all these papers?"

"Found them in her room, Sangster," said the DI. "Now then, do you have any other information pertinent to all this?" I shook my head. "Sure?" I shook my head again. "Very well, Eccles, please escort Miss Ustrix to a car and take her to the holding cells at Crownhill. I'll be along presently."

DC Eccles nodded to a WPC who escorted Jane Ustrix from the room (she gave another imploring look as she passed me and mouthed something in what sounded like German), followed by the other uniformed officers. Eccles then collected the papers from the billiard table and left as well.

"How did you know about her being Polish?" DI Hawke asked me when he'd gone.

"Oh, er, it doesn't matter, bit of luck."

"Hmmm…" The DI looked hard at me. "Not sure about you, Sangster."

"And how did you move so quickly, Inspector? We only spoke at lunchtime."

"Did a background check on a Miss Jane Ustrix and all sorts of alarm bells rang. We got instructions, from the Met, no less, to apprehend immediately."

"What will you do with her?"

"Keep her locked up at the station for now. Seems MI5 already have operatives in the area, and they'll take over in due course."

"Alright, Inspector," said Sir John, rubbing his hands together. "Now is there anything else we can do for you?"

"Not right now, but if there's anything you haven't told me, Sangster, anything at all, then—"

"I'm just here to find Christopher De Coverley."

"Then please keep to that brief, understood?" I nodded. "Both of you," she then added, looking at Sir John.

"Now just a minute, I—"

"Sir John says yes," I interrupted, placing my hand on his shoulder as his faced turned blue. "Goodbye, Inspector."

*

"Well, Sangster, I don't know why you humoured that one-eyed harridan of a detective."

"Because she's the law, and we'll do well to remember that."

"Alright, Sangster," he said, pulling his jacket on. "Suppose you're right, now come on, quick drink and you can fill me in on the rest before I go on to Truro."

We walked to the bar, where Joe Gurney served us whisky at Sir John's insistence (twelve-year-old Macallan, I was relieved to see – 'put it on Mr Sangster's room tab, would you please, barman').

"So, Sangster," Sir John said, whilst lighting one of his enormous trademark cigars ('good enough for Churchill, good enough for Granville') and beckoning to Polly, who brought him a small basket, which he proceeded to put on the bar counter, then open and take out a plate, cutlery, tin of beluga caviar, jar of foie gras, dry toasts, and a pot of fig preserve, "that was a bit rum, with a Polish spy and all."

"Mmmm." I sipped my whisky, thinking just how 'rum' it really was, and used to Sir John's eating habits whilst travelling, not paying attention to the words round me.

All of a sudden Sir John shouted out, "Yes, it is my bloody hamper, and no, I won't put it away."

"But sir," Joe said as quietly as he could whilst pointing to a sign behind the bar, "all food and drink consumed on the premises must be bought at the Wyvern Arms."

"Poppycock. I always bring me Fortnum's Hamper on trips, don't I, Polly?"

"Well," said a very flushed Polly, "I suppose—"

"Well, I do," Sir John shouted again, as if the habit made it fair and legal.

At this point, as Joe was about to say something else, Anton the chef appeared. "So, my food is not good enough for you, eh?"

Sir John looked the diminutive chef up and down, then patted him on the head. "Now I'm not saying not good enough, I just mean, well…"

Oh God I thought, he's going to say something. "This isn't personal, Anatole, but I couldn't be sure you'd meet my, how do I say it, culinary standards down here."

"My name is Anton, I am French, and my country is the home of cuisine."

"That's as may be, André, but I need good London food," Sir John replied, whilst taking a large portion of caviar on a piece of toast and rather theatrically placing it in his mouth. "Like this wonderful caviar here, or the foie gras there." He pointed at the pot of goose-liver pâté.

"That caviar is from Persia, whilst your foie gras," shouted Anton. "All foie gras… is French." I watched his face go redder and redder as he spoke. "You dispute that, you big, how you say… ignorant nincompoop, and I'll punch you on your big British nose, which, by the way, is distended from too much of our good French wine." Anton held his fists up like a prize fighter, although a flyweight at best.

"Now calm down, lad," said Sir John, rearing up to his full height, a head and a half taller than Anton. "Or Vassen here," he pointed to the chauffeur, "will need to teach you some manners."

Vassen stood up and Anton faced him, half Vassen's height, or so it seemed. For myself, I usually humoured Sir John, but right now I felt for Anton, and with everything that had gone on I didn't have the spare room to humour him anymore. It would have been so easy to be polite, but somehow I couldn't. Stepping between Vassen and Anton, the thought already crossed the back of my mind that I'd acted rashly. Besides there being a good chance of losing my job, Vassen had three inches on me and about fifteen years.

"Go to the car, Vassen. There's nothing for you here."

"You're just the hired help, Sangster," Vassen replied with a sneer. "You want to make something out of it, happy to step outside."

I pushed my face close to Vassen's and heard myself speaking, out of body, as if it was a radio show. "Whenever you like, I'll—"

"Now stop it." Polly stood between us. "You're behaving like scrapping schoolboys in the playground."

"I mean it, Vassen," I said, stepping back.

"Sir?" said Vassen, looking at Sir John, who I saw smiling to himself, not with humour, I felt, but with satisfaction at two of his employees vying for supremacy.

"Alright, go on, lad." Sir John jerked his head towards the front doors.

"And you, Sir John," I shouted, "this is a damn good chef. Acknowledge him like the gentleman I know you to be." I gulped, wondering what would happen next, as I suppose so many have before me when standing up to their boss. "Please, apologise to Anton and Joe here. You insulted Anton, and Joe was only trying to do his job." I was amazed.

"Both of you, I was bang out of order, so you, little Frenchy, please—"

"*Moi?*"

"Yes," said Sir John, closing up his hamper after placing the items inside. "Polly, put this back in the car, and Chef, please bring me your best pâté."

"*Bien sûr. Vous êtes le chef.*" Anton then marched off towards the kitchen with a massive beam on his face, whispering to me, I think, that I was a '*bon gentle homme*', whilst Polly quietly came to Sir John's seat and took the basket away.

"And you."

"Me, sir?" answered Joe Gurney.

"You, sir. I'll take a glass of the best port wine you have. Alright?"

"Alright," said a smiling Joe, reaching for a very ancient-looking, and I imagined very expensive, bottle of port. At this point I remembered I was still standing up and shuffled backwards, sitting down next to Sir John.

"I'm sorry, Sir John, I just couldn't—"

"Don't thou worry, lad." He clapped me on the shoulder so that I felt hammered into my seat cushion. "You spoke your mind, and you know what?"

"No, what?"

"I've all the more respect for you for doing it." He took a draught of the port Joe Gurney had provided. "Ah… good stuff, I was right to trust the victuals in this place. Now, as I say, respect providing you don't ever face me off again in public."

I thought for a moment that Sir John was joking, then looked at his eyes, which were deadly serious in that manner even the most manipulative, confident, and controlling of individuals occasionally exhibit. I realised he wasn't joking, and just having someone contradict him had clearly made Sir John pause for thought. We sat in silence for some seconds.

"Anyway, Sangster," Sir John eventually said, "distractions aside, how close are you to finding this missing lad?"

"Um…"

"Now, Sangster, I'm being leaned on. Had another call from Whitehall today."

"I'm doing the best I can, I don't know what else to say."

"Well, Sangster," he said, raising his voice so that others in the bar looked around, including the Dikes, who peered at us from their usual corner seats, "it's already Wednesday and you haven't found the boy yet. I need a result, and I need it soon. They really are leaning on me."

"PM again?"

"Yes, and worse, you don't want to know."

He sounded desperate (an emotion I couldn't recall Sir John displaying before), so I felt this a good time to bring up the ten thousand-pound indemnity for the ground-penetrating radar.

"They want how much, Sangster?" he shouted, voice now even louder.

"As I say, ten thousand, Sir John, but it's just a guarantee. No money need change hands."

"And you really need this ground-penny… tracing, er…?"

"Ground-penetrating radar. Yes, I believe so."

He then grudgingly agreed, whilst making it clear the ten thousand would come out of my salary every month for as long as it took to pay back if anything happened to the navy's GPR rig.

"I really do hope you're close to finding this boy, Sangster."

"Well, I have some ideas, Sir John, but there are still pieces missing. Perhaps I'll know more this time tomorrow."

"You'd better." He drained his whisky glass. "Polly," he then called across the room, "get Vassen and we'll be going."

With that Sir John strode to the front door and Polly followed, whispering, "Good luck," over her shoulder as she passed me, with me mouthing back, "Thanks for cooling everything down just then." She seemed to understand me.

I then stood by the open door as the white Rolls-Royce silently (except for the crunch of its tyres on the gravel) pulled away down the drive. Watching the car go, I cursed under my breath, realising I'd once again missed talking to Sir John about the May expenses.

6:30 PM

Once Sir John's car had disappeared, I went back into the common room to see Mercy waving from the bar.

"Jack, I…" She looked at the floor and coughed.

"Mercy?"

"There's something I do once a week, or most weeks at least, and tonight I'd like to share it with you." She pointed towards the corridor leading to her rooms.

"Er… of course."

"Sorry, it's just about what I think of as 'me time'. There's a private dining room, and I have a formal meal served in there every Thursday."

"On your own?"

"Yes. It's nice to be on my own now and again."

"I can imagine."

"Well, tonight I'd like you to join me." Mercy looked at me sideways, her usual confidence suddenly diminished, almost as if she were an uncertain teenager hoping for confirmation that a new dress looked pretty. "If that's alright, of course?"

"I'd love to." Here was another opportunity to talk, to question her. After all, I still hadn't managed to speak to Mel, and I couldn't help feeling Mercy didn't really want me to. Perhaps a relaxed dinner with Mercy would help me to get closer to what might be going on underneath the façade. "What time?"

"Half eight. Allows time to let the staff get things going in the restaurant first, then serve us."

"It's a date then." I immediately regretted the choice of words. "And the menu?" I asked, keen to change the subject.

"I usually leave it to Anton, that OK?"

"Perfect, as long as there's no tripe." I again regretted the choice of words.

"I'll make sure there isn't." She laughed. "Oh, and Jack?"

"Yes?"

"Dress for dinner. Don't want you looking sloppy."

I touched my forelock. "Yes, Missus."

8:30 PM

I walked past the TV lounge and billiard room to find the next door ajar and entered to see Tilly lighting candles on an enormous oak refectory table.

"Missus will be along in a minute," she said, blowing out a long taper.

"Did you set this?" I asked, looking at the candelabras, glinting crystal glasses, shining crockery, and cutlery arranged with geometrical precision.

"Yes, sir."

"Well, it's immaculate."

"Thank you, sir." Tilly gave a slight curtsey.

"And Tilly, your surname's Omodiagbe, right?"

"Yessir," she answered, stepping back a little as she answered. "Why?"

"Oh, it's just that my doctor's name is Omodiagbe, and I never heard it anywhere else before. He's from the south-west of the country."

"Devon, sir?"

"Nigeria, near Cross River."

"Me too, sir."

"But you've been here in Devon a few years now."

"How d'you guess, sir?"

"You speak like a local."

She smiled. "My mother's still there, though, and I'm saving to bring her to England, but it's ever so difficult." She sniffed a little. "Takes a long time to save up and then there's lots of paperwork. I…" She looked at her feet. "Sorry, sir, not my place to tell you all this."

"Of course it is. And if you keep going the way I've seen you work these last few days, you'll have your mother over here in no time. Remember, you can do anything, with a bit of luck, and as long as you give it everything."

"Thank you, sir." She beamed. "Nobody's spoken to me like that before."

"They do, er… treat you with respect here?"

"Oh yes, sir," Tilly said with another curtsey. "Well, most of them, but…"

"But who?"

"That Mr Edgerton from the hunt, sir, he treats me like… badly, I mean… like some people did in our village did back in Nigeria."

"Anything, er… untoward?"

"Perhaps, sir, but I never let him do anything."

"Then if he tries it again tell Mrs Merrivale, OK?"

"I'd rather tell you."

"I won't always be here."

"Thank you all the same," she said, smiling again. "Are you a detective, sir?"

"No, but similar."

"Well, a maid hears a lot in a place like this, so if I hear anything I'll let you know." She then left the room, just as the 'Missus' arrived.

Tonight, Mercy wore a high-necked scarlet minidress, the material giving the appearance, so it seemed to me, of fish scales, each sparkling with a separate reflection in the candlelight. Her hair was swept back, held from her forehead by a matching head band, and her shoes, also matching the colour and texture of the dress, were high-heeled, so that she stood tall in front of me.

"I suppose I don't have to tell you how nice you look," I said as she closed the door behind her. "And I'm sorry I only have one semi-smart outfit with me," I added, looking down at my blazer, which I'd chosen to wear with an open shirt and silk cravat as a nod to Mercy saying 'dress' for dinner.

"You look just fine, Jack, and thank you. I haven't worn this dress for, oh, I don't know how long." She walked across the room to a buffet (also oak) with cut-glass decanters and tumblers laid out on the top. "G&T?"

"Why not?"

"Here you are, now what shall we toast?"

"To Christopher De Coverley, found safe and sound before the week's out." We clinked glasses.

"Your boss would probably drink to that as well." She laughed. "I couldn't help overhearing earlier."

"I think the whole of the common room overheard Sir John."

"Well, he seemed very agitated that Christopher's still missing. Eccentric sort of a chap, if you don't mind me saying."

"Eccentric's a good word." I sipped my gin and she sipped hers. "By the way, Mercy, I haven't seen Melissa this evening. Is she staying in Plymouth again? Because if she is, the police won't approve."

"No, she has an evening study session at school. Due home on the last bus, I—" Mercy was interrupted by a knock on the door. "Come."

It was Tilly, pushing a serving trolly. "Sorry, Missus, you'm not ready yet?"

"No, please go ahead and serve." Mercy nodded towards the chairs. "Let's sit Jack.,"

And sit we did, at either end of the table, which was almost (but not quite) too long to permit conversation.

"Anton says this is game and potato consommé," said Tilly, removing the lid of a vast, florally decorated porcelain tureen, ladling thick brown liquid into my dish, then pouring a spiral of cream on top before sprinkling with fresh parsley. "And here's his home-made bread." She placed a white roll on my side plate using a pair of silver tongs and, after serving Mercy, held up a bottle of wine.

"Ah, the '59 Côte du Beaune, just as I asked."

"Yes, Missus. Mr Gurney says it's the last bottle. He also says he's already let it breathe for half an hour."

"Let me taste," said Mercy. "Unless you want to, Jack?"

"Oh no." I shook my head, as Mercy lifted her glass, swirled the shining red fluid within, sniffed, then sipped. "Mmmm…" She nodded at Tilly, who proceeded to pour half glasses for each of us. "I remember Dad driving over to Burgundy and coming back with that wine."

"Main course in twenty minutes, Missus?"

"Yes, thank you."

Tilly took the trolley and, rather elegantly, I thought, backed out of the door.

"So, Jack," Mercy raised her glass, "a toast to Anton's peerless game and potato consommé?"

"And his unparalleled home-made bread."

In fact, both toasts were justified, with the soup and the bread amongst the most delicious I could remember. Tilly then returned with the main course, a fillet steak, served with, as she confidently stated, 'garlic butter, new potatoes, and sautéed field mushrooms, all sourced from within five miles of the hotel'. She was accompanied by Jenny, both waitresses simultaneously lifting silver 'voila' dishes to reveal the delicately prepared meat below.

"Anton says it's from a Red Ruby Devon they slaughtered over in Yelverton last month, meat dry aged for twenty-eight days," Tilly usefully informed us as she raised my dish. I wondered if she might go on to tell us the cow's name and blood group as well. "And Anton insists it must be cooked medium rare."

Mercy thanked the waitresses, and we were left alone once again, eating in near silence, the quiet only punctuated by the occasional 'mmm' in appreciation of Anton's main course.

"This is an interesting room," I said after a time, looking around at the oak-panelled walls, on which were hung several fine-looking oil paintings of Dartmoor landscapes.

"It was Dad's favourite place in the hotel." Mercy gestured to the pictures and several hunting trophies in glass cases, including a stuffed otter and a beady-eyed pike of gigantic proportions. There was also a nod to farm animals of the locality, with one particular painting in the corner catching my attention, an enormously fat-bodied pig, painted in profile with implausibly tiny legs, standing in front of a long, low building with the moor in the background. 'Pride of Princetown' said a label underneath.

"Liked his country pursuits, I see."

"Yes." She paused for a moment, looking up at the ceiling. "It was during a hunt up near Wistman's Wood that he died."

"A fall?" I asked, suddenly feeling I might have overstepped the mark. "Sorry, don't mean to pry."

"His heart burst actually." Mercy looked up at the ceiling again. "I remember Mum's face when they brought Dad home that day, laid across the back of his horse."

"I'm sorry."

"She was never the same afterwards. It's what turned her to… well, you've seen for yourself."

"And you took over running the hotel?" I said, trying to brighten the conversation.

"Al and I did together, yes."

I'd heard various people vaguely refer to the slightly mysterious Aloysius Merrivale, father of Melissa and conspicuously absent from the Wyvern Arms. Assuming he and Mercy separated some years previously (and perhaps emboldened by the burgundy), I asked her if she knew where Aloysius was now.

"Looking up at us, if I know Al." She grimaced, pointing to the floor.

"Pardon?"

"Killed, four years back."

"I'm sorry, I didn't realise."

"I suppose you thought," she said slowly, "that he'd left me."

"I did wonder."

"Might have been better if he had. Died drunk at the wheel, but only after having damned nearly run this place into the ground first."

She said this with clenched teeth, looking down into her coffee cup. "Perhaps I'm being harsh, though. Al had never really recovered from the war."

"I know how that feels. Lost my ship in '45, torpedoed from under me." I paused, looking down at the table, thoughts of that dreadful day clouding my mind. "Still gives me nightmares."

"Oh no." Mercy laughed, seemingly indifferent to my emotion. "Al wasn't traumatised, he just never adapted to peacetime. If anything, he wanted to hang on to the excitement."

"I suppose some people do."

"My dad always said Al thought the world owed him a living, and, well…" she frowned into her cup, "I'm afraid some of that's rubbed off on Mel as well. She basically does what she likes."

"I meet plenty of kids like that in my job, Mercy. She'll grow out of it."

"Perhaps, but I do worry for her, Jack, I really do."

We ate without speaking at all after that, perhaps because of the awkwardness at talking openly about two recent tragedies in Mercy's life, but mostly I think due to the impracticality of trying to converse across twenty feet of table, with the silence only broken when Jenny arrived to remove our plates. Once these were cleared, Tilly wheeled in the serving trolley again, which this time held an ornate copper flambé burner, along with a glass jug of white liquid and several liquor bottles.

"Crepe suzette, Missus," said Tilly, lighting the burner then pouring the white liquid into a small copper frying pan. "Anton has prepared the mix according to his own family's recipe. Asks me to tell you that it's the same one as was first discovered when his grandfather, an under waiter at the time, set fire to the sauce by accident at the, er…" She stood in thought for a moment. "Yes, the Café de Paris in Monte Carlo in the year, um… I can't remember when, Missus, but last century. His grandfather was serving a prince when it happened, Anton says."

"Please tell Anton that's very interesting," said Mercy, winking at me as Tilly poured various liquors and juices into the pan, then set them alight before jumping back as flames instantly leapt upwards.

"Woof, you alright?" I called from my end of the table.

"Too much Cointreau, sir," Tilly replied as the fire subsided, serving the pancake to Mercy before wheeling the trolley along to me and repeating the ceremony (thankfully with a lot less Cointreau this time).

"Coffee's on the side, Missus," said Tilly once my pancake was cooked and served, accompanied by the faint aroma of singed eyelashes. "You can pour for yourselves when you'm mind." She pointed to the top surface of the buffet, where a bone-china coffee service had been placed, then repeated her backward exit from the room.

"Your Tilly's a treasure," I said to Mercy as the door closed. "And did you know she's saving up to bring her mother over from Nigeria?"

"No, I didn't, people do talk to you, Jack."

"Oh, I, er… just try to… she's not having much luck, you couldn't do anything to help her, could you?"

"I'll speak to Tilly about it, try and assist if I can."

I smiled. "And she really knows her stuff, Mercy, I mean, all that about Anton's grandfather and Monte Carlo."

"She's had a good teacher, Jack. A couple of months ago Anton had the waitresses telling guests he was a foundling, left on a doorstep in Marseilles and brought up by a widowed miller's wife in the Camargue."

"Never spoil a good story for the truth, isn't that how the saying goes?"

"It was Oscar Wilde, and no doubt by Christmas Anton will be Oscar's long-lost grandson."

"Well, wherever the recipe comes from," I said, savouring my first taste of the pancake, with its bittersweet sauce, "it's delicious."

"Then, Jack," she said, eyes sparkling almost as much as her scarlet dress, "let's just enjoy the crepe suzette and the moment."

Mercy then spooned some of the sauce onto a large piece of crepe, placed it on her tongue, and, closing her eyes, letting out a long 'mmm' before lifting her chin, the scarlet choker on her neck moving slightly as she swallowed.

And looking at this beautiful woman, whom a few days ago I'd never met, the table with its cut-glass and bone china, ornate paintings hanging on oak-panelled walls, and all flickering with shadows and reflections from the light of the candelabra, one overriding thought came to mind, particularly when I glanced at the Pride of Princetown, corpulently silent as he hung in the corner.

I was being fattened up for the kill.

*

"That really was," I said, dabbing my lips with a serviette as Mercy brought me a coffee cup from the buffet, the question still niggling my mind as to why I was receiving all this hospitality as she did so, "the nicest meal I've had in… well, a very long time."

"I'm glad." She poured herself a cup then pulled up a chair beside me. "And I'll sit beside you, if I may." She laughed. "Otherwise I'll go hoarse, shouting from the other end of the table."

"Me too, and there was already enough shouting earlier."

"Certainly was, Jack." Mercy sat forward and looked at me, eyes and dress sparkling in the now-flickering candlelight. "You don't smoke, do you?" I shook my head as she took a cigarette from a silver case and lit it from one of the candles. "By the way, did you believe Jane Ustrix, or whatever she's really called, about not knowing what's happened to Christopher?"

"Not sure." I remembered the imploring look on Jane's face as she was led away, and her enigmatic last comment, mouthed to me and, as far as I could tell, unheard by anyone else.

"*Die Glocke verändert alles,*" which, even with my very basic German, I'd managed to translate.

The Bell changes everything.

"And Jack," Mercy continued, leaning even closer, "have you any ideas as to where he might be, and whether any local people are involved?"

"I've some ideas, but they're…" I considered whether to mention some of my more outlandish thoughts. "No," I eventually said. "Too odd, not properly formed. Need more investigation."

"I'm intrigued by your job, Jack. I mean, how do you go about an investigation?"

I explained my methods much as I had to Jane Ustrix and Professor Frere, emphasising the importance of talking and listening to people.

"And you came into this line of work how?"

"Just fell into it. When I joined the Granville, they found I have, as someone wrote in my last company assessment, 'an aptitude for solving the insoluble'. At least where missing kids are concerned, that is."

"Very impressive," said Mercy, shaking her head and winking.

"Sorry, sounds like blowing my own trumpet. It's as much intuition and luck as anything else."

"And does Jack Sangster always get results?"

"Mostly."

"And here, on Dartmoor?"

"It's a baffler." I shrugged.

"There must be someone you suspect, Jack." I shrugged again. "You can tell me, surely?"

"No," I answered, sitting back a little and suddenly feeling I was being subtly interrogated. "Not ready."

"My uncles, for example, Septimus and Peregrine. John De Coverley too. You've spoken with all of them, and so have the police."

"Yes, and by the way, could I have a chat with Melissa?"

"Er..." Mercy hesitated. "Why?"

"Oh, she knows Christopher well. Always good to talk to the peers when a kid goes missing, and being home-schooled, the lad didn't have many. Peers, that is."

"Of course then, but there won't be time tomorrow morning."

I wondered if she was evading.

"What time does your daughter get the bus into Plymouth?"

"Oh, quite early. Before seven."

"I'll tell you what I'll do then, I'll give her a lift to school. That way Melissa can leave later in the morning, and I'll have longer to chat with her."

"Alright, I'll let her know, but Jack, you didn't answer me."

"Answer what?"

"Do you suspect someone?"

"Look, Mercy, I can't say anything more for now."

"Alright, I'm sorry," she said, stroking my arm. "How about we take a brandy outside, on the bridge, like the other night?"

11 PM

We stood on the crest of the bridge, glasses in hand, watching the fireflies put on their nightly show, the air calm and quiet as the shining creatures glided above the river.

"Wonder if Old Soldier will make an appearance." I peered into the water below.

"No fish tonight, so probably not," Mercy replied, pointing under the bridge, then looking up towards the road, where the lights of an approaching bus could be seen. "Must be eleven already. Mel will be back, let's go over and meet her, I'll introduce you properly, oh…" We watched as the bus passed the hotel gates at speed, its engine noise and lights fading quickly away into the night. "The bus isn't stopping."

"Perhaps she caught an earlier bus, went straight to her room while we were eating."

"Yes, Jack," said Mercy, staring towards the hotel. "That must be it. Shall we walk back too, I want to—"

Suddenly, and all at once, the hotel lights went out.

"Must be one of those damned electrical surges we keep getting. Main fuse has likely gone."

"What's that?" I pointed to the field behind the hotel, where a red glow momentarily illuminated the silhouette of the building before disappearing and leaving the night black again, save for a slight moonshine.

"Maybe to do with the power surge. That's the field with the standing stones, it's... oh my God, look."

The field was lit again, first with a series of sparks, then a criss-cross of blue filaments that danced and changed as they threaded around the stones, so that the ancient monoliths almost looked alive. And soon after this came what seemed to me unquestionably the same blanket of sound, although further away, so quieter, that had filled Wistman's Wood two nights before. And this time possibly, I wondered afterwards, because we were in the open rather than sheltered by woodland, the noise was followed by a wind, rising rapidly to a howl as it raced across the roof of the hotel.

Almost falling myself, I saw Mercy buffeted by the powerful gusts, hair blown almost horizontal, legs giving way as she grabbed in vain for the bridge parapet. There was a shattering sound, her brandy glass crashing to the ground, I later realised, then a cry as she fell against the wall, feet now off the ground, back arching over the side of the bridge. Senses confused by the fury of the squall, I nevertheless knew that in seconds she would fall into the river, which now raged white with foam. I lunged, throwing my arms around Mercy's waist, feeling her slide despite this, so that for a moment I thought my grip lost. I locked my arms tighter, sensing them blocked from slipping by the curve of Mercy's hips, and in a daze staggered backwards, pulling her, after what must have been a second but seemed like an hour, back onto the bridge.

Then, as we stood breathlessly staring at each other, the light, noise, and wind subsided as quickly as they had come, the river running calm and still again, so that peace returned to the Wyvern Arms.

"Get me inside, Jack." Mercy's voice wavered as she pulled down her skirt and fingered a rip in the dress material. "I don't want to be out here."

"Me neither," I gasped, as, arm in arm, we walked quickly back to the front door, opening it just as the hotel lights came back on.

"Joe must have fixed the fuse," said Mercy, grabbing my hand and pulling me across the threshold. As she did so I looked back at the river.

All of the fireflies had gone.

*

"Thanks again, Mercy," I said as we walked across the common room, which was empty except for a couple sitting in the window settle, Joe Gurney washing glasses behind the bar, and Tilly wiping down the tables. "For a delightful dinner."

I'd wanted to bring back some normality but immediately felt my words banal.

"I'd have remembered it anyway," I went on. "But after that, er… I can't say what we just saw out there, but well…" I laughed as best I could, "I'll definitely remember it."

"No, it's me who should thank you, Jack," she replied, still smoothing her dress, voice still wavering. I saw the couple by the window stare at the tear in the material, which was now a jagged gash at least six inches long. "For er… whatever you just did out there. Oh, and Joe?"

"Missus?"

"Pour me a brandy, please," she continued to smooth the gash in her dress. "Large one. I dropped my glass up on the bridge."

"I'll send Tilly out with a brush and dustpan, Missus," Joe replied, placing the drink on the bar, then silently watching as Mercy, with trembling hands, downed it in one.

"No, in the morning, when it's safe… I mean, when it's light." She looked fearfully at the door and the windows. "Ciggy, please, Joe." The barman passed an open packet to her, she took one then waited as he struck a match. "Thanks," she said, inhaling deeply. "Now, Jack, drink for you?" I shook my head, and Mercy turned back to the barman. "Did you get all the lights back on, Joe?"

"No, Missus, most of the bedrooms are still out, so I got these from the cellar." He pointed to a row of candle holders on the bar, then lit two, handing one to Mercy. "We've already taken some up to the guests."

"We'll call the electricity board in the morning, and they can check the upstairs fuses then." She took the candle from him, hand still trembling slightly, then turned towards the hall that led to the private rooms.

"And I enjoyed dinner too, Jack," she said over her shoulder, her voice now calm and soft. "More than I have for a long time."

*

I watched Mercy disappear down the hall, red dress still sparkling, then took my candle in hand and climbed the stairs to my own room.

"Damn," I said out loud as my door key turned. "Forgot to check what time I need to take Melissa tomorrow." Walking back down to the common room, I saw Joe locking up the bar.

"Is there a phone I can use to call Mercy's room?"

"No phone in the Missus's room, sir."

"I just need to check a time for tomorrow morning."

"Should catch her if you're quick. Fifth door down, on the right at the end."

"Thanks."

I walked past the TV lounge, billiard room, and private dining room, before coming to a wide-open door. Looking inside, the flickering light from my candle revealed what must surely have been Melissa's bedroom, with posters of pop stars on the walls, a record player on a desk, and a guitar standing in the corner.

But the bed was unslept in, and the room empty.

Then I heard sobbing, a woman's sobs that echoed from the end of the hall. There, through an archway, I could see Mercy sitting at a table, head bowed, chin held in her hands, cigarette burning in an ash tray next to her.

*

"Is everything OK?" I placed my hand on Mercy's shoulder, making her start, then look up.

"Jack, what are you doing here?"

"Sorry, I, um… I just came to find out what time you wanted me to pick up Melissa tomorrow morning."

"No point in that now." She dragged on the cigarette then blinked, eyes filled with tears.

"Is there not?"

Mercy stood up, dabbing her lids and cheeks with a tissue paper then waving a note in the air.

"She left this, listen…"

I've gone away for good, somewhere neither you nor anyone else will be able to find me so please don't try. And don't worry, I'm going to follow my destiny. I'll be safe and happy.
I love you, Mum,
Mel

"…and I'm afraid," Mercy began to sob again, "I've not been entirely straight with you, Jack."

"Haven't you?"

"Let me just change out of this poor old dress." She touched the gash on the side, that had now extended up to her shoulder. "Can you wait here a little?"

Mercy returned ten minutes later wearing a dressing gown, make-up removed, and eyes, as far as I could see them in the candlelight, still red but no longer crying. She picked a briefcase up from beneath the table and opened the clasp, tipping out a number of papers. I jolted when I saw a press clipping with my name on it.

"Please, would you sit down?"

"OK, but what's all this?" I pointed to the documents strewn across the table.

"We'd better start at the beginning…"

Melissa, it seemed, had taken her father's death very badly, and the years leading up to it had already been difficult. Aloysius's drinking, and Mercy trying to keep the business afloat despite this, had made for an unhappy home life, and Melissa, naturally headstrong, had inevitably fallen into trouble.

"She was always a bit of a daddy's girl, and she… she blamed me for Al's death."

"I'm sorry. May I ask why?"

"Oh, he was more drunk than usual that night, we'd had an argument, and when I told him to get out, he took the car. You can imagine the rest."

I nodded, and she continued, telling me that soon after Aloysius's fatal car crash, Melissa, aged thirteen but already very tall and also old in other ways for her years, began spending more and more nights away from home.

"I'd been worried sick, but with the hotel to run, and Mother to deal with, I didn't spend the time on Mel I should have. It all came to a head two years ago, when she… well, she fell in with some bad people." Mercy sniffed and dabbed her eyes. "The police found her in a squat down near the docks, she'd been helping with robberies, muggings, even getting money for drugs by—"

"It's alright, you needn't spell it out," I said as Mercy began to sob again. "I deal with kids like that a lot. They usually come back round given half a chance."

"Yeah, well, Mel didn't. Refused to take any help and was taken into care."

"And then?"

"They cleaned her up and she was forced to come home, under a binding order to stay with me until she was eighteen. I thought we'd reconciled, and I thought everything was OK, but since Christmas she's started spending more and more time away again."

"Back in Plymouth?"

"No, I don't think so. She became friendly with Christopher when he stopped going to school. Funny, really."

"Funny how?"

"Because he was an academic lad and a year younger than Mel. Not her type at all, I would have said."

"So," I said, taking all this in as best I could, "you say you haven't been straight with me."

Mercy shuffled the papers on the desk. "Look, when I heard that you were coming to look for Christopher, I panicked." She lifted up the press clipping, which was from the previous month's *West Briton*. "The police didn't seem too bothered, but I worried you'd get to the truth, just as you did with that missing girl in Cornwall."

"Why panic?"

"Because I'm sure Mel has been involved in something serious with Christopher, and social services would take her back into care in an instant if they found out." She held up another paper, this time a magazine article about the Granville Institute. "You're pretty close to being social services yourself, aren't you?"

"Not really." I laughed. "We do work with them, that's true, but we're independent and I would never blindly follow procedure if I thought it against a child's best interests. Anyway…" I picked up a scrap of paper with notes scribbled in Melissa's handwriting, "I'm not mandated to look for Melissa, just Christopher." I pointed to the notes. "So what's this, a list of some sort?"

"Hidden in her dressing-table drawer. I don't know what to make of it, Jack."

The notes looked like a series of dated events, although the writing was often indistinct. The lines began in December, with dates following almost up to the present, and with one cryptic description, '*Tonight changes everything*', written next to a smudged date that could have been March the 25th. That date seemed to jog my memory, but the hour was late, and the day had been long, so that, try as I might, I could not recall why.

There was also a hastily sketched diagram, perhaps of a building like a school or office block that stood inside an oval wall. There was a street leading up to what might have been front gates, with a cul-de-sac forking off to one side. An 'X' was marked at the end of this fork and the building outline also seemed vaguely familiar, but again, my memory failed me.

At the bottom of the sheet, a note simply stated: '*And I will follow, at sundown four days after the sun stands still*'.

"That last line, would it mean something special to Melissa?"

"No idea." Mercy shrugged.

"May I keep this?"

"Of course." I folded and pocketed the paper. "But Jack, about not being straight with you. What I wanted to say was—"

"I know." I held up my hand to stop her talking. "You've been over-attentive since I arrived, getting close so you could ask questions. And to seem more plausible, you even let slip you were the anonymous caller reporting the boy missing, and that you thought Melissa had been lying."

"Oh God," she muttered, cheeks reddening. "You knew all along?"

"More or less."

"And I thought it was working. I even wore that bloody red dress, so tight that one little tear soon became a great hole. I could hardly breathe during dinner." Mercy laughed, only a little, but for the first time since I'd found her sobbing. She then picked up a photograph, eyes welling up with tears again. "I took this of Mel and Chris just before Easter."

The picture showed the two standing outside the hotel, holding an anti-hunting placard. I remembered Septimus Frere's menacing comment: "Swore he'd happily kill anyone who got between him and Old Soldier. By the look on Miles' face, I think he meant it as well."

"How did all this anti-hunt stuff sit with Miles Edgerton?"

"Not well." Mercy shook her head. "And it wouldn't do for me to upset him too much."

"Hunt's good for business, I guess?"

"Yes, and I spend enough time having to fend Miles off whilst making sure we keep his custom without having to worry about his spats with Mel and Chris."

"I can imagine, Miles did, er… tell me to keep clear of you. Now how did he put it… oh yes, that the county understood you were spoken for, and so should I if I knew what was good for me."

"The county, spoken for, he said those things?" I nodded. "Oh my God, the man really is deluded." She threw her head in the air. "Sorry, Jack."

"Don't be, but would Edgerton… you know, go to extreme lengths?"

"Heaven's no," Mercy shouted. "Not Miles, I've known him all my life and he's a pain alright, but I won't think that." She put her hand over her face and returned to sobbing.

"Alright," I said, offering a handkerchief and glancing at my watch. "It's midnight, so I think it would be best to turn in, but before we do…"

"Yes, Jack?"

"I'm not sure we have much time, so is there anything else, anything at all you can think of, that might help?"

"I don't know whether this matters," she said, still crying. "But I followed Mel to Foxtor House one evening a few weeks ago and saw John De Coverley talking to her in the garden. When I challenged her the next day we had a dreadful row, and all she'd say was that I couldn't possibly understand."

"Nothing more?"

"No, we didn't talk for a few days after that, except… hmmm, now I come to think of it, she did say something odd while we were arguing." Mercy blew her nose. "Mel shouted quite a few times that even Whiddon would know better, that Whiddon… what was the word she used, yes, 'remembered'. Just felt like a clumsy insult, but now it seems strange."

"Certainly does." I stood up, making a mental note to talk again with Whiddon. "I'll go now, if I may. Will you be OK on your own?"

"Yes, I think so." She rose from her chair and kissed me on the cheek.

"What's that for?"

"Not judging me, or my silly attempts to get around you. You must think me such a fool."

"Never, now goodnight, Mercy."

"Goodnight, Jack, and for what it's worth, I meant it about enjoying dinner more than I have for a long time."

As I walked back along the hall, I heard Mercy begin to sob again.

THURSDAY, JUNE THE 25TH
1 AM

I lay on my bed, face up to the ceiling, eyes wide open.

"It's Wednesday and you haven't found the lad yet," Sir John had blustered at me earlier. "Time's running out, Sangster."

Perhaps it was running out, but the main pieces of the jigsaw, I sensed, were now in front of me, and I would be shown how they fitted together before too long.

But unlike completing a jigsaw by adding pieces, solving cases like this also involved throwing pieces away. These unwanted pieces beguilingly looked the right shape and colour at first, but as the solution became clearer, just didn't seem to fit. I listed them in my head:

- I'd wondered about Miles Edgerton, perhaps having had some altercation with Christopher that turned violently wrong, but this seemed unlikely, especially as Melissa had now disappeared as well.
- Then there was Jane Ustrix, now unmasked as a Polish agent, and convinced some kind of wonder weapon had been brought to the Highmoor Centre after the war, but without a shred of evidence, and following a story scoffed at by mainstream science.
- And Detective Inspector Hawke, who I had thought might be keeping things from me because of resentment or orders from her

superiors. And although her eccentric manner and looks might say otherwise, the DI seemed to be merely carrying out orders, aided by the long-suffering Eccles.
- My last jigsaw piece to discard was Mercy, her attempts to seductively gain my confidence motivated by no more than a mother's instinct to protect her only child.

Now the distractions were eliminated, and the puzzle was reduced to its key pieces, I listed these in my head:

- Christopher De Coverley, whose disappearance was the reason I was here, purportedly gone missing a few days ago, allegedly seen since, but not firmly identified for around twelve weeks.
- Doctor John De Coverley seemed at the heart of it all, with his connection to Melissa and the Freres. De Coverley's long service at the Highmoor Centre also seemed to matter, but I couldn't say why.
- Melissa Merrivale, wild and headstrong, and now run away, surely to be with Christopher.
- Peregrine Frere, in charge of an atomic research centre and reliant on De Coverley to manage technology he didn't fully understand.
- Septimus Frere, tutor to Christopher and obsessed with Sir Francis Drake.
- And Drake himself, dead almost four hundred years, and yet somehow still key to the case, whether leading the Wild Hunt or talking of vanquishing the Armada with his own wonder weapon.

Then there were the odd events and throwaway words that I hoped would help me slot these pieces into an overall picture:

- Electrical disturbances in the field with the standing stones and Wistman's Wood, and according to the papers, in many other places as well.
- Modern ordnance found in the Elizabethan armoury at Reynard's

Hall, that looked very like the shells I'd seen all those years ago in Donegal. The analysis results of both were due later today.
- The theft of a machine gun and maintenance kit from the Devonport Arms Depot, perpetrated by people that looked very like Doctor De Coverley and his son.
- The Polish authorities being interested enough in Doctor De Coverley to bother sending an agent to investigate. Jane Ustrix might no longer be a key piece of the puzzle, but the very fact of her being sent here rang alarm bells in my mind.
- And what, according to Melissa, did Whiddon know and remember?

Yes, most of the pieces were all there, I thought, but not the one that solved the puzzle, and that piece would only present itself if I could answer a single question.

Why were the British and Eastern Bloc governments so keen to find Christopher De Coverley?

Something to do with the work at the Highmoor Centre, that much seemed certain. I tried to concentrate on this, hoping other ideas might follow, but all reasoning was clouded by thoughts of Mercy racing through my mind. I told myself her attentions had all been an act, but somehow, they still felt real.

"This place, it's getting to you, Sangster," I said out loud. "Stay on top of the case, remember who you are, and stop imagining things."

I then heard Sarah's voice in my head: "I can't wait to get home, darling."

I shook myself, determined to clear my mind, and, with lips pursed, turned over, blew out my bedside candle, and pulled the bedclothes up high.

*

Moments later I began to dream I was back in the squall on the bridge, but this time powerless to move towards Mercy as she fell, my legs seemingly fixed to the floor. I cried out to her, and she to me, but try as I might, I couldn't lift my feet, and watched, powerless, as she disappeared over the parapet.

Then I found myself looking down at the water, where a woman's body lay, lifeless eyes staring upwards, dress, a full white gown rather than Mercy's red minidress, billowing in the current, black hair drifting around her face.

I let out a scream. It was my wife I saw beneath the surface of the river.

Sitting up and awake, I wondered whether I had screamed out loud, but there was no sound of other bedroom doors opening or footsteps on the landing, in fact, no sound at all. The scream, I decided, settling back under the bedclothes, was a scream of the mind.

Sleep was fitful after this, incoherent dreams waking me every few minutes, until, too tired even for these garbled images, my mind fell into an exhausted slumber.

2 AM

I heard a rapping noise which made my temples throb, and, opening my eyes, realised the sound was not from a nightmare but real, just outside the room. Heart pounding, I called out in that timorous voice we so often use when awakened by something unknown in the dead of night.

"Come in, whoever you are."

The bedroom door opened, casting a shadow across the floor.

"Jack, I couldn't sleep."

Mercy stood in front of me, the folds of her floor-length white nightdress irradiated by a candle she held.

"It's Mel," she said, closing the door silently then walking across the room. "I can't lose another loved one."

I looked up as she stood next to my pillow, blonde hair falling loose to her waist, angular features reflected in the candlelight. The white gown now looked almost translucent, her figure within outlined where skin touched the material.

"Make me happy, Jack, just for tonight."

As she said this, in soft tones I'd grown so used to over the last few days, and in my half sleep, nature offered no choice. The delirious desire that swept over me seemed, as far as I could think at all, a throwback to the fever of teenage days and quite beyond anything

I could immediately have controlled. Temples now throbbing like thunder, I sat up and turned aside the bedclothes. Mercy gave a hint of a smile, placed the candle holder on the bedside table, then lifted her hands to unbutton her nightgown, which fell with barely a rustle from her shoulders. I wanted to speak but she pressed a finger to her lips, and I was almost lost when Sarah's voice came back to me.

"You're not here, Jack, and I'm burying Bubba, she's all I had."

"I... I... can't, Mercy."

"What?" She took a step back and looked down at the nightdress.

"I can't. You are beautiful and everything any man would want, but I can't. My wife, I..."

"Wife?" was all she replied, and I nodded. Then without speaking again, Mercy picked up the nightdress, pulled it roughly over her shoulders, and walked out of the room, slamming the door after her.

8 AM

I blinked from the sunlight that streamed through the bedroom window and began fumbling around the bed, vainly feeling for Mercy. The vacant sheets made me begin to wonder if her coming to the room had simply been a dream. Then, feeling a plunging sensation in my stomach despite the drowsiness usual for this early hour, I remembered my rejection of Mercy.

My alarm clock showed eight, as, still half asleep, I climbed out of bed, stretched, and walked to the bathroom, where a rather tired version of myself stared back from the mirror.

Pulling on a T-shirt, shorts, socks and running shoes, I went downstairs and out into the morning, setting off at a faster pace than usual, up and across the old bridge, then turning right towards Postbridge and Wistman's Wood. I kept running at speed, feeling driven, with a sense that today would bring me answers. I also sensed that perhaps I wouldn't want to hear some of those answers.

Then there was Mercy.

I had almost let happen what I'd promised myself, on the day I'd proposed to Sarah, would never happen, and, I assumed now, to boot had sent all the wrong signals to a lonely and very much a good woman. I also wondered if my investigative style, happy to get close to, socialise with, and even enjoy romantic meals or car trips with useful witnesses, had added to those wrong signals. With these thoughts, the guilt of it all began to tear through me as I ran, and I found that pushing my legs harder helped dull the immediate angst a little. Thus inspired, I increased my step even more, and within a short time was crossing the bridge where I had almost crashed two days before. Today the place was silent and calm, and I slowed, carrying on at a gentle jog up the mild slope that would eventually take me to the woodland track and Whiddon's caravan.

"Even Whiddon will know more," was what Melissa had repeatedly shouted at her mother. "Whiddon will remember." What could she mean?

*

I leaned against the side of the caravan for a full minute before knocking on the door, my breath gradually becoming less laboured.

"Who's that?"

"Sangster," I gasped. "Can I come in?"

There was a grunt from inside which I took to be a yes, so I opened the door to find Whiddon, head still bandaged, sitting up and drinking tea.

"Morning, Mr Whiddon," I wheezed. "Are you well?"

"I should ask you that the way you're breathing."

"I've been running."

"Running after who?"

"Nobody."

"Someone after you then, shall I say you're not here if they knock?"

"No, I run most mornings." Whiddon looked at me, mouth open. "I do it to keep… oh, never mind, may I have a cup of tea?"

"Help yourself." He pointed at a battered old enamel teapot and then to a cupboard above it. "Up there." I opened the cupboard and took down a cup, then regarded a half-opened, slightly rusty-looking condensed milk can.

"I'll just take it black, thanks."

"Please yourself."

I sat opposite him and sipped, the hot liquid soothing my parched throat.

"Ahh," I sighed. "That's good."

"So you're alone?"

"Yes," I answered as he winked at me.

"No woman with you this time?"

"No, not this time." I laughed.

"Did that nurse ask you to look in on me again?"

"Not exactly."

"I'd rather she visited than you." He rubbed his hands together and spat on the floor. "The hem on that starched uniform shows off her nicely turned ankles, I…" Whiddon's voice trailed off and he stared at me again, mouth now open even wider. "Why are you here on the moor?" He asked this quite some seconds later.

"I'm here to try and find Christopher De Coverley."

"I heard that boy'd gone missing, but isn't it a copper's job to find him?"

"I'm helping the police, and I was just wondering if you could help me."

"You'd better pour me another cup then, milk and three sugars." He gestured to the cupboard, and I took down the sugar bowl and milk can.

"There you are, Mr Whiddon," I said, pouring from his teapot, and over this a trickle of thick, creamy liquid from the can into the cup. "Oh, you've ants in the sugar bowl."

"Don't mind them," he said, brushing off the insects then shovelling three heaped teaspoons into his cup. "They get in the Carnation tin as well sometimes, never affect the flavour, though." He took a draught of tea. "Now what is it you think I can do for you?"

"Did you ever work at the Highmoor Research Centre, when you were younger, perhaps?"

He shook his head. "That blocky place. Never."

"Really, I thought—"

"You thought wrong," he said, eyes glazing and mouth falling open again. "Now who are you?"

"Whiddon's thoughts do wander a little, but pay no mind," Nurse Pickles had said.

"I'm Sangster."

"Course you are." Whiddon's glazed look passed and he leaned towards me. "Now I never worked at that new place, but I did have a job at the Old Centre. Sent there after I was demobbed."

"That would be 1945?"

"That's right. I only stayed a few months, didn't like being cooped up underground."

"Underground?"

"That's right, most of the place was underground, built on top of an old mineshaft, they reckoned."

"And what did they do there?"

"Can't rightly say, but it…" Whiddon then spoke of military comings and goings, odd machinery that he couldn't recognise, and parts of the compound being closed off to all but a few staff.

"Can you remember…" I paused, suddenly feeling the question I now wanted to ask would perhaps sound very foolish, "er… a strangely shaped machine being brought to the place that year, something the army guarded more heavily than usual, something bell-shaped, perhaps?"

"We were sworn to secrecy, so how d'you know about that?" I shrugged. "Mr Sangster, I remember that night well…"

Whiddon and some others had, it seemed, been asked to work overtime one very stormy winter night. And this particular night was especially memorable, he said, because the storm brought down all the power lines, but the people at the centre insisted he and his fellow workers stay nevertheless, even setting up diesel generators to provide light. In the early hours of the morning, despite the weather now having degenerated into a blizzard, a convoy of army trucks arrived. Amongst these was a heavy transport vehicle with low clearance that struggled along the uneven road that led to the centre, so that more than once the convey stopped while soldiers cleared the way.

Once the transporter was safely in the centre's compound, Whiddon and the others had watched as tarpaulins were removed to reveal a black metallic object, perhaps twenty-five feet high, and shaped like a bell.

"We'd never seen the like, Mr Sangster, never. Something about that thing made your eyes hurt when you looked at it. Doctor had us help unshackle that satanic machine."

"Doctor John De Coverley?"

"That's right, he was just a young'un then. Ran the place with that Henry Weaver bloke. Never took to Weaver."

"Why not?"

"Oh, I dunno, but... funny way of talking for a start, didn't really sound local, didn't really sound English."

"And the Bell, what happened to it?"

"We placed it on rollers and helped the troops take it on inside. Never saw the thing again, and we were told never to speak of it."

"Did they ever ask you to keep things secret before?" Whiddon shook his head. "And was there anything about the Bell that seemed odd?"

"Apart from it being a twenty-five-foot bell?"

"Yes, Mr Whiddon," I laughed, "apart from it being a twenty-five-foot bell."

"Well, like I say, your eyes hurt to look at it. Seemed to shimmer, even in that awful snowstorm. It was rigged up to a power cable on the transporter, then they swapped this for a line to one of our portable generators. Seemed like they wanted that Bell plugged in all the time, almost as if it was on one of them hospital things, what are they called?"

"Life-support machines?"

"S'right."

"Anything else?"

"There were markings on the casing that I couldn't make out, but there was something, I..." Whiddon's mouth opened again, his head lolled, and he went silent.

"What, man?" I said, shaking his shoulders.

"On the side of the Bell I saw... a..." He muttered a word, and although the sound was indistinct, I was fairly sure of what I'd heard.

"And have you told anybody else about this?"

"No, I never did, except…"

"Yes?"

"Well, young Mel told me she'd been up to the place a few weeks ago, and, well, I told her to keep away. Told her I had bad memories, told her about the Bell."

*

So, I thought to myself as I turned from the lane onto the main road, Mel knows about the Bell. I wondered just how much Whiddon had told her, then spoke out loud the word he had muttered to me when I pressed him about the Bell's markings.

"Swastika."

*

The hotel car park was quiet when I arrived, with no hunt, delivery vans, or frantic police to disturb the morning. In fact, the only sign of life was the Dikes walking through the gates as I ran in from the road.

"Fine morning," I said, thinking it polite to stop and greet them whilst wanting only to get in a hot bath.

"Fine morning indeed," said Ballar. His wife, who was standing behind him, sullenly carried their oversized rucksack whilst he leaned on his staff. "Been up by Wistman's Wood?"

"Close by."

"Ah, very strong ley lines converge up there." He made a spiralling hand gesture. "We can feel the power of them, Fidelma and I, telluric lines, dragon lines, song lines, all meeting to magnify the might and majesty of Mother Earth. Wistman's Wood's a truly exciting spot if you're a druid, Mr Sangster."

As he said this, I watched Fidelma looking at her husband with what could only be described as complete disdain. She turned away when she caught my eye, and I was reminded of Jane Ustrix's comment

('The Dikes talk absolute rubbish. It's as if they've read a couple of books on witchcraft and picked out some words to bandy about.').

"Probably not as exciting as this spot was last night."

"Sorry?" said Ballar, with a look of genuine bafflement.

"All that police activity. I only arrived later, but you two must have seen it all."

"Ah yes," he said. "Er… of course, very exciting. Anyway, we're hiking towards Fox Tor today, so we'll bid you a good morning."

"Was it you who got caught up with the hunt there the other day?"

"It was," growled Fidelma. "Ruined our morning's ramble, they did, so we're going back there for a proper hike." She turned and carried on walking, her husband tapping behind her with his staff.

"Well, remember the mires," I called after them. "Where rushes grow, ponies fear to go."

*

"Didn't see you at breakfast, Jack."

"No, Mercy," I said from the cockpit of the car. "I had a tray sent up."

"And now?"

"I'm going to the Highmoor Centre, talk to Sir Peregrine."

She suddenly leaned forward. "Take me with you. I can help, show you round Foxtor House, maybe."

"Look, Mercy, about last night, I—"

She opened the car door and sat beside me, stroking my arm in her customary manner. "It never happened, Jack, don't worry. I'm worried sick about Mel, and I… I just needed… well, you know." I nodded. "So will you take me?"

"If you like."

"OK, I'll be ten minutes." She kissed me on the cheek then ran inside. I was glad Mercy had cleared the air to the point where there would be no awkward silences ('It never happened, Jack'), but I still felt emotional turmoil. And why was I letting her come with me?

"Get a grip, Jack," I shouted out loud.

"Grip of what?"

I looked up to see DI Hawke, hands resting on the goat's head of her walking stick.

"This case," I said, stepping out of the car. "How's your prisoner?"

"She wants to see you, Sangster, heaven knows why."

"And you came all this way to tell me in person?"

"I didn't," she said, tapping the stick several times on the gravel. "No such honour for you, I'm afraid."

"Then what?"

"It's the De Coverley boy. The powers that be finally decided he merits a full-scale search. Even as we speak, officers and canine units are spreading out across the moor around Princetown. Thought I'd drop in to see you, being nearby. Face to face is always better than the phone."

"You think something really has happened to him?" I asked, wondering if I should report Melissa missing despite my promise to Mercy. "You don't think he's just run off?"

"Not sure either way," she said, shaking her head. "But he's been missing long enough to merit a search, and with the interest in the case from on high we've got no problem getting local police resources. Drafted a hundred or so extra people in from Dorset, Cornwall, and Somerset too."

"OK, well, I—"

"Your movements today," she interrupted. "What are they?"

"Er… Highmoor Research Centre for eleven, then I'll drive over Yelverton way after lunch. No other specific plans, although I'm thinking of looking at Foxtor House."

"Then," DI Hawke said, looking at her watch, "could you come to us at six?"

"Er… yes. Where is it I'm to go exactly?"

"Crownhill station is just off the Tavistock Road when you come into town, can't miss it. Ask for Eccles when you arrive."

With that she limped over to a waiting police car, which pulled away just as Mercy returned.

"Police again, Jack?"

"The inspector. She's here because they're doing a full-scale search of the area for Christopher. Over a hundred officers apparently."

"You didn't, er… did you?"

"If you mean tell her about Melissa, then no," I said as we drove away. "I should have, though."

"Oh, Jack, we'll find her on our own, won't we?"

I pulled the car to a halt, brakes screeching. "Is that what last night was for?"

"What do you mean?"

"Butter me up with fine food and wine, a little flirting, brandy on the bridge, then bang, you've got me, eh?"

"No," she shouted back. "It started out like that at first, but not when I got to know you, and not now. And I wasn't going to speak about us again, but last night was, well… I didn't know you were married, really."

A horn tooted from behind the car.

"Alright, we're going." I waved to an irate-looking bus driver, before hitting the ignition and pulling away.

"Jack, I mean it."

"Hope you do," I said through gritted teeth, remembering that I'd very nearly betrayed everything I held dear. "Now let's just get on with things."

*

"I'll go to Highmoor on my own," I said to Mercy as we drove into Princetown. "You'll have to wait somewhere."

"Are you still cross with me?"

"They won't have a badge for you," I sighed.

"But he's my uncle."

"You need special permission because the place does nuclear weapons research, so I don't think even the great Sir Peregrine Frere can break security rules."

"Alright, drop me at Jay's, I'll have a cup of tea."

We pulled up outside the store to see Verity arranging magazines on a rack on the pavement next to the shop door.

"Morning, Mrs Merrivale, Mr Sangster."

"Morning, Verity," I replied, as Mercy got out of the car.

"How long, Jack?"

"An hour, maybe more."

"Then Verity," said Mercy, looking up and down the magazine stand, "a copy of *Woman's Own*, a pot of tea, and a toasted tea cake, please."

*

"Cigarette?"

"No, thanks."

"Smoking too many of the things myself these days," muttered Sir Peregrine, gesturing to a chair by his desk. "So, Sangster, take a seat and tell me how your investigation is progressing. Jones will be in with coffee in a minute."

"Moving along, Sir Peregrine, but still some way to go."

"Police everywhere today. Dogs, officers with sticks prodding bushes, must be hundreds of people. Do they really need you as well, Sangster?"

There was a knock on the door and Jones entered, carrying a tray.

"Just set it down on my desk, Jones," Sir Peregrine said, mopping his brow with a handkerchief. "And make sure we're not interrupted again, I can't manage any more questions this morning." He passed me a cup as Jones left the room.

"As I've not been taken off the case," I answered, taking a sip of tea. "I assume they do need me, and I'm anyway here to look at things the police might miss."

"You're that good?"

"That's not what I meant. Just different."

"I'm sorry. Now how can I help you?"

"That map you showed me the other day, you called it a geo—"

"Geological survey map."

"Yes, showing the something-or-other batholith."

"Cornubian. The map's here in the cupboard, like to see it again?" I nodded, and he pulled down the rolled-up map, stretching it out on the table in front of us. "Awkward to read, tends to curl up." He proceeded to hold the corners down using the coffee set; pot, milk jug, sugar bowl, and biscuit plate. "Anything particular about this map?"

"We're here, right?" I pointed to a red patch.

"Yes, that's the Dartmoor pluton."

"A place where volcanic rock outcrops, right?"

"Correct, and this is the site of Highmoor." He placed his finger on a black ink dot. "De Coverley drew that spot on the map, I think."

"I see, and sorry to be a pain, but you don't have a larger scale map of this area, do you?"

"Ordnance or geological?"

"Oh, er… geological."

"One moment." Several more rolled-up maps fell out as he scrabbled in the cupboard. "Here we are." He brandished a rather jaundiced-looking scroll. "Haven't seen this in an age. From my predecessor's time, I think."

"Henry Weaver?"

"Indeed, now…" He carefully untied two ribbons from the scroll and opened the map, which showed a faded representation of the rocks that made up the area of moorland around Princetown. "Oh," Sir Peregrine exclaimed, pointing to several ink spots, "De Coverley's been writing on it too, see."

The spots seemed to be in a familiar pattern, but I couldn't be sure, as the map was concerned with geology, not geography. There were no place names.

"You said the rocks here are perfect for your research, Sir Peregrine." He nodded. "Why is that?"

"Several reasons. There's the mineralogy for a start. Makes for very good conductivity."

"Electrical?"

"I suppose so, you'd have to ask De Coverley for details."

"And the other reasons?"

"There's a series of vents, natural tubes within the granite. They spread out in an underground network, and this allows for the safe dissipation of the massive energy we sometimes need to generate. We couldn't do that if the Highmoor were built on, say, a sandstone or limestone formation."

"I see."

"Anything else, Sangster? I really am very busy. We've had two generator outages in as many days and De Coverley's not been around since Tuesday."

"Do you know where he is?"

"No, disappeared off the face of the earth, and I really am at my wits' end."

"I'll not keep you long then. I just wanted to ask about the original facility here." I pointed out of the window towards the hill and the Old Centre. "What kind of a man was Henry Weaver?"

"I never knew him, I'm afraid. He passed away and they appointed me to oversee the build of this place. You'd have to ask De Coverley, the two of them were very close."

"And this Weaver's research?"

"Very hush-hush. MOD stuff from the end of the war. After Henry Weaver died, they stopped using the Old Centre, shut down its reactor, stripped out anything worth salvaging, then bricked the place up and surrounded it with barbed wire."

"Seems strange not to knock it down."

"As I said last time we met, De Coverley lobbied that it be kept as a shrine to commemorate Weaver's work."

"Very laudable of the MOD to accommodate him, Sir Peregrine."

"I always say in front of De Coverley that it might have been cheaper to knock the place down, but I actually think, Sangster…" he said this with a wink, "the decision had far more to do with saving the pennies than De Coverley thinks. Cost of completely demolishing a former nuclear site would be prohibitive, so better merely to contain any residual radioactivity." He lit another cigarette. "A fully-functioning reactor in a place accessible to the public's not something they'd want generally known, though, all those protestors around and so on." He winked again. "Far cheaper just to wall it up and keep the place off-limits." He stood up. "Now, if there's nothing else, I really must be getting on."

"I'll leave you in peace, Sir Peregrine," I said, also standing up.

"Jones," he shouted down his intercom, "Sangster's leaving."

"Goodbye, and thank you for your time." I held out my hand. "Oh, would you, er… mind awfully if I kept this for a while?" I pointed to the faded map with the ink spots.

"A bit irregular, but very well. Jones?" he called, rolling up the map and retying its ribbons.

"Sir Peregrine?"

"Make sure Sangster signs for this." He handed me the map, then turned back to his desk, muttering quietly that it was high time De Coverley came back to work.

"Just sign here, sir," said Jones, passing me a pen and paper from his desk outside the office door.

"Is Sir Peregrine under particular pressure right now?" I asked, scribbling my signature.

"He's, er… missing Doctor De Coverley. Sir Peregrine's really a political figure, no eye for detail."

"But De Coverley's been gone what, two days at most?"

"We've had unexplained power outages twice during that time."

"And nobody else can help?"

"Doctor De Coverley, now how can I put it… likes to keep control by only telling people what he thinks they need to know. That way, nobody has the overall picture but him, not even Sir Peregrine."

"I see, well, thank you."

"Thank you, sir."

12:30 PM

The tinkling doorbell of Jay's store rang as I entered, and I looked across at the café to see Mercy sitting in the corner, magazine held against her face, blue smoke curling up from behind it.

"Ahem." I coughed, walking towards her as she lowered the magazine.

"Don't sit down."

"Sorry?"

"I've been in here well over an hour, Jack," she said, stubbing out her cigarette. "My left leg's gone numb and I can't stay any longer."

"But I'm starving."

"Look, there's a little pub on the way to Yelverton and they do a nice ploughman's lunch, OK?"

"OK," I nodded, as Mercy stood up and Verity came over to the table.

"May I clear this away now, Mrs Merrivale?"

"Yes, please, Verity. Now, Jack, I'm just popping to the loo. Three pots of tea take their toll."

"Alright." I laughed. "Let me get the bill and I'll see you outside."

I went to the counter and waited for Verity.

"That'll be four and six, please, Mr Sangster."

"Here's five bob, can you give me a receipt?"

"Thank you," she said, placing my coins in the till. "And you will find him, won't you?" She lowered her voice to a whisper and rubbed her belly. "Every day I worry Dad will find out. I can't hide it forever."

"I'm doing everything I can, and so are the police. If Christopher's to be found, we'll find him."

Verity handed me the receipt as Mercy reappeared.

"Here's my *Woman's Own*, Verity," she said, passing the magazine over the counter. "I've read the thing from cover to cover, so someone else might like it."

"Kind of you, Mrs Merrivale."

"Alright," I said to Mercy as we left the shop. "I was longer than I expected with Sir Peregrine, but I learned a lot."

"Can you tell me what you learned?"

"Let's wait until lunch," I said, holding the car door open as she stepped inside.

"Whatever you say, and Jack, don't you notice anything different about me?"

I sat down in the driver's seat and looked at Mercy as she displayed her even white teeth in the broadest of smiles.

"Er..." All the usual differences, new hairdo, clothes, etc., surely didn't apply, so I couldn't imagine what she meant. I even wondered if she'd put on a lot more make-up, but it didn't seem so.

"I'm smiling, for heaven's sake."

"So you are."

"It's Mel, she's come back." Mercy shook her head with exasperation. "I called the hotel while you were up at the centre, and they put her on."

"Do you know why? I mean, after she wrote that note—"

"I'm not questioning what's happened, Jack," she said, punching my shoulder. "I'm just grateful to know she's home."

"Do you want me to take you back now?"

"No, Mel said she wanted to rest, so I'll see her later this afternoon. Oh, what's that?" She pointed to the glove compartment, which was open, and touched the protruding cassette.

"Oh, er... cassette tape player. They just fitted it for me."

"We have one of those at the hotel, bought it for dictation actually, help with Mel's studies." She touched the cassette again, almost caressing it. "I didn't know you could have one in the car, so play something on it, Jack, please?"

"Oh, no, I've only one cassette, it's not very—"

"No, go on."

"Alright." I pushed in the tape and Mantovani's soft, orchestral string music filled the car.

"I know that tune, Jack." She lifted her hair and cocked an ear. "Now what's it called again?"

"Um… *Elizabethan Serenade*. I'm going to get something more modern when I—"

"No, no, shush…" She put her finger to her lips then closed her eyes. "The sun's shining, Mel is back home, I love it."

As the strings rose to a fine crescendo, I inwardly admitted I rather loved it too. And with thoughts of Septimus Frere and his Drake obsession, I couldn't help feeling *Elizabethan Serenade* to be as appropriate as anything we could have listened to.

1 PM

"Here we are, Jack," said Mercy as we pulled up outside the Black Talbot Tavern, an ancient-looking stone-built pub standing alone by the edge of the moor. The outline of the building and the landscape behind it looked familiar somehow.

"Could I have seen this on a picture somewhere?"

"Er…" Mercy scratched her head. "Of course you have, it's in the background of that pig picture in the dining room."

"Ah yes." I regarded the long, low building, which, besides being remote (we had bumped about a mile up a track from the main road to reach it), also looked one step away from being condemned. "Are you sure about this place?"

"Don't worry, the Talbot's mostly renovated inside, and I know the landlady. Her food and beer make up for the state of the outside."

"Hope so." I grimaced, looking up at the patched slate roof. "Wouldn't like to be under that in a thunderstorm."

"Now come on, Jack, you go inside and order us a couple of ploughman's lunches."

"Where are you going?" I asked as she stepped out of the car.

"Privy," she called, running round the side. "All that tea."

"Drink?"

"Just a shandy, and Jack," Mercy shouted, as she disappeared behind a shed to the side of the pub.

"Yes."

"You're not on the tourist trail here. Mind your Ps and Qs."

I looked above the pub doorway to see a sign ('M. Cobley, licensed to sell liquor, beer, and cigarettes'), and above that, a moss-covered stone, engraved with the almost illegible characters '1596 AD'. Stepping forward, I twisted the knob on the door, but it didn't move, the only sound to be heard a slight creaking from the pub's wooden sign, which hung from the wall on a metal sprit and bore a picture of a prancing black dog. The paint was faded and flaking, and the animal's proportions seemed crudely wrong, but for all that the artist had caught something, the dog's wicked red eye staring down at me as if to say, 'I'm watching you, mate'.

I went to try the knob again but, before I could turn it, fell forward as the door opened.

"You better come in, sir," called a high-pitched voice from within. "Knob's a bit stiff with all the damp weather we've had, eh, lads?"

I heard murmurs of agreement and, blinking in the dim light, entered the pub to see a diminutive and expressionless woman standing before me. The room itself matched her demeanour, with low ceilings, oak beams, and nicotine-coloured plaster. There were few decorations, just a pair of tarnished horse brasses, a yard of ale and a horse collar hanging on the walls, while in a stone niche behind the bar, someone had placed an ancient-looking leather shoe. A group of men, all over seventy, I guessed, sat in one corner next to an enormous fireplace, which was hung with several blackened iron pots that dangled above the unlit grate. Next to the bar stood two younger men, both tall and, I guessed by their dress, farmhands or engaged in some other kind of outdoor work. Other than that, the room was empty of customers.

"Is there something you'd like, sir?" asked the landlady.

"Er... a half of shandy?" Sniggers echoed from the fireplace. "A pint of your ale there," I added quickly, pointing to a polished wooden beer pump. "And two ploughman's lunches if you have them."

"Yes, we have them," the woman said flatly, pouring my pint. And as she did so, I became more and more uncomfortable with the atmosphere (and not just because it was choked with blue smoke), the men by the fireplace staring directly at me, and the two by the bar doing the same.

"That your car outside?" said one.

"Yes."

"Fine-looking motor," said the other. "We watched you pull up just now." He pointed to a small window next to the door. "But I'm surprised you could get a low-slung thing like that up the lane."

"Be even more surprised if he can get it back down the lane, eh, Clive?" said the other.

They both laughed.

"Oh, I'll manage," I said.

"I wouldn't be too sure if you don't know the road," said Clive with a smirk. "Now if you just give me the keys," he said, holding out his hand, "I can drive her down to the Tavistock road for you."

"Thanks, but no thanks," I said with a sigh.

"You saying you don't trust my brother Clive's driving?"

"No," I said, turning away. "Now how much is that?"

"Eight and six," said the landlady, looking at the two by the bar apprehensively.

"Don't you turn you back on us, mister high and mighty," said Clive, placing his hand on my shoulder.

"Listen, friend, I don't want any—"

Clive then seemed to lunge at me, and I side-stepped so that he sprawled across the bar, knocking over the pint and the shandy glasses in the process. I then jumped backwards, partly to avoid my trousers getting a soaking but mostly to be ready for whatever happened next. They were both big men with at least twenty-five years on me, and nobody else in the bar seemed prepared to intervene. The landlady stood stock still with her button mouth closed, and the old men by the fireplace simply grinned and puffed on their pipes.

I gulped, then tensed myself, fists raised and expecting the worst.

"I broke my nose, Marty," cried Clive, lifting himself up to reveal an untouched nose but a bruised forehead and bloody lip. Marty put his arm around Clive, who had begun to cry, then looked at me.

"Look what you done to Clive," he said, almost crying himself. "He only wanted to help."

"Your brother tried to hit me," I shouted. "I just jumped out of the way."

"You're a cruel man, that's what you are."

The old men by the fireplace murmured 'cruel man' in chorus.

"Come on, Clive," coaxed Marty. "You sit down here on this stool and Mildred will fetch you a nice rejuvenating glass of scrumpy, won't you, Mildred?"

Mildred's button mouth remained closed as she turned the tap on a cider barrel behind the bar and filled a jug with cloudy-green/brown liquid. Clive, meanwhile, continued to blub as Marty dabbed blood from his lip with a bar towel.

"You'll be wanting new drinks?" asked Mildred once the scrumpy was poured.

"Er... you know," I said, turning towards the door, "actually, I'd better be—"

"Hello, Mildred, that knob still sticking in the damp?" Mercy's willowy frame appeared in the doorway, shafts of sunlight shining into the room from behind her.

"Afternoon, Missus," said the landlady, the old fireplace men murmuring the same.

"Clive and Marty Eggins," Mercy then exclaimed, looking at the two brothers. "What have you been doing?"

"I'd rather not say, Missus," said Clive, lifting his head up and pointing to me. "You better ask him."

"Everything alright, Jack?"

"Er... fine." I shrugged.

"That's alright then. Mildred, did Jack order for us?"

"Pint of bitter, half of bitter shandy and two ploughman's. I already poured two new drinks after the first lot got spilled."

"Oh dear, anyway, can you bring the food into the snug, please?"

"Right you are, Missus."

Mercy led me into a narrow, L-shaped room that seemed protected from the thick atmosphere in the main bar. I took my first breath of relatively fresh air since entering the pub, then sighed as she lit a cigarette.

"This is a friendly place," I said, taking a long and well-earned, I felt, drink of ale.

"What happened?"

"That Clive character started ragging me, then he lunged and tripped on the bar."

"Are you alright?"

"Oh, I'm alright, but the whole place now has me down as some sort of bully."

"Jack," she laughed, stroking my arm, "Clive and his brother are, as my mother might say, a bit ninepence to the shilling, but harmless."

"Have you seen the size of them?"

"Oh yes, they do odd jobs for me now and again."

"And everyone in here called you Missus, even the landlady."

"That's er…" Mercy smiled, "because I own the place. It's tied to the Wyvern."

"Then I'm glad," I laughed, "that I didn't end up paying that landlady, what's her name?"

"Mildred."

"Yes, paying Mildred eight and six."

"Jack, you miser," Mercy said with mock sternness, "Mildred's got a living to make, and I don't take any money out of this pub. In fact, if you must know I paid to have it renovated a couple of years ago."

"God knows what the place must have looked like before," I muttered, as Mildred appeared with our lunches.

*

"So Jack," said Mercy, pushing her plate to one side, "Uncle Perry, what did he tell you?"

"A big part was what he didn't tell me."

"Sorry?"

"Well, your uncle seems stumped without De Coverley. Couldn't answer some of my questions and was struggling with the day-to-day running of the place."

"Yes, I'm afraid he always was more politician than hands-on."

"That's what his assistant Jones said."

"Is that…" she pointed to the ribbon tied scroll I'd brought into the pub from the car, "from your visit as well?"

"Yes," I said, untying it. "I was wondering if you could shed any light on the thing, look." I spread the map out across the table and pointed to the ink spots. "Do you know where these are?"

"Is that one the Highmoor Centre?" Mercy asked.

"Yes, so can you tell where these places are?"

"This one," she said, pointing to the nearest dot, "is in Princetown itself, right under St Michael's Church, I'd say."

"And the others?"

"Well, this is Wistman's Wood."

"Yeah."

"And this is…" She stopped, then put her head in her hands.

"What, Mercy?"

"This is the bridge on the Postgate road, where we swerved that time. Remember?"

"And this other spot?" I said, deciding not to press further about the bridge.

"Oh… that's right behind the hotel, in the field with the standing stones."

"Right, well, come on, we'd better be getting going."

"Do these places mean anything to you?"

"I think they do, Mercy, yes."

"Care to tell me?"

"Not yet, now I'd better go and pay."

*

"That was eight and six, wasn't it?" I asked the landlady, who silently took my money.

"And for the two spilled drinks," Mercy reminded me.

"Of course," I said, handing over a further half-crown.

"Where are Clive and Marty, Mildred?"

"Gone outside, Missus. Clive's upset, I…" She leaned forwards and whispered, Mercy nodding back to her.

"Come on, Jack," Mercy then said loudly. "Let's go."

"Before we go," I asked the landlady, "I have to know. Why is there a shoe there behind the bar?"

"For luck, sir."

"Luck?"

"Aye, sir. When we were doing the renovations two years back, builders found that shoe bricked up inside a wall. Blokes from the museum in Plymouth said it would have been placed there deliberately, hundreds of years ago, to bring the house good luck. Then the museum men took it away, and after that we had all sorts of troubles. Roof fell in, our deep well got poisoned, chimney collapsed, septic tank sprung a leak, even the cat got run over, all sorts. Missus here asked the museum to return the shoe."

"And did it bring back the good luck?"

"Works all went as smooth as can be after that, sir. Look around for yourself." She glanced across the smoke-filled bar room. "Got a new cat as well." She pointed at a tabby, curled up by the fireplace. "Beautiful room now, isn't it?"

"Oh, er… yes." I nodded, mustering what enthusiasm I could.

"Jack, I think you should touch it," said Mercy.

"The cat?"

"No, silly, the shoe?"

"Er… should I?"

"Yes, you need all the luck you can get right now."

Mildred muttered her agreement, so I walked behind the bar and placed my hand on the shoe, which felt oddly warm, the rough surface of the material making my fingertips tingle.

"OK, Mercy," I said, pulling my arm away with a shudder. "That's done, now let's get on to Yelverton."

As we walked towards the door, the old men by the fireplace nodded deferentially whilst Mercy whispered to me, "Clive Eggins is known as 'Clumsy Clive' around here. Mildred said he was just leaning towards you and, as she put it, 'he came over all wrong'. He's very upset."

"Well, Clive and his brother were ragging me like I said, being sarcastic about driving the car down the lane. That wasn't clumsy, it was simply spoiling for a fight."

"Oh, Jack, you really are a long way from home. The Eggins brothers might be big, but they've got children's minds and they wouldn't know sarcasm if it bit them on the elbow."

"Alright, I'll say something," I said as we walked out into the sunshine to see the brothers standing by my car. "Clive," I called, "are you alright now?" He nodded. "Want to take the Jag for a turn round the car park?" He nodded again, vigorously this time, and I passed him the keys.

"You do have a licence, Clive?" asked Mercy.

"My brother can handle a car, Missus," said Marty, as Clive sat down in the driver's seat smiling, eyes wide with a look of glee. I suddenly wondered whether I shouldn't have offered to be the driver.

"Turn the key then press that button." Clive started the car with a massive rev. "Just stay in first and easy on the throttle," I shouted, my muscles tensing as he bumped off in a series of circles across the asphalt.

"Keep an eye on him, Mercy," I yelled across the car park as the Jag continued to rev. "I need to use that privy."

"Too much beer?" she called after me.

"No, but Clumsy Clive's driving's playing havoc with my bladder."

2 PM

"Clutch seems to have survived." Mercy laughed as we sped down the main road.

"Hopefully my touching that shoe saved the car from Clive's less-than-gentle touch," I answered, but with no real conviction, remembering the grating sound of Clive changing gear.

"Perhaps touching the shoe will do more than that – after all, it worked for Mildred."

"Maybe it will work for Christopher De Coverley then." As I spoke, it occurred to me that if my work on the boy's case turned out anything like the renovations at the Black Talbot Tavern, I'd better get another job.

*

Once again, the sign *'Closed to visitors'* hung on the open gates of Reynard's Hall.

"You're sure Uncle Septimus is in?" asked Mercy as we continued up the driveway.

"The navy's delivering some equipment to him today, so he should be in. Likely closed up so he can use it without being disturbed, yes…" I pointed to a dark blue van with *'RN'* on its side. "They'll have brought the gear in that."

We pulled up next to the van to see a uniformed rating leaning against the door and smoking a cigarette.

"Excuse me, is Lieutenant Jolly here?"

"Who wants to know?"

"Commander Sangster."

"Sir," said the rating, stubbing out his cigarette under foot and standing to attention. "They went that way, to the kitchen garden, I believe." He pointed in the direction of the dig.

"Thank you… er?"

"Ordinary Seaman Brown, sir."

"Thank you, Brown," I said, looking at a white estate car parked behind the naval van, its door bearing the words:

Plymouth Polytechnic
(Incorporating Plymouth Institute of Marine Studies)

"And is there someone else with them?"

"Yes, sir, a Doctor Stewer."

"Should be interesting," I said to Mercy as we walked across the lawn. "Stewer and your uncle hate each other."

"I know." She laughed. "Stewer's the one whose been rubbishing Uncle Septimus in the newspaper."

*

As we arrived at the kitchen garden wall I heard raised voices and, walking through the entrance, saw Septimus Frere, arms flailing wildly. He was shouting at another man, tall, thin, of early middle age, and wearing a brown trilby, underneath which a mop of black hair protruded.

"The whole point of using this equipment, Stewer," Frere yelled, "is so I can prove you wrong."

"I can't be wrong," the other answered. "You found modern shells in the cache. That's all we need to know."

"Someone's put them there, Stewer. Wasn't you, was it?"

"How dare you, I'll—" Frere's tall antagonist raised his fist, and I suspect would have punched Frere despite their age difference if Lieutenant Jolly hadn't intervened.

"That'll do, gents," he said, stepping between the two warring academics. "We're here to try and resolve any issues beneath the ground, not above it." He pointed to a pair of uniformed ratings, who were wheeling what looked for all the world to me like an enormous child's pushchair, I noticed 'Fisher GPR' was printed on the side, taking the machine to and fro over the area of the cache and the surrounding land.

"Everything alright, Jolly?"

"Commander Sangster," the lieutenant replied. "Good to see you again, sir."

"And is it?" I said, looking at Frere and Stewer, who were still looking daggers at each other. "Alright, I mean."

"Mr Jack Sangster," sighed Frere, taking a step backwards, "may I introduce Doctor Thomas Stewer. And Stewer, this is my niece, Mercedes Merrivale."

"Heard of you, Sangster," said Stewer, holding out his hand before visually appraising Mercy, whose slim figure and breeze blown yellow hair clearly drew his attention. She linked her arm into mine and stared back at him.

"Ahem…" Stewer coughed. "A pleasure to meet you, Mercedes." I thought by this he felt contrite, but he then turned back to Frere. "And thank God she doesn't get her looks from your side of the family, Frere."

"Why you…" This time Frere raised his fist, whilst Mercy looked at me and rolled her eyeballs.

"Gentlemen, please," said Jolly. "Any more of this and we're packing up."

"Why all the arguing, Uncle?" Mercy asked.

"Stewer here doubts my contention that the weapons cache we found is Elizabethan, and all I've done is invite him here today so he can see for himself that it is."

"How will you know?"

"The equerry's diary clearly says they buried something else here, so if that, er…" he pointed to the wheeled GPR unit and its two operators, "contraption gets a hit, and we can dig it up, then we're in luck."

"Look, Frere," said Doctor Stewer, "I'm not saying all the contents of this cache are modern, I just doubt they were buried here by Drake."

"By that line of arguing," Frere said, voice raised and arms waving again, "whatever we find, you'll doubt it."

"What about…" I said, a little unsure of myself but remembering an article I'd recently read, "radiocarbon dating? Wouldn't that settle it?"

"No good," said Frere and Stewer in unison, shaking their heads (I guessed the two had far more in common than they would ever dare to admit).

"Why not?"

"Too much room for error," said Stewer, Frere nodding in agreement. "Could be contamination as well," added Stewer. "It wouldn't be definitive."

"So Doctor Stewer, what really would satisfy you?"

"Corroborative evidence, such as a document detailing some event, not directly related to Drake or Reynard, so we could fix a precise date to it."

"Sadly," said Frere, "they didn't write much down in those days."

"But even if you found such a document, how would you know that was genuine?"

"We can carbon date the paper fairly well," said Stewer. "But not the actual ink, which means there can be modern forgeries using genuinely old paper. So… it's the independent event that we need, like, say, a documented eclipse at a specific date or time or… or something." He shook his head. "And I'm afraid Septimus here," he looked at Frere with disdain, "doesn't have any corroborative evidence through such an event and hasn't even found his precious hidden artifact, in fact—"

Doctor Stewer was cut short by a whistle blowing, and I looked across the kitchen garden to see one of the ratings holding up his hand.

"Hit here, sir," he shouted. "About eighteen feet below the surface."

"Can you tell what it is?" Jolly called back.

"No, sir, but we can check for metal."

He took up a long pole with a flat disc about a foot in diameter attached to the end, then plugged in a pair of headphones and began sweeping across the ground.

"What on earth's that sailor got in his hand?" Mercy whispered to me.

"Is that what I think it is, Jolly?"

"Yes, sir, mine detector, borrowed from the Marines. I wanted to be prepared."

"Very commendable, carry on."

"Yes, sir," Jolly answered with a grin, as the rating in the headphones raised his hand again.

"Metallic object," he called out. "And like I said, sir, eighteen feet under."

"Could your men, er… possibly dig it out for us?" Frere asked.

"Sorry, Professor Frere, beyond my remit. I was instructed to bring the GPR rig here and help you find what you were looking for, that's all." Jolly waved to the ratings. "Alright, chaps, pack her up and we'll be on our way back to Devonport."

The ratings planted a small red flag in the ground where they had made their 'hit' then quickly dismantled the 'contraption', as Frere called it, and left, along with Lieutenant Jolly. Before the lieutenant went, however, I reminded him that we had a call organised later on about the origin of the two fifty-cal shells.

"Of course, Commander Sangster. We're pretty short-staffed right now, but I saw the lab techs working on them this morning, so it should be fine for five this afternoon."

*

"Let's just agree to disagree," said Stewer to Frere, in what I felt was intended to be a conciliatory voice, as we watched the blue naval van pull away down the drive.

"Very well," said Frere. "And I don't want to fight over it either, Stewer," he added, as Mercy, standing behind the professor's back, nodded to me and mouthed the words 'yes, he bloody well does'.

"But I am convinced this cache is Elizabethan and of profound importance to our proper understanding of Drake and the Armada."

"Find your artifact and get your corroborative evidence then, Frere," said Stewer. "And I, for one, will be your biggest supporter."

"Ha, easier said than done. How am I going to dig eighteen feet down after what may be a wild goose chase?" the professor said, almost crying.

"Ah," said Stewer, wagging his finger at Frere. "So you admit it might be a wild—"

"Have you a phone I can use?" interjected Mercy.

"Er… yes, Mercedes. Maisy?" Almost before Frere shouted, Maisy Whiddon appeared at the door. "Take my niece to the office, would you? She needs to make a call."

Mercy returned with a smile a few minutes later. "There'll be two blokes along with spades in twenty minutes. They'll dig out whatever's under your kitchen garden, Uncle, and you can leave it to me to pay them."

"Thank you, my dear." Frere beamed.

"Mercy, it…" my mind flashed back to the Black Talbot Tavern, "wasn't the Eggins brothers you called, was it?"

"They can do the job and they're free this afternoon, so yes, Jack, it was the Egginses."

"Good luck with the dig, Professor."

"Thank you, Sangster," Frere replied, my irony clearly lost on him. "And you, Stewer, I'll see you eat your hat."

"Glad to eat it if anything turns up, and you two can be my witnesses," he answered, nodding to Mercy and me, then taking off the apparently edible trilby in question before opening his car door.

"Oh, and Stewer," said Frere, squinting at the doctor's tie, "I perceive you ate smoked haddock for lunch."

"How on earth could you know that, when you haven't even been close enough to smell my breath?"

"Elementary observation, Stewer, I detect traces of fish skin on your tie, and haddock scales are unmistakable."

"Well, I am impressed, I... hang on a minute, we both had finnan haddock for lunch." He shook his head. "Miss Whiddon served it in your refectory."

"Oh," wailed Frere. "I suppose she did."

"Now if you don't mind," Stewer said, opening his car door, "I need to be getting back to the Poly." He started the engine, then wound down his window. "And remember, Frere, you don't just need your artifact." He began to wind his window up again. "You need your compelling event as well, fully documented and dated, otherwise... we... won't..." His voice trailed off as the window closed.

"Whippersnapper," shouted Frere after Doctor Stewer's car as it drove away.

3 PM

"I'll take you back to the hotel now, Mercy," I said as we drove out of the gates.

"Was that your last visit of the day?"

"No, last one's with the police. But that's not until six and you've Mel to see and a business to run."

We drove silently through Yelverton and back onto the road to Princetown, passing the track that led to the Black Talbot. This time I noticed a sign with an arrow stating:

Black Talbot Tavern Freehouse
Good Beer & Food
Warm Fire & Welcome

I smiled inwardly at the last line.

"That's a very old pub, how long's it been in your family?"

"What makes you think the Talbot's so old?"

"Keystone over the door has '1596' carved into it."

"Ah, well, no, you see…"

Mercy went on to tell me that although the building dated back almost four hundred years, it was just an old Devon longhouse until her grandfather ('he was a "Jack", just like you') bought the place around the turn of the century and turned it into a pub. And this Jack Curtice, it seemed, named the pub for his favourite dog, an otter hound called Talbot.

"But Jack, less of the history lessons, are you any nearer to finding out about Christopher?"

The only ideas I had were outlandish in the extreme, and still very ill-formed, so I said nothing and drove on, Mercy looking sideways at me for a moment then staring straight ahead.

"What time's your appointment in Plymouth again?" she asked a few minutes later, as we drove past Princetown.

"Six."

"Well, Mel will still be resting, and the next right turn takes us down to Foxtor House. Might be worth having a check around there?"

I looked at the car clock. Three fifteen. There would be time, and Foxtor House was the last place mentioned in the police file left to visit. I'd been waiting until John De Coverley reappeared, but my instinct now was that the wait to see the absent doctor would last until at least tomorrow, which, I'd had drummed into me at school, 'never comes', so why not have Mercy show me today? Like many times before, I felt right then she might somehow help me get to the bottom of things, and if Melissa was really resting, the thought didn't sit right somehow, and I felt as anxious to see the girl as to see De Coverley, perhaps even more so now I had spoken to Whiddon about her, then there was plenty of time to visit Foxtor House.

"You know the place well, I guess?"

"All my life, Jack."

"Alright." I swerved hard right and down a track even narrower than the one leading to the Black Talbot Tavern. "Let's have a look at Foxtor House then." I slowed down to a crawl as the hedges either side of us tickled the car wing mirrors. "If we make it that far."

*

"So is this it, Mercy?"

"Yes, Jack, Foxtor House is one of the first big houses built in the area. Sixteenth century."

"Looks like something dreamed up by Edgar Allen Poe," I said, as we passed through granite gateposts topped by rampant gryphons, beaks agape and staring with either surprise or hostility, I could not decide which. The stone creatures had presumably stared like this at every visitor during the last four centuries.

The house itself was no less eerie-looking, a 'rambling gothic pile, Jack', as my wife Sarah would likely have said, built of dark Dartmoor stone, complete with turrets, mullioned windows, and arched doorways, its roof boasting crenelations and gargoyles in equal measure.

"Look over there," Mercy said, pointing down the valley towards a grassy open area, where distant figures could be seen slowly walking in a line. "Must be the police search."

"Certainly seems to be," I said, stepping out of the car. "And here's a copper now."

We walked up to a uniformed officer standing by the front door.

"Sorry, sir, this is being treated as a crime scene, no entry, and I must ask you to leave the way you came."

"Oh, come on," said Mercy. "I know the owner, and I come here all the time."

"Nevertheless, Madam, I must insist that—"

"Will this do?" I said, pulling out the Granville Institute's mandate document.

"And you are this…" the constable scrutinised the paper, "Special Investigator J.G. Sangster?"

"I am," I said, showing him my driving licence.

"Very well, sir," he eventually said, gesturing to the front door, which, I now saw, was slightly ajar, with a splintered lock that must have been broken open by the police. "Please proceed, but don't touch anything, like documents or whatnot." I wondered what the 'whatnot' might be, but simply nodded. "And let me know when you are leaving, Mr Sangster."

*

"Ooh, Jack." Mercy shivered, linking her arm through mine as we entered Foxtor House. "This place doesn't feel lived in at all."

"You been here recently?" I asked, looking around at the hallway, a large, panelled room with a wooden staircase and gallery above, around which were hung numerous portraits.

"No, Jack, not for a while, but it used to be, well…" she pointed to a chandelier, which was unilluminated and covered in cobwebs, "a bit more inviting."

"Copper on the door said the lights were all fused, didn't he?"

"Yes, Jack, but even so, this house feels… well, no longer wanted."

The ground floor showed little sign of habitation, with dusty furniture and a kitchen that, judging by its dusty sink, clearly hadn't been used for some time. We then climbed the stairs and walked across the landing, past empty bedrooms with some of the doors hanging open in a way that further accentuated the sense of emptiness.

"Looks like there's nothing to be found here," I said, as we opened a last door. "This is just a broom cupboard."

"Do you know what you are looking for, Jack?"

"Apart from Doctor De Coverley and his son, no, not really."

"It's almost as if John hasn't been living here, and yet we've all seen him."

"Yes, I—"

"Hey, I remember there's an attic up here." Mercy walked into a small side landing and pointed to a trapdoor with a ring on it, high in a corner of the ceiling and almost completely obscured by a wardrobe.

"Easy enough for the police to miss, but if we're going to get in up there, we need something to pull the door open, and a ladder."

"Hang on a minute." She walked round the corner and opened the broom-cupboard door again. "Voila," she then said, lifting a window pole and folding stepladder out. "Help me, will you?"

We both heaved the wardrobe to one side, then Mercy lifted the pole and pulled the trapdoor, which opened to a shower of dust and cobwebs. Given they had been searching today, it seemed clear the police had indeed missed it.

"I'll go first."

I followed Mercy up the ladder and into the attic, which was dark except for a brittle beam of light from a tiny window at one end. I gazed around and made out what looked to be cisterns and piping, but not much else. I saw a single light bulb hanging from the centre roof beam and clicked a switch on the wall, but to no avail.

"This should help." Mercy lifted up a tilly lamp, then lit the wick with a match from her pocket. "That's better… oh."

The light from the lamp showed the attic as it really was. Down the centre stood a long table, strewn with papers. Next to this were signs that people had been living here recently, including two unmade camp beds, a small gas stove, saucepans, cups, plates, cutlery, bottles, and tinned food. There was also a white porcelain sink, cold tap only, as I found when I tried it, with a mirror behind.

"There's a loo up here as well," said Mercy, drawing back a curtain in the corner to reveal a toilet.

"Is that lipstick on the shelf under the mirror?"

Mercy picked up a gold-coloured cylinder and unscrewed the top. "Hmmm… Revlon Kissable Pink." She turned to me with a frown. "And unless Doctor John De Coverley has a whole other side to him, my guess is that Mel has been here as well."

"Really?"

"Yes, I bought that lipstick, or one exactly like it, for her a few weeks ago."

"And what's this?" On one end of the table stood several bottles, some with pills and some with liquid, as well as a leather case, which, on opening, revealed a syringe and several vials of liquid.

"Drugs," said Mercy. "I knew I couldn't trust Mel."

"Er, no," I said, picking up one of the bottles, its handwritten label stating:

Codeine Phosphate 30mg
1–2 tablets every four hours or as needed
Max 240mg per day

Another bottle's label stated:

Flurazepam 15mg
1 tablet orally per day women, 1–2 men

"At least not those kind of drugs. These tablets are probably for insomnia and pain relief, and the syringe for insulin. Melissa's not diabetic, is she?"

"No."

"And these papers on the table…" I picked up the nearest, a faded blueprint entitled '*Die Glocke*'. "I've seen something like them before, amongst the papers confiscated from Jane Ustrix. And these," I said, picking up a sheaf of handwritten notes, "all seem to relate to Drake and the Armada."

"I'd like to get back soon, Jack. See Melissa."

"Sure."

"Better leave everything as we found it, police didn't want anything touched."

"Alright, Mercy," I answered as she replaced the lipstick on the shelf. "And look here." Behind a screen was another window, this time completely covered by wooden shutters. "Let me open these." I turned the catch, which was broken so that the shutters were actually hanging loose, and looked out, to see a narrow iron fire escape leading down the wall and obscured by a pine tree. "This would be the way in and out if you didn't want to be seen."

"But why would John live up here, and for quite a few months if the state of the house is anything to go by?"

"Didn't want to be seen, I guess, although judging by all those pills he might have gone a bit…"

"Crazy?" Mercy finished my sentence with a question and a whisper.

*

"Thank you, Mr Sangster, Mrs Merrivale, we'll have the attic looked at as you suggest. Search team aren't knocking off until sundown, but after that there'll be plenty of people to check it out."

"We'll bid you a good afternoon then, Officer," I said, as we turned towards the car. "And that would be the Old Centre?" I pointed to a small hill about two hundred yards away.

"Yes, sir. Search team already found De Coverley's car there, abandoned in some bushes."

"Would you mind if we walked up to it, Mercy? I'd just like a quick look around."

"It's all closed up, but OK." She shrugged. "As long as we're not too long and you watch out for those dark patches."

I looked across the flat meadow that lay between us and the building. "Mires?"

"That's right. Always boggy here, no matter what the weather. Not sure why."

We walked on, carefully avoiding the wet patches, then began to climb.

"Can you hear water, Jack?"

"Under the ground by these bushes, yes, I can, and it's… oops, hello."

I started, taking a jump backwards as a whiskered face stared out at me from the undergrowth. The whiskers' owner, an otter, four, perhaps even five feet long and standing on hind legs, then turned, and with a swish of its tail, disappeared again.

"Where'd he go?" cried Mercy.

"Down here." I parted the bushes to see a rusting metal wheel on top of a stone hatch, where a slab, presumably intended as a cover, was slightly displaced. From within, the sound of running water could be heard. "Give me a hand," I said, and we both gripped the slab then pushed, the stone slowly scraping open to reveal an underground stream and a metal ladder leading down to the remains of a sluice gate.

"So that's how Old Soldier escapes from the hunt," gasped Mercy as we stood up and caught our breath. "A hidden culvert running down from the hill and into the mires."

"You'd still think the hounds would find him, though."

"Yes, you would, Jack."

"Let me climb down."

"Careful," said Mercy as I descended the ladder, which creaked as if it might give way at any time. Holding on to the bottom rung, I bent down and placed my hand in the water, withdrawing it quickly again. "This stream is hot," I shouted up to Mercy. "Look, there's steam rising."

"That might put dogs off the scent," she called, as I climbed back to the surface. "Miles told me once they can't smell in hot water."

"Wonder where it comes from."

We walked on, finally arriving at the compound walls surrounding the Old Centre, which were topped with barbed wire and high enough to largely obscure the circular building within.

"Entrance is on the other side, Jack," said Mercy, leading me to a pair of padlocked metal gates bearing a sign:

Keep Out
Property of Ministry of Defence
Trespassers Will Be Prosecuted

On the wall next to the gates was a small brass plaque, relatively new, judging by the shine on it, with the words:

Original Highmoor Research Centre Building
Operational between 1946 & 1956
Superintendent – Henry Weaver
Listed under the Town and Country Planning Act (1947)

I also saw that there was a track, laid with wide concrete slabs and now weed-infested through lack of use, that led from the gates to the main road. This was consistent with Whiddon's story of a military convoy bringing the Bell to the centre in a blizzard, all those years ago.

"Where does that go?" I asked, looking at a fork in the track with an offshoot that led further around the hill.

"Oh, a dead end, just to some bushes, I think." She pointed to thick foliage at the side of the building. "So if you've seen enough, let's go, I really must talk to Mel."

"Of course," I said, looking at my watch. "I'll drop you off now."

4:30 PM

"Where the hell is she then, Gurney?" shouted Mercy at the barman.

"I don't rightly know, Missus. Melissa left over an hour ago."

"I must check her room," Mercy cried, running away down the corridor. I followed, to find her standing over the dressing table in Melissa's bedroom. She held a folded note in her hand.

"Read it to me, I can't…"

She covered her eyes with her hand as I took the note and read out loud:

Mum,
I had to come back to get something, and saying I'd decided to
come home seemed the easiest way.
I'm sorry for lying to you, and now I really am going to follow my
destiny.
By the time you read this I'll be far away.
Love you always,
M

"She's really lost now, Jack," Mercy sobbed. "And there's nothing I can do."

"I'll be back later, and we'll do what we can," I said, not knowing how else to comfort her. I slipped quietly out of the door, beginning to feel overcome with emotion myself.

Melissa's coming back home had been one positive event in a week of uncertainties, and now she was gone again.

5 PM

I squeezed into the call box outside Jay's general store, pulled out the slip of paper with the Devonport number from my pocket, then dialled.

"Lieutenant Jolly, please." After the usual questions I was transferred through.

"Commander Sangster, glad you called, I've the ballistics results you wanted."

"And?"

"As I said when we met, both bullets looked to be ordnance stolen from the armoury a few nights ago."

"We knew that," I shouted, impatient to hear about the Ballyshannon bullet. "Less spleen, Jack," I muttered under my breath, angry with myself for losing control.

"Sorry, sir, I was getting to the next results. It seems…" I heard him rustling papers, "that the barnacle-encrusted shell was indeed fired from the stolen M2."

"Can you be certain?"

"Well, it's not me, sir, it's the lab techs, and they gave a ninety-nine per cent certainty."

"How could they know?"

"That M2 was test fired fairly recently, and apparently…" Jolly then read an extract from the report, detailing how shells that were test fired into a water tank had been kept. This then enabled the lab to compare those shells with mine. I then felt myself jolt when he told me this recent test firing had been suggested by Doctor De Coverley himself.

"Was the gun used during the war?" I asked after a breathless pause.

"Don't think so, sir, but can you hang on a minute…" I heard the clunk of the receiver being placed on a desk, the sound of his footsteps walking away, the minute or so wait until I heard him returning feeling like an age. "You still there, sir?"

"Yes, Lieutenant, still here," I answered, now feeling distinctly dizzy and anything but 'still here'.

"Well, I'm reading an inventory note saying the gun was taken out of service in 1932 and placed on display the same year as the first example of its kind to be used by the navy."

"Could there be a mistake?"

"The records are pretty meticulous, so no, that particular M2 couldn't have been used during the war."

"Sorry, but I think you'll find it was." I tried to speak with authority but heard my voice waver, the thoughts fighting in the depths of my mind now beginning to overwhelm consciousness.

"I'll double-check, sir."

"Please do that, Lieutenant, and contact me when you know for sure." I sensed beads of sweat popping out of my forehead, then felt my legs give way, relieved I happened to be in a phone box as I clawed myself upright again. "And thanks for the, um… good, er… work." I leant against the glass windows to try and catch my breath.

"You alright, sir?"

"No, I'm not…" I dropped the receiver and staggered out into the sunlight. If the lieutenant was right, there was no rational explanation I could offer for this.

Walking back to the car, I kept muttering, "Impossible," as the shrill voice of Lieutenant Jolly repeatedly called my name from the dangling phone. I then sat breathing deeply for a full twenty minutes before feeling ready to drive again.

6 PM

"Jack Sangster, Granville Institute," I said, passing my card to the desk sergeant. "Inspector Hawke's expecting me."

"Hmmm…" He ran his finger along the entries in an appointment book. "Ah yes, just take a seat."

There was little to look at as I sat, just some public information posters about protecting one's house from burglaries and a police recruitment poster. The air in the station was quite oppressive, and smelt of new paint, so that I began deliberately breathing through my mouth to avoid the smell. With all this, my mind began to wander, and I thought of Sarah, vulnerable and lonely in Israel. She knew the country's religion and customs as an academic but had by no means been brought up orthodox. She would be a stranger in a strange land, and I suddenly had a vision of my wife standing in Jerusalem, alone and surrounded by a baying mob. Sarah was screaming out my name and I was there, but impotent, unable to reach her. I screwed up my eyes and winced.

"Mr Sangster, come with me, please." I opened my eyes quickly, suddenly realising where I was again, looking up to see the familiar face of Constable Eccles, who gave me an odd look. "DI's waiting for you in the interrogation room."

I followed him as he navigated several corridors, eventually arriving at a windowless room where DI Hawke sat at a table, its top bare except for a notebook and what I assumed was some sort of tape-recording device.

"Evening, Inspector," I said.

"And good evening to you, Sangster, although I hear the Merrivale girl's gone missing."

"That's right."

"And as it's not for the first time, why weren't we told?"

"It was, er… delicate. She has form, you see, and the family didn't want her taken back into care."

"I'm sure your motives were for the best, Sangster," the DI said, fixing her good eye on me, "but don't withhold anything else from now on. This De Coverley case is turning into a nightmare, with massive police resources up on the moor and the seniors all breathing down my neck for results."

"Understood."

"Good," she said, before shouting at Eccles to go and get Jane Ustrix. "Any news on De Coverley?"

"Which one?"

"Either of them, or both, you know what I mean," she snapped.

"Well, here's what I have so far…" I told her about the attic at Foxtor House, the drugs and syringe, as well as the documents.

"Do you know if De Coverley or his son might be diabetic, Inspector?"

"Let me see," said the DI, paging through a loose-leaf folder. "Yes, Doctor De Coverley needs regular shots of insulin to stay alive."

"So if De Coverley left his supply at Foxtor House, and couldn't return because of the police presence, he'd have to get more from somewhere else."

"Right. I'll have Eccles ring round all the local chemists, see if anyone's been asking for insulin." She then picked up her goat-headed stick and laid it on the table. "Now tell me Sangster, what do you think's really going on?"

"Alright, here are the facts as I see them, and here's what I think…"

This was the first time I'd put everything together, even in my mind, let alone out loud, so I stumbled a little, but in summary told the DI the following:

- Melissa Merrivale regularly absconded from home, despite her care order, and had likely been staying overnight at Foxtor House.
- Christopher De Coverley had allegedly been seen in the company of Doctor De Coverley in the preceding weeks, but only from a distance, and my suspicion was that people were actually seeing Melissa, not Christopher (the two were similar in height, hairstyle, and build). Christopher himself hadn't been definitively seen since Easter.
- Doctor De Coverley had almost certainly been conducting his own experiments, unknown to the authorities, the current superintendent of the Highmoor Centre being unaware of operational details to the extent that De Coverley could probably use the facility's considerable resources to do what he liked. These experiments were probably responsible for the electrical anomalies recently experienced in the locality.

"And what is the nature of these experiments?" DI Hawke asked me once I'd finished speaking.

"I don't know, but I believe they relate to advanced technology, perhaps recovered from Germany after the war."

I waited for some sarcastic reply from the inspector, but none came.

"And you really think Doctor De Coverley could do all this secretly at the Highmoor Research Centre, right under the nose of Sir Peregrine Frere?"

"No, I think somehow De Coverley's managing to use the Old Centre for his work."

"But it's deserted, and we have over a hundred officers in the Fox Tor area. Someone would surely see him."

"Nevertheless, I think there's something going on there." I told her about the underground culvert with its stream of hot water.

"Well," she said, looking at a clock on the wall, "it's a bit late now, but I'll talk to the search team tomorrow morning, and we'll give the place more of a going-over. Anything else?"

"The whole thing seems to revolve around Reynard's Hall and people obsessed with Sir Francis Drake."

Once again, the inspector didn't flinch at what must surely have sounded outlandish. "How do you mean?"

"I don't exactly know, but both De Coverleys, senior and junior, seem to have been consumed by their interest in Drake, as is Professor Frere." DI Hawke nodded. "Then we have the weapons cache Frere found, full of stuff taken during that break in at the Devonport arms depot. Did anyone own up, by the way?"

"No." She shook her head. "We've trawled the whole country, including help from the Met, and drawn a complete blank. The IRA, European anarchists, crime groups, the lot. Nobody knows anything, it's a complete—"

"Ma'am," interrupted Constable Eccles, opening the door, "here's Miss Ustrix for you."

Jane Ustrix walked in behind him, followed by a uniformed WPC. Jane held her head down and looked quite forlorn, wearing a blue prison smock and no make-up.

"For God's sake, knock next time, Eccles," said DI Hawke. "Now go away and call round any chemist shops within a half hour bus ride of Princetown. Check if they sold insulin to anyone in the last couple of days."

"Right away, Ma'am," said Eccles.

"Alright, Miss Ustrix, take a seat." Jane duly sat down. "So I'd better explain to Mr Sangster here that you have agreed to, how shall we say, cooperate with the authorities in return for safe haven in Britain."

"That's right. Asylum."

"In short," I said, "you're defecting."

"That's right."

I'd wondered why Jane Ustrix had been so forthcoming about her mission, even when we'd met in the hotel billiard room the night before. Now I knew.

"So is there anything you can tell us about this artifact, this Bell?"

"Not much more than I've already said, Inspector."

"Do you know its purpose?" I asked.

"Oh, yes, of course, perhaps I forgot to mention that with everything else going on. It's an anti-gravity device, and also designed to be stealthy."

"Stealthy?" said DI Hawke.

"I've heard of this stealth, Inspector. It's when they build something, like a war plane, to be invisible to radar."

"Invisible?" The DI made the trademark eyebrow raise above her good eye. This time, it seemed, her credulity had been stretched too far.

"Done, I think, by reducing sharp angles or coating with a reflective paint."

"Thank you for that gem of detail, Sangster."

"Ha." Jane laughed. "The Bell was designed to be invisible, not just to radar but so you couldn't see it at all."

"Are you joking with us, woman?" shouted DI Hawke.

"Do I look as if I'm joking?" Jane shouted back. "Can you imagine what your generals would do with a craft that can float silently in any direction and enter the ranks of the enemy unseen?"

"Certainly explains a lot," I said. "And I, anyway, believe you, because we know from other sources that a massive bell-shaped device bearing German insignia was brought to Dartmoor in 1945." Jane smiled slightly. "Now one other question, if I may."

"Yes."

"This Heinrich Weber, are you sure he came to Britain with the Bell?"

"Oh yes, and stayed with it for ten years until he died. Changed his name, of course."

"Of course he did, I should have realised before, he's—"

"I thought I told you to knock, Eccles," screamed the DI as the door opened again. "So why didn't you do as I… oh, hello, Chief Superintendent, but who are you two?"

A senior-looking uniformed officer, with crown and diamond motifs on his epaulettes, was followed into the room by a man and a woman. The man was dressed in a dark suit, shirt, and tie, whilst she sported a black leather jacket and trousers tucked into knee-length boots. Both had slicked-back dark hair, and although I'd never seen them dressed like this, the pair were nevertheless familiar to me.

"These people are from the security services, here to collect the prisoner," said the chief superintendent. "Paperwork's in order, so she goes with them now."

"Mr and Mrs Dike," I said to the two figures standing behind him, "you look, er… different."

"Evening, Sangster," said Ballar. "I'm afraid we have a little explaining to do."

"Except," said Fidelma, "that in our line of business we never explain anything." Ballar nodded. "But suffice it to say if I'd had to act out that arguing druid couple charade any longer, somebody might have found themselves minus a few fingers one morning, or worse…" She looked at Ballar with much the same expression I'd seen when she was dressed in her sandals and sackcloth robe, 'acting' out an argument with her handfasted husband. "So come along, Miss Ustrix."

"Where are you taking her?" I asked, as Jane stood up with a look of resignation and walked over to the Dikes.

"Oh," Ballar laughed, "you don't need to know that."

"And I suppose your name's not Dike, or even Atkinson?"

"Course it's Dike." Ballar again laughed. "We were… what was it called, my dear?"

"Handfasted," said Fidelma with a sigh. "On the solstice… my dear." She emphasised the 'r' of the word dear.

"Ah yes." He laughed yet again. "Solstice, ridiculous word."

"Even a fool of a fake druid like you," Jane said with a shake of her head, "should know solstice comes from the Latin for 'sun standing still', as in the sun appearing to hang in the sky at midsummer."

"I should be very polite to me, given where you're going." Ballar's laughter was replaced by a slight snarl, and I once again felt fear for Jane.

"Where is she going?"

"Mr Sangster, please, no more questions," Fidelma sighed again. "Now we'll be back late to the hotel tonight, so I'd like a debrief tomorrow. You're not leaving, are you?"

"No, case isn't solved, the De Coverley boy and the Merrivale girl still not found."

"We'll say ten o'clock in the morning then?"

"Fine," I said as the Dikes, the chief superintendent, and Jane Ustrix walked out, leaving me alone with a stunned-looking DI Hawke.

"Don't know why we bother, Sangster," she finally said.

*

"Oh, Mr Sangster, before you drive away…" I turned to see Eccles standing on the steps of the police station. "DI says to tell you that Melissa Merrivale bought insulin using a prescription made out for Doctor De Coverley at the chemist's shop in Princetown."

"When?"

"About two hours ago."

"Thank you, that really is a help," I said as Eccles turned back up the steps. "And DC Eccles?"

"Mr Sangster?"

"You've done some good police work, getting the details on Jane Ustrix so quickly, and now finding out about this prescription."

"Thanks, I appreciate you saying that."

"So why do you do it?"

"Sorry?"

"This job."

"I, er… enjoy police work, sir, always have."

"No, I mean put up with abuse from DI Hawke."

The young detective looked hard at me. "Do you know how she got that limp, and the eye patch?" I shook my head. "She was a rising star in the Met, you see, one of the youngest and certainly one of the first women DIs."

"She certainly does have drive, but what happened?"

"The DC fell foul of some serious criminals. Working undercover, no idea how they found out she was a copper, but anyway, she was thrown from a second-storey window and broke her back. Lucky ever to walk again."

"And the eye?"

"Just before she was, what's the word…"

"Defenestrated?"

"Yes, well, before that they decided to add insult to injury by throwing acid in her face."

"That's terrible."

"Hence all that make-up," said Eccles, pausing for a moment. "And she's not going to tell you, but as a result, the DI's in more or less permanent pain, so don't judge too harshly."

"Sorry, I didn't know." It was my turn to pause. "How does she hold her job down?"

"Takes medication, and 'keeps buggering on', as she likes to say. Devon born and bred as well, so they gave her this posting when she recovered. Maybe as a thank-you, I don't know."

"Well, I appreciate you explaining that, Constable, I—"

"And she cares enough that she doesn't take all the pain relief drugs she could. Says some tablets make her delusional."

"That's, er… very brave."

"And DI Hawke gave me a chance in CID, Mr Sangster, when nobody else would, so as I say, don't judge too harshly." I nodded. "Well, good evening, sir."

Eccles went back into the station, leaving me feeling more than a little embarrassed, but also wondering about his comment that 'some tablets make her delusional'.

Doctor De Coverley took long-term pain medication.

Did that make him suffer from delusions?

7:30 PM

"Three messages for you, Mr Sangster," said Joe Gurney, handing me a slip of paper. "One from your wife in Tel Aviv saying she's all ready to come home as planned on Sunday."

"Thanks."

"And a woman from the admiralty in London called for you, but… sorry, I don't recall her name."

"Yorke, perhaps?"

"Yes, that's her, and she asked if you could collect Admiral Anson at four o'clock tomorrow from the main entrance at Devonport Naval Base. He's booked in to stay the night here apparently."

"And the other message, Joe?"

"From Professor Frere, over in Yelverton. Wants you to call him, I wrote the number down for you."

"Thanks," I said, and went to the telephone alcove. "Miss Whiddon… yes, the professor please… Jack Sangster, I'm returning his call." I waited for a moment, then heard Septimus Frere's voice.

"Sangster, marvellous news."

"You've found something buried under the kitchen garden then?"

"Oh no, the two men Mercedes sent over haven't finished yet. Whatever's down there is buried very deep, and that's partly why I called you."

"Oh yes?"

"Well, I think I've found my compelling event, as our friend Doctor Stewer might say, so just hang on." I heard Frere rustling paper. "Now then, I was having another look at the Peter Pearce diary."

"Drake's equerry?"

"Yes, and I found this, now, ahem…" He cleared his throat and read from the diary. "Says here that *'Reynard Hill commanded that Jehovah's Wind be buried deep, no less than three fathoms below ground'*, so don't you see?"

"Er…"

"Three fathoms, so eighteen feet, the depth of the object we picked up on radar."

"Hardly a compelling event, Professor, and you haven't dug anything up yet. Stewer's point, if I may say so, was that the whole diary might be a fake, even if it's written on genuinely old paper. You need something that proves the date of the diary."

"Oh, I know. That's mainly what I called to tell you."

"And?"

"Well, let me read this entry: *'Today I, and others from the hall, were asked to help with the building of a longhouse near Hoo Meavy. The bricklayers followed the Devon custom of leaving a shoe within the walls to bring good luck. I was honoured to be asked to place the shoe, which was well worn, as is tradition, into a cavity at the base of the north wall.'*"

"And you think this place he mentions might be the Black Talbot Tavern?"

"I don't just think so, Sangster, I'm almost certain. That building's a traditional longhouse, built in 1596, near Hoo Meavy, and a sixteenth-century shoe was found in its north wall a couple of years ago. So…" I heard him laugh down the phone, "unless that rascal Stewer can prove Peter Pearce's diary was written less than two years ago, he can't dispute its authenticity."

"Er…" I said, trying and failing to find a hole in Frere's logic. "Yes, you're right. Congratulations."

"Thank you, Sangster, and don't forget to come to the hall

tomorrow around three. Those two chaps Mercedes sent reckon they'll have dug down to the eighteen-foot mark by then."

"I'll come if I can, Professor. Good evening."

8 PM

As I changed for dinner, my thoughts turned over and over in a vain effort to link the things I knew held the key to finding Christopher De Coverley. And of these, foremost in my mind was the shell from the shipwreck in Ballyshannon. How could it possibly have been fired from a gun kept here in Plymouth? I tried to convince myself that Jolly must have been wrong about the antique M2 not being used in the war, but without success.

Mind still spinning as I entered the common room, I saw Mercy standing by the bar.

"Jack, I'm sorry, with everything else I forgot." She held up a sheaf of papers, including a photo of Melissa. "Police have asked for these, pictures, list of people and places she knows, and so on. I promised we'd drop them off. I know it's asking a lot, but you couldn't run them up there, could you?"

"Not all the way back to Plymouth, surely?"

"No, no," she said with her usual stroke of my arm. "Just Princetown. Police station's on the main street, a bit past the store, and if you get to the church, you've gone too far."

"I know where it is," I said, looking at her red eyes. "You just concentrate on getting ready for dinner, and I'll drive straight there now." I took the papers from her. "And save me a nice table for when I get back."

"Of course, now…" She slapped her thigh. "Dammit, Jack, they asked for a handwriting sample as well. Let me just have a look in Mel's room."

"It's alright, I've still got that page from her notebook in my jacket. They can use that."

*

"Sir," called Tilly, as I was about to get into the car.

"Yes, Tilly?"

"You're looking for that Christopher De Coverley boy, aren't you, sir?"

"I am."

"Well, it's just that…" Tilly then described how she had overheard Melissa on the phone earlier telling whoever was on the other end that she would be joining Christopher tonight.

"Are you sure?"

"Sure as I stand here, sir."

"Did she say where she would meet him?" Tilly shook her head. "Thanks, that's very useful."

"Yessir, now I'd better get back inside before I'm missed."

Where would Melissa meet Christopher, I wondered as I started the car? Somewhere far away she had said, so not in this locality. And as I drove away, the sky above the moor now a deep blue as dusk began to settle, the exchange between Ballar Dike and Jane Ustrix in the interrogation room also began to nag at the back of my mind.

She had corrected him about the meaning of 'solstice', that much I remembered.

"Solstice comes from the Latin for 'sun standing still,'" she had said, but why was that important?

I felt the pieces of the jigsaw beginning to fit. You're close now, Jack, I thought as Princetown came into view, but you're also tired. Best just to drop the papers off with the police, have a quiet night then start again in the morning, when things will hopefully become clearer. I looked down at the passenger seat, where the sheet from Melissa's notebook lay on top of the papers Mercy had given me. Then I slammed on the brakes.

"That's it," I shouted out loud. "And I will follow, at sundown four days after the sun stands still."

Whatever fate had overtaken Christopher, wherever he had gone, the girl was to follow, tonight, four days after the summer solstice, and at sundown. I looked at my watch, remembering Mercy saying the sunset around nine thirty at this time of year.

Eight thirty-five already. With the stark realisation that I had less than an hour to find Melissa, I looked at the diagram above the notes, and thanked providence the outline was now recognisable. This wasn't a school or an office block, but a plan of the Old Centre, with its forked approach road, one side leading to the main gate, the other to the blind lane by the bushes.

Driving away again, I ignored the turning to Princetown, arriving at the turn-off to Foxtor House. Too long a way round, I thought, better to take the concrete road to the Old Centre. Once at the entrance, I jumped out of the car and pulled a metal gate open, which swung on its hinges surprisingly easily despite the barbed wire all around it and the superficial look of disrepair. This made me think that the gate, despite the prominent MOD sign next to it telling people to keep out, had been in regular use.

After a tricky drive up to the centre, my car's clearance once more proving barely adequate for moorland tracks, concrete or otherwise, I parked along the blind fork. Climbing out and checking my watch again, then looking across to the west, where the sun lay low in an ever-darkening sky, I realised there were now only forty-five minutes to sunset.

Melissa's sketch showed a cross at the end of this road, so the place must have held some significance for her, but all I could see was bushes. I picked up a stick from the ground and began to beat my way through the thicket, where after a short time the splitting of branches gave way to the clank of metal. As the leaves parted, it became apparent that the clank was from a navy-blue Land Rover, parked so it couldn't be seen from the road, a large yellow sticker across the windscreen stating that the owner of the vehicle was to contact Devon and Cornwall Police immediately. I thought back to the provost marshal's comment that De Coverley and his son had climbed into a dark grey or blue or van, and the police constable at Foxtor House ('De Coverley's vehicle parked up by the centre').

Surely De Coverley was here somewhere, but where?

Time was running out, and there seemed nowhere else to look. The compound itself was clearly inaccessible, and this place was definitely a cul-de-sac, with the concrete road stopping at a small wall that stood a couple of yards or so further on. On the other side of that, it just was greenery.

The dusk was now settling, making detail hard to see amongst the foliage, so I took a torch out of the boot and shone it 360 degrees. Perhaps there was a back door to the centre hidden in the trees, I wondered, but the beam of light showed nothing.

"Idiot Jack," I then muttered as my foot caught a tree stump, making me stagger and drop the torch, which rolled under the Land Rover. Bending down and reaching under the vehicle, I immediately sensed a dip in the ground and touched something that felt like the edge of a carpet. Next to that was a surface, hard and cold. Peering down low, I could see the torch lay on a leaf-covered mat that had been pulled aside to reveal a metal door set into the earth. A ring was set into the door, which, when pulled, like the outer gates to the road, moved far more easily than I expected. In fact, it was a steel cover rather than a hinged door, with the leaf mat just a thin layer designed to conceal its presence, so that I was able to lift both mat and door completely away from the Land Rover. Seeing steps below, I then lay face down and eased my legs into the opening, just managing to slide head and shoulders below the underside of the vehicle.

The steps led down about ten feet into a square room with concrete walls, which at first seemed to have no exit. I then saw buttons on one of the walls and realised I was looking at the door to a lift. I pressed and waited, listening to the whir behind the door as the lift ascended. After a long enough time to tell me the shaft must be deep, the door opened, flooding the room with light. I stepped inside and pushed a single button, this lift clearly had only one destination. As the doors shut and the lift began to descend, I looked up to see a round lens that could only have been part of a closed-circuit TV system, making me involuntarily clench the stem of the torch, thinking that whoever was down below probably now knew I was coming. It then occurred to me that nobody else did.

How rash could I have been?

About a minute later, the lift door slid open, and I drew breath, confronted by an enormous space, the roof three storeys high, with roughly circular walls perhaps one hundred feet in diameter. All around the sides lay a mass of equipment and furniture, consoles with numerous dials and switches the purpose of which I couldn't begin to imagine, a desk covered in papers and notebooks, several TV screens, one of which showed the interior of the lift, and metal containers of all sizes, from massive boxes to ones the volume of a suitcase. Here and there were ladders and scaffolding, and mounted next to the largest container was an iron wheel similar to the one by the concrete culvert hatch I'd seen down the valley.

But this was all surely, and literally, peripheral equipment, I thought as I looked towards the centre of the room, where suspended from a crane over a gaping hole was something that almost defied comprehension. I blinked several times at the sight, half expecting my vision to correct with each drop of the eyelids.

"So that's the Bell," I whispered, gazing upwards at the Nazi *'wunderwaffe'* Jane Ustrix's father had helped design, a device far ahead of its time, spirited away from Poland at the end of the war by Heinrich Weber, then finally perfected all these years later by Doctor John De Coverley.

And Die Glocke, which emitted a low hum that pervaded the entire room, was well named, being more or less conical with a bulging lower rim and sides that curved upwards a full twenty-five feet. The surface was a deep matt black that nevertheless glistened in a manner that was uncomfortable to the eye, and one side of Die Glocke was embossed with a dull scarlet swastika (just as Whiddon had said). On the opposite side I saw a metal walkway leading from the edge of the shaft to a door in the Bell, from which muted voices could be heard. Looking into the interior of the machine, which was bathed in a violet light that seemed to cast shadows in all directions, I saw De Coverley standing over someone sitting in what looked very much like a coffin. It was hard to recognise the face through the lighting, but I guessed I had finally found the elusive Christopher, who, as I watched, took a glass of liquid from De Coverley, put something in his mouth and swallowed.

"What are you doing?" I shouted.

De Coverley turned and looked at me, then let out a shriek. "How can you be here?" he cried, whilst closing the coffin lid as his son lay down again. "I must complete my work, it is time." I watched him adjust some levers by the door of the machine and felt the hairs on the back of my neck stand up as the hum from the Bell grew louder.

"No," I yelled, walking up the gangway. "Whatever you're doing, think twice, that's your only son in there."

"You'll not stop me now," De Coverley bellowed, running down the gangway towards me, eyes wild, hands outstretched. I held my arms up to fend him off, but he had the advantage of the slope, the full force of his body pushing me back so that I staggered and fell, only avoiding a fall down the shaft by clinging on to the rail at the edge.

De Coverley then went over to the main console and began frantically throwing switches. I thrashed around with my legs, eventually finding a ledge on the pit wall with which to push myself up. Running up behind him, I grasped his waist, the two of us wrestling whilst De Coverley kept grabbing at the console. Eventually, just as he was pulling one of the largest levers, I managed to wrench his body backwards, the shaft of the lever pushing upwards to its limit then shearing away in his hand as we fell.

De Coverley sat on the floor as sparks began to jump across the console, holding the broken lever in his hand and laughing. "Do you know what you've just done, Sangster?"

I slumped against the console and shook my head.

"You've pushed the power up to maximum, and without this lever, there's nothing we can do to stop it." He waved the lever shaft at me. "Circuits will short soon, and that'll be the end."

"Got to get your son out then." I pushed past him, walked up the gangway, then entered the Bell, as the hum it emitted continued to grow all around us. The coffin-like box lay in front of me and I knelt then heaved open the leaden lid.

"Christopher, you must come with me, it's… oh." I looked into the face of Melissa Merrivale and froze. "Not… not safe here, Melissa," I eventually managed to say.

She looked up at me, eyes rolling. "Oh, Mr Sangster, have we arrived?"

"Yes, now come on out." I lifted her up, and with my arm round her shoulder, she stepped out of the box.

"What did you give her?" I asked as we walked back down the gangway.

"Just sleeping pills for the trip," he replied, as the sparks behind him spread across every piece of equipment and the hum from the Bell grew louder, almost drowning out our voices.

"Is your son here as well?"

"No, no." He shook his head and waved his hands. "Not here." The tone of De Coverley's voice somehow rang true.

"I'm going to take her to the surface, then come back for you," I shouted, walking the very compliant but unsteady Melissa to the lift.

"No need," he called back as the lift door opened. "Just get out yourselves, go as far from here as you can."

The door closed, and the lift began to ascend, Melissa slumped against the corner. After what seemed a lifetime the doors opened, and I led her out.

"Now, Melissa, can you hear me?" She faintly nodded. "Then climb these steps and find help, flag down a car, anything. Get the police, alright?" She nodded again and I pushed her up the steps, watching until she slithered out from under the Land Rover.

Then, taking a deep breath, I entered the lift again.

De Coverley was still leaning against the console when I reached the bottom, but now the entire bunker was lit with blue sparks, just like those I'd seen in Wistman's Wood. I held my hand out to pull De Coverley up, but he merely laughed.

"Gonna short any time now, Sangster, here it goes…"

I closed my eyes and waited for oblivion, but all I heard was a damp hiss.

"Is that it?" I said, opening my eyes to find the bunker in semi-darkness, lit by weak red lights, the blinding blue sparks now gone, along with the hum from the Bell. "No fires, no nuclear meltdown…" I threw my hands in the air. "And no, er… gas explosions?"

"That's it," De Coverley said, still laughing. "We've no gas main within a mile of here, all the electrics have fried except these back-up lights, and no meltdown… yet." He pointed up at the dim red bulbs hanging from the ceiling. "But that still means curtains for you and me."

"Come on, I'll help you into the lift, there's still time."

"It won't work, try it if you like."

I ran across and pressed the lift button, but there was no reaction, no sound or light inside, no movement from the door.

"Isn't there an emergency generator?"

"Look," he said, pulling himself to his feet, "we just pushed the power up to full at the very point I was about to launch the Bell. None of the systems are built to withstand that kind of surge. We're finished."

"But if the power's gone surely we're not in danger?"

As I spoke, there was a crashing sound from above and the crane began to slip, the Bell moving lower down the shaft so that the gangway broke away, clanking into the depths until we could hear it no more.

"Is the Bell likely to explode?"

"It's inert without power, so no, now sit down." He sighed, gesturing to two chairs by the side of the shaft. "Our problem is that." He gestured to the largest container. "Tank holding half a million gallons of water. Without electrics it will slowly fill to bursting point."

"Is there nothing we can do to empty it?" I pointed to the iron wheel.

"Nothing," he said. "That wheel does operate a drainage sluice, but it's power-assisted. You can't turn the wheel by hand alone when the tank's full."

I noticed De Coverley's voice begin to slur, and remembered he was diabetic.

"You need any medicine?"

"Nothing you can give me," he replied, with an infectious tone of hopelessness, so that I began to wonder whether Melissa would be able to find help in her drugged state and, if by some miracle she did, when that help might come. I decided the best thing would be to talk with De Coverley, keep him awake.

"I had the Bell explained to me, you know." I sat down next to him and looked at the machine, trying to use the same words as Jane Ustrix to describe it. "Deflects gravity, doesn't it, and Die Glocke can also generate a cloak of invisibility, effectively letting it move unseen."

"Anti-gravity machine, cloak of invisibility, is that what they still think?" De Coverley laughed, almost wailing in his semi-coma, then looked around the bunker. "We're going to die here, Sangster."

"There's always hope, if Melissa can get help, they might—"

"Oh, come on, man." He pointed to the collapsed lift shaft. "She's drugged up to the eyeballs, we're buried over a hundred feet below ground and the pressure's building up to critical…" He gestured to a gauge on the side of the water tank, where a needle on the dial was moving closer and closer to a red-coloured zone. "Tank could blow at any time now."

"Then what happens?" I gulped.

"Water will flood into the drainage culvert behind the tank and there'll be none to cool the main reactor housed a further sixty feet below us, which will overheat in a matter of minutes. Then, poof…" He held up his arms and made a sound that I assumed was intended to be an explosion.

"I won't give up hope, De Coverley."

"Good for you." He lifted up his shirt and patted the needle-marked skin of his abdomen. "But you're not running out of insulin."

"Is there none here?"

"Melissa brought me the vials, but the syringe kit's in the Land Rover. I was going to go up and get it as soon as the Bell was launched."

"Alright, things don't look too bright."

"Not too bright at all." He laughed again, eyes beginning to roll and head lolling forward.

"Come on, De Coverley," I said, pushing him upright again.

"Thanks, Sangster." He took a deep breath and looked down the shaft at the Bell. "So, I might as well spend my last minutes explaining what that thing actually is, and what we've done with it. Pass me that, will you?"

He pointed to an oblong device on the desk, which I recognised as a cassette tape recorder. The machine had a small microphone attached to it.

"May as well record this," he said, setting the microphone down on the floor next to him. "Just in case someone finds it."

De Coverley then pressed two buttons on the box simultaneously and told me a most fantastical story…

*

He had first seen the Bell almost a quarter of a century before, when the device arrived at the centre by military convoy, along with a senior Nazi scientist by the name of Heinrich Weber.

"Henry Weaver in English?"

"Very good, Sangster, anyway…"

Weaver had taken De Coverley under his wing, and with almost unlimited resources from the government, they had continued to work on the Bell for another ten years.

"We did that in parallel with other projects to keep the MOD happy, but the Bell was always our passion. I still remember when Henry revealed its true purpose to me, something he had always kept from the British." De Coverley looked up at the roof, mouth open. "An epiphany, Sangster."

"And its true purpose was?"

"I'm coming to that…"

Weaver had, it seemed, known he was going to die for some time and, as a result, made sure the bunker, which for many years only he and De Coverley had ever entered, was hidden during the months leading up to his demise. This he achieved by using numerous building contractors from other parts of the country, for everything from the concealed lift to the power supply, and even the hot water drainage culvert that Old Soldier found so useful. Everyone did a separate job, none seeing the whole, so that by the time Weaver died, only De Coverley knew how to access the bunker, how to control the power, and, most importantly, what the Bell was capable of.

And the Nazi machine did indeed, De Coverley said, have gyros that defied gravity, although these were merely a by-product of its main function (I became increasingly impatient to find out what this primary function was each time he alluded to it). Another by-product was the illusion that the Bell could disappear, and both these strange effects had been used in demonstrations to show the authorities that progress was being made.

But the Bell had a far more disturbing and epoch-changing purpose, De Coverley whispered.

It was capable of time travel!

At this point I felt certain the doctor, as Sir Peregrine had hinted, had lost his reason, but I decided to go along with him for now. Perhaps he would say something that would help us find a way out, or hint at the true fate of his son.

And I nevertheless jolted at the words 'time travel', as he went on to say that the Bell was capable of moving backwards through time to a given point and then returning to the present, its creation inspired by a dream, apparently, of the German high command, to change history. And in 1969, thirteen years after the death of Henry Weaver, Doctor De Coverley, working in the secret bunker, and using modern components and levels of power unimaginable in Nazi Germany or even in Henry Weaver's time at the centre, finally managed to make the device operational.

"But," I said as De Coverley stressed the word 'operational', "you can't go back in time and change history."

"Why not?"

"I could, er…" I vaguely remembered reading a magazine article entitled 'Time Paradox', "that's it, go back and kill my own grandfather, meaning I could never be born to go back in time and kill my own grandfather. There."

"It doesn't work like that. How can I explain to you…?" He gave me a look that said he was talking to a child. "If you go back in time, whatever you do is just a part of things. The past has already happened so you simply can't change it. Kurt Godel worked it all out, and he influenced Henry Weaver's work."

"Kurt who?"

"Austrian physicist, embellished Einstein's theories. Godel mentored Henry in… oh, what's the point?" He threw his arms in the air. "Just suffice it to say the Bell worked but had a major drawback." De Coverley then held his finger up and wagged it at me. "I couldn't control when it would land, Sangster."

"Sorry?"

"The Bell would go back to a fixed point in time and then return, but I couldn't say in advance when that fixed point would be." I continued to look blankly, and he threw his arms in the air again. "I didn't know how far back in time I would go."

"So what did you do?"

"Just, er…" He laughed again, eyes rolling and voice wavering so that I now really feared he would slip into a coma. "Got in and tried it out, and d'you know what?"

"No."

"The Bell landed in the year 1587, mid-afternoon on Christmas Day."

"And you know this, I mean, you walked amongst Elizabethans?"

"Oh no, if I'd opened the door, I'd have lost the protection of the Bell, but I saw the date on the instrument panel and realised its significance."

"The year before the Armada. Ah, I think—"

"You think rather too much, Sangster," De Coverley said, eyes facing forwards in their sockets again and voice back to normal. "Otherwise you wouldn't have ended up stuck down here with me."

"Suppose not."

"So…"

Once De Coverley knew that the Bell operated in precise 388-year cycles, a plan began to form. The Armada, as far as his studies told him, should have been invincible on paper, at least when fighting the English fleet. Now, with careful preparation, he could give an edge to Drake that would render any Spanish warship defenceless.

"And you chose a machine gun?"

"Exactly, Sangster. I am sure some sort of bigger weapon could have been better, but I just needed something effective, simple to maintain, easy to mount on a sixteenth-century ship, and, of course, available."

"The twin-gun M2 Browning in the museum?"

"Right again, and we took it, along with some fifteen thousand rounds of incendiary ammunition and a maintenance kit."

"You and your son?"

"The gun, yes."

"And the ammo?"

"Ah, that was different. I ordered it through the Highmoor Centre, filled all the forms out myself, no questions asked. We do some ballistics research, you see."

"But that much ordnance, De Coverley, surely it would be noticed?"

He laughed. "It's amazing what can slip through the net if you follow the red tape, and Perry Frere struggles so much with paperwork he never noticed."

I remembered Sir Peregrine fretting over costs for an outsize ordnance order, and Jones's comment that 'Sir Peregrine will sign anything you put in front of him'.

"In fact…" De Coverley continued, "I was more worried that Perry's brother might work things out, living at Reynard's Hall, studying Drake, digging in the grounds, and so on."

"Why worry about the professor?"

"Shouldn't have been worried," he muttered, almost to himself before looking me in the eye. "Buffoon imagines himself something of a Sherlock Holmes, but he couldn't deduce the filling in a cheese sandwich."

"Yes," I laughed, "I've seen the professor's, er… deductions first hand." I began to wonder what threat De Coverley did imagine might come from Septimus Frere. "Anyway, I suppose that recent break-in at Devonport was for the maintenance kit?"

"Yes, Melissa Merrivale and I took the kit. Christopher was, ah… already out of reach by that time."

I asked what 'out of reach' meant, whereupon De Coverley's story became more outlandish by the minute, reinforced by a drugged demeanour which made the man look and sound increasingly delirious. The Bell, he said, protected its occupants providing they stayed within the capsule. Once outside, or even if the door was opened, there would be no going back.

"If you ventured into the world of 1588, then returned to the present using the Bell, you would age commensurately. The Bell is a one-way ticket, Sangster."

"And there was no insulin in 1588."

"I could have taken a diesel generator and refrigerator but still only would have had enough insulin and the other medications I need for a couple of months at most. After that…" he made a cutting motion across his throat, "the trip would have been a death sentence for me."

"So you sent your only son back almost four hundred years on that one-way ticket?"

"Chris begged me to let him go, begged me."

"Really?" I said, guessing De Coverley had in reality, like so many parents do, tried to transfer his own desires onto his child.

"You think I influenced the lad, I can tell." I nodded. "But you're wrong, Sangster, my son jumped at the chance."

"But a fifteen-year-old," I said, continuing to humour De Coverley in the hopes he might yet give away what had really happened to the boy. "How could he be prepared for life in another time, or to be able to meet Sir Francis Drake, let alone persuade England's greatest sailor to listen to him?"

"Losing his mother changed things for Chris. He wanted to make a difference, even at that young age." I watched De Coverley's face become even more drawn when he mentioned his wife. "So I took him out of school and arranged tutoring from Septimus Frere specifically so my boy could learn as much as possible about the Elizabethan age, about the Armada, about Drake."

"And being a hunt saboteur was all an act to stop the Miles Edgerton and co following that otter and finding the culvert."

"You really do think too much, Sangster."

"And you trained Christopher in the use of the Bell?"

"Trained him in the use and maintenance of the weapons as well, so he was all prepared when the time came."

And that time came, said De Coverley, just before Easter. The Bell was prepared for its human cargo and Christopher was successfully transported in the same lead-lined coffin Melissa had so recently lain in.

"How can you possibly know Christopher survived the journey?"

The machine, De Coverley said, was able to carry written messages back to the present ('on plastic sheeting in a lead-lined box, Sangster, although it was only used once, see, there's the box on the desktop'). And according to Henry Weaver, De Coverley went on to say, the Bell would operate with optimal efficiency only at given times of the year, four days after each equinox and solstice, and at sunset. De Coverley wasn't sure that Weaver was right, especially as the Bell had not yet been used at that time. However, when the machine was ready to launch in late 1969, he still preferred to follow these guidelines ('just in case, Sangster, just in case'). Hence De Coverley's first voyage was on

Christmas Day, Christopher's on March 25th, the quarter day, and the final trip, where Melissa would join Christopher, today, June 25th, four days after the summer solstice. This meant she would arrive in 1588 less than a month before the Armada was due to sail up the English Channel.

"I suppose that maintenance kit was due to go with her, so it's still in the Bell?"

"Yes."

"So how could the M2 ever have been used against the Armada?"

"Oh, the gun was operational when Christopher took it. Without that kit it could only have been used for a limited time but still long enough to beat the Armada."

Thus far, De Coverley's story, whilst preposterous, was consistent, but I could nevertheless identify another issue that surely proved it fantasy.

"You say the Bell travels in time, but can it move?"

"How do you mean, move?"

"Er… travel through space," I said, hoping this was the appropriate jargon.

"The machine travels along world-lines via closed time-like curves." I looked blankly at him. "So yes, it travels through time, and no, it does not travel through space."

"But," I said, deciding not to ask him what any of that meant whilst at the same time feeling triumphant, "even if the machine itself doesn't move through space, with the rotation and orbit of the Earth and the Solar System you would move. Surely travelling just a few minutes in time, let alone four hundred years, would mean ending up somewhere other than where you started."

"World-lines, Sangster, it's hard to explain."

"Alright, somehow you've cracked that problem, but even so, landscapes change. How could you have been sure, even on that first trip, that the machine wouldn't materialise within some solid object?"

"Ha. The more you try and think the further you get from the truth."

"Why?"

"Because, Sangster," said De Coverley, still laughing whilst gesturing towards the pit, "you're actually looking at a Roman mine working that predates the Elizabethans by something like fifteen hundred years. Henry Weaver seemed fairly certain the Bell's CTCs would be less than—"

"Sorry?"

"Henry thought the range of those closed time-like curves," he said slowly, "would be less than five hundred years, so even before I knew precisely when the Bell would land, it was clear the machine would probably materialise safely if suspended in the mineshaft." He shrugged. "Anyway, it was a risk I was prepared to take."

"And the shaft's deep connections to the natural underground granite vents all around this area help dissipate the staggering energy expended when the Bell is operational?"

"As I said, Sangster, you really, really do think a bit too much."

"Seems fairly obvious," I said. "Based on that geological map of Sir Peregrine's you marked with the ink spots." I suddenly pictured Mercy, laid across the parapet of the old bridge, red dress rent down one side, blonde hair blown sideways. "And I've seen for myself the effect when you start that infernal machine up, in places like the Wyvern Arms and Wistman's Wood."

"Er... yes, I suppose so, and that unpredictable surface charge was an unfortunate side effect that manifested itself every time we ran a test, let alone an actual voyage." He looked down at his feet, and I fancied tears welled up in his eyes. "Very unfortunate." Then he looked up again and rubbed his hands together, apparently reanimated.

"So, Sangster, as I was saying, by the time Christopher sought out Sir Francis Drake," De Coverley nodded at the machine, which, even in its damaged state, still shimmered so that I found it hard to look at, "the Bell had done its work, and everything was ready. Can you imagine, Sangster?"

"Imagine what?"

"The first time the gun was deployed, mounted on the *Revenge*, Drake's flagship." He looked up at the roof again, mouth agape, eyes wide. "Twin M2s opening fire on a Spanish galleon at over one thousand yards. Perhaps Drake himself manned the guns, peppering the Dons with five hundred incendiary rounds per minute. Oh, what I would give to see that." He continued staring upwards with glazed ecstasy.

"But the Merrivale girl, how did you persuade her to follow your son?"

"I didn't. She thought I would just transport her somewhere, far away, to be with Christopher. Melissa never knew the Bell could travel through time."

"So you tricked her into going, why?"

"Because…" he pulled out a rolled-up piece of plastic from his pocket and handed it to me, "the message Christopher sent back in the Bell was this."

On the sheet, which was intact but certainly had a feel of great antiquity, were the three words…

So lonely, Dad

…written in faded black felt-tipped pen.

"How could I leave him there alone, Sangster, how could I?"

"But you tried to send the wrong girl."

"What do you mean? Chris told me he was in love, and I'd seen the Merrivale girl with him numerous times."

"She had feelings for him, yes, but your boy…" I told him of Verity, and he listened, without questioning any part of the story. In fact, for the first time I sensed De Coverley was emotionally engaged with something other than the destiny, real or imagined, he felt so driven to fulfil.

"So," he said when I finished explaining, "I'm to be a grandfather and nobody thought to tell me."

"That's unfair. Christopher never knew, and Verity doesn't dare speak to you or anyone else."

"I suppose you're right, Sangster," he sighed. "But if only I'd known, I could have done something." He walked over to the desk and picked up a paper, pen, and envelope. "And if this place isn't entirely destroyed, then perhaps I still can do something." De Coverley then furiously scribbled for some minutes, before folding the paper and sealing it in the envelope. On the front he wrote:

To be opened in the event of my death

"Pretty likely in one way, Sangster," he said, placing the envelope in the lead-lined box, "but at the same time unlikely." De Coverley walked back to his chair, sat down again, and took off his right shoe and sock. "You see that?" He held his foot up and pointed to a birthmark on the instep.

"Yes."

"It's the mark of my bloodline. Chris had one, my father had one, his father before that, and so on."

"Oh, er, yes."

The lack of medication had clearly made my reluctant companion's mind wander further, I thought, as he pulled sock and shoe back on before once again staring into the depths.

De Coverley then stayed like that, saying nothing, for what seemed an eternity, before speaking again, this time with a further revelation that shocked me to the core, not least because his face told me he believed every word to be true.

*

"Now make your peace with God, Sangster, whatever you perceive him to be," whispered De Coverley. "And before you do, just pop this in the lead-lined box as well, would you?" He clicked open the cassette recorder, passed me the tape, and I duly walked across to the desk and opened the box.

"Needle's well in the red now, she'll blow any time." De Coverley stretched his hand out towards the cooling tank.

"And when that happens, we'll only have a few minutes, right?"

"That's right, Sangster, just a few minutes, I—"

"I know," I said, hearing my voice waver, "that we're finished, but what about the people nearby? After all, we're talking about a nuclear reactor. What about the blast radius, fallout, and so on?"

"Oh, it won't be like Hiroshima, Sangster, the reactor's deep under the moor and surrounded by granite." He sniffed, as if my question was of no consequence. "More like an earthquake when it goes, I shouldn't wonder, and a very local one at that. Might damage a few foundations, but there'll be no blast and the rock will contain any fallout or radiation poisoning."

De Coverley's voice was drowned out by a deafening groan, and I watched as the side of the water tank began to bulge, then rip open, the metal tearing like paper before spewing a torrent. I stood up and braced myself, grasping a metal bracket on the wall in the full expectation of half a million gallons enveloping us both. But although the water frothed and cascaded across the floor, pouring down the shaft in a steaming waterfall, the flow subsided almost as quickly as it came. All the while, De Coverley continued to sit on his chair, apparently unconcerned.

"I… I thought there'd have been more water." I released my grip on the bracket.

"Most of it will have escaped down the culvert, look." He pointed through the broken wall of the tank. "See, the drainage sluice is shattered."

Peering inside, I saw mangled metal hanging either side of a circular aperture, perhaps six feet in diameter.

"And that's the entrance to the culvert, open to us?"

"For what it's worth, yes."

I felt my heart leap. "Then come on," I shouted.

"Culvert's blocked downstream by a metal grill that can only be opened from above ground, so we'd still be trapped. Might as well die quickly here as slowly down a drain."

"That grill's broken, De Coverley, I've seen it. We can get through."

"Hey, what are you doing?" he cried, as I grabbed my torch then pulled him up from the chair.

"Getting us out of here."

I continued to drag him, first through the hole in the wall of the tank and then into the culvert, which sloped away in a series of bends. I struggled, the steepness of the winding drain, as well as its circular shape, making balance difficult, especially with De Coverley, now clearly delirious, screaming at me and refusing to walk. The stench was also difficult to bear, years of heat from the tank water having encouraged algae to grow in a thick layer of sludge against the concrete lining of the pipe.

We staggered on and I looked at my watch. Two minutes since the tank burst. Surely the grill and the concrete hatch weren't far away now, and if we could climb that ladder to the surface, it might just be possible to reach safety before the power plant blew.

"Only want to go to sleep," De Coverley moaned, lying down in the trickle of water that still flowed beneath our feet.

"Don't give up." I pulled De Coverley by the arm, almost dragging his now-limp body, which banged as he lurched against the slime-covered walls. I gasped for breath, continuing along the culvert like this until I thought my sinews would snap and my lungs would burst. Turning a particularly sharp bend that I thought might be as far as De Coverley would go, I shone my torch ahead and there it was, the broken grill and the ladder.

I looked at my watch. Four minutes since the water tank burst.

"Leave me here," slurred De Coverley as I tried to push him up the ladder.

"No," I shouted. "Now climb." I pushed him from behind and he slowly began to ascend, rung by rung, each step taking several seconds. Then I heard a rumble, first like distant thunder, then closer, until it filled the air, the sound rushing through my ears. I gave De Coverley a final heave, sending him out through the hatch, then followed, as the noise grew to an unbearable level and the smell of burning sulphur began to replace the stench of algae. Dragging the concrete cover slab as far as I could across the opening in the hope of containing the blast and fumes, I grabbed De Coverley and dived onto the grass.

I'll never forget the sound that came next. It was louder than anything I could have imagined, even the noise of naval gunfire I'd once heard on a battleship during the war, which I knew could kill someone inadvertently standing next to an active turret. But loudness alone wasn't what indelibly etched the experience into memory. This was a sound that emanated deep below me, making the very ground vibrate, a monstrous groan from the earth that seemed to know no end.

I lay for seconds, minutes, or hours, I could not tell which, hands held against my ears, whilst watching De Coverley, who was writhing on the ground next to me, do the same. Then, just when my head could take no more, the din lessened, only to be replaced by crashing from the hill above us.

I remembered De Coverley's comment ('oh, it won't be like Hiroshima, Sangster, the reactor's deep under the moor surrounded by granite – more like an earthquake when it goes, I shouldn't wonder').

A moment later I looked up, to see the Old Centre in its death throws, the perimeter walls collapsing first, followed by the main building, which fell in on itself in a matter of a few heartbeats. Soon after that, the disintegrating walls and implosion of the compound threw up a vast plume of dust, visible despite the dark night through a red glow, which then faded along with the last of the underground noise.

De Coverley and I now lay in darkness and, bar our laboured breathing, complete silence.

I felt in my pocket and smiled, pulling out a crumpled envelope. Lack of light prevented me from reading what was written on the front, but no matter.

"To be opened in the event of my death," I said to myself.

MIDNIGHT

"Mr Sangster," shouted a familiar voice as torchlight dazzled my eyes.

"DC Eccles?"

"Yes, sir, let me help you up."

I took his outstretched hand, pulled myself to my feet, then blinked. All around me were uniformed police, and in the distance by Foxtor House, a mass of lights, including a powerful searchlight pointed in my direction, showed the outlines of vehicles and more people.

"Come along, sir. We're to bring you over to the house. DI's waiting there, along with those two spooks. Can you walk on your own?"

"Yes, thanks," I said, following the line of officers as they tramped down the valley. Behind me, De Coverley was being carried on a stretcher, and behind him, brought into relief by the beam of the searchlight, glowed the remains of the Old Centre, now barely visible above the crest of the hill. As we approached the house, it became clear that quite a crowd was gathered there, along with numerous vehicles, including police and unmarked cars, vans, and an ambulance. Standing by one of the cars was DI Hawke, who came forward when she saw me, goat-headed stick in hand and limping at speed.

"I suppose," she said, tapping her stick on the ground in front of me, "you simply didn't have time to tell the police where you were going, Sangster?"

"That's right. I had no time."

"Not even a few minutes to dial 999?"

"No, I'd have called if I could, but every minute counted. I'll explain when things are a bit quieter."

"And any sign of the boy?" I shook my head. "Well, at least we've found the Merrivale girl." I looked behind her to see Melissa wrapped in a blanket and sitting on a stool next to the ambulance. "And the doctor as well?" DI Hawke pointed to the stretcher.

"That man needs insulin urgently."

"Eccles," she shouted.

"Ma'am?"

"Check with the ambulance, they should carry insulin."

"Ma'am." Eccles ran to the ambulance and shouted through the open rear doors. A moment later a medic appeared with a box, as De Coverley's stretcher was laid down in front of her. I breathed a sigh of relief as the injection was administered.

"And you, Sangster, are you alright?"

"Glad to know you have my best interests at heart, Inspector."

"Don't be funny, you know what I mean."

"Yes, thanks, I'm fine."

"I'm so pleased," said a voice behind me. "Gas explosions can be quite dangerous."

I looked around to see Fidelma and Ballar, once again without their robes and dressed in dark clothing.

"It wasn't gas, it was—"

"Shhhh." Ballar put his finger across his lips. "Now, if you don't mind, we'll be taking charge of the patient on the stretcher." He and Fidelma went to pick up Doctor De Coverley, who now seemed to be conscious.

"Come along, sir," said Ballar, lifting and then frogmarching the dazed De Coverley past the DI and me to a waiting van, the side of which was marked with a crest and the words HM Prison Dartmoor. "We're going somewhere they can help you."

The doctor looked imploringly at me as he was manhandled into the van, mouthing some words just before the door slammed shut. I still wonder to this day exactly what he said, but I think it might have been 'don't tell, please don't tell'.

Ballar walked back over to me. "Still on for a debrief, Sangster, ten o'clock tomorrow?"

"Is that necessary now?"

"Essential, and don't talk to anyone about any of this until you and I have spoken again. As far as you are concerned, Sangster, Doctor De Coverley was killed in that unfortunate gas explosion blast and no longer exists."

As he finished speaking, the phrase 'no longer exists' reverberated around my mind. How could someone 'no longer exist' on the mere say-so of government agencies that asked permission from nobody? Because they can, came the reply in my head and I resolved to say nothing, in a situation I knew I couldn't influence, at least not right now.

"Can we meet a bit later?" I eventually sighed, looking at my watch. "It's already past midnight."

"Noon then."

*

"Let me through," a voice screeched. I looked across to the police cordon, where officers were holding their hands up as a woman tried to push past them. "Let me through."

"Excuse me, officers, that's the girl's mother."

The tape was lifted, and Mercy ran towards me.

"I just got the call, where's Mel?" I pointed, and Mercy sprang forward then threw her arms around Melissa. The two remained like that for some minutes, their embrace broken only by a tap on Mercy's shoulder from DI Hawke's cane.

"Excuse me, Mrs Merrivale, but we need to have a word with your daughter."

"Can't you wait, I'm…" Mercy looked imploringly at me.

"The detective inspector's got to do her job, Mercy," I said. "But Inspector Hawke, perhaps this could wait until tomorrow?"

"Quite impossible, Sangster."

"Oh, come on, what harm can there be in—"

"Alright, alright." DCI Hawke held her goat-headed stick in the air. "We'll leave any interviews until tomorrow or the next day then." She looked hard at Mercy. "At your hotel, so stay put there in the meantime, please." She then turned to me. "And don't take liberties because some people think you're a hero, Sangster," DI Hawke said, pointing her stick at my chest before walking away. "On your head be it if this girl flies off before we can talk to her."

"On your head, Sangster," Eccles echoed, before following his boss.

*

"You'll come back with us, Jack?"

"I'm actually parked up there," I said, looking at the still-smouldering hilltop. "But I don't fancy the walk."

We climbed into Mercy's car, Melissa sitting silently in the back seat and still wrapped in her blanket.

"Here we are then, Mercy," I said as we arrived in front of the remains of the Old Centre. "See you back at the hotel."

"Alright, the front door will be open and I'll…" She pulled at my arm as I went to open the car door. "You brought me Melissa back," she then said quietly, glancing briefly at her daughter, sitting behind us, head bowed against her knees. "I don't know how, but…" Mercy wiped away a tear, "it means more to me than anything, I can't say enough…"

"Then don't say anything." I climbed out of the car. "And I'll see you at the Wyvern Arms in a few minutes."

FRIDAY, JUNE THE 26TH 12 NOON

"Both back in your robes, I see."

"Cover still needs maintaining, Sangster," said Fidelma, smoothing her sackcloth skirts. "Just until we leave, this afternoon."

Ballar muttered something to the effect that it wouldn't be before time.

"Too right." She nodded. "Now, shall we go for a little walk?"

"As long as it's just outside, by the river, in full view of the hotel."

"Don't worry, Sangster," Ballar laughed, "we won't spirit you away."

"Oh, but I do worry." I laughed back.

"So," said Fidelma as we walked across the lawn, coming to a pair of benches by the water's edge, "everything we say here, and everything you know about this case, must remain totally confidential. Your employers will be receiving letters to that effect, but for the time being, just sit down and tell us what happened last night."

"Well…" I related how I had found the concealed entrance, the bunker with the mineshaft and the Bell inside it, and Melissa helping Doctor De Coverley. I then told of the struggle, and how it had shorted the electric circuits, setting off a chain of events that would inevitably mean the destruction of the Old Centre and everything in it and below it, including the Bell.

"And what put you onto all this, when even the police were stumped?"

I told them of my discussions with Sir Peregrine, the electrical anomalies in Wistman's Wood and other places nearby matching up with points on the geological map, and Whiddon witnessing the arrival of the Bell back in 1946.

"You see, Henry Weaver built that bunker in secret, and when he died the Bell was forgotten by all but Doctor De Coverley and a few old retainers like Whiddon."

"And you say you found your way into this bunker using a sketch left by the Merrivale girl?" Fidelma asked.

I nodded.

"And you escaped down a drain?" said Ballar with an incredulous frown.

"That's right, we were very lucky."

"And the Bell itself," asked Fidelma. "What did you make of it?"

"Certainly an odd-looking thing." I shuddered at the memory. "And of Nazi origin."

"How would you know?"

"By a dirty-great swastika on the side."

"Ah yes." Ballar looked knowingly at Fidelma. "And the machine's purpose, Sangster, any ideas?"

"Anti-gravity and stealth device, wasn't it?" I answered, deciding to say nothing of the Doctor's outlandish claims of time travel, or links to the stolen machine gun and the apparently out-of-time fifty-cal shells.

"That's right," said Ballar, something in his voice telling me that he might anyway know the Bell also had a darker purpose. "And not something that could ever fall into the wrong hands. Would change the face of warfare for ever."

"And the boy?" asked Fidelma. "What of Christopher De Coverley?"

"I don't know. Perhaps he was somewhere nearby and died in the blast, perhaps he died in an earlier experiment of his father's, or perhaps he really did run away. I just don't know."

"Well, he's now listed as officially missing, and his father is—"

"Yes, why did you take De Coverley away in a Dartmoor Prison van?"

"Sangster," said Ballar, looking me directly in the eye, "now listen carefully. Doctor De Coverley died in the explosion. The man on the stretcher we took last night was somebody else."

"Understand?" added Fidelma.

"Yes, but—"

"And for what it's worth, that somebody else can never go free."

"The man has lost his wife, his son, and suffers from dementia. He even has advanced cancer, for heaven's sake."

"Yes, unfortunate, that," she said. "Exposure to the Bell seems to cause it. Henry Weaver died of that same type of cancer."

"He'll be well looked after, if that's important to you," added Ballar. "Doctor De... er, the man on the stretcher, has a psychotic condition made worse through long-term medication to manage pain from the cancer and damage from diabetes."

"How do you know?"

"Oh, we came from the prison this morning. The man's had a full medical, including a psychiatric assessment. The quack says he's not got dementia, but he is a... what was it?"

"Schizophrenic," said Ballar.

"That's right, imagines all sorts of crazy things, but the prison doctors will treat him."

"Why do they bother to do that?" I asked.

"He's a valuable resource, and we want him in as good a shape as possible."

"May I ask a question?"

"Perhaps," said Ballar.

"How did you get onto all this?"

"Can we answer?" He looked at Fidelma for approval and she nodded. "It was the Polish agent."

"Jane Ustrix?"

"If you want to call her that, yes. Our intelligence from Warsaw told us she was assigned to look for a Nazi *wunderwaffe* in England, and after that it wasn't difficult to trace her, or her handler."

"Handler?"

"Yes, she met him in Princetown this week."

"Ah," I said. "That explains why she was dressed in the height of fashion when she claimed she'd been walking out on the moor."

"You're an observant one, aren't you, Sangster?" said Fidelma. "Ever want a job with us, just let me know."

"Did you catch this 'handler'?" I asked, shaking my head with a grin.

"We've a tail on him. More useful if he doesn't think he's been sussed."

"Sussed?"

"Found out, cover blown, exposed, compromised, you know the jargon from the TV. We need to learn whatever we can about all this, from De Cov… ahem." She checked herself with a cough. "Sorry, the man on the stretcher, but also the agents of the other side. Last night's explosion set us back years, and it was pretty public. People will remember and some things will get back to the other side, I'm certain."

"Surely it's all over now, and people don't remember for very long. Nine-day wonder and all that?"

"We're having the remains of that centre demolished, as well as the concrete trackway up to it from the road, so pretty soon there won't be anything much left there to remember."

"Yes, but you said, 'set us back', not finished."

"You don't think that machine in the bunker was the only one of its kind, do you?"

I suddenly felt fatigue overcome me, and slumped back, swallowing hard at the idea that the Dartmoor device was not the last of Die Glocken, so that even now, perhaps a second Bell lay in the hands of some malevolent group. And what if De Coverley was not deranged, and these people really had acquired the power to change history?

"Then where's the other one?" I finally said. "Russia, America, here?"

"Time to go back inside," the Dikes said to me in unison.

2 PM

"Call for you, Mr Sangster, you can take it in the phone chair as usual."

"Thanks, Joe," I said, picking up the receiver. "Sangster here."

"Commander Sangster, Lieutenant Jolly, do you have a moment, sir?"

"Of course, Jolly, what can I do for you?"

"Well, sir, it's about those two fifty-cal shells we analysed for you…"

"Yes," I said, sensing he was finding it difficult to talk.

"It's all a bit embarrassing, you see…"

The lieutenant went on to say that with the shortage of laboratory staff, records appeared to have become confused, so it wasn't clear now whether or not the Ballyshannon shell had been fired from the stolen machine gun.

"Can we test the shell again, Jolly?"

"No, sir, we can't."

"And why not?"

"It's been destroyed, sir."

"What?"

"Got mixed up with a batch of out-of-date ordnance scheduled for incineration, sir."

My heart sank. That barnacle-encrusted shell I'd kept all those years was the only tangible evidence that De Coverley's story contained even a grain of truth. I even wondered for a moment if there were more such shells, languishing in some obscure Irish museum amongst the crumbling timbers of the Santa Extrana, perhaps I could… Then I shuddered and cleared my mind. Time to let all this go.

"Sir," Jolly called down the phone at my silence.

"Sorry, yes."

"You, er… don't need to report this to Admiral Anson, do you, sir?"

"No, Jolly," I said, remembering my white lie that the analysis request was on the admiral's express orders. "He won't hear anything about it from me."

"Thank you, sir."

"Oh, and Jolly, did you double-check whether that M2 was used during the war?"

"Yes, sir, of course, I forgot to tell you. Definitely not."

"How can you be so sure?"

"Well, apart from our written records, the gun was actually photographed in its display case for a local newspaper article. There's a copy that's been kept at the depot."

"Any idea of the date the picture was taken?"

"Yes, sir, the 29th of April 1944."

3 PM

"So this is what you found, Professor Frere?"

"You mean, what me and my brother found," said Clive Eggins, leaning on his spade next to a massive pile of earth and rock, beside which was a tarpaulin covering some sort of angular object.

"That's right," Marty added. "Been digging a good twelve hours, we have, day before yesterday and all today."

"Sadly, Sangster, it seems our arms thieves have been making free with the Reynard's Hall gardens as a dumping ground. First all those shells, now this." Frere pulled away the tarpaulin to reveal a metal shape, rusty and soil-encrusted, but still unmistakable, with twin barrels, a metal mounting, and ammunition belt feeds either side. "Our good friend Doctor Stewer will have a field day when he finds out."

"The navy's stolen machine gun?"

"I believe so, but someone's coming to confirm… ah, here they are now."

I looked around to see Lieutenant Jolly walking towards us, accompanied by several ratings. One I recognised as Ordinary Seaman Brown.

"Commander Sangster, I didn't realise you'd be coming here when we were talking on the phone."

"And is this your lost gun, Lieutenant?"

"We'll just see…" He knelt down and rubbed the side of one of the guns with a rag. "It's a Belgian model M2 alright. Read me out the serial number, please, Brown?"

Brown read out a series of numbers which Jolly repeated.

"Yes, this is the stolen M2, but look at the state of it." He ran his finger across the barrel, which was heavily corroded, pockmarked with rusting holes. "How did the thieves store the gun when they buried it, Professor?"

"Found it in this," said Clive, holding up a sackcloth and some shards from what must have once been a wooden box.

"The sub-soil here is full of ammonia," added Frere. "So highly corrosive. The thieves clearly didn't know that."

"No, they didn't," said Jolly, picking up one of the wood shards, then throwing it back to the ground. "And our valuable antique gun's pretty much destroyed as a result, but at least we have it back. Er… Commander Sangster," he then said, whilst simultaneously instructing the ratings to carry the gun away. "May I have a quick word?"

"Everything alright, Jolly?" I asked as we walked away from the dig.

"Yes, sir, but I just wanted to apologise again for the cock-up at the lab with that shell."

"These things happen, Lieutenant. It's forgotten now."

I watched Jolly visibly relax as I spoke, remembering some of the dressing-downs I'd received at the hands of senior officers for minor mistakes. I felt good for a moment, that I'd done the right thing in not telling Phil Anson. Anyone as diligent as Jolly should be allowed at least one gaff, and as a private citizen I was under no obligation to report anything to anyone, not even De Coverley's delirious revelations during those last minutes in the bunker.

5 PM

"Remember when we first sailed into Plymouth on *Victorious*?" said Phil Anson, pointing out to sea from the Hoe.

"You mean when we brought the old carrier back from being on loan to the Yanks, when they'd renamed her the *Robin* of all things?" He nodded. "Autumn of '43?"

"Think so." Phil looked up at the statue of Francis Drake, gazing out over Plymouth harbour towards the small island that bore his name. "And old Drake would have had a heart attack if he'd seen the navy's firepower during the war, let alone now."

"Maybe he would." I looked up at the statue as well, wondering if De Coverley's rantings had been anything other than the those of a man, already mentally fragile, pushed to madness by grief, his mind and body ravaged by exposure to radiation, prescription drugs, and denial of insulin. "Then again, Phil, maybe he wouldn't."

"Ever the enigmatic one, Jack, just like this chap." Phil patted the base of the statue. "Anyway, sun's making its way over the yard arm, so what say we drive up to the hotel and partake of this marvellous Dartmoor hospitality you've told me so much about?"

"Yes, let's," I answered, looking one more time at Drake as we walked towards the car, musing as to what he really knew and where his body now lay. I even addressed the questions directly to the old mariner in my mind, but he continued his silent gaze out to sea, giving nothing away.

"And you say they have a billiard table?"

"They certainly do."

"Then I'll take you on at a frame of snooker," said Phil with a wink. "And beat you, just like I did that spring we were stationed in Belfast."

"You couldn't beat me then," I winked back, "and you won't beat me now."

6:30 PM

"Oh no," I said, as we arrived at the hotel.

"What on earth's the matter, Jack?"

"Look, it's JG 1." I pointed to the number plate of Sir John's white Rolls-Royce, parked by the main doors.

"Ah, Sir John Granville."

"The very same, Phil, here to check up on me, I bet. Let's just hope he hasn't decided to stay the night."

"Hats off and best foot forward." Phil laughed, getting out of the car, and pulling his bag from the boot.

"Sangster," boomed Sir John as we entered the common room, "come over here." I walked across to the bar, where my outsized boss was leaning against the counter, cigar in one hand, glass of scotch in the other. "And you would be…" Sir John looked at Phil's jacket sleeves, with their gold bands, three thin and one thick, "Admiral Philip Anson."

"Sir John Granville, I presume," Phil responded, holding out his hand.

"Aye," said Sir John, taking Phil's hand then grabbing mine and shaking it vigorously. "And good job, Sangster. Heard all about the explosion. De Coverley boy and his father were killed, but we can't win 'em all. You alright?"

"A bit bruised, but—"

Sir John didn't wait for my answer, mouthing to me 'PM's happy', before turning to Phil. "Now I would like to have a chat with you, Admiral, about a little piece of business I discussed with the Home Secretary."

"May I check in to my room and change first?"

"Of course, of course." Sir John waved vaguely towards the reception area. "I'll still be here when you come back down."

"Doesn't mess about, your boss," said Phil, as we walked across to the desk, where Mercy was waiting, already dressed for the evening in a blue three-quarter-length frock (elegant enough, but nothing like the outfits she'd worn earlier in the week).

"Er… no, he doesn't mess about, sorry," I said. "Now let's get you signed in, this is Mercedes Merrivale, the owner."

"Pleased to meet you, I'm Philip Anson."

"Call me Mercy, Mr Anson." She turned to the pigeonholes behind the desk, took down a key, and handed it to him. "We've put you in room ten, so if you could just give me a signature…" Phil signed the visitors' book. "Everything except your bar bill is prepaid, and dinner's at eight. Oh, and Jack, are you going upstairs?"

"Yes," I answered, as Phil gave me a sideways look.

"Good, then could you show Mr Anson where his room is?"

7 PM

"So, Sangster," said Sir John, "if I could just borrow the admiral for a few minutes…"

"Of course."

"Good stuff, now, Admiral, how about a scotch?" Phil nodded. "Another Macallan," Sir John then yelled to the barman. Joe Gurney was standing next to us behind the bar and jumped back at the noise.

Drinks in hand, Phil and Sir John walked over to the settle in the bay window and sat down. I saw Sir John immediately make his customary arm gestures, no doubt, I thought, overflowing with some business proposition that would involve the navy contributing further to his already unspeakably large bank balance.

Meanwhile, I was left high and dry.

"All alone and wanting someone to talk to?" I looked around to see Polly Darlow standing at the end of the bar.

"Pretty much."

"Will I do?"

"Always, Polly, let me get you a drink."

"Just a tomato juice, if you don't mind."

"Two Virgin Marys, please, Joe."

"Worcestershire sauce, salt and pepper, slice of lemon?"

"Yes, give it the works."

"Thanks," said Polly, as Joe passed us the glasses. "Now, Mr Sangster, what shall we drink to?"

"You're driving back to London tonight?"

"Yep, 'fraid so."

"Then let's drink to safe travels, Polly."

I felt a wave of relief as we raised our glasses and sipped the spicy concoctions. Polly driving back tonight meant Phil and I, and the rest of the hotel for that matter, would be foregoing the dubious pleasure of Sir John's company over dinner.

"So I hear it's been a tough case, Mr Sangster."

"Call me Jack, please, Polly."

"There's nothing I'd like better," she said brightly, then hesitated. "Er… I mean, I can't, it's one of Sir John's things, calling executives by their surnames. If I call you Jack now, I'll forget and do it in front of him."

"I'm an executive?"

"He seems to think so. Rates you as the best we've got."

"Hmmm…" I sipped the tomato juice, tongue stinging so that I wished Joe hadn't been quite so zealous with 'the works'. "I didn't find the boy, though."

"But you did find the hotelier's missing daughter and saved her from that gas explosion."

"And the boy's father, I—"

"You mustn't blame yourself for everything, Mr Sangster."

"Suppose not," I said, remembering De Coverley's face as he was led away, and the comment from Ballar Dike: "As far as you are concerned, Sangster, Doctor De Coverley was killed in that blast and no longer exists."

"By the way, Polly, I still have those outstanding—" I was about to ask her again if she could push through my May expenses when I heard Sir John's blustering tones behind me.

"Polly, is Vassen in the car?"

"Yes, Sir John."

"Good, I need to have a chat to Sangster here before we go."

With that he strode across the common room, and I followed, mouthing over my shoulder to Polly that I still needed to talk to her.

"So, Sangster," said Sir John as I sank into the rear seat of his car, "I'd like a confidential word, very confidential."

"Confidential," I said, pointing to the back of the chauffeur's head. "In here?"

"Good thinking." Sir John lifted the top of the centre arm rest to reveal a console. "This thing's supposed to be sound-proofed…" He pressed one of the console buttons and a glass screen whirred upwards, closing off the rear seats. "Vassen," he then boomed, "can you hear us?"

The chauffeur remained silent and still, peaked cap facing directly forward.

"That should do it," said Sir John, lighting a cigar from an ignitor in the console, then offering me one as an afterthought. "You, er… don't, do you?" I shook my head. "Didn't think so." He put the cigar back in its case, then sat back as the car began to fill with smoke.

"Now then, Sangster, I've just had an interesting chat with your friend Admiral Anson, and…"

Sir John then explained that he had received a message from the Home Office to talk with Phil on a matter of national importance relating to the De Coverley case, hence them both coming to the hotel at the same time.

"I thought you were dropping in to see how I was, and that Phil's visit was social."

"No, lad, I'm sorry." He clapped me on the shoulder with what I supposed he thought was a comforting hand. "You haven't told anyone about all this, have you, Sangster?" he then asked, voice raised and anxious.

"Not the whole story, not to any one person, not by a long way."

"Good." Sir John clapped me on the shoulder again, even harder this time. "And that's the way it must stay. You don't, er… have any, ah… concrete evidence about what happened?"

"No, how could I?"

"Just asking, because woe betide you if you did and the authorities found out."

"I take it you won't need my written report then, Sir John?"

"No, not a word in writing and you shouldn't say anything, understood?"

I thought for a second whether I could answer this question truthfully.

"Of course, but why?"

"Because this business has gone up to the very highest level in the land."

"All the way to the PM?" I asked.

Sir John took a long drag on his cigar and whispered his answer to me through billowing smoke. "Even higher, Sangster, even higher."

I think this was the first and last time I ever heard him properly whisper.

*

Dinner that night was a quiet affair, which, after everything that had happened, suited me well. Phil and I took a table in the corner and spent the time largely reminiscing about our days together at sea. Mrs Curtice seemed to have the night off, whether voluntarily or not Mercy didn't say, and was replaced by a familiar figure, who played, if not with Mrs Curtice's particular brand of gin-fuelled gusto, both classics and modern pieces equally well.

"Can you excuse me a moment?" I said to Phil as we sipped our coffee. "Need to talk to the pianist."

"Bit young for you, old chap," he laughed, "but don't mind me."

*

"Verity, that was a lovely performance. May I have a word?"

"Let's go somewhere quieter," she said, standing up from the piano and leading me out through the common room, where I saw Melissa glare at us from behind the bar.

"I'm not showing too much, am I?" She patted her stomach as we stepped outside.

"No, nothing noticeable as yet, but it's that that I need to talk to you about."

"Is it Christopher, do you have a message?" She looked at me, eyes wide with anticipation.

"I'm sorry, but I'm pretty sure you won't see him again."

I watched her eyes fill with tears.

"Did he die with his father?"

"Perhaps, but I need to ask, do you have any proof your baby is Christopher's?"

"Er... no, but it's his. I didn't go with anyone else."

"You don't have..." I thought hard for inspiration, "love letters with dates, anything like that?"

"No." She sniffed.

"And I suppose no witnesses the night it, er... happened."

"Of course not."

"Sorry, I meant a signed register at a hotel or something?" She shook her head. "Well, anyway, come with me." I walked to the car and took De Coverley's note from the glove compartment. "This is for you."

To be opened in the event of my death

She gingerly took the envelope from me. "What's in it?"

"Something that may be to your advantage, Verity, read it."

"Will you read it, please?" she said, passing me back the envelope with an unsteady hand.

"Very well." I opened out the note and began to read De Coverley's spidery handwriting, which was only just legible in the dim light of the car park:

For the attention of Verity Jay, Jay's General Store & Tea Rooms, Princetown, Devon

Dear Miss Jay,

Today I have been told you carry my unborn grandchild. If you truly do, the baby will bear a birthmark on the instep of its right foot, chocolate brown in colour and heart-shaped, about the size of a half-crown in an adult. We De Coverleys all have this, so no birthmark, no De Coverley.

Once the child is born and providing said birthmark is visible, get it medically certified as genuine. You may then take this note to my solicitors, Badcock and Jackman of Plymouth, and claim ownership of Foxtor House and all other residual parts of my estate in the name of the last of the De Coverleys, this estate to be placed in trust for the child until it comes to majority. Trustees will be yourself and Silas Badcock (and his nominated successor if needs be), you being entitled to take income from the estate of three thousand pounds per annum (or its inflationary equivalent in future years), with the right to reside at Foxtor House in perpetuity.

For the benefit of that old pedant Badcock, let it be known I consider this note my Letter of Wishes, prevailing over my previous will. I confirm I am of sound mind as I write and am witnessed in doing so by Jack Sangster of the Granville Institute. Mr Sangster is not aware of the precise content of this note.

John R. De Coverley, June 26th, 1970

Verity continued crying whilst I read, then took the note and the envelope.

"Thank you, Mr Sangster, this is a shock, too much to take in, but—"

"Just keep it safe, Verity," I said. "And tell no one until you visit the solicitor after the baby's born. No one, alright?"

"Alright."

We walked back inside, to find Mercy waiting in the common room.

"Ah, Verity," she said, staring at me rather than the girl, "I was looking for you."

"Just telling Verity how delightfully she plays."

"I'm sure."

"Snooker then, Jack?"

Saved, I thought, as Phil appeared from the dining room.

"Raring to pick up a cue, so lead on. And could, er, someone bring us coffee and a nice whisky?" I asked Mercy.

"Come with me, Jack, and you can tell Tilly exactly what type you want."

"See you in the billiard room Phil," I said over my shoulder, as Mercy ushered me from the room. "And goodbye, Verity."

"Jack," said Mercy as soon as we were on our own, "I don't want to ask you, but I suspect you're my best bet for an answer."

"Why me?"

"Someone, never mind who, saw you walking and talking with Verity in Princetown."

"Alright."

"Anyway, there's some sort of spat between Melissa and that girl."

"Really?"

"Yes, really. When I mentioned Verity Jay would be replacing Mum on the piano tonight, Melissa went mad with me. You don't know what it's about, do you?"

"Both keen on the De Coverley boy, I guess."

As I said this, my fists clenched involuntarily. Did Melissa somehow know of Verity's condition?

"I can't help feeling there's more to it," said Mercy, looking down at my white knuckles. "What do you think?"

"Them both liking the same boy would be reason enough on its own," I replied, hoping she wouldn't press me into overtly lying. "Wouldn't it?"

"Suppose so. Now Jack, coffee for two and whisky in the billiard room, on your tab?"

"Yes," I laughed, "on my tab."

11 PM

"They do say it's a sign of a misspent youth," said Phil as I potted the last black ball. "Did you misspend your youth?"

"Perhaps, but not playing snooker, although…" I thought back to our time together in Northern Ireland during the war. "I won quite a few quid at this when we were in Belfast." I took the black ball from the pocket and held it up. "Anyway, it's game over for you, Admiral Anson."

"Yes, Jack." He leaned on his cue and sipped from his whisky glass. "And you know, well played and all that, but…"

"But what?"

"You were always too good at everything."

"Too good?"

"I don't need to win so much, that's one reason why I—"

"Why you're an admiral?"

"Dunno, but I don't challenge the people in charge."

"And I do?"

"Yes, Jack, and it's also game over for you now, in more ways than one. We need to talk, it's, er… political."

My friend was generally jovial, keeping conversation light whenever we met, so his current tone worried me. I had been expecting Phil to say something given Sir John's warning, but now, feeling recovered from the events of the previous night, and the evening being so convivial, I'd pushed the conversation in the Rolls to the back of my mind.

"Sounds ominous, Phil, but alright. Another whisky?"

"Thanks, mate."

I poured him a generous measure from the decanter Tilly had left with the coffee service.

"So," said Phil, cupping the glass, "been quite a week, eh?"

"It has," I answered, sensing even more of an edge in his voice.

"And I suppose, well…" He stopped talking, pulling out a handkerchief and polishing his glasses.

"Suppose what, Phil?"

"Jack," he said, "I can't lie to you. The authorities got wind that I was due to be down here inspecting the Antarctic survey ship and asked for a favour."

"What favour?"

"Called first thing this morning. Wanted me to make sure you keep in line."

"What line?"

"The one that the powers that be have drawn up." Phil then told me that I mustn't discuss the De Coverley case with anyone, and that he needed to go back to London with a cast-iron assurance to that effect.

"And can you get that assurance, trust me, I mean?"

"You tell me, Jack."

"How much do you know about the whole thing?"

"Nothing except the basics." Phil shrugged. "And it's better that I know as little as possible." He then smiled. "I can tell you they're really pleased with how it all panned out. You've got quite a rep, you know."

"I'm so glad for them and so flattered, Phil." I hoped my irony was crystal-clear, also wondering as I spoke whether he had been responsible for making sure the report on the Ballyshannon shell was lost, and the shell itself destroyed. I then thought better, remembering Lieutenant Jolly's words: "You don't need to report this to Admiral Anson, do you, sir?"

"These powers that be, Jack, they, er… just need to feel safe."

"And if 'they' don't," I said through gritted teeth, "feel safe, that is?"

"Not good for you…" He looked down at his feet. "And not good for your marriage either."

"Sarah?"

"Well, there are a couple of things on that front." He continued to look downwards. "For a start, they think you've told her too much about the case."

"How would anyone know that?"

"Someone overheard you talking to her on the phone, it seems."

"Then if I get hold of them, they can…" I thought of the Dikes, then picked up a cue and smashed it against the side of the table, "er…" I felt my control returning, "think again."

"Whoa," Phil said, holding his hands up. "As I say, Jack," he then went on more softly, "all that the authorities want is to feel safe, and all that takes is your silence."

"What about some of the other people here? They know things."

"Only you have the overall picture, that's what these people said to me."

"These faceless 'people', eh?"

"Yes."

"So what do I need to be silent about, exactly?"

"You must never mention…" he took a paper from his pocket and unfolded it, "er… Foxtor House, burglaries from Devonport Armoury, Doctor De Coverley's scientific work, matters relating to… oh, that's an odd one." He held the paper at a distance. "Sir Francis Drake, it says here, and there's a whole lot more, so you mustn't say anything, really."

"Well, is that all?" I almost snarled.

"No."

"There's more, Phil?"

"Sadly yes. It's absolutely essential that you go along with the story that Doctor De Coverley was killed in the, er…" he squinted at the document, "gas explosion."

"Huh." I remembered De Coverley's comment and was tempted to mention there was no gas main anywhere near the Old Centre but said nothing.

"Oh, and…" he rubbed his chin, clearly finding the conversation more and more awkward, "you need to avoid the Princetown area, and anyone you've met while you've been here, at least for a few years."

"Years?" I shouted with incredulity. "I've had government warnings before, but never anything like this, it's disgraceful, I—"

"You were given a government warning after that case last month with the missing girl," Phil interrupted.

"You know about that?"

"I've been briefed on your background, even if they didn't give me particulars of this case," Phil answered glumly. "And this one really is as serious as it gets, mate."

"So I can't talk to anyone here about it, not even, er…" I remembered his comment about Mercy, "the owner, for example?"

"Especially the owner. They're worried you might have got, er… how shall I say, a little too close to Mrs Merrivale."

"What?" I shouted, taking new meaning from his comment about it not working out well for my marriage.

"Sorry, mate, and for what it's worth I told them they'd overstepped the mark with that one. I would never do anything to hurt you and Sarah."

"Wouldn't you?"

"No." He looked hard at me. "But they might, Jack."

I looked back at Phil, who, although his career had skyrocketed in a way I could never have dreamed of, was still my oldest friend.

"And they sent you, of all people."

He nodded. "Must confess, when they gave me the paper for you to sign, my glasses weren't to hand, so I didn't read it properly until today. Was a bit shocked when I did."

"You didn't think to check what it said until now?"

"Er… no, sorry, Jack." He coughed. "Ahem… all that's not much of an excuse, is it?" I shook my head. "They leaned on me too, you know."

"How?"

"I'm, er… well, they're considering… I mean, taking my service record into account, the PM wants to…" He stumbled, uncharacteristically, for words. "This is confidential, OK?"

"Of course," I answered, whilst wondering how much more confidential things could possibly get.

"I'm up for First Sea Lord, and they made it clear that if I acted as messenger to you and Sir John, it would—"

"Don't tell me," I interrupted, my earlier conversation with Sir John in the car now making complete sense. "Help make up Her Majesty's mind in your favour."

"If you want to put it like that, yes. They also said, in so many words, that my career in the service will be over if I don't come back with a signature. But… I…" Phil stumbled again. "I'll understand if you don't sign, it's—"

"What if you tell them I simply refused to sign? That wouldn't be your fault, would it?"

"You have to sign, Jack." Phil placed the document and a pen on the green baize surface of the billiard table, then turned away. "For all our sakes."

SATURDAY, JUNE THE 28TH 12 NOON

Until I left the Wyvern Arms on that last Saturday of June, I hadn't realised it was possible to become so attached to a place or its people in the space of less than a week.

*

"Thanks, Joe," I said, leaning on the reception desk to sign my bill. "I think you just need to send that on to the institute and they'll transfer the money directly."

"We will do, Mr Sangster."

"Oh, and I'll take one of these," I added, looking at a rack of postcards. "How much?"

"Oh, just pick one, Mr Sangster. On the house."

"Thanks." I chose a scene of the Wyvern Arms in winter, the surrounding moorlands snowbound, giving the already remote hotel a look of complete isolation.

"Long drive ahead?"

"Yes, all the way back up to Chester," I answered with a grimace, remembering the trip down, where it seemed almost all of the roads between Devon and Cheshire were being dug up.

"Well, I heard the roadworks out by Mortonhampstead have finished, so at least you could take the Postbridge Road across to Exeter this time."

"Thanks, but even so, I won't be home until late this evening."

"Then I won't keep you." Joe Gurney extended his hand. "But drive safe if you do go via Postbridge, keep your hands on the wheel, and if you see any other hands on your wheel, however hairy, take no notice."

"Hairy?"

"It's been a pleasure, Mr Sangster." Joe was clearly avoiding my answer and I sensed a slight undertone that made me uncomfortable. Nevertheless, he spoke with conviction, and after he said this he beamed. "And I'll hope to see you back at the Wyvern before too long."

"I, er… I'm not sure when I'll be back, but it certainly has been good to meet everyone here." I shook his hand and picked up my bag. "Well, goodbye, Joe."

*

"Oh, Mr Sangster?" I turned around to see Tilly skipping down the corridor. "My mother might be coming, just like you said."

"That's wonderful news."

"Yessir, you said we can do anything, with a bit of luck, and as long as we give it everything."

"That's right," I said, happy at her smile but worrying I'd perhaps given Tilly a rather simplistic view of things.

"Missus promised to help me bring her over." She looked at my bag. "You leaving, sir?"

"I'm afraid so, my work here is done."

"But you'll come back?"

I smiled and, bag in hand, walked towards the common room.

*

"I won't see Chris again, will I?"

Melissa Merrivale, tall as her mother, blocked my way to the front door.

"No, I don't think so, but—"

"No need for buts," she said. "I felt it, even when I went to his dad. I hoped, but I knew, deep down."

"It might not be quite what you think." I saw her eyes lift and felt that pang which accompanies disingenuity, however well meant or half-believed it may be. Christopher De Coverley hadn't left Melissa in any romantic sense of the word, and either died in the explosion or went who knows where. But for all that his heart was still with another, and that other now bore his child.

"Perhaps," she said, looking down at the floor again. "Anyway, I'm going to carry on with my studies now. That's a good thing, isn't it?"

"A very good thing."

She pointed at my bag. "You're leaving?" I nodded. "Without saying goodbye to Mum?"

"Haven't seen her this morning."

"She's out picking up Whiddon. Back in a few minutes, and the rest of the committee's out front as well."

"Committee?"

"Hunt Committee, in the car park right now, they're doing some planning over lunch today."

"Oh, well, I—"

She was stopped from saying more by a high-pitched Gallic squeal. "Monsieur Sangster, Monsieur Sangster."

"Yes, Anton?"

"I hear from Missus you are leaving us?"

"I am," I sighed.

"Then you must take this for your journey." He thrust a small hamper into my left hand, then earnestly, and with unexpected vigour, shook my right. "Monsieur Sangster, you are a gentleman," he said breathlessly. "A gentleman."

Melissa then put her hand on his shoulder. "That's nice that you prepared a picnic for Mr Sangster Anton, but please, we've got twenty people for lunch in a few minutes."

"D'accord, Mademoiselle." The chef scampered away towards the kitchen, shouting as he went, "Bon voyage, Monsieur Sangster, et au revoir."

"I'm not sure we will meet again, Anton," I called after him. "But anyway, thank you for the hamper."

Once more, and now with the hamper in my other hand, I walked towards the front door, and once again my path was blocked by Melissa. "But Mum, she wants—"

"What does she want?"

"You must say goodbye."

"We already said our goodbyes last night," I said, thoughts of that conversation still fresh in my mind.

*

I'd bid Phil Anson a good night and was sitting on my bed, still shocked from his words during our snooker game, when Mercy had knocked and then slowly pushed open the door.

"Jack, I know we said… well, I just thought—"

"I'm… tired, it's…" I stuttered, not sure what I wanted to say next, remembering Phil's veiled threat: "They're worried you might have got, er… how shall I say, a little too close to Mrs Merrivale."

And then his next comment: "I would never do anything to hurt you and Sarah."

I knew without a shadow of a doubt I loved Sarah, but that night Mercy had needed me and it would have taken only the gentlest of pushes to have fulfilled that need. It was also the first time in our marriage I'd felt even close to being unfaithful, and the two emotions conflicted, my only clear sense being that of wronging both women.

"Mercy, I can't."

"I know you're married, so I have to ask myself whether I care, and, well…"

She stood in front of me, not dressed seductively, not dressed for anything really, and I felt a wave of warmth. Then I thought again of Phil's warning. What else could I do?

"I'm a married man, Mercy. I need to leave tomorrow and not come back, I'm sorry."

She said nothing, turning to leave the room, shutting the door with the merest hint of a slam. My heart felt unbearably heavy as she went, and I slumped back down on the bed.

What else could I have done?

*

"And Melissa," I put the bag and the hamper down and waved my hand at her, "I'll say goodbye to you now as well."

"You mustn't worry too much, Mr Sangster," she said, waving back. "It's just that Mum seemed to think you were different from the others, that's all."

"Others?" I asked, but although I pierced Melissa's eyes for an answer, she merely raised her eyebrows and walked away.

*

I wasn't immediately sure whether the glare outside the hotel came from today's rare blue Dartmoor sky or the crowd that stood waiting. Melissa, who followed me through the door, had mentioned the Hunt Committee was meeting for lunch, but it never occurred to me that so many people I'd met in the recent frenetic days would right now be standing together in the hotel car park.

Then I looked, and there they were, eyeing me in unison, the nearest, Miles Edgerton, smiling, but more with a gloat than a fond goodbye as he saw my travel bag.

Then there were the Frere brothers, seated at one of the outside tables, beaming at me with a glint in the eye that seemed to say, "Will I be found out?" Peregrine and Septimus, I was sure, peered at me like this for very different reasons. Their sister, Letitia Curtice, up and about despite what to her must have seemed an ungodly hour, sat between them, sipping a glass of tomato juice, virgin or not, I couldn't tell.

And behind the Freres, outside the bay window that housed the common room settle, were the Egginses. Both wore white overalls, with Marty atop a stepladder, paint pot and brush in hand, whilst Clive stood below him, holding the rungs steady. I watched Marty turn his back to the window frame when he saw me but continue with vigorous brush strokes, so in a few seconds the window glass was smeared with paint. I smiled as Marty unwittingly whitewashed the windowpane, whilst the Egginses, taking this as a goodbye smile, grinned back and waved.

"Seems you made quite an impression in the few days you were here."

I looked around to see DI Hawke stepping out of a car, followed by Detective Constable Eccles. "Judging by the turnout, Sangster."

"Oh, they're not for me, it's the Hunt Committee lunch."

"I wouldn't bet on that, but anyway, you're leaving?"

"Excellent detective work." I laughed, holding up my bag.

"Let me walk you to your car. Eccles, bugger off for a minute, would you?"

"Goodbye, sir."

"And to you, Constable Eccles," I said, then crossed the car park with the DI, whose goat-headed stick crunched on the gravel as we went.

"Can I help you with that car hood, Sangster?"

"No, it's fine."

"Then let me just say thanks. You got us a great result, in fact I'm not sure I've ever worked on a case quite like this." I said nothing, continuing to button down the car hood. "Um… Sangster?" she then asked slowly.

"Yes."

"I, er… just wondered, did anyone say anything to you about, you know… confidentiality?"

I sighed. Not another lecture on the Official Secrets Act. "How do you mean?"

"Well…" she leaned towards me with both hands on her goat's head, "cards on the table, I was given all sorts of forms to sign, and basically told to shut up about this case on pain of death."

"Me too." I climbed into the driver's seat and started the engine.

"Any idea why, Sangster?"

"I couldn't tell you if I did know, could I?"

"I suppose not, but Sangster?"

I'd already moved the car forward as she spoke so stopped again and turned my head. "Yes?"

"I, er… could you turn the engine off for a moment?" I did as I was told. "I felt safe with you on this job, Sangster."

"Hmph…" I cleared my throat, suddenly feeling a warmth towards this rather different police officer. "Eccles told me a little of what happened to you. You're very brave to continue on as a copper."

"I do what I can," she whispered, and if a blush had been possible through her make-up I felt sure her cheeks would have reddened. "And Sangster, as I tried to ask before, you couldn't tell me why this is all so hush-hush?"

"No, I couldn't, it's above my clearance level, as they used to say in the navy."

She made a snorting noise which I could almost equate to a laugh, then stepped away from the car and shook her head. "No, I don't suppose you could or would, and I don't suppose we'll be seeing you down here again."

I wanted to say, 'never say never', but all that came out was a weak 'goodbye'.

*

I took the Postbridge Road, just as Joe Gurney advised, instinctively holding tight as I neared the bridge, where another car approached from the opposite direction. I recognised Mercy at the wheel, with

Whiddon and Maisy sitting in the back. Slowing up, I waved as we passed each other. The two Whiddons waved back, but Mercy stayed staring ahead, hands firmly on the wheel.

EPILOGUE

"Come on, darling, we need to go," my wife called to me from the hall. "Tell me you're not still sitting in the study?"

"Sorry, yes," I called back.

"Right, I'm coming to pull you out. It won't do if we're late, I... oh, you're looking at that old postcard from Dartmoor."

"Er, yeah," I said, placing the card in the desk drawer and standing up. "Coming now."

"How do I look?" she asked as we left the house, her breath pale in the winter air.

"You look lovely, Sarah."

"Let me straighten you up." She adjusted my bow tie, buttoned my overcoat, then stood up on tiptoe and kissed me on the cheek. "You know, it's been nearly six months now, and I still sometimes see you looking at that postcard."

"Just liked the place, I suppose." I felt the familiar pang of guilt that always came when she asked me about the Wyvern Arms.

"We could go back to Dartmoor if you like, stay a couple of days."

"No, there's not that much to do there, and plenty of other places to go."

"Oh," she said, speeding up her step, a sure sign in Sarah of exasperation. "I give up. One minute you're looking longingly at the place, the next you say you don't care about it."

We walked on in silence through quiet streets and past festive lights, the sound of our shoes the only thing to be heard, especially the clacking of Sarah's high heels on the frosty pavements.

"Here we are," I eventually said as we arrived at the steps of the Grosvenor Hotel. "It's the first of December and the institute's Christmas party only comes once a year, so let's enjoy Sir John's hospitality."

"Jack?" said Sarah as we walked through the revolving entrance doors, waved into the lobby by the concierge.

"Ballroom for the Granville reception, sir, straight ahead."

"Jack," Sarah insisted as we walked on, "I want to know what really happened on Dartmoor."

"This is it." I guided her to the double doors of the ballroom. "Commander and Mrs Sangster," I then said to a uniformed Master of Ceremonies.

"Commander and Mrs Sangster," he repeated deafeningly as Sarah slipped her arm through mine and we entered.

"Should call it the bawl room," I whispered to her. "And I meant what I said before, you really do look lovely."

"Don't fob me off, Jack, I want to know. Why won't you tell me?"

"Because," I said, squeezing her hand and managing, I hoped, to avoid the question with at least a half-truth, "I don't really know myself."

*

In fact, whenever I'm asked what I was doing on Dartmoor I have to bite my tongue, with the gagging order and ban on my visiting the Princetown area still firmly in place, and likely to stay that way for as long as the government sees fit.

But the government can't stop my mind visiting the Wyvern Arms, which, at this time of year, if not actually covered in snow like the postcard, will still look bleak, the countryside around the hotel bereft of midsummer's foliage and very different from the green landscape of my memories.

I like to think of Joe Gurney, Tilly, and the rest of the staff going about their daily business, and now that it's out of season, attending, as Joe used to say, to all those 'pesky jobs that you never have time to do when you're busy'.

Meanwhile, Maisy Whiddon doubtlessly walks the panelled corridors of Reynard's Hall to the sound of Septimus Frere talking with Drake's portraits when he thinks nobody's looking, whilst Septimus's brother Peregrine covers up, as best he can, the struggle to manage Highmoor Research Centre without De Coverley.

As the sun begins to set, Mrs Curtice is still in bed preparing for the evening's recital, Melissa is dutifully studying, whilst Miles Edgerton sits in the common room planning next year's hunting season and secretly imagining Mercy is simply playing hard to get. And Miles' nemesis Old Soldier, his hidden and heated accommodation in the culvert now destroyed, is, I assume, holed up in a new home, safe, warm, and waiting for the Dartmoor spring.

Later on, when the evening's work at the hotel is done and the moon shines on the river, a woman, tall and blonde, may quietly pull on a coat and slip outside. Taking her brandy glass to the crest of the old bridge, she looks down into the icy water and pauses a moment in reflection. And as she does so, I hope Mercedes Merrivale thinks, at least a little fondly, of me.

Foxtor House will be deserted and frozen, its doors and shattered windows boarded up until someone comes forward to claim the property. And perhaps Verity Jay watches the house from some vantage point in Princetown, waiting as Foxtor's rightful owner grows in her belly, day by day.

The ruins of the Old Centre, long given over to bulldozers and the elements, are doubtless already no more than a mound of rocks and grass on a nearby hill. This wild place, away from any beaten track, will now only be frequented by a few hardened ramblers, unaware that the ground they walk upon harbours secrets that will likely now be concealed forever, the true nature of the hill's interior forgotten by all but a few.

We'll probably never know what became of Jane Ustrix, and perhaps I'm being naïve, but I do hope that rather than incarceration, the government offered her a fresh start. Either way, other than a formal communiqué from the Home Office reminding the Granville Institute that all matters pertaining to this woman are subject to the Official Secrets Act, we've heard nothing.

We don't hear much about Doctor John De Coverley either, probably because he doesn't officially exist. But, as far as I do know, the doctor, imprisoned under the name of Roger Hill, now spends his days alone in a cell, incarcerated so close to his beloved Foxtor House and yet unable to see it. According to the last Home Office report, sent to the institute with another stern reminder of the Official Secrets Act, prisoner Hill seems contented enough, responding well to cancer treatment, although his long-term prospects are not good. The report adds that he still refuses to make a statement as to the true fate of his only son.

*

And even as I think back, my midsummer time on Dartmoor fades like the colours of the year, with boundaries between reality, illusion, and conjecture ever more blurred.

What I can't forget, though, are the words De Coverley spoke just before the culvert split open, as we both sat trapped under the Old Centre, with the pressure gauge on the cooling tank creeping ever higher, and all hope of rescue seemingly gone. And all I need to do to be sure those words were not a dream is wait until I'm alone in my car, then listen to the cassette tape I took, along with the letter to Verity Jay, from De Coverley's lead-lined box.

He had stared silently into the abyss of that bottomless shaft for some minutes, before looking up at me and speaking, the sudden sound of his voice a shock as it reverberated around the sealed stone bunker that I felt sure would become our mausoleum.

"You see, Sangster, you can get over most things given time, even the death of a wife."

"My first wife passed away a couple of years ago." I nodded. "So yes, I do see."

"Do you?" He laughed, not with any mirth but in a high-pitched manner that evoked in my mind both a bitter irony and utter despair. "Because I take it you didn't kill your wife."

"No, and neither did you kill yours."

He gave his hollow laugh again. "I admit I hadn't known how the energy from the Bell would dissipate underground, or where it would emerge."

"How is that connected with the death of, oh…" I remembered swerving out of control by the bridge where Irene De Coverley fatally crashed.

"It was the first time I fired up the Bell," said De Coverley, tears now clearly in his eyes. "Irene was driving home, and the pulse must have caught her as she passed. A million-to-one chance."

"That's terrible but still an accident."

"Oh no, I killed her, Sangster."

I said nothing for a minute or so, trying to take in what he had said, trying to imagine how I would have felt.

"Did your son know?" I finally asked.

"Oh yes, it's partly what drove Christopher to join in with my plans. We both wanted to make it so that Irene's death wasn't in vain." He put his head in his hands and whispered, "But I'm beginning to wish I'd never let him near the Bell."

"Why ever not?"

"Because something like this… well, it's too much at odds with the way things should be."

As he was speaking, a rumble came from the shaft, the mangled crane and its sinister cargo below beginning to slide lower, emitting deep groans, buckling, and scraping as they went. The groans grew to roars, as a series of metallic bangs came echoing up from the earth. Then, with a rasping crack, the chain hanging from the crane broke completely, the noises below growing fainter as the great machine broke free and ricocheted against the rock, sinking deeper and deeper until no sound could be heard.

The Bell, whatever it really was, had fallen, irretrievably, into this man-made gateway to hell.

"That's that," said De Coverley, staring down the shaft. "Gone."

"Perhaps, but what did you just say… something about being too much at odds with the way things should be?"

"Ha." He laughed again, rubbing the gash in his forehead, staring at the blood on his hand then turning to me, wild-eyed.

"Is it too much to bear that you think you averted England's defeat at the hands of the Spanish Armada?"

"No, Sangster," he sighed, almost, I felt, in exasperation.

"Then do you mean the loss of Irene, and afterwards Christopher?"

"Not the loss of my wife, and not even my son, not exactly… you wouldn't even know where to begin."

"Try me."

"Is this the first case where you have failed?"

"Failed?"

"To find your missing child?"

"Melissa is safe."

"But remember, it was my son you came here to find."

"Suppose so."

"Well, you haven't failed."

"Haven't I?"

"Didn't you wonder about that name on the gravestone at Reynard's Hall?" I shrugged. "Oh, Christ, do I have to spell it out?" he then yelled. "Use Fox for Reynard and Tor for Hill and you get 'Fox Tor', Sangster."

My heart missed a beat. It seemed so obvious now that when De Coverley said time and time again that Christopher wasn't far away, he merely meant his son was buried close by.

"So you found your missing child after all, Sangster, Reynard Hill, lying six feet under at Reynard's Hall."

"You really think that's Christopher?" I said, trying to speak softly but raising my voice, nevertheless.

"Such is my torment, and so I ask you this…" De Coverley shook his head and continued to laugh. "Could your soul ever be at peace if you were… no, I can't say it, even here, even after everything that's happened."

"Tell me, man…" I was shouting now, almost screaming. "If I were what?"

"Descended from your own son."

ALSO BY THE AUTHOR
THE FACE STONE

Do ancient rocks and woodlands really harbour a secret that could bring about worldwide catastrophe? And can saving the health, life, and even mortal soul of one missing boy avert that catastrophe?

It is Easter 1969, and Jack Sangster, only recently appointed as a special investigator for the Granville Institute, is sent to an elite school, where the son of wealthy local family has disappeared.

Sangster, despite his talent for dealing with people and problems, only comes upon more mysteries as the case unfolds, struggling to reconcile his natural pragmatism with disturbing questions.

Follow as he navigates clues and red herrings, learning at every turn that if his eyes and ears are to be believed, the stakes linked to this case are rising at an alarming rate. Sangster tries to do the right thing even as his uncertainty rises; all the while a seemingly well-ordered and rational world is slowly revealed to perhaps be older, darker, and more chaotic than he ever imagined…

ANGEL'S BLADE

A profound secret that echoes down the centuries is uncovered by a uniquely gifted girl, who in doing so jeopardises her own life and that of the only person who can protect her…

It is the spring of 1970. When a beautiful and precociously talented pupil goes missing from a residential school in Cornwall, Sangster, with his reputation for sleuthing, is assigned to help police find her.

At first nonplussed by the girl having apparently disappeared into thin air, Sangster gradually gains an understanding of local people, legends, and landscapes that helps him unravel mysteries far, far deeper than could have been imagined, so that despite initial scepticism, he wonders…

Could events from two thousand years ago in this remote corner of Europe really have repercussions that might rock the very foundations of western society?

Governments on both sides of the Iron Curtain, and even hallowed religious institutions, certainly seem to think so.

It will take all of Sangster's nerve, skill, and determination, as well as a generous measure of luck, to discover the truth before it's too late…